阿昌族非物质文化遗产丛书

英汉对照

阿昌族民间故事集(一)
Folk Tales of Achang Nationality
Volume I

成 功 杨叶生 ◎ 编著
叶佳旖 (Jessica Jiayi Ye) ◎ 译
姚思琪 (Cindy Siqi Yao) ◎ 插图

知识产权出版社
全国百佳图书出版单位
—北京—

图书在版编目（CIP）数据

阿昌族民间故事集. 一：汉、英/成功，杨叶生编著；叶佳旖译. —北京：知识产权出版社，2025.5
（阿昌族非物质文化遗产丛书）
ISBN 978-7-5130-9304-0

Ⅰ.①阿…　Ⅱ.①成…②杨…③叶…　Ⅲ.①阿昌族—民间故事—作品集—中国—汉、英　Ⅳ.①I277.3

中国国家版本馆CIP数据核字（2024）第034363号

责任编辑：高　超　兰　涛　　　责任校对：谷　洋
封面设计：姚思琪　　　　　　　责任印制：刘译文

阿昌族非物质文化遗产丛书

阿昌族民间故事集（一）（英汉对照）

成功　杨叶生◎编著
叶佳旖（Jessica Jiayi Ye）◎译
姚思琪（Cindy Siqi Yao）◎插图

出版发行：知识产权出版社有限责任公司		网　　址：http://www.ipph.cn	
社　　址：北京市海淀区气象路50号院		邮　　编：100081	
责编电话：010-82000860 转 8383		责编邮箱：morninghere@126.com	
发行电话：010-82000860 转 8101/8102		发行传真：010-82000893/82005070/82000270	
印　　刷：天津嘉恒印务有限公司		经　　销：新华书店、各大网上书店及相关专业书店	
开　　本：720mm×1000mm　1/16		印　　张：17.25	
版　　次：2025年5月第1版		印　　次：2025年5月第1次印刷	
字　　数：292千字		定　　价：88.00元	

ISBN 978-7-5130-9304-0

出版权专有　侵权必究
如有印装质量问题，本社负责调换。

编 委 会

丛书总主编： 成　功（中央民族大学）

编　　委（按姓氏拼音首字母排序）：

　　　　　　曹先强（阿昌族）　　成　功

　　　　　　孙　媛（阿昌族）　　许本学（阿昌族）

　　　　　　杨叶生（阿昌族）　　袁钰莹

生态环境部生物多样性调查、观测和评估项目（2019—2023年）
Project Supported by the Biodiversity Investigation, Observation and Assessment Program of Ministry of Ecology and Environment of China
(2019—2023)

阿昌族非物质文化遗产丛书

阿昌族是我国人口较少的民族之一，主要分布在云南省德宏傣族景颇族自治州的梁河县和陇川县。阿昌族具有自成一体的传统文化与生活方式，但是目前阿昌族传统文化仍然没有得到足够的重视，也缺乏必要的保护。为此，本丛书尝试将阿昌族的既有研究与未来发展纳入公众视野之中，力争呈现阿昌族传统文化的方方面面，为保护文化多样性，促进阿昌族社会生态系统可持续发展，略尽绵薄之力。

Achang Ethnic Intangible Cultural Heritage Series of Books

The Achang people, one of the China's smallest ethnic minorities, are primarily settled in Lianghe and Longchuan counties within the Dehong Dai and Jingpo Autonomous Prefecture in Yunnan Province. The Achang people possess unique traditional culture and lifestyle of their own, however, these cultural expressions have not yet received adequate recognition and protection. In response, this series of books seeks to bring current studies and future development of Achang heritage into public view. Through an exploration of various aspects of Achang traditional culture, this series of books endeavors to contribute modestly to the preservation of cultural diversity and the sustainable development of the social and ecological systems of the Achang people.

阿昌族非物质文化遗产丛书
总序

　　序言应该简短，不宜喧宾夺主。一套丛书的总序，更是应该克制，好像路边的指示牌即可。

　　现代社会有一个迷思，仿佛不同的社会和文化，不过是同样的现代人在不同的自然地理环境中的适应现象。如果把不同社会中的人放在一个具体的时空范畴内，他们就会复原为基本的样式，从而表现出一种混合的文化现象。

　　基于上述想象，人类获得了某种平等与一致性，而这既有着生物学的分类学的支撑，还为现代社会的文明提供了"不言自明"的基本框架。

　　这样的信念引导着人们确信现代意义上的"人同此心，心同此理"，为此，在表面上尊重不同文化的客气表象之下，潜伏着某种解构一切文化差异的野心。

　　这套丛书希望发出一丝微弱的声音，提醒读者意识到文化多样性比我们的想当然要深刻复杂得多，跨文化交流像跨物种交配一样，很容易产生不马不虎的马马虎虎。有两个基本的解决方案可以化解这样的尴尬。

　　其一是重生方案，就是一个人可以在一个社区里出生，具有这个文化的内部视角，然后机缘巧合，他在另外一个社区里得以重生，获得新社区的文化身份和认同。例如，一个孩子出生在中国的洛阳，10岁开始在澳大利亚的墨尔本人家里借宿读书，他有可能拥有完整的中国文化认同，也有全面的澳大利亚文化惯习。

　　这其实是人类学家梦寐以求的获得社区新身份的过程，虽然大多数人类学者内心很早就放弃了这种努力，毕竟"人已经老了，如何能重生呢？岂能再进母腹生出来吗？"

　　其二是退而求其次的同情性理解方案。这需要先承认自身已经很难获得真实的异文化身份与认同（更遑论从来没有存在过的纯粹不杂），那么不妨接受这现实，然后怀有克制的好奇心和善意的同情心来理解异文化，进而可以具有对于自身固有文化的审视能力和批评精神，跳出自以为是的狭隘视野，不再做井底之蛙。这方案的侧重点在于对自身的反思和批判，"他山之石可以攻玉"。

本丛书就是希望读者获得后者的助益。子曰："益者三友——友直，友谅，友多闻。"以不同的声音提醒自己，世界很大，价值很多，人生很短。

阿昌族是一个人口很少的民族，2010年人口统计还不到4万人，大部分生活在中国和缅甸边界附近的德宏傣族景颇族自治州。但是这个民族并不小，因为他们具有自成一体的文化，在他们的世界里，有宇宙创造的图景，有社会运行的途径，有人类生存的价值。所以不能用小来形容这样的一个民族。

遗憾的是，阿昌族的传统文化正如同江河东流一样逝去，年轻的一代人无意传承古老的歌曲，更无法相信古老的信仰。等到某一天，他们不再年少，纵然意识到非物质文化遗产的价值，很可能为之晚矣。

现在，我们想做一些力所能及的工作，记录下某些东西，给出我们的声音，让一种文化不至湮没无音。同时，也请我们的读者不要用学术的冷漠来阅读，不妨用孩子的耳朵去聆听。

如果不是有一些不得不说的话，实际上大可不必有这篇序。

丛书主编：成功
中央民族大学生命与环境科学学院

General Preface to the Series of Books of Achang Ethnic Intangible Cultural Heritage

Perface should be brief and serve the content of the book. A preface to a series of books should be as concise as a roadside signpost.

There is a myth, or perhaps a misconception or an assumption in modern society, which holds that different societies and cultures are nothing more than what would come about when modern people adapt to a physical environment they are relocated to. In other words, if people in different societies were placed in a certain time and space, they would restore the basic norms of that environment, hence presenting a mixed cultural phenomenon.

Based on this assumption, human has achieved a certain sense of equality and uniformity, which is supported by the biological taxonomy of the natural sciences and provides a "self-evident" basic framework for civilization in modern societies.

Such a belief leads to the conviction of the modern expression (term) that "People of similar natures and emotions will have similar understandings". Beneath the polite facade of respecting different cultures lurks the ambition to deconstruct all cultural differences.

This series of books hopes to make a faint sound against what is taken for granted, reminding readers that cultural diversity is profound and complex, and cross-cultural communication, like cross-species breeding, is prone to produce something that is neither fish nor fowl. To avoid such an awkward result, there are two basic solutions as follows.

One way is the rebirth solution, in which case a person can be born into one community and develops an internal perspective of that culture. Then, by chance, he was born again in another community, acquiring the cultural identity and recognition of the new community. For example, a boy was born in Luoyang China, and at the age of 10, he started to live and study with a Melbourne family in Australia. The boy might have a complete Chinese cultural identity and a full experience of Australian lifestyle.

This is an anthropologist's dreaming process of acquiring a new identity in a community, although most anthropologists had given up on this endeavor long before. After all, "How can someone be born when he is old? Surely how he can enter a second time into his mother's womb to be born?"

Another way is to settle for the second best option of empathetic understanding. It is necessary to confess that it is hard enough to obtain one's own identity and identification with a different culture, (not to mention genuine identity and identification of a different culture, which is technically non-existent). We may as well accept the fact and understand alien cultures with restrained curiosity and well-intended compassion, which then helps us to examine and criticize our own culture, leave our narrow-mindedness behind and embrace a broader view on different cultures. The emphasis of this project is on self-reflection and criticism, that is, "Stones from other hills can be used to polish local jade".

It is the benefit of the latter for the readers that serves as the purpose of this series of books. Confucius said, "Three kinds of friends are beneficial to a person—friends who are straightforward, friends who are sincere, and friends who are knowledgeable". Amidst so many different voices, we remind ourselves that the world is vast, values are various, and life is short.

The Achang ethnic group is a minority with a very small population. The majority of them live in the Dehong Dai and Jingpo Autonomous Prefecture, Yunnan Province. But these people are not insignificant, because they have a self-contained culture, and in their world, there is a picture of the creation of the universe, a way of society operation, and the value of human existence. The word "small" doesn't do justice to such an ethnic group.

Unfortunately, the traditional culture of the Achang people has paled into history or faded with time. The younger generation has no intention of passing down the old songs, nor can they observe the faith of the old people. Perhaps one day when they are no longer young, they will realize the value of intangible cultural heritage, but it will be too late.

At present, we want to do what we can to record all that matters and make our voice heard in hope that this ethnic culture won't be lost without even being known to the world. At the same time, we request our readers not to read like an indifferent academic, but to listen like an attentive child.

This preface wouldn't have been necessary if there were not anything that had to be said.

Editor-in-Chief
Dr. Cheng Gong
College of Life and Environmental Sciences
Minzu University of China

前　言

《阿昌族民间故事集（一）》的来由

人类在没有文字的时代，如何创造、传承、拓展知识与认识世界？

最重要的方法，应该就是口头表达。世界知识产权组织有一个机构，叫作"知识产权与遗传资源、传统知识和民间文学艺术政府间委员会"（Intergovernmental Committee on Intellectual Property and Genetic Resources, Traditional Knowledge and Folklore, IGC）。其中的民间文学艺术，狭义上就是民间故事。

考虑到在人类的历史中，大多数的时间，大多数的地方，大多数的人都不使用文字。即便是现在，绝大多数的人的大部分交流仍然采用口头表达。那么，我们可以正视口头的民间故事的价值所在。

阿昌族被学术文献记录为一个没有文字的民族。实际上在笔者的调查中，不但发现了阿昌族的文字系统，而且还有三套文字方案。可惜的是，这些文字并没有被广泛采用，而是在个人水平上艰难传承。即便在阿昌族内部也没有什么人知道这些文字方案。

所以，阿昌族的文化，就更多依托于口传史诗、民间故事、歌曲唱词等口头叙事进行存储与传承。我们对这些内容进行了全面的收集整理，并非因为我们是民俗学或者民间文学的研究者，而是因为我们希望借助这样的工作，去理解淹没在层层叠叠累积起来的历史中的上古文化。1923 年 5 月 6 日，顾颉刚在《努力周报》的副刊《读书杂志》上发表《与钱玄同先生论古史书》，提出了"层累地造成的中国古史"的观点。这个学术观点迄今已有百年，成为我们解读中国古史绕不开的界碑。

因为阿昌族的口传民间故事，呈现了更真实的无文字信息传播、传承与传创形态。这样就为从口头到文字的跨文化理解提供了有价值的方案。

以上是我们从事阿昌族民间故事收集、整理、编撰、发表和翻译的目的。下面需要介绍一下具体的工作分配。

杨叶生先生是我的忘年交，他是阿昌族培养的第一代大学生，也是阿昌族口传史诗的唯一译介者。他以毕生精力，在耄耋之年搜集整理了阿昌族各种民间文学表达，包括口传史诗、口头叙事诗、动物故事集、民间故事集、民俗故事集、阿昌族古歌。其中，《阿昌族动物故事集》（中英文对照版）已经由知识产权出版社于2021年出版。

笔者作为阿昌族非物质文化遗产丛书主编，非常荣幸地参与了这本《阿昌族民间故事集（一）》的编撰工作。笔者的主要任务是对这些民间故事进行注疏性的导读。因为涉及云南的少数民族文化，很多背景差异会造成读者无法理解故事的指涉，甚至具体词汇的所指与能指，对于读者也会有难以逾越的隔阂。通过"编者按"的形式，提供阅读理解民间故事的钥匙，打开文化交流互动的门。

这本《阿昌族民间故事集（一）》由上海的叶佳旖女士（Ms. Jessica Ye）翻译。自2022年年底她接受翻译的委托之后，在繁忙的学业之余，一字一句地对这些故事进行汉译英翻译工作。译者自小对文字和语言表达极为敏感。她于2024年获得全国英语辩论联赛冠军、最佳辩手。其亦热心于保护文化多样性、女性平权及生物伦理方面的学术研究及写作，于2023年获得哈佛国际评论学术写作比赛（Harvard International Review Academic Writing Contest）最佳写作奖（Best Writing Award），于2024年获得约翰·洛克写作竞赛（John Locke Essay Competition）论文竞赛写作推荐奖。译者致力于为保护和传承少数民族传统文化尽绵薄之力，这亦是她参与翻译此丛书的初衷，希望此丛书成为一个有质量、有温度的读物，让更多的人可以分享阿昌族的传统文化。

按照阿昌族非物质文化遗产丛书的惯例，我们希望通过插图来增强趣味，提高美感，也形象地呈现出故事里的角色。故此邀约了姚思琪女士（Ms. Cindy Yao）来为本书设计插图和封面。她擅长中国传统绘画中的花鸟主题，按照她对于故事的感受和理解创作插画，使画面弥漫民间故事的讲述现场氛围。这样的艺术创作，使得本书在中英文对照之外，还获得了视觉表达的新空间。尤其是对于广大读者来说，阿昌族的人物形象和传统服饰得以生动表现。

  感谢扬州大学王世弘的汉语校对，感谢汉诺威高中（Hanover High School）的成了（Selah Cheng）的英文校对。感谢知识产权出版社的高超编辑和兰涛编辑对于本书的付出。

  最后，希望《阿昌族民间故事集（一）》收录的 36 个异彩纷呈的阿昌族民间故事，既是大俗大雅，亦是雅俗共赏。

本书编者：成功
于碧山居
2024 年 9 月 4 日

Foreword

The Origins of Folk Tales of Achang Nationality (Volume I)

How did Human create, transmit and develop knowledge and understanding world in eras without writing?

The most important method was likely oral expression. The World Intellectual Property Organization (WIPO) has a institution known as the "Intergovernmental Committee on Intellectual Property and Genetic Resources, Traditional Knowledge and Folklore" (IGC). The term "folklore" here, in narrower sense, refers to folk tales.

When we consider human history, in most of the time, in most places, the majority of people did not use writing. Even today, the vast majority of communication still takes place orally. Thus, we should recognize the value of oral folk tales.

The Achang people are recorded in academic literature as a ethnic group without writing system. However, in my investigations, the author discovered that not only do the Achang people have a writing system, but also have three different writing systems. Unfortunately, these writing systems have not been widely adopted, and are passed down with difficulty by individuals. Even within the Achang community, very few people are aware of these scripts.

As a result, the Achang culture is largely preserved and transmitted through oral epics, folk tales, songs and other oral narratives. We have undertaken the work of comprehensive collection and compilation of these materials, although we are not researchers of folklore or folk literature, we seek for using this work as a way to understand the ancient culture buried beneath layers upon layers of accumulation. On May 6, 1923, Mr. Jiegang Gu published "A Discussion with Mr. Xuantong Qian on Ancient Historical Texts" in the supplement of *The Weekly Effort* called *Book Magazine*, where he proposed the concept of "layered construction of Chinese ancient history". This academic viewpoint, now a century old, has become an unavoidable landmark in the interpretation of Chinese ancient history.

The oral folk tales of the Achang people present real form of non-verbal transmission, inheritance and innovation of information. Thus these stories offer valuable insight for cross-cultural understanding, from oral to written traditions.

This is the purpose of our collection, compilation, editing, publication and translation of Achang folk tales. Now, I'd like to briefly introduce the division of labor involved in this project.

Mr. Yang Yesheng is a lifelong friend of mine. He is the first-generation undergraduate student come from the Achang people and the only translator of Achang oral epics. With his lifelong dedication, he has, in his old age, painstakingly collected and compiled various forms of Achang folk literature, including oral epics, narrative poems, collections of animal stories, folk tales, folk stories and ancient songs of the Achang people. His *The Achang Collection of Animal Stories* was published in a bilingual Chinese-English edition by the Intellectual Property Publishing House in 2021.

As the chief editor of *the series of books of Achang Intangible Cultural Heritage*, I am honored to have participated in the compilation of *Folk Tales of Achang Nationality (Volume Ⅰ)*. My primary responsibility was to provide annotations and guided readings of these folk tales. Since this work involves the culture of a minority ethnic group from Yunnan, many cultural differences may cause readers to struggle with understanding the references to the stories, as well as the meanings of specific terms. Through editorial notes, I aim to provide readers with the keys to understand these folk tales, open doors to cultural exchange and interaction.

Folk Tales of Achang Nationality (Volume Ⅰ) was translated by Ms. Ye Jiayi (Jessica) from Shanghai. Since accepting the translation commission on the end of 2022, she has worked diligently, despite her busy academic schedule, meticulously translating these stories word by word from Chinese to English. Jessica is highly sensitive to words and language expression. She earned the championship and the Best Speaker awards at the National High School Debate League Competition in 2024. Additionally, she is passionate about academic research and writing in the fields of cultural diversity preservation, women's rights and bioethics. She has received the Best Writing Award in the Harvard International Review Academic Writing Contest in 2023 and a Commendation in the John Locke Essay Competition in 2024. Her participation in this translation project stems from her dedication to the preservation and transmission of traditional cultures of ethnic minorities. She hopes that this series of books will become a work of both quality and warmth, allowing more people to appreciate the traditional culture of the Achang people.

In line with the tradition of *the series of books of Achang Intangible Cultural Heritage,* we aim to enhance the appeal and aesthetic quality of the book through illustrations, while vividly portraying the characters in the stories. So we invited Ms. Yao Siqi (Cindy) to design the illustrations and cover for this book. Specializing in the traditional Chinese Bird-and-Flower Painting, she created watercolor illustrations based on her own impressions and understanding of the stories, bringing to life the atmosphere of storytelling scenes in folk narratives. This artistic contribution adds a new dimension of visual expression to the book, complementing the bilingual Chinese and English text. For readers, in particular, the characters and traditional attire of the Achang people are vividly brought to life on the pages.

We would like to extend our gratitude to Wang Shihong from Yangzhou University for his Chinese proofreading, and to Selah Cheng from

Hanover High School (Hanover, NH) for her English proofreading. Special thanks to editors Ms. Gao Chao and Ms. Lan Tao from the Intellectual Property Publishing House for their contributions to this book.

    Last but not least, we hope that these 36 vivid and colorful folk tales included in *Folk Tales of Achang Nationality (Volume I)* truly embody both the profound and the popular, being enjoyable for both refined and common tastes alike.

Dr. Cheng Gong
In Green Mountain
Sep. 4, 2024

目录

1…开辟漕涧坝

3…The Establishment of the Caojian Plain

5…神奇的龙桌子

7…The Miraculous Loong Table

9…蜈蚣克蟒蛇

11…Centipede Restrains Python

13…祭龙求雨的故事

18…The Story of the Rain Ritual Sacred to the Dragon

23…皇阁寺的传说

26…Legend of Huangge Temple

29…小黄龙

31…The Little Yellow Dragon

33…曹扎和龙女

39…Caozha and the Dragon Girl

47…腊银和腊康(一)

52…Layin and Lakang Ⅰ

57…腊银和腊康(二)

62…Layin and Lakang Ⅱ

69…腊银和腊康(三)

72…Layin and Lakang Ⅲ

75…阿昌族不信鬼的由来
78…The Origin of Achang's Disbelief in Ghosts
81…老实人
83…The Honest People
85…继母
89…The Stepmother
94…猎人过生日
97…A Hunter's Birthday
99…白鸡姑娘
102…The White Hen Girl
105…爱撒萨
108…Yuan Sasa
111…大蛇的故事
115…A Story of the Great Serpent
120…双妹俩
124…The Two Sisters
129…万能的鼓
132…The Magical Drum
136…眉间长旋儿的姑娘
140…The Girl with a Swirl Between Her Brows
144…奢三和线二
146…She San and Xian Er
149…一筒竹子通梢的故事
152…A Story of a Bamboo That Is Hollow All the Way Through the Top
156…螺蛳妹
163…The Story of the Snail Girl

171…宝剑
176…The Precious Sword
181…神奇的拐杖
184…The Magical Cane
188…瞎子弟弟
192…The Blind Younger Brother
197…负心的干兄弟
202…The Godbrother with an Unfaithful Heart
207…弟兄分家
209…Brothers' Separation
212…弟兄俩的银子盒
214…The Silver Box of Two Brothers
217…偷银罐
219…Steal the Silver Pot
222…各人心肝各人带
224…Everyone Has Their Own Intentions
226…腊良和腊洪
228…La Liang and La Hong
230…仙草
232…The Miraculous Herb
235…姊妹三人
239…The Three Sisters
243…狗头国
246…Dog Head Kingdom
248…白狗代嫁
250…White Dog Replaces a Person to Get Married

开辟漕涧坝

在很古以前,漕涧这个地方原是一块荒无人烟的草坝子。坝子里到处长满了茫茫的芦草和杂木丛,坝子四周都是密密麻麻的大树林,一排一排,一层一层地把坝子围住。

一天,住在下面澜沧江边上的人家放养在山上的牛群不见了,他们找了三天三夜,找遍了江两岸的大小山头、青沟也不见牛群的影子。最后他们在一处山脚下发现了一串牛蹄印,就顺着蹄印翻过一个一个山包,来到了澜沧江西边最大的雪冲山下。一看,天呐!牛蹄印竟朝雪冲山上去了,高高的雪冲山顶上一年四季都积着雪,牛群到山上去做什么呢?大家商量了一下,就顺着蹄印朝山上爬去。爬啊爬,终于爬到了山顶,这里没有树,也没有草,只有白皑皑的雪。在白森森的雪地上有一串清晰的牛蹄印,翻过山梁到山的那边去了。人们翻过山梁一看,哎——哟哟,山下有一块大大的坝子,坝子里的绿草丛中有一个一个亮晶晶的水塘,失踪的牛群正在水塘中打滚呢。人们高兴得忍不住大声地喊:"瞧见了,瞧见了,牛群,牛群。"后来大家就把这草坝取名为"瞧见坝",后来不知怎么会叫别的了,就成了现在的漕涧坝。

大伙来到坝子里,找到了正在水塘中打滚的牛群,见一个个牛肚子都吃得滚圆滚圆的,就像是一面面大鼓,几天不见的牛群不仅没有饿瘦,反而个个膘肥毛亮、十分健壮。到了第二年,牛群又不见了,大家又来到坝子里找牛,只见在去年牛群打滚的烂泥塘边,长着一簇一簇的谷子。长长的谷穗沉甸甸地低着头,在微风中不停地摇晃,仿佛是在向人们招手。

原来去年牛群到这里时,身上沾了谷种,在泥塘里打滚时就把谷种无意中栽在这里了。大伙马上七手八脚地在烂泥塘四周开挖了一丘丘水田,派人回家去拿来了谷种种下去,第二年就长出了一片片金黄的谷子,比山下江边的谷子还要好。从此大家就陆续把家迁到这里来,绕围着这个烂泥塘又开出了很多很多的田,后来大家就把这个第一次长出谷子的烂泥塘叫作"田母子"，因为它像母亲一样生出了许许多多的田，生出了现在整个漕涧坝子的田。

讲述：左春胜
搜集整理：李淳

编者按： 阿昌族有开天辟地的创世型故事，就是口传史诗《遮帕麻和遮咪麻》，为他们提供了最基础的世界观解释；阿昌族也有具体而微的地方性故事，比如本文"开辟漕涧坝"，说明了一个地方的发现和开发。

首先需要解释"开辟漕涧坝"里的"坝"。这是一种云南常见的地理表达方式，指众山环绕之间的一片平原，故此英文译为"plain"。云南多山多水，生物多样性极为丰富，但最适合人类居住的，是山间平坝。

在阿昌族主要分布的滇西高黎贡山，平坝具有更好的粮食生产能力，往往是傣族和其他民族的聚居区，而阿昌族村寨坐落在地势相对平缓的山坡上。因此，对于阿昌族来说，平坝是非常难得的理想家园。

"开辟漕涧坝"这个故事讲出了一群阿昌族人翻山越岭、筚路蓝缕，发现和开发一个坝子的历史记忆。

虽然采用故事的结构呈现这个历史过程，但是，这个故事对于地理和生态的描绘，是非常精确的。例如，第一段中间的芦草，说明这里是一个湿地；杂木丛，是湿地演替的后续阶段；边缘的树林，是陆生植物长期发展的顶级群落。第二段中间的绿草丛里的水塘，无疑是湿地演替过程中残留的水体，烂泥塘也指出了水成土的特征。而这个坝子被崇山峻岭环绕和隔离，山是大雪山，终年积雪，山顶不长树，也不长草，对于低纬度高海拔的山峦刻画非常到位。

如果引申一下，我们可以从故事中，感受到阿昌族作为一个具有"游耕"传统的迁徙型部落的很多线索。对于牛群的重视，从谷子的生长中，发现新的迁居可能，这些都是"游耕"部落的生活方式。

故事以"田母子"结尾，这个生生不息的田地，不仅是谷子的母亲，也是赖以为生的阿昌族的大地妈妈。

The Establishment of the Caojian Plain

In the old times, Caojian was originally a barren grass plain. The plain was full of weeds and bushes and surrounded by a dense forest.

On the riverside of the Lancang River, there was a family. One day, they lost their herd of cattle in the mountains. They have searched for three days and three nights, going through all the hills and ditches on both sides of the river, but there was no signs of the herd. Finally, they found a trail of hoofprints at the foot of a hill, and followed it across one hill after the other, to the largest snow mountain on the west side of the Lancang River. Oh dear! The trail was heading towards the snowy mountain where snow piles up all year round. Why did the herd go to the mountain? After discussing the matter, they followed the hoofprints and climbed up the mountain. They climbed and climbed, and eventually they reached the top of the mountain, where there were no trees, no grass, but only pure white snow. There was a clear trail of hoofprints on the white snow, over the mountain ridge, and all the way to the other side of the mountain. The family looked beyond the mountain ridge. Oh my god! There was a big plain at the base of the mountain, and among the green grass in the plain was a shiny pond where the missing herd was wallowing and playing around in the waters. They were so happy that they couldn't help but shout, "Look! Look! It's the herd!" Later, the people named this grass dam "Qiaojian Ba" (Qiaojian means "look" in Chinese). Subsequently, it somehow got named incorrectly and became the current Caojian Plain.

People came to the plain, and found the herd rolling in the pond, bellies full like large drums. The herd was not starving and skinny at all, but fat, shiny, strong and healthy. In the following year, the herd disappeared again, and everyone went to the plain to look for them once more. By the side of the muddy pond where the cattle frolicked last year, there were growing clusters of big barley. The ripe grains lowered their heads in the breeze and swayed slowly, as if they were waving to the people.

But how can there be grain here for no reason? Ah, it turned out that when the cattle came here last year, they got grain seeds on them and shed them here unintentionally when they were playing in the muddy pond. People immediately dug rice paddies around the muddy pond and sent some men home to bring grain seeds to plant them here. The next year, patches of golden grains grew, even better than the ones that grown by the riverside under the mountain. From that time onwards, people moved their families to this pond one after another, and many paddies were opened around this muddy pond. Later, people called this muddy pond, where grains grew for the first time, the "mother of the paddies", because it was like a mother that gave birth to many paddies and gave birth to the entire Caojian Plain as it is now.

神奇的龙桌子

阿昌族聚居的云龙县漕涧坝，有很多美丽诱人的自然景观和神奇的传说故事。

漕涧坝的东南边，世袭上司早氏宅居的后山小梁上，就有一座风景秀丽的高山，称为苗丹山。山脚下有一寺庙，寺庙后有一座圆形的小山头，山上只长青草，不长树木。小山头上堆着整整齐齐的石头，石堆上有一块圆形的大石板。大石板的直径有9尺2寸，厚2尺1寸。石板平面光洁如洗，酷似石匠精心雕琢而成的圆桌。石桌北边有一个光脚板脚印，这脚印把圆桌踩陷6寸多深，而桌面没有半点破损的痕迹。这就是当地传说的神奇的龙桌子。

传说，漕涧坝西北边的志奔山上有一个老龙王，它和居住在漕涧坝的阿昌族酋长做朋友，志奔山龙王经常在这张桌子上宴请阿昌族酋长和外来的高人贵客。

有一天，志奔山龙王邀请了永昌府（保山）睡佛寺的睡佛老爷和阿昌族酋长到志奔山游览九十九龙潭。游览结束，志奔山龙王宴请睡佛老爷和阿昌族酋长，品尝志奔山龙家风味。三个好朋友围在这张石桌子边吃边喝边聊，时间过得好快，不知不觉天色暗淡，夜幕降临。睡佛老爷想：今天我若不能赶回永昌府，保山坝一定会发大洪水，就会淹没庄稼和房屋，那时候回去一切都完了。现在若要赶回去，时间已经来不及了，因此睡佛老爷心里很焦虑。志奔山龙王看在心眼里，便上前去劝慰睡佛老爷说："你别着急！我会马上送你赶回永昌府的。你先蹬上桌子看看你所行走的线路。"睡佛老爷听了老龙王的话，马上蹬上石桌，他万万没想到，一只脚刚蹬上大石桌边，他就腾云驾雾飞了起来，他还没来得及向志奔山龙王和阿昌族酋长告辞，一转眼就回到了永昌府。于是桌子上就留下了永昌府睡佛老爷的一只脚印。

编者按： 谁才是土地的主人？有一个故事曾经提及，澳大利亚一位土著酋长听说自己的家乡居然是远在天边的大不列颠岛上的女王属地，就义愤填膺地说，她从来没有涉足过这些土地，也讲不出这片大地的来历，说不出一草一木的故事，怎么可能是这地的主人？

故此，土地和人的关系，并非简单的资源和利用者的经济联系，而是丰富多彩的各方位筋脉相连。

漕涧坝的政治中心早氏土司的后面有苗丹山，山脚下有一个宗教中心寺庙，山头有一个神迹遗存"龙桌子"。讲故事的人对于桌子的形态描述得无微不至，几句话就可以在听众的心里刻划出一个明确的样子出来。

故事里在这"龙桌子"上请客吃饭的，居然不是地处漕涧坝东南的苗丹山的神明，而是漕涧坝西北的志奔山龙王。这个细节颇值得品味，显然这是代表了本地社会生态系统中的生态系统之神，可以抽象地称之为"龙"，或者在汉族传统中的"社"。故事发生在这个"龙"和更大的政治权力中心"永昌府"的睡佛老爷之间，但是作陪的，是本地的阿昌族祖先，一位酋长。这显示了阿昌族在这个地区的角色举足轻重，人在大地和神明之间的位置。

虽然"永昌府"早已在地图上改为"保山地区"，但是在民间，仍然作为一种符号，存在于口传故事和历史传说之中。

The Miraculous Loong* Table

In the place where the Achang people live, which is the Caojian Plain, Yunlong County, there are many beautiful and enchanting natural landscapes, as well as miraculous legendary stories.

On the southeast side of Caojian Plain, there is a scenic mountain called Miaodan Hill, located behind the ancestral house of the Tusi of Zao (Tusi, often translated as headmen or chieftains, were hereditary tribal leaders recognized as imperial officials by the Yuan, Ming and Qing Dynasties of China.). At the foot of the mountain, there is a temple, and behind the temple, there is a circular hill, which is covered with grass but no trees. Stones are neatly stacked on top of the hill, and there is a large circular stone slab on the stone pile. The diameter of the stone slab is 9. 84 feet and 2 inches, and is 2. 19 feet and 1 inch thick. Its surface is smooth and clean, resembling a round table carefully carved by a stonemason. On the north side of the stone table, there is a barefoot print that has sunk about 6 inches into the table. Yet there is no sign of damage on the tabletop. This table is the legendary magical Dragon Table of the local folklore.

It was said, on Zhiben Mountain, which is in the northwest side of Caojian Plain, there was an old Dragon King. He was a good friend of the Achang tribal ancestral leader who lived in Caojian Plain. The Dragon King of Zhiben often feasted with the Achang tribal leader and other distinguished guests at this table.

One day, the Dragon King invited the Sleeping Buddha Master of the Sleeping Buddha Temple in Yongchang (Baoshan's former name) and the Achang tribal leader to visit the Ninety-Nine Dragon Pools on Zhiben

---

* Note: The dragon mentioned in this book refers to Chinese dragon or Loong. The same as bellow.

Mountain. After the tour, the Dragon King hosted a banquet for them, serving them the specialties of Zhiben Mountain. The three good friends sat around this stone table, eating, drinking and chatting. Time flew by, and they didn't realize that it was getting dark and night was falling upon them. The Sleeping Buddha Master thought to himself, "If I can't make it back to Yongchang today, there will be a big flood in Baoshan Plain, which will destroy the crops and houses. Everything will be ruined when I get back." But now, it was too late to get back in time. The Sleeping Buddha Master felt perplexed. Seeing this, the wise Dragon King approached the Sleeping Buddha Master and comforted him, said, "Don't worry! I will send you back to Yongchang immediately. Firstly, you must step onto the table and recall the route you have traveled". Hearing the words of the Dragon King, the Sleeping Buddha Master immediately stepped onto the stone table. Unexpectedly as soon as one foot touched the edge of the table, he ascended into the clouds and flew away. He didn't even have time to bid farewell to the Dragon King and the Achang tribal leader. In the blink of eyes, he returned to Yongchang. Thus, a footprint of the sleeping Buddha Master from the Sleeping Buddha Temple of Yongchang was left on the table.

蜈蚣克蟒蛇

明洪武十六年，明廷授予漕涧阿昌族首领早纳"土千总"之职。"土千总"统治区域后来得到扩展，东至雪山，与旧州段氏土司辖地接壤；南至栗柴坝，与保山瓦窑相连；西至孙足河底，与保山瓦马相邻；北至分水岭，包括现在的老窝乡、民建乡等地，管辖面积达1000多平方公里。

漕涧"土千总"世袭延续了475年，直至清朝咸丰年间才被废除。由于土司政权内部争权夺位，加重赋税，导致统治区内的百姓日益不满。传说有人便从外地请来一位堪舆大师，请他察看仁山苗丹早氏土司衙门的风水地脉，找克制土司衙门的办法。

堪舆大师登上苗丹村对面的嘎窝山头，仔细观察苗丹山的来龙去脉和土司衙门位置。堪舆大师经过几天的观察研究，终于发现：苗丹山势如卧居崇山山脉中一条巨大的蟒蛇，气势汹汹地正要下山吸食漕涧坝里的人畜。土司衙门就建在这条巨蟒的头部，要克制这条蟒蛇，必须在漕涧坝的空讲河上架一座桥，桥的模型要像一条蜈蚣，抬头看着苗丹山。蟒蛇看见蜈蚣就不敢动了。风水地理学上叫蜈蚣克蟒蛇。凑足50两银子的那些人听了堪舆大师的这番解释后高兴极了，马上一传十、十传百、百传千，积极策划建造蜈蚣桥。

原来在保山瓦窑通往泸水六库的必经驿道上，漕涧空讲河上有一座人畜通行的简易裸体木桥。由于雨水冲刷，经常复修，甚至被洪水冲毁多次。

堪舆大师离开漕涧以后，漕涧街上的村民请来一群手艺高超的石匠，在旧桥两端支砌两个高大的桥墩，河心建三个桥墩，设4个流水孔，工匠用厚厚的栗木大方搭起一座长5丈多、宽1丈有余的大桥，桥身采用木屋架形式。上顶用筒瓦盖成两边出水的风雨廊桥，在上层屋檐底下的两边再用筒瓦各加盖一屋一片厦。酷似蜈蚣身子下长出一对儿翅膀来。桥两侧用密密直立的圆木支撑着桥身木架。又像蜈蚣密密麻麻的脚杆露出来。桥的东边中梁顶上设有一个石灰做成的蜈蚣头。蜈蚣头正对着仁山苗丹村的土司衙门。这就是当地人叫的"蜈蚣桥"。

据传:"蜈蚣桥"建成几十年后,苗丹村土司也就逐渐走向崩溃了。

编者按: 历史未必是任人打扮的小姑娘,也可能是打抱不平的神话传说。1382年是洪武十五年,大明帝国封立段保(汉人)为云龙州土司。本故事指名道姓地见证说一位阿昌族首领"早纳"于洪武十六年被册封为"土千总",就是能够管理一个区域的半独立行政司法单位。这两者是一致的,还是矛盾的,有待商榷。虽然在第一段里,对于这个"土千总"的管辖范围刻画得具体而微,但是其实际影响力也是很难证明的。我们可以从这个故事里看到的是,一个远方的更大更高的权力中心介入遥远的漕涧坝。对于当地的阿昌族来说,出现了一个延续475年的本土治理政权。

这个权力的出现就不依赖当地人,也不是为了服务本地,故此异化为一个争权夺利、盘剥百姓的政权也就不足为怪了。由于这样的霸权,阿昌族苦难深重,自然生发出抗争的意识。但是由于没有先进的思想引领,走向了以风水对抗暴政的路线。故此,既要肯定他们的反抗,又要反思他们反抗的方式。

这种反抗被耶鲁大学的詹姆斯·C.斯科特称为"弱者的武器"。在同名的《弱者的武器》中,斯科特以东南亚的山地民族为例,指出了当普通人在这样的处境下,会采用传统文化的方式,进行消极抵抗。

本文就是阿昌族用建造一座貌似蜈蚣的廊桥方式,克制了如同蟒蛇一样吸食民脂民膏的土司政权。有意思的是,故事里强调"凑足50两银子的那些人听了堪舆大师的这番解释后高兴极了,马上一传十、十传百、百传千,积极策划建造蜈蚣桥"。这既是某种共谋,也是某种隐蔽。这种对于暴政的反抗,融化在人民群众的汪洋大海之中。而这些人没有出卖这个秘密给土司,更暗示了土司的不得人心。

Centipede Restrains Python

In the sixteenth year of Hongwu's Period (1383 A.D.), the court of Ming Dynasty appointed Zao Na, the leader of the Achang ethnic group in Caojian, as the Local Chiliarch or Tusi of Thousand. The Tusi Zao's jurisdiction expanded eastward to the Snow Mountains, bordering the territory of the Jiuzhou County of Duan the Tusi. To the south, it extended to Lichai Plain, adjacent to Baoshan Wayao. To the west, it reached the bottom of Sunzu River, neighboring Baoshan Wama. To the north, it stretched to the watershed, including the village that present-day known as Laowo Village, Minjian Village, and other areas, with a total area of over 1,000 square kilometers.

The governance of hereditary lineage of the Tusi Zao in Caojian has lasted for 475 years until it was abolished during the Xianfeng Period of the Qing Dynasty. Due to power struggles and increased taxation within the dominant of Tusi system, the people in the domain area became increasingly dissatisfied. Legend has it that someone invited a *Fengshui* master from a faraway region to come to survey the Tusi Zao's official governance in Renshan Miaodan territory and find a way to restrain the official governance of Tusi.

The *Fengshui* master climbed to the top of *Gawo* peak, which was on the opposite side of Miaodan Village, and carefully observed the origin and position of Miaodan Mountain and the chieftain's office. After several days of observation and study, the *Fengshui* master finally discovered that Miaodan Mountain was like a giant python lying among the Chongshan Mountains, angrily preparing to descend to prey on the people and livestock in Caojian Plain. The chieftain's office was built on the head of this giant python. To restrain it, a bridge was need to be built over the Kongjiang River in Caojian Plain, modeled after a centipede, raising its head and looking at Miaodan Mountain. When the python saw the centipede, it wouldn't dare to move. This method is called Centipede Restrains Python in *Fengshui*. The people were overjoyed after hearing the *Fengshui* master's explanation and immediately spread the news. They actively planned to build the Centipede Bridge.

Originally, there was a simple wooden bridge for people and livestock to pass over the Kongjiang River in Caojian on the must-pass post road from Baoshan Wabao to the Lushui Liuku. Due to erosion of rain, the wooden bridge needed frequent repairs and was even washed away many times by floods.

After the *Fengshui* master had left Caojian, the villagers invited a group of highly skilled stonemasons. They built tall bridge piers on both ends of the old bridge and three bridge piers in the middle of the river, with four water holes. The craftsmen used thick chestnut wood to construct a bridge that was over 17 meters long and more than 3 meters wide, bridge body adopted the building structure of house. On the top of bridge was covered with barrel tiles, forming a covered bridge with water outlets on both sides. Underneath the upper eaves, two tiles were added on both sides. It looked like a pair of wings growing under the body of a centipede. The sides of the bridge were supported by densely arranged vertical logs, like the legs of a centipede. On the east side of the bridge, there was a lime-made centipede head on top of the middle beam. The centipede head faced the local village of chief's office in Renshan Miaodan Village. This is what the locals call the Centipede Bridge.

According to legend, several decades after the completion of the Centipede Bridge, the chieftain of Miaodan Village experienced a gradual collapse of power.

祭龙求雨的故事

阿昌之源——云南省大理白族自治州云龙县漕涧镇仁山村，是大理州的西大门，又是大理、怒江、保山三个地州的接合部，阿昌族人民就世居在漕涧这块风水宝地上。阿昌族人世代以农耕为生，在这里繁衍生息，演绎了无数动人心弦的故事，给后人留下了多少神奇美丽的传说。

漕涧坝的东南面，背靠着一座风景秀丽的苗丹山。苗丹山的半山腰，有一个方圆300多米的青草坪，草坪周围生长着鲜艳的映山红和茂密的翠绿灌木丛林，草坪中心有一潭四季不涨不退清澈如镜的大水潭。水潭的左侧有一块长10多米、宽4米多的光滑如洗的天生大石板，又叫"磕头板"，"磕头板"上端有一块长4米多、高1米多的天生石板，酷似一张石桌子，又叫龙桌子。这里就是世代留传的阿昌族人祭龙求雨潭。求雨潭往里走就是龙王潭。行人每到此处都低声细语，唯恐唤醒沉睡中的龙王，否则，不一会儿天空就会乌云密布，接着就会下起瓢泼大雨。这个缘故还得从下面说起。

相传，有一天，有个乡绅左老先生去漕涧赶街，在经过弹弓坡时被一个浑身长满疥疮的陌生男子拦住了去路，让他帮忙挠痒痒，犹豫再三，善良的左老先生答应了他的要求，替他挠痒痒。当他脱去衣服时，天哪！全身上下哪有一寸完好的皮肤！这怎么办呢？既然已经答应他，看来难以推辞了，左老先生于是就坚持帮他挠痒痒，挠了一会儿左老先生就走了。

第二天，当左老先生经过弹弓坡时又遇见了昨天那个人，他要求左老先生继续给他挠痒痒。左老先生想了想，昨天已经帮过他了，再帮一次也无所谓，反正闲着也是闲着，帮人就帮到底吧！就再一次替他挠痒痒，在挠到胳肢窝时，看到有颗小痣，咦！太奇怪了，怎么在这个地方会有痣呢？左老先生把脸凑近一看原来是只虱子，左老先生小心翼翼地把它掐住，捉了出来。就在这一刻令人不可思议的事情发生了，这位浑身长满疥疮的人身上的疥疮一下子就消失了，显露出他的真面目，变成一个英俊潇洒的男儿。左老先生心中不禁惊叹，真是一表人才呀！惊喜中又持疑惑，于是便问其故，可是这男儿没说事情的缘由。道过别之后，各自走了。

第三天，当左老先生再次经过弹弓坡时，这男儿又在那等他，并向他招手，示意左老先生走向他，与他靠近些，好像有话要说。他告诉左老先生：自己是一条龙，原本是志奔山龙王的三太子，在经过仁山时由于被虫子叮咬，体力透支过度，无法回去，只得化成人栖息在此，不料遇到善良的左老先生不嫌弃自己一身长满了疥疮，救了自己。昨天在这里担心身份暴露带来祸事，立即回到志奔山。父亲问起他最近去了哪里？于是，他将情况如实向父亲说了出来。这次回来是要邀请左老先生到志奔山家中去做客，父亲有礼物相送以回报救子之恩。

三日后，他们来到漕涧坝西北面一座海拔3000多米，方圆数十公里的大高山，当地人称为志奔山。

凹凸起伏的山顶被原始森林覆盖，在森林茂密的山间，漫山遍野开满了红的、紫的、白的各色杜鹃花，香柏苍翠，花繁草绿，犹如地毯，志奔山共有九十九个小龙潭，龙潭水幽深，净洁无比。据传，九十九个小龙潭是志奔山龙王的居住地和游耍潭，一般人既找不到龙潭也不敢去龙潭玩耍。志奔山富丽堂皇，仿佛是人间天堂，应有尽有。龙王热情地接待了他，并让他挑选一个宝物作为答谢，可是这里有数不尽、道不完的宝物，该选什么好呢？龙王的三太子告诉他，父亲有这么多的财宝，最贵重的要数那尊龙马，它有神奇的力量。左老先生就想，若能得之，它能呼风唤雨，家中百亩良田不就可以浇灌了嘛！再说回去路途遥远，带其他的宝物也带不动，于是就选了一尊黄金龙马。可是如果就这样带回去，路上若遇上盗匪不就丢了宝物，岂不是辜负了龙王一片心意，弄得不好搭进了自己的性命也难说。龙王父子也看出他的心思，于是就将此尊黄金龙马变成了铜龙马。几天之后，左老先生带着铜龙马回到莲花村（今仁山丹梯村）。

相传，居住在漕涧坝的阿昌族人生性忠厚，直爽，为人公道朴实。所以，志奔山龙王很喜欢和阿昌族酋长交往，经常往来，龙王和酋长就成了相交甚密的好朋友，龙王还经常邀请酋长到志奔山九十九个小龙潭游耍。逢年过节，酋长也邀约龙王变形化装后到家里来做客，相互间有求必应，无所不帮。后来，在云龙的阿昌族人对志奔山龙王十分崇敬，鼎敬龙王为神，奉龙似仙。

漕涧坝有一万多亩稻田，自古以来，由于干旱缺水，当地人叫"雷响田"，全靠老天下雨来种庄稼。如遇大旱年，过了农历五月十三，天还不下大雨，水稻无法移栽，阿昌族酋长就要组织人马到苗丹山求雨坪求雨了。求雨前，村里要请一位德高望重，早姓改左姓的土司后人来主事，要精通求雨秘诀的人并带领三十五个属龙的童男子，在仁山村东、西、南、北、中五处各取一担水到求雨坪，还要搭建起一丈多高的"五方龙王坛"。童男子们背上牲礼：鸡、鸭、鹅、鱼，贡品：香、烛、钱纸、食物等祭祀用品，顶着烈日爬上苗丹山到求雨潭祭龙求雨。烧火煮饭，等待牲礼祭品煮熟后，就把贡品和牲礼供献在求雨潭边那张龙桌子上，来祭奠龙神。上山求雨的每个人都要恭恭敬敬在那张"磕头板"桌上三跪九叩，怀着诚心默求志奔山龙王降雨，保佑阿昌人当年五谷丰登。主事者边念咒边画符，吟诵求雨"秘诀"，恳请志奔山龙王及时施云布雨，以便按时栽插，不延误节令。通过祭师求雨、裸男献礼、裸男狂吼、裸果狂奔，请求龙王发大水。

祭奠龙神结束，接着就是一顿饱餐，求雨人酒足饭饱时，太阳已经偏西了。这时，求雨的男子汉们脱光衣裤，选1个或2个小孩和年长者背衣物外，其余人的脸上和全身糊上稀泥巴，让别人看不清本人面目，然后，往山下的田坝里跑，做农活的人看见求雨的人迎面跑过来了，连忙大声喊叫："老天要下大雨了！老天要下大雨了……"直到太阳落山，求雨人才到僻静处，洗净身上的泥巴，穿衣裤回到各自家中。

最为神奇的是即使前晌午烈日当空，但是祭雨之后就会下起瓢泼大雨，这也成为仁山一带的一个未解之谜。

云龙漕涧阿昌族的祭龙求雨做法一直延续至20世纪50年代初。当地60岁以上老人大都参加过祭龙求雨。新中国成立后，党和政府高度重视水利建设，漕涧坝沟渠密布，水源得到充分利用，万亩水稻能按时栽插，阿昌族祭龙求雨的真实故事也逐步被人们遗忘了。

讲述：赵龙父子
搜集整理：左骞　左续忠

编者按：这个祭祀求雨的过程，与农业发展有很深的关系。农业分为两个基本的模式，粗放型农业和集约型农业，前者代表性的是刀耕火种,后者代表性的是精耕细作。刀耕火种经常在降雨比较少,或者不稳定的环境中,种植旱作作物,例如五谷里的黍和稷。精耕细作是在水量较大,相对稳定的环境中,种植湿生植物,例如五谷里的稻。

故此,稳定和充足的水量是阿昌族极为关注的问题。在没有大型的水利工程的情况下,各自为政的村寨需要解决一个超过他们能力的挑战。而龙王作为一位司水的神明无疑是阿昌族特别敬重的对象。

在这个讲述中,并没有一般故事的前因后果,线索与逻辑都飘忽不定,这是口头故事的讲述特征。但是总体脉络里仍然围绕着龙王故事。

开篇"阿昌族人世代以农耕为生",指出了阿昌族的生存背景,也点明了阿昌族敬奉龙王的文化根源。不过这种表述多少有点不识庐山真面目,只缘身在此山中。因为阿昌族从族源上,具有氐羌谱系,很可能是在从北向南的迁徙过程中,从游牧转向游耕,只是在最近的几百年,才相对稳定地采用了定居农业的生活方式。当然,哪怕只有 200 年,在口传文学中,就会自然表达为"世代如此这般"。故此,在很多非物质文化遗产领域,需要区分记忆中的古老和历史上的革新。

实际上这个龙王故事包含了三个片段,第一个片段讲了左先生和龙王之子的奇遇;第二个片段讲了志奔山龙王和阿昌族酋长的交情;第三个片段讲了向龙王求雨的方式和应验。如果看到了这三个层面,也就理解了故事的某种潜在线索:行善产生了私人恩德,并且有名有姓的左先生,家住莲花村,还有铜龙马为物证;阿昌族人的公道朴实,让志奔山龙王欣赏,并与阿昌族酋长有了领导人级别的交往,建立了互利的关系;最后顺理成章地说明阿昌族酋长在苗丹山求雨的过程和灵验,这都是建立在前两个故事的铺垫基础之上的。

故事重心其实是求雨的过程,特别是裸体狂奔这个独特的风俗。《伊川易传》卷四:裸以求神,荐牲而祈。这显示裸体求雨这个方式,是非常古老的民俗。恐怕与传说之中旱魃是裸体有关。《神异经》记载:"南方有人,长二三尺,袒身,目在顶,走如行风,名曰魃。所见之国大旱,赤地千里,一名旱母。"关键的信息来自董仲舒的《春秋繁露·精华》:"大旱雩祭而请雨,大水鸣鼓而攻社。""雩祭"是求雨的祭祀活动,特征是舞蹈,例如,《论语·先进》曰:"暮春者,春服既成。冠者五六人,童子六七人,浴乎沂,风乎舞雩,咏而归。"另有记载显示,如果长期不雨,就会把巫觋赤裸放在太阳下暴晒。

这个讲述者格外强调裸体的都是男性，但是如果按照上古的文化传统，以及目前仍然在印度、尼泊尔等地的风俗，求雨的裸者应该是女性。故此，应该有学人专门去这些故事流传的区域，认真进行田野访谈，以求证此事。

The Story of the Rain Ritual Sacred to the Dragon

In Renshan Village, Caojian Town, Yunlong County, which is the origin of the Achang people, We finds the western gateway of Dali Prefecture and the combination of Dali, Nujiang and Baoshan. The Achang people reside in Caojian, which has been a beautiful place for generations, have been making a living for many generations. They have been prosperous here, creating countless touching stories and leaving many magical and wonderful legends for future generations.

The southeast side of Caojian Plain is situated next to the scenic Miaodan Mountain. Halfway up, there is a green lawn of more than 300 meters in width, with bright rhododendrons and dense green bushes growing around, and a large pond of crystal-clear water in the center of the lawn that remains full in all seasons. On the left side of the pond, there is a smooth natural stone slab of more than 10 meters in length and 4 meters in width, also called the Kowtow Slab. Above the Kowtow Slab there is a 4 meter-long and 1 meter-high natural stone slab, which is called the Dragon Table. This is the Pond used for Achang people's ritual, sacred to dragon for rain. Further in the Rain Pond is the Dragon King Pond. Whenever the people come here, they whisper in fear of waking the sleeping Dragon King, otherwise the sky will soon be covered with dark clouds, and then it will rain heavily. And the story starts from the following.

According to legend, one day an old gentleman, named Zuo, went to Caojian to go to the market. And when he passed the Dangong Slope, he met a strange man covered with scabies, who stopped him in his way and asked him to help scratch the itch. Zuo hesitated, because of his kind heart, he finally agreed to help. When the man took off his clothes, oh my goodness, there was not a single inch of healthy skin on his entire body! Zuo was astonished and felt unwilling to help this man. But because he had already promised him, it seemed difficult to back out. So he helped him, scratched for a while and then left.

The next day, when Mr. Zuo was passing through the Dangong Slope, he met the man again, who asked him to continue to scratch his itch. Zuo thought about it, he had already helped him yesterday, so it really does not matter if he helped him the second time, he was idle anyway. So Mr. Zuo scratched the man's itch once again, when scratching his armpit, he saw a small mole. Huh? That was odd, how can there be a mole in this place? He leaned in closer to look at the mole, and it turned out to be a louse, he carefully pinched the bug and took it out. At that moment incredible things happened. This man's scabies disappeared at once, revealing his true appearance as a dashing and handsome man. Surprised and doubtful, Mr. Zuo asked for the reason, but the man did not explain. After saying goodbye, they went their own way.

On the third day, when Mr. Zuo passed the Dangong Slope again, the man was waiting for him there and waved at him, telling Mr. Zuo to walk towards him, as if he had something to say. He told Mr. Zuo that he was a dragon, originally was the Dragon King's third prince from Zhiben Mountain. When passing the Renshan, due to the insect bites and physical exhaustion, he couldn't return to the Mountain. So he turned into a human and stayed here, but unexpectedly met the kind old gentleman—Mr. Zuo, who did not mind his scabies, and kindly saved him. Yesterday he feared that his identity might be exposed and brought misfortunes, so he immediately returned to Zhiben Mountain. When his father asked where he had been recently, he told him the truth. This time, the man came back to invite Mr. Zuo to visit his home in the Zhiben Mountain, because his father had a gift for Mr. Zuo in return for saving his son's life.

Three days later, they came to the northwest side of the Caojian Plain, where there was a large mountain with an altitude of more than 3,000 meters and covering 10 kilometers, locally known as Zhiben Mountain.

On the top of the mountain, trees grew abundantly. The mountains are covered with red, purple and white azaleas, cypresses, lush flowers and green grass, just like a carpet. There are ninety nine small dragon pools on Zhiben Mountain, and the water in the pools was deep and pure. According to the legend, the ninety nine small dragon pools were the residence and playground of the Dragon King of Zhiben Mountain, and the people can neither find the dragon pools nor dare to play in them. Zhiben Mountain was so rich and beautiful that it seemed to be a paradise with everything you need. The Dragon King welcomed Mr. Zuo warmly and let him pick a treasure as a reward. But there were countless treasures here, what should he choose? The Dragon King's third prince told him that the most valuable among his father's treasures was the Dragon Horse, which had magical power. Mr. Zuo thought, "If I can get that, I can create wind and rain, so I can water my farmland at home! Besides, it was a long way back, and I can't take other treasures with me". So he chose a golden dragon horse. But then he thought, What if I encounter some bandits on the way back home? They would rob my golden dragon horse and would even take my life! The Dragon King and his son also saw what was on his mind, so they turned the golden dragon horse into a bronze one. A few days later, Mr. Zuo returned to Lianhua Village (now was called Renshan Danti Village) with the bronze dragon horse.

According to the legend, the Achang people who lived in Caojian Plain were loyal, honest, fair and simple. Therefore, the Dragon King of Zhiben Mountain liked to interact with the chief of the Achang tribe, and after meeting frequently, the Dragon King and the chief became good friends. The Dragon King often invited the chief to visit the ninety nine small dragon pools of Zhiben Mountain. On festivals, the chief also invited the Dragon King to visit his home and they helped each other in difficulties. Later, the Achang people in Yunlong had great respect for the Dragon King of Zhiben Mountain, and worshiped the Dragon King as god and honored the dragons like deities.

There were more than 10,000 acres of paddies in Caojian Plain. Since ancient times, due to the drought problem and water shortage, the locals called them "Leixiang Paddies" and it all depended on rain to grow the crops. In case of a severe drought, rice can't be transplanted. On the 13th day of May in the lunar calendar, if it has not yet rained heavily, the chief of the Achang tribe would organize people to go to Miaodan Mountain to pray for rain at the Qiuyu Meadow. Before praying for rain, the village would ask a highly respected descendent of the Zuo family to take the lead, and a person who was proficient in the magic secret of praying for rain would lead 35 young men who belong to the zodiac of dragon to take a basket of water from each of the five places: the east, west, south, north and middle of Renshan Village to the Qiuyu Meadow, building a 3 meters high "five-sided Dragon King altar". The young men carried chickens, ducks, geese, fish, tributes, incense, candles, money, paper, food, and other ritual supplies on their backs and climbed up Miaodan Mountain in the hot sun to pray for rain. After the rice and the offerings were cooked, the tributes and animals were offered on the Dragon Table to worship the Dragon King. Everyone who went up to the mountain, praying for rain must respectfully kneel three times and bow nine times on the "Kowtow Slab", and sincerely begged the Dragon King of Zhiben Mountain to bring down rain and blessed the Achang people with abundant crops throughout the year. The priest recited spells and chanted the "secret words" to pray for rain, asking the Dragon King of Zhiben to bring rain as soon as possible, so that the plants can be planted on time without delaying the harvest.

At the end of the rituals for the Dragon King, a good meal would follow until the praying people were satisfied, when the sun was Set to west. Then the men who prayed for rain got undressed, selecting 1 or 2 children and old people to carry their clothes, and the rest people had their faces and their whole body covered with mud, so that others can't see their faces. After that, they ran down the hill to the rice paddies. People doing farm work saw the people who prayed for rain running towards them, and hurriedly shouted: "It is going to rain! It is going to rain heavily…" It was not until the sun went down that the people praying for rain went to a secret place, washed the mud off their bodies and returned to their homes in their clothes.

The most amazing thing was that even if the sun was blazing in the midday, rain would still pour down after the rain ritual, which has become an unsolved mystery in the area of Renshan.

Caojian, Yunlong's Achang people's rain ritual continued until the early 1950s. Most of the local elderly people who are over 60 years old have ever participated in this ritual. After the foundation of P.R.C, the government paid great attention to hydraulic construction. The Caojian Plain was densely covered with ditches and canals, so water sources could be used fully. 10,000 acres of rice were able to be planted regularly, and the true story of the Achang people's rain rituals was gradually forgotten.

皇阁寺的传说

传说每年农历正月初九是玉皇大帝的诞辰,陇川县户撒皇阁寺庙会活动隆重热烈,边疆民族俗语叫"赶摆"。户撒阿昌族主要信仰小乘佛教,但为什么对道教的皇阁寺那么信奉诚心呢?水有源头,树有根,关于户撒朗光村皇阁寺,还有一段民间传说。

明朝初年,西南边疆封建领主割据,互相争夺,引发各少数民族的不团结,那时兵荒马乱,民不聊生,各地社会秩序比较混乱。据传,明朝皇帝朱元璋派明将沐英率明军入云南,调停领主争端及民族不和的纠纷,以武力统一边疆各少数民族。

沐英接受命令,深感命令重如山,工作艰巨,任务繁重,但怎样完成呢?他有一片忠心诚意,决心要平息领主间的争端,完成边疆统一的任务。他想有志者事竟成,但有志无恒要畏缩,有恒无志乱碰撞,任务都是难以完成的,要有志必有恒,统一军队。

当时,行道未通,交通工具欠缺,行军全靠脚走马驮。翻越重重高山,跨过条条江河,攻破层层障碍,安顿地方官员,平息一个地方前进一步,经过三年多时间的迂回作战,克服了许多困难,终于到达了户撒。

当时的环境条件很艰苦,莫说解决纠纷,平息争端,就连食宿行军作战都碰到很大困难。任务远远没有完成,兵员越来越少,翻越高黎贡山已经筋疲力尽,到了进退两难的地步。下层将士一部分产生动摇情绪,而沐英意志坚强,他想,不遇艰苦不会发愁,发起愁来办法有。于是组织将士整顿队伍,要大家出主意想办法。

沐英在愁思当中,趴在战图上疲倦地睡着了。他的决心意志最终感动了上苍,醒来时,一只白马鹿出现在他的眼前,抓又抓不着,跟也跟不上,部队每行动一步,它就移动一节,始终相隔一段距离。

从此,白马鹿便成了沐英部队征西的向导。宿营停下,行军在前,始终看得见,摸不着。在白马鹿的引导下,他们沿着高黎贡山而下,跨越陇川江，经过风吹坡，来到了户撒朗光，白马鹿再也不走了。

那时边疆部落领主互相械斗，盈江地区领主兵强势壮，常常强占别的地方。而户撒地区民穷势弱，经常有被别人侵吞的危险。沐英到户撒安营扎寨后，面临盈江方面领主的威胁，便发动组织阿昌族等当地民众配合部队随时出动抵抗。

一天，盈江地区领主突然率兵攻打户撒，来势凶猛，情况十分紧急，各寨鸣锣发动群众，当时又连日阴雨，兵器不足，众人手持长刀、木棒，披上搭扇（避雨用具），仓促上阵，冒雨直奔盈江方向山梁。幸好户撒战士发觉及时，出动迅速，不等盈江领主率兵来到，就抢先爬上山，占领了山头。待盈江兵士爬到半山腰，在雨雾蒙蒙中，向上看时，只见山顶黑压压一片，每个人披的搭扇长有两只翅膀，像要飞一样。盈江兵未见过长着翅膀的军队，吓得不敢再前进，连跑带滚地退了下去，从此"飞军"出了名，又得了势。

这次出兵抢占山头抵御，本来准备要浴血牺牲，决一死战，只因为每个官兵民众都披了一张搭扇，成了神奇的"飞军"，吓得犯者不进反退了。这一仗未有交战，就告大捷。从此，对方认输，不敢再来侵犯，民众才得以安居乐业。

沐英率兵征西，经过艰苦曲折的作战，克服了重重困难，有白马鹿的指引，完成了明朝廷交给的任务，实现了自己的理想诺言。经过沐英的发动，对凶恶敌人侵略的抵抗，以长有翅膀的神奇"飞军"吓垮了敌人，不战而胜，完成了任务，这时白马鹿也不见了，民众得以安居乐业，专心专意地生产……这一切的神奇偶合，大家认为都是玉皇大帝的安排。

因此，白马鹿出没的户撒朗光山坡，被认为是玉皇大帝的家，户撒人便在此修建了皇阁报恩寺，以表达敬意和报恩。

故事带有一定的神话色彩，但它也表达了边疆各族人民要统一、要和平的美好愿望。

搜集整理：郑嘉才

编者按： 这个故事从本身来说，故事性很弱，一旦脱离了户撒乡的范围，估计没有人会讲，更没有人会想听。

但是，编排出这样一个没有多少故事性的故事，一定有比故事情节更重要的信息，隐含在这个叙事里。因为这样，这个故事才能流传下来。

这个故事与其说是民间故事，不如说是一个历史故事，记载了明帝国开疆拓土的功绩，以及各民族之间文化与信仰的融合。

有明一代，在云南很多地区都建立了土司制度。这样的土司制度是与明军的武功震慑力相辅相成的。而云南省德宏州陇川县户撒阿昌族乡正好位于汉文化影响力的边缘，今天也是国境线上的地区。

在这样的民族杂居区，我是谁就成为一个问题。在国境边缘地带，我属于哪里，也可以成为一个问题。在这样的区域，宗教信仰不仅仅是个人问题，也是一个社会认同的标尺。

故事开篇介绍的小乘佛教也称为"南传佛教"，是户撒乡本地傣族人的主要信仰，也是部分靠近傣族区域的阿昌族信仰。而一山之隔的梁河县阿昌族有自己的民族信仰，传承以活袍和撒杂为代表的萨满文化。皇阁寺位于两者之间，却是更接近汉族的道教寺观，可见这个宗教多样性背后的复杂关系。

皇阁寺背后是沐英的军队，沐英的军队背后是一个开疆拓土的大明帝国。这才是皇阁寺的故事，而白马鹿是解释皇阁寺位于朗光村的由头。盈江兵与户撒战士的一次不流血的对峙，依稀勾勒出土司制度下权力空间的争夺。

Legend of Huangge Temple

Legend has it that it is the birthday of the Jade Emperor on the ninth day of the first lunar month. Every year, a grand temple fair is held at Huangge Temple in Longchuan County, also known as the "Ganbai" Festival in the ethnic dialect. Although the Achang people in Husa hometown mainly believe in Buddhism, they have deep respect and devotion for the Taoist Huangge Temple. Just like water has its source and trees have their roots, there is a folk legend about Huangge Temple in Husa hometown.

During the early Ming Dynasty, feudal lords in the southwestern border were in constant conflict, leading to problems and disunity among the various ethnic groups. At that time, there was chaos, and people were suffering, with social order being disrupted in many places. It is said that Emperor Zhu Yuanzhang of the Ming Dynasty let General Mu Ying and his troops to Yunnan to mediate the disputes between feudal lords and the ethnic conflicts, aiming to forcefully unify the ethnic groups on the border.

Accepting the order, Mu Ying knew that this task would be difficult. How could he accomplish the task? He had the loyalty and the determination to solve the conflicts of the local powers and believed that where there is a will, there is a way. Yet, without persistence would lead to aimless wandering. He understood that completing the mission of unify the army required both determination and perseverance.

At that time, there were no roads, and transportation was very inconvenient. The troops had to rely on walking and had to carry their supplies on horses. They needed to overcome numerous mountains and rivers, break through obstacles, and establish local government officials. Gradually, they made progress in one place after another. After more than three years of maneuvering and overcoming many difficulties, they finally arrived at Husa.

The conditions were harsh at that time, and they faced great difficulties not only in resolving disputes and conflicts but also in terms of food, accommodation and military equipment. The task was far from complete, and the number of troops was dwindling. After climbing the Gaoligong Mountain, they were exhausted and faced a dilemma. Some of the lower-ranking soldiers began to waver, but Mu Ying remained resolute. He believed that they should not worry when hardships came, because where there are difficulties, there are solutions. So he organized the soldiers and asked everyone to come up with ideas and solutions.

Lost in thought and fatigued, Mu Ying fell asleep on the mat. His determination and will eventually were being seen by the gods. When he woke up, a white deer appeared before him. No matter how he tried to catch it or keep up with it, the deer stayed at constant distance, moving forward with the troops as they took each step.

From then on, the white deer became the guide for Mu Ying's army as they ventured westward. They could see it when they camped, and marched, but they could never touch it. Guided by the white deer, they descended into Gaoligong Mountain, crossed the Longchuan River, and passed through the Fengchui Slope, finally arrived at Huangge Temple in Husa. And there, the white deer stopped running.

Back then, the leaders of the border tribes were constantly fighting each other. The powerful leaders in the Yingjiang area frequently invaded other territories. In contrast, the Husa region was poor and weak, often at risk of being invaded by others. After Mu Ying set up the camp in Husa, he faced threats from the leaders in Yingjiang. So he encouraged the Achang people and other residents to cooperate with the army.

One day, the leader of Yingjiang suddenly launched a harsh attack on Husa. As the situation was urgent, the villagers banged the gong to gather the people. It was rainy for days, and they lacked proper weapons. Everyone held long knives and wooden sticks and wore the Dashans, which used for shelter from rain, as they rushed towards the mountains in the direction of Yingjiang. Luckily, they discovered the attack in time, and swiftly climbed up the mountain, taking the hilltop before the soldiers from Yingjiang. In the mist and rain, when the soldiers from Yingjiang looked up, they saw a crowd on the mountain top, every person wearing the Dashan, making them look like they had wings, as if they were ready to fly. The soldiers from Yingjiang had never seen an army with wings and were so frightened that they dared not go forward. They retreated in haste and fear. From then on, the "Flying Army" became famous and gained power.

However, because every soldier wore a Dashan, they became the magical "Flying Army", which frightened the enemy. This battle was won without single shot fired. From then on, the enemy surrendered and did not dare to invade again, and the people could live in peace.

Mu Ying led his troops on a mission to the west, overcoming numerous difficulties and fighting many battles. With the guidance of the white deer, he fulfilled the task assigned to him by the Ming Court and realized his own ideals and promises. The "Flying Army" terrified the enemy and achieved victory without fighting. The task was completed. At that point, the white deer also disappeared, and the people were able to settle down and live happily. All these magical coincidences were believed to be the arrangement of the Jade Emperor in heaven.

Therefore, the slopes of the Mountain Langguang in Husa, where the white deer had appeared, were believed to be the home of the Jade Emperor. As a gesture of respect and gratitude, Huangge Temple was built.

This story not only carries certain mythical charm, but also expresses the longing for unity and peace among the ethnic groups of the border regions.

小黄龙

从前，有一条小黄龙到处游玩。有一天，它游到了户撒，一路走，一路玩，走一段路它就伸出头来，看看是否到了皇阁寺。每次它伸出头的地方，就会留下一个洞，人们就叫它龙洞。洞里的水流得清清的，农田有水灌。它来到芒弄寨子，发现寨子背后有个拱母，它知道拱母不能为民造福，想把它毁掉。于是它从拱母的坡脚打通一个洞进去，想一下子把它从根底掀翻。可是它力量不够，不但没有把拱母掀翻，反而滑到边上去了。从此，拱母旁边就留了一条弯弯曲曲的小沟。

它又一直走呀走，走到了朗光村皇阁寺那里。皇阁寺后面有一个深水塘子，它就在那里住了下来。一天，它又出来玩，看见皇阁寺正在兴建，老师傅们正忙着竖柱子呢。小黄龙想皇阁寺盖起来也不能为民众造福，而是劳民伤财。它想：如果他们竖不起柱子来就不会盖了。于是它在暗里使劲，使师傅们几天都竖不起一根柱子来。老师傅们感到很奇怪，没有信心再竖了，就只好这样搁下了。

一天，一位老师傅闲着无事，想来想去，认为一定有什么妖怪在作怪。于是，他就拿一截树枝刻了一条木龙，满身扎上些钉子，丢到后面水塘里。不几天，木龙真的活了。一天，木龙碰上了小黄龙，就跟小黄龙在水里打起架来，打了很长时间不分胜负，但是木龙遍身是铁钉，把小黄龙刺得到处鲜血直流。小黄龙流血过多，血把水塘都染红了，不久小黄龙便身疲力竭也就死去了。小黄龙死后，皇阁寺也就盖起来了。所以，朗光村就有了皇阁寺。

搜集整理：张亚萍

编者按： 这个小黄龙故事需要和前面一个皇阁寺故事对照理解。

这条小黄龙是一个好龙，它钻出来的龙洞都是水源，可以灌溉利民。当小黄龙在芒弄寨发现一个不好的"拱母"的时候，它见义勇为，打算除害。虽然最后没有清除"拱母"，但是仍然留下了一条弯弯曲曲的水沟，哺育着当地的作物。

故事的精彩之处在于，小黄龙一眼就识别出来，皇阁寺不是什么好东西。讲述者当然不会这么直白，只能含混不清地说，"小黄龙想皇阁寺盖起来也不能为民众造福，而是劳民伤财"。如果结合前面的皇阁寺故事，就指出了封建主义的明朝，在当地人心目中实际的形象了。

小黄龙采用了某种抵抗的艺术，在暗地里破坏建设过程，而不是大张旗鼓地宣战。

但是，在技高一筹的老师傅面前，小黄龙还是失败了，并且惨死在皇阁寺的水塘里。皇阁寺也就盖起来了。

这个故事是含蓄地表达了当地人对于一个强加于人的权力不满而无奈的心绪。如果没有同理心，可能会感觉这个故事有点云山雾罩。但是如果心有同感，那么故事的默契就达成了。

The Little Yellow Dragon

Once upon a time, there was a little yellow dragon wandering around. One day, it swam to Husa, walking and playing along the way. It walked for a while and stretched out its head to see if it had reached the Huangge Temple. Whenever it stretched out its head, a hole was left behind, so people called it the Dragon Cavern. The clean stream flowed smoothly, and the farmland was irrigated with water. When it came to the Mangnong Village, it found that there was a Gongmu behind the village. It knew that the Gongmu could not benefit the people, so the little yellow dragon wanted to destroy it. So the little yellow dragon dug a hole through the foot of the slope of the Gongmu and tried to lift it off from the root in one go. However, it did not have enough strength to overturn the Gongmu, instead it slipped to one side. From then on, a small, curved ditch was left next to the Gongmu.

The little yellow dragon kept on walking and walking, and came to the Langguang Huangge Temple. There was a deep pond behind the temple, so it settled and lived there. One day, it came out to play again, and saw the Huangge Temple being built, and the engineers were busy putting up pillars. The little yellow dragon thought that the temple would not be built for the benefit of the people, but rather as a waste of money. So it thought, if they set up the pillars, they would not be able to build the temple. So it secretly caused trouble and hindered the progress of the construction. The engineers couldn't even erect a single pillar in a few days! The engineers felt strange, and as time progressed, they did not have the confidence to set the pillars again, so they had to put the construction work aside.

One day, an engineer, who had nothing to do, thought about the odd things that happened with the pillars. He thought that there must be some sort of monster playing tricks on him. So he took a section of a free trunk to carve a wooden dragon, and covered the body with nails, then threw it into the pond. Within a few days, the wooden dragon really came to life! One day, the wooden dragon came across the little yellow dragon, althogh they had fought for a long time in the water, unable to determine victory or defeat. But the wooden dragon, covered in nails, stabbed the little yellow dragon. Blood oozed out of the little yellow dragon's body, and stained the pond red. The little yellow dragon died shortly of blood loss. After the death of the little yellow dragon, the Huangge Temple was finally built. Therefore, that is why the place of Longguang has the Huangge Temple.

曹扎和龙女

这个故事发生在很久以前,不知什么时候!

有个阿昌族青年,他的名字叫曹扎。曹扎很小就死了阿帕(父亲)、阿妮(母亲),成了一个孤苦伶仃的孤儿,无依无靠,只好靠上山砍柴、割草和下河拿鱼卖为生。

有一天,曹扎在河里拿得一条鱼。这条鱼,小巧精干,头像娃娃面,身子有一道道花斑,扎实好看。曹扎给它取名叫"小花鱼"。曹扎把小花鱼拿回家,舍不得吃,放进水缸里养起来。曹扎每天出外做活,都要先到水缸边看看小花鱼。看见小花鱼在缸里欢快地游来游去,他才放心地锁上门,拿着用具走了。晚上回家,他把柴担、草担一卸下,打开门,就先跑到水缸边看小花鱼。看到缸里的水脏了,马上就换,水少了,就立即添满,然后,才烧火煮饭。

一天,曹扎挑柴上街,晚上回家,开了锁,打开门一看,十分惊讶,屋里的鸡屎扫干净了,床上的破被子补好了,并折得整整齐齐地放着,灶洞里燃烧着红红的火炭,锅里支着甑子。曹扎打开甑子一看,甑里是雪白的大米饭。饭上炖着一盘肉,一股香气直扑鼻子。曹扎认为是自己的眼睛发花了。闭上眼睛,睁开一看,白花花的米饭、喷香的肉还在。曹扎想:可能是邻居哪个好心的妮央嫫(大妈),看到自己早出晚归,无人煮饭,悄悄来帮自己煮的。现在肚子正饿,我先吃了后,再去找煮饭的人感谢。

曹扎饱饱地吃了一顿饭,然后去问隔壁邻舍,都说不知道。曹扎觉得有些奇怪。

第二天,曹扎早早出门上山割草。晚上回到家时,锅里照样炖有肉饭。他吃了后,又去问邻居。邻居说,你的门用锁锁着,哪个进得去帮你煮饭。

是呀,我回到家时,我的门是好好锁着的,哪个能进得去呢?曹扎更觉奇怪。我明天去近处拿柴,回来早点,看看到底是哪个好心人帮我煮饭。天刚花花亮，曹扎早起，拿着大刀就上山去。日头正当顶时，曹扎挑着一担柴走到寨边，看到自己的茅草房顶冒起了炊烟。曹扎连忙加快脚步往家走。到家门时，他轻轻放下柴担子，走到门边一看，门上的锁照样锁着。曹扎打开门一看，只见一个十八九岁的姑娘，慌忙放下手中炒菜的锅铲，低着头，快步向水缸走去。曹扎进门要过去细看，那姑娘到缸边就不见了。曹扎跑到缸边一看，只见水缸里的小花鱼，游来游去，用珍珠般晶莹闪亮的眼睛，看着满脸露出惊奇神情的曹扎。

　　曹扎回到灶边，饭已煮好，菜已炒在锅里，他一边吃，一边想。这姑娘到底是什么人？她热心为我煮饭，但为何一见我就走掉？曹扎连忙吃了两碗饭，就去水缸边坐着。天黑了还不见那姑娘出来。曹扎又烧起了一堆松树明子火，还在水缸边坐着。明子火熄了又添，添了又熄……

　　"喔喔——"山里的老公鸡，唱起了第一支歌，曹扎还不见那姑娘出来，才去睡觉。

　　天蒙蒙亮，曹扎又背着鱼网，下河拿鱼。走出寨子，看见两只喜鹊落在路边一棵攀枝花树上喳喳喳地叫。他又想起昨晚上的那个姑娘。我不如回去躲在家里，看看那姑娘到底是哪个？这样，曹扎就背着鱼网，折回家悄悄爬上房顶，扒开茅草，盯着屋里。

　　日头像被绳子拴着一样，老是不见走。曹扎觉得这天的时光走得特别慢。好不容易才熬到响午时候，只听得屋里的水缸"哗哗"地响，不一会儿，昨天晚上帮他煮饭的那个姑娘，像一棵青竹笋似的，从水缸里慢慢冒出来。然后离开水缸，就去打扫屋里，收拾床铺，之后就去抱柴烧火。一股浓烟升上屋顶，呛得曹扎直咳嗽，那姑娘听到有人咳嗽，就抬头向屋顶上看。看见曹扎瞄她，她急忙低下头，快步向水缸走去。这时曹扎着急了，他慌忙拿起压屋顶的一个石头，向水缸砸去，等那姑娘走到水缸边，缸烂了，水淌光了，露出缸底，小花鱼不见了。

　　"你呀，这样莽撞。"姑娘微嗔地说。

　　"贤妹，你不要生气，你有心来为我煮饭，我有意和你做一家。我喜欢你有颗善良的心！"

　　曹扎跳下来，向姑娘表真情。那姑娘用深情的眼光看了曹扎一眼，羞涩地低下头。曹扎看看姑娘的脸，像一朵刚刚开放的火红的攀枝花。

　　曹扎和那姑娘，在门前一棵青松树下，磕了三个头，结为夫妻。晚上，那姑娘告诉曹扎，她是龙王家的三小姐，因在龙宫里太寂寞，游到龙宫外的小河里玩耍,却被曹扎拿回家养在水缸里,看到曹扎勤劳、诚实可信,就出来给他扫地煮饭……这样,两人的感情更好。你体贴我,我关心你。曹扎仍然上山砍柴、割草,下河拿鱼,三小姐在家纺线、织布、做饭,曹扎家里充满了温暖。

一天晚上,三小姐对曹扎说,"人间虽然自由自在,比龙宫好,但离家的时间长了,也想回去瞧瞧父母和兄弟姐妹"。

"我送你一段路,你快去快回。"曹扎爽快地说。

"你跟我一起去吧,我一个人去,怕父王不让我再出来。"小姐难舍地说。

"你家是在龙宫里,我去得了吗?"曹扎担心地说。

"你跟着我。我叫咋个做,你就咋个做。"三小姐说。

曹扎和三小姐来到河边,小姐叫曹扎拉着她的裙子,闭上眼睛。霎时,曹扎像长了翅膀一样,身子轻飘飘地飞了起来。过了一支烟的工夫,三小姐叫曹扎睁开眼睛,金碧辉煌的龙宫,已出现在眼前。

龙王一见三小姐领回一个打柴汉的女婿,大发雷霆,马上命令虾兵虾将,要把曹扎抓去杀死。

三小姐知道父王是说得出口,做得出手的,他每年要糟害无数百姓。三小姐对龙王说:"曹扎是个很能干的人,他要和父王打赌。父王叫他做哪样,如果他做得出,他就赢,我们就做一世夫妻。要是曹扎做不出,他算输,我们就此完结这世夫妻。"

龙王暗想:一个穷打柴的我不用费吹灰之力就叫你输,因此他答应了三小姐的要求。

晚上龙王把曹扎叫去。龙王叫曹扎第二天要把九山十八凹所有的树木砍完。如果砍不完就要吊死曹扎。曹扎觉得自己闯了大祸。九山十八凹那么多树,咋个砍得完。急得他心里像烧了一团火。一回到屋,就躺倒睡觉,不住叹气。三小姐问他,龙王叫他做哪样。曹扎痛苦地拉着三小姐的手,说出龙王叫他做的事,并说:"我们恩爱夫妻怕要结束了。"三小姐笑了笑,安慰曹扎说:"你不要急,我帮你想办法。我找四把斧子给你。明天早上,你把四把斧子,拿去摆在四座山顶。然后,你就在山边睡觉。"

"卖死命砍也怕要砍半个月,睡觉更砍不完了。"曹扎难过地说。

"你就照我的办法去做。"三小姐说。

曹扎急得一夜没有合眼。天一亮,就拿了四把斧子上山,摆在四座山的山顶上。他把斧子摆好后,就坐到山草窠里想歇一下,但一坐下他就睡着了。一觉醒来,日头已偏西。天边已涌出一片片火红的晚霞,一群群白色的鹭鸶,在晚霞里飞着归巢去。曹扎一看山,啊呀!九山十八凹,原本是浓浓密密的森林,现在都已砍倒。曹扎高兴地回去告诉妻子。小两口正高兴着,龙王派虾兵来把曹扎叫去,要曹扎第二天把所有砍倒的树木烧光。烧不光,就要烧死曹扎。曹扎脸都气白了,一回到屋里,就把龙王反悔的事说给妻子。妻子三小姐说:"你不要心焦。你明天拿上四泡干牛屎上山,摆在山的四个角落,点上火就睡觉。"

砍,这关是过了,烧,这关能不能过?第二天一早,曹扎心中忐忑不安地背上四泡干牛屎上山,支在山的四个角落。他点上火,到山洞里想坐下歇歇,但刚一坐下,他就睡着了。等他醒来,出山洞一看,日头还高高地挂在天上,一群群小燕子,在他头顶嬉戏地飞着。他一看山,啊!九山十八凹被砍倒的树木都烧光了,一层厚厚的火灰铺在山上,曹扎脸上绽开了笑容,像燕子一样欢乐地唱起歌回家。他想:这回龙王该认输了吧。曹扎刚回到家,水都还不得喝一口,龙王又派虾兵来把曹扎喊去。要曹扎把九山十八凹铺着灰的山地都挖完,挖不完就要乱棍打死。曹扎听了很生气。龙王说话不算数,回去给三小姐一说,三小姐说:"父王就这样,诡计多端,你明天扛上四把锄头上山,摆在山的四个角落,就在山中睡一觉。"曹扎照三小姐的主意去做,第二天天黑时,九山十八凹的坡地被挖完了。

龙王又要曹扎背上九斗九升芝麻,把九山十八凹挖出的坡地撒完。撒不完,龙王就要用箭射死他。三小姐叫曹扎把九斗九升芝麻,分装在四条口袋里,背上山,支在山的四个角落,然后睡觉。曹扎照三小姐的办法去做,天刚晌午时,芝麻就撒完了。龙王又命令曹扎把撒下的芝麻拾起来,如少了一粒,就要把曹扎放进油锅煮死。曹扎一听,十分气愤地说:"龙王的话,不如放屁,一次一次地反悔。"三小姐说:"我既然自愿做你的妻子,跳大海过血河,也要相扶相爱。你有难,我一定尽力帮助。"她告诉曹扎,明天拿着四只口袋上山,把口袋放在山的四角落,打开口袋口,就放心地睡觉。第二天,曹扎就照三小姐的办法做,到傍晚醒来时,四只口袋装满了芝麻,一数,少了三粒。曹扎慌了,忙回家告诉三小姐。三小姐叫曹扎背着箭上山,有一群斑鸠落在地边的一个大石头上,哪只叫,就射哪只。曹扎慌忙背上弓箭上山,只见五只斑鸠落在一个大石头上,这时有一只公斑鸠，咕咕，咕咕……地叫起来。曹扎瞄准那只斑鸠，一箭射去，正射着那斑鸠的脖子，曹扎剥开斑鸠嗉子，三粒芝麻还好好地在斑鸠嗉子里。曹扎高兴极了。他想：龙王这回总该认输了吧。曹扎回家向三小姐说了自己的想法，三小姐也很高兴。小两口正欢欢喜喜地交谈着，龙王又传来一道命令，要曹扎第二天跟他比赛造水，龙王在河上头造，曹扎在河下头造。曹扎感到：龙王不把自己整死心不乐。三小姐也十分气愤，逼到这一步，只好这样了。她对曹扎说："龙王想尽千方百计，要把我俩拆散，他想用大水把你淹死。但纯真的爱情，是哪个也拆不散的。你明天背上一把长刀，坐在一只竹筏上，从下游往上划。你看到上游河水淌下来的物件，冲向你的竹筏，你就用长刀砍。"

第二天，比赛开始，曹扎身背长刀，站在竹筏上，从河下游慢慢往上游划。不多时，只听上游雷声大作，暴雨像用瓢倒一样从天上泼下来。隔了一会儿，一股洪水向下游冲来，波浪像小山一样，一个又一个向曹扎的竹筏冲来。接着，一条五桠八杈的怪东西，往曹扎的竹筏撞来，那东西刚接触竹筏，说时迟，那时快，曹扎马上举刀向那怪东西砍去。曹扎手起刀落，把那怪东西砍成两截。顿时，乌黑的腥血，淌满了一条河。原来那怪东西是龙王变的，他想把曹扎的竹筏撞翻，让曹扎淹死在河水里。哪知反而弄巧成拙，龙王被砍死了。

曹扎和三小姐，回到了原来的家。曹扎仍然每天上山砍柴、割草，下河拿鱼。三小姐在家种园子、纺线、织布、煮饭，过着安居乐业的幸福生活。

讲述：赵安贤　曹德春
搜集整理：赵洪顺　孙加申

编者按： 这是一个很长的故事，也是一个非常典型的民间故事，穷小子娶仙女。这个故事与牛郎织女传说是一个类型的，而且也有女方的家长从中作梗。

曹扎和龙女，是把这个典型的民间故事给本土化了，场景、道具、语言都是云南西部的阿昌族社区风格。

这个类型的故事已经被分析得非常多，所以我们就不赘言了。我们从这个故事里找到一个颇有地方特色的地方，就是龙王给曹扎的五次难题。这五道题明显是分为两个阶段，第一个阶段是让穷小子知难而止，是前四道题目；第二个阶段是让穷小子彻底毁灭，杀心顿起，但是因为有龙女的告诫，结果反转成为龙王自寻死路。

在第一个阶段的四个考验，实际上是阿昌族传统农业的四个阶段。阿昌族在传统上是从事刀耕火种农业的群体，这个群体很多时候居无定所，但是已经有了铁制工具，可以有效地清理林地，在晾晒几个月之后，用火把干枯的林木转变成种植需要的肥料。清理林地是一件极为费力的工作，经常是整日工作，汗流浃背才能收拾旋踵之地。故此，第一个难题就是让曹扎砍伐茂密的丛林。只有干过这个工作的人，才理解这个挑战多么不可思议。而听这个故事的阿昌族人，正好是知道这种痛苦的。

第二个难题是焚烧砍伐的树木。这对于只在电视上看过森林大火的人来说，似乎轻而易举，只要点火即可。但是这个难题不是这么简单的。如果有实践经验，就知道刚刚砍伐下来的树木是无法焚烧殆尽的。而用四坨牛粪，点燃这些树木，是正确的方法和错误的时间。然而在龙女的帮助下，曹扎顺利通过了这一关。

第三个挑战是撒芝麻。就是从这个难题中，我意识到这个故事背后的结构是刀耕火种这样的粗放型农业的隐喻。之所以称之为刀耕火种，就是因为在种植之前需要用刀砍伐森林，用火清理场地，之后还需要用长刀在土地上挖一个小坑，种入种子，再用脚把一点点土壤回填。

第四个挑战表面上是拾回种子，实质上是收获。这样就构成了一个砍伐、焚烧、种植和收割的循环。这是阿昌族传统农业的主要工作，也是最辛苦的部分。

如果接受四难题是刀耕火种四流程的比喻，就需要一个更有想象力的对最后也是决定性的比赛的解释。

编者受到《逃避统治的艺术》的影响，认为这个最终决赛代表灌溉农业试图控制刀耕火种的失败。管理水的神明龙王（代表灌溉农业）和砍柴割草捕鱼的阿昌族小伙子（暗示游耕阶段），通过龙王女儿的背叛家庭和投身婚姻，停在了男耕女织的社会状态，进入了定居农业阶段。

Caozha and the Dragon Girl

This story happened a long time ago,and nobody knew the exact time!

There was a young man from the Achang ethnic group, whose name was Caozha. Caozha lost his father and mother at a very young age and became a lonely orphan with no one to rely on. So he had to went up the mountain to chop wood, cut grass and caught fish from the river to sell for a living.

One day, Caozha caught a fish in a river. It was a small, fine fish, with a head like a doll's face and a body with a pattern of spots, firm and beautiful. Caozha named it "little flower fish". Caozha took the Little Flower Fish home, but could not endure to eat it, so he put it in the tank and kept it. Before going out to work every day, Caozha went to the tank to see the little flower fish. After seeing the fish swimming around happily in the tank, he was able to lock the door, feeling assurance, and leave with the tools he needed for work. In the evening, when he came home, he set the wood and grass loads down. He opened the door and ran to the water tank to look at the little flower fish. When he saw that the water in the tank was dirty, he immediately changed it. And when the water was running low, he immediately filled it up. And then, only then, did he start the fire to cook.

One day, Caozha carried the wood and went to the street, returned home at night, unlocked the door, opened it, and was very surprised. The house was cleaned up, the tattered quilt on the bed was mended and neatly folded, the stove was burning red coals, and the big pot was holding a kettle. Caozha opened the cauldron and saw that it was filled with white rice. The rice was stewed together with a plate of meat, a delicious fragrance wafted straight to his nose. Caozha thought that he must be dreaming! When he closed his eyes and opened them, the white rice and the fragrance of meat were still there. He thought, "Maybe it was the kind-hearted lady in the neighborhood who saw that I left early and came home late, and no one was cooking, so she came quietly and cooked for me. But now that I'm hungry, I'll eat first and then go to the person who cooked the rice to express my thanks."

Caozha had a good full meal, and then went to question the neighbors. But they all said they didn't know who was responsible for. Caozha felt a bit strange.

The next day, Caozha went out early to cut grass in the mountains. When he returned home in the evening, there was meat and rice stewed in the pot just as before. After eating, he spoke to his neighbor about this thing, who replied that Caozha's door was locked, so he wondered who could get in to help him cook.

"Right, when I came home, my door was properly locked, who could get in?" Caozha felt even more strange. "I'll go to get wood from a place nearby tomorrow and come back early to see who helps me cook." Just after the day dawned, Caozha got up early and went up the mountain with a big axe. When the sun was shining right at the top of sky, Caozha carried a load of wood to the village and saw smoke rising from the roof of his house. Caozha quickened his pace and went home. When he arrived at the door, he gently put down the wood and walked close to the door, but the door was locked as usual. Caozha opened the door, saw a girl of 18 or 19 years old, in a panic, put down the spatula in her hands, lowered her head, and walked swiftly to the water tank. Caozha entered into the room to take a closer look, but the girl disappeared by the tank. Caozha ran to the tank to check, only saw the little flower fish in the tank, swimming around, with crystal shiny eyes, looking at Caozha with a face full of wonder.

Caozha returned to the stove. Rice had been prepared, vegetables had been cooked in the pan, he ate and thought: "What kind of person is this girl? She was so kind to cook for me, but why did she walk away as soon as we met?" Caozha hurriedly ate two bowls of rice and went to sit by the water tank. It was dark and the girl still didn't come out. Caozha started a fire and sat by the tank. Again and again, he rekindled the fire, but there was still no sign of the girl.

"Cock-a-doodle-doo! Cock-a-doodle-doo!" The old rooster sang the first song of the day, but Caozha still did not see the girl, so he decided to go to bed.

At dawn, Caozha carried his fish net again and went down to the river to catch fish. Walking out of the village, he saw two magpies landing on a kapok tree by the roadside chirping... He thought of the girl from last night again. "I might as well go back and hide at home and see who that girl really is." Thinking this way, Caozha carried the fish net, went home and quietly climbed on the roof of the house, peeled away the thatch, and stared into the house.

Time was like being tethered by a rope, slow and long. It was already noon when he heard the water tank in the house was making a chattering sound. Not long after, the girl who helped him cook last night, like a bamboo sprout, slowly emerged from the water tank. Then she left the tank and went to clean the house and the bed, then went to carry wood for the fire. A thick smoke rose to the roof, choking Caozha and causing him cough. As the girl heard someone coughing, she looked up to the roof. Seeing Caozha glancing at her, she hurriedly lowered her head and walked quickly toward the water tank. Caozha got anxious, so he hurriedly picked up a stone and chucked it at the tank, and as the girl reached the tank, it was broken, and the water dripped out. The bottom of the tank was revealed, and the little flower fish was gone.

"Oh you, acting recklessly like that." The girl said with a slight anger.

"My dear, don't be angry. You have the heart to cook for me, and I want to become a family with you. I like that you have a kind heart!"

Caozha jumped down and expressed his true feelings to the girl. The girl looked at Caozha with deep love and shyly lowered her head. Caozha looked at the face of the girl, which was just like a flaming red kapok.

Caozha and the girl bowed three times in front of the door under a green pine tree, and got married. At night, the girl told Caozha, she was the third daughter of Dragon King. Because living in the Dragon Palace was too lonely, she swam to the river outside the Dragon Palace to play but was taken home by Caozha and raised in the water tank. Seeing Caozha was hardworking, honest and trustworthy, she came out to sweep the floor and cook for him. By this way, the two persons became even closer. They were considerate and cared for each other. Caozha still went up to the mountains to chop wood and cut grass, and down to the river to get fish, while the girl was at home weaving, spinning and cooking, and Caozha's house was full of warmth and love.

One night, the girl said to Caozha, "Although the human world is free and better than the Dragon Palace, I have been away from home for a long time, and I want to go back to see my parents and siblings".

"I'll go with you a short way. You go and return quickly." Caozha said readily.

"Why don't you come with me, if I go alone, I'm afraid my father won't let me return again." The girl said with hesitation.

"But your home is in the Dragon Palace, how can I get there?" Caozha said worriedly.

"Follow me. I will tell you what to do." The girl said.

When Caozha and the girl came to the riverside, the girl told him to hold onto her and close his eyes. Suddenly, Caozha felt as if he had grown wings, his body gently drifted up. After some time, the girl told Caozha to open his eyes, and the glorious Dragon Palace, appeared before him.

When the Dragon King saw that his daughter had returned home with a son-in-law who was a woodcutter, and he was furious, and immediately ordered his soldiers to capture Caozha and kill him.

The girl knew that her father truly wanted to kill Caozha, since he had already harmed countless people in years past. The girl said to the Dragon King: "Caozha is a very capable person, and he wants to make a bet with you. Just tell him whatever you want him to do. If he can do it, he will win and we will be husband and wife for a lifetime. If he can't do it, he will lose, and we will end our marriage here. Deal?"

The Dragon King secretly thought,"He is only a poor woodcutter, and I do not have to spend much energy to make him lose". So the king agreed to the girl's request.

In the evening, the Dragon King called Caozha to his place. The Dragon King told Caozha to cut all the trees in the nine mountains and eighteen alleys the next day. If he could not finish cutting, he would be hanged. Caozha felt that he had gotten into big trouble. "There are so many trees in the nine mountains and eighteen alleys, how can I possibly cut them all?" He was so anxious that his heart felt like a burning ball of fire. As soon as he returned to the house, he lay down to sleep and sighed repeatedly. The girl asked him what the Dragon King told him to do. Caozha painfully took her hand, and repeated what the Dragon King said, and said, "I am afraid our marriage is going to end here". The girl smiled and comforted Caozha and said, "Do not be anxious, I will help you think of a way. I will find four axes for you. Tomorrow morning, take the four axes and set them on top of the four mountains. Then, you just go to sleep on the edge of the mountain".

Caozha said sadly,"Even if I try my best, I'm afraid it will take half a month to cut all of these trees, and it will take even longer if I sleep"!

"Just do what I told you." The girl said.

Caozha was so anxious that he can not sleep all night. As soon as it was dawn, he took the four axes and climbed up the mountains and placed them on top. After the axes were set up, he sat down in the grass bushes and intended to take a break, but he fell asleep. When he woke up, the sun was already in the far west and the sky was already full of the flaming red sunset. A flock of white herons could be seen flying in the evening sunset to return to their nests. Caozha looked at the mountains. Ah! The nine mountains and eighteen alleys used to be covered with thick and dense forests, but now they all had been cut down. Caozha happily went back to tell his wife. The young couple was delighted when the Dragon

King sent a soldier to call Caozha. He asked Caozha to burn all the trees that were being cut down the next day. If he couldn't burn them all, then the Dragon King would burn Caozha. Caozha's face turned white with rage, as soon as he returned to the house, he told his wife about the news that Dragon King would going back on his word. His wife replied, "Don't be so distressed. Tomorrow you will take four portions of dry cow dung up to the mountains, place them in the four corners of the mountains, set them on fire and go to sleep".

The chopping task has passed, but can the burning task be passed? The next morning, Caozha carried four portions of dried cow dung on his back to the mountain and placed them in the four corners of the mountain. He lit a fire and went to the cave to sit down and rest, but as soon as he sat down, he fell asleep. When he woke up, he came out of the cave and saw that the sun was still high up in the sky and a flock of small swallows were flying playfully above his head. He looked at the mountain. Ah! The trees that were cut down in nine mountains and eighteen alleys were all burned up, and a thick layer of ash spread across the mountain. Caozha's face blossomed into a smile, and he sung joyfully on his way to home like the swallows. He thought, "This time the Dragon King should admit his defeat". Caozha had just returned home, not even having the time to have a sip of water, when the Dragon King sent soldiers to call him again. He wanted Caozha to dig up the nine mountains and eighteen alleys in one day, and if he could not finish digging, he had to be beaten to death with a stick. Caozha was very angry when hearing this. The Dragon King broke his promise again, so he went back to the girl, who said, "My father is like that, sneaky and tricky. Tomorrow you will carry four hoes up the mountains, set them in the four corners of the mountain, then go to sleep". Caozha did what the girl said, and when it was nightfall the next day, the nine mountains and eighteen alleys were dug up.

The Dragon King asked Caozha to carry nine buckets of nine liters of sesame seeds, and finish spreading the slope of the nine mountains and eighteen alleys in one day. If he could not finish spreading, he was to be shot with arrows. The girl told Caozha to put nine buckets of sesame seeds in four sacks, carry them up the mountain and put them in the four corners of the mountain, and then sleep. Caozha did what the girl told him to do, and at noon, the sesame seeds were completely spread. The Dragon King further ordered Caozha to pick up the sesame seeds that had been scattered, and if one seed was missing, Caozha was to be boiled to death in a frying pan. Caozha was furious when he heard it and said, "The words of the Dragon King are no better than a lie, and they are repeatedly retracted"! The girl said, "Since I choose to be your wife, I love you no matter what If you are in trouble, I will try my best to help". She told Caozha to take the four sacks up the mountain tomorrow, put the sacks on the four corners of the mountain, open the sack mouth, and sleep at ease. The next day, Caozha did as the girl said, and when he woke up in the evening, the four sacks were full of sesame seeds, but when he counted them, three seeds were missing. He panicked and went home to tell the girl. The girl told Caozha to carry arrows up the mountain, while there was a group of turtledoves on a big stone on the ground and shoot whichever bird chirped. Caozha hurriedly put on his bow and arrows and went up the hill. He saw five turtledoves landing on a big rock, and then a male turtledove chirped "Cuckoo..." Caozha aimed at the dove and shot an arrow, hitting the neck of the dove. Caozha peeled the dove's neck open, and three sesame seeds were in it. Caozha was very happy and thought, "The Dragon King should admit defeat this time". Caozha went home, and told the third princess what he thought, and the third princess was also very pleased. The two of them were talking cheerfully when the Dragon King sent an order to compete with him the next day to create water. Caozha thought: "The Dragon King will not be happy unless I am dead." And the girl was also enraged. She said to Caozha, "The Dragon King tried every possible way to break us up, and he wanted to drown you with water. But true love cannot be torn apart. Tomorrow you will carry a long knife, sit on a bamboo raft, and row upstream. When you see an object coming down the river from upstream and rushing toward your raft, cut it with your long knife".

The next day, the competition began, Caozha carried a long knife, stood on the bamboo raft, and rowed slowly up the river. In a short time, he heard a loud sound of thunder upstream, and a heavy rain came pouring down from the sky like a waterfall. After a while, a flood came downstream, and the waves were like small mountains, one after another rushing towards Caozha's raft. Then, a strange thing with five branches and eight twigs came crashing into Caozha's raft. When it touched the raft, Caozha immediately raised his sword to cut the strange thing. Caozha's knife fell and cut it into two. At once, blackish red blood filled the river. It turned out that the strange thing was the Dragon King, who wanted to knock over Caozha's raft and let Caozha be drowned in the river. But it turned out to be a botched attempt, and the Dragon King was killed.

Caozha and the third princess returned to their own home. Caozha still went up to the mountains every day to chop wood, cut grass, and down to the river to catch fish. The girl planted a garden, spun yarn, wove cloth, cooked rice, and they lived peacefully and happily together.

腊银和腊康（一）

很久以前，有一家兄弟两个，哥哥名叫腊银，弟弟名叫腊康。他们很小就失去了父母。父母死后，上无片瓦，下无寸地，兄弟俩只好去拜师学打铁，练武艺。几年后，腊银和腊康学得了一套打铁本领，练就了一身武艺。他俩肩挑打铁工具，身背弓箭，走乡串寨，以修打小农具为生。

有一次，腊银和腊康来到一个叫猛岗的寨子打铁。猛岗寨的百姓，知道兄弟俩打的板锄很好铲，打的条锄很好挖，打的镰刀很好割。因此，很喜欢腊银和腊康。

有一天夜晚，猛岗寨子里的黄牛，跳出厩，闯烂栅栏门，钻进兄弟俩的打铁炉房，把炉房的工具弄得乱七八糟，把打铁的砧桩闯倒，把铁砧子摔在石头上砸烂了。寨子里的百姓知道后，就来向腊银和腊康道歉。腊银说："铁砧子烂了倒没有哪样事，只是我们兄弟俩不能在这里打铁了。"腊康说："我们只好先回家做个砧子。"猛岗寨的老人们在一起商量，一个老人说："这两个小伙手艺好，打出的农具好用，又热心，穷苦的人家去找他们修农具，钱多钱少他们不计较。我们要想办法留他们在我们寨子再打一些日子。"另一个老人接着说："我们各家凑一滴滴钢铁，给兄弟俩打个铁砧子，咯要得？""合啰合啰，我一家一户去找缺刀烂锄，凑来给腊银和腊康打铁砧子。"第三个老人说。大家都同意了。

第二天，猛岗寨的人，给腊银和腊康送来了三挑箩碎钢片、破铁块。兄弟俩很感激，做好铁砧，"叮叮当当……"又在猛岗寨打起铁来了。

月亮圆了又缺，缺了又圆，腊银和腊康在猛岗寨打农具两个多月，看着寨里的百姓都有了使用的农具，兄弟俩才搬到九湾河河边的一个寨子——河边寨。

腊银和腊康在河边寨支起炉子，为百姓修打农具。兄弟俩看到河边寨的百姓来修农具时，衣衫很破烂，愁容满面。寨子里的房子都是用树木搭起的茅草棚，河边的田园，盖满了沙石，长起蒿枝杂草。所以，兄弟俩收修打农具的钱更便宜。有的穷人来修农具,干脆工钱也不要。河边寨的穷苦人,非常感激兄弟俩。

有一天,河边寨南面的山顶上,厚厚的乌云翻着,"轰轰隆隆"的炸雷,一声比一声响得大。隔了一会儿,一阵狂风刮得山摇地动,飞沙走石。随后,暴雨像瓢泼似的,从乌云里倒下来,霎时,九湾河河水猛涨。河水夹沙带石,乱滚乱翻,"哗啦哗啦"冲进河边寨的田园……

暴雨过后,龙王的大太子,带领二十名虾兵蟹将,背弓带箭来打腊银和腊康。兄弟俩不知为哪样,就问龙王大太子:"我们为百姓打农具,不占你们的地盘,也不伤你们的一兵一卒,你们为哪样要来打我们?"

大太子恶狠狠地说:"嘿!你这两个穷鬼,还说不占我的地盘。你知道我的地盘有多宽?你们走遍天下,光脚板踏的地,毛虫头顶的天,都是我的!你们在这里打铁,那'叮叮当当'难听的声音,吵得我家睡不着觉。"说完,就命令那些虾兵蟹将去砸兄弟俩的炉房。

腊康说:"大太子,请你们不要乱动。我们打铁人,是拿手艺和汗水,换点银钱过时光。你把我们的炉房砸了,叫我们咋个活。我们井水不犯你河水,做事何须那么狠毒!"

"呸!像你们这些黑不溜秋的打铁汉还想过时光!我今天叫你们两个死无葬身之地。"阴险狠毒的大太子,张弓搭箭,就向腊银和腊康射来。腊康顺手把太子射来的箭接在手,两手轻轻一掰,箭断成两截。腊康把断箭丢进九湾河里。"虾兵,快砸烂这两个黑铁匠的炉房!"大太子恼羞成怒,凶神恶煞地命令虾兵蟹将。

虾兵就冲进炉房,乱砸乱抢。蟹将就扳弓搭箭,射穿了炉房的篱笆,射烂了炉房的屋顶。虾兵砸烂了兄弟俩的风箱、砧子,打坏钳子,抢走了锤子……

腊银和腊康满胸的怒火冒起十丈高。他们想,如若不把这些不听好言相劝,凶神恶煞的暴徒除灭掉,今后他们还要肆无忌惮地来伤害、欺压百姓。据河边寨的百姓讲:"荒芜的田地,破烂的园子,就是龙王家糟蹋的。"于是,兄弟俩弯弓搭箭,向龙王太子的兵将射去。一箭倒一个,两箭倒一双。不一会儿,太子的兵将有十五个中箭倒地,再也爬不起来。这时,骄横的太子吓慌了手脚,他想不到兄弟俩武艺这么高强!他的十个兵将还不抵一个黑铁匠。他牙齿一咬,眼珠一转,马上变成一条鲤鱼,就往九湾河里钻,想逃回龙宫搬兵来战兄弟俩。腊银和腊康猜中龙王太子的诡计,追到河边。腊银一箭射中太子的眼珠,腊康一箭射中太子的咽喉,鲤鱼太子马上死了。五个虾兵蟹将,仓皇逃回龙宫去了。

逃回龙宫的虾兵蟹将,向老龙王报告了情况。老龙王气得眼喷金星,嘴冒白沫,马上传令找来二太子、三太子,命令他俩带兵去把兄弟俩捉进龙宫斩首,祭大太子。

腊银和腊康早有准备,又有河边寨百姓的帮助,把二太子、三太子的虾兵蟹将,打得死伤遍地。二太子的左手也被打断了。三太子见二太子受伤,慌忙后逃,只带回十个残兵败将。

老龙王见二太子断了手,回去十个兵将,都是断脚少手的,肺都快要气炸了,胡须倒竖、眉毛直起,眼睛瞪得比鸡蛋还大,两道凶光射来扫去。龙王抖动胡须吼道:"我倒要去看看他们的脑壳是铁铸的,还是钢打的!"马上调集一百员虾兵蟹将,老龙王披挂铠甲,拿着砍山刀、梭山篾,背着金筒帕,驾着拂晓的浓雾,浩浩荡荡迎战兄弟俩。

老龙王带兵将出动时,雷声大作,暴雨如注,一时间山洪暴发,河水猛涨。九湾河边的百姓,看到可恶的老龙王又出来祸害百姓,还要捉拿兄弟俩,就一起来保护腊银和腊康。他们拿起锄头、镰刀、棍棒跟龙王的兵交战。

老龙王驾着雨,恶声恶气地命令:"不论哪个兵将,只要捉拿着腊银和腊康,偿给两个金筒帕。"虾兵蟹将一窝蜂向腊银和腊康冲来。兄弟俩在九湾河边百姓的支持下,脸不变色,心不跳。他们弯弓搭箭,射向老龙王的兵将,一箭倒一个,两箭死一双。不一会儿,龙王的兵将死伤过半,剩下的兵将都吓得小腿直打哆嗦。老龙王大发雷霆,举起砍山刀,向兄弟俩劈来。

腊银和腊康想,老龙王是总祸根,兄弟俩拉开满弓,瞄准老龙王射出愤怒的利箭。腊银的箭射中老龙王的右手。老龙王"哎哟"一声惨叫,砍山刀掉了。腊银夺得了老龙王的砍山刀。腊康的箭要射老龙王的梭山篾,但因一道刺眼的闪电,刺了腊康的眼睛,箭没有射中梭山篾,却射中了老龙王背着的两个金筒帕。老龙王慌了手脚,匆匆忙忙发出了一道涨水的命令,逃回了龙宫,再也不敢来战兄弟俩了。

腊银和腊康,夺得了老龙王的砍山刀以后,除了打农具外,还打砍山长刀。在九湾河边打了后,又到户撒山区打,一辈接一辈,一代传一代,阿昌的铁农具和砍山长刀,越打越出名。

如今，在阿昌族地区，阿昌人民背起长刀上山，就想起长刀的来历。想起长刀的来历，就要讲祖先腊银和腊康战老龙王的故事。

搜集整理：赵洪顺　孙加申

编者按： 阿昌族的铁制品远近闻名，甚至在王小波的成名作《黄金时代》里，还反复借用了这个产品。而这里的阿昌族特指陇川县户撒阿昌族乡的阿昌族，他们生产的长刀是中国少数民族三大名刀之一，其余两个是保安族腰刀和英吉沙小刀。

在云南，历史上铁器制作一直是重要的核心技术。因为云南地处云贵高原，山多水深，交通不便，农业大多数停留在刀耕火种阶段。而刀耕火种的关键设备就是一把锋利的长刀。这把刀既可以开山辟路，也可以切菜割肉，还可以开荒种地。

阿昌族的长刀是反复淬火锻造的，韧性极强，可以完成多种任务。刀头是月牙形的，可以当作锄头用。刀的前部分可以砍砸，削铁如泥。展示的时候，把很多铁钉放在砧板上，一刀下去，脆断。刀的后部分磨得异常锋利，吹毛断发，就是把头发放在锋刃上，吹一口气，头发就会断。阿昌族人给我讲解的时候，用了一个说法，可以刮脚毛。他们看我不懂的神色，马上撸起裤脚，用刀把小腿上的毛刮干净。我才知道他们称小腿是脚，所以刮脚毛就是可以当作剃刀用。

作为阿昌族最著名的民族产品，也是首批国家级非物质文化遗产，阿昌族的户撒刀是他们的荣誉。这样的东西，自然需要一个传说来解释。

这个故事就是把长刀追溯为老龙王的武器，为了让这个来历显得高贵，反复铺垫了很多情节。

这些情节都不是节外生枝，实际上是反映了底层人民与那些宣称占有土地和天空的外来权力的对抗。

从阿昌族的角度来看，外来的老龙王宣称自己对于天地的霸权，还通过祸害百姓来彰显自己的力量，这是蛮不讲理的。于是，把长刀从老龙王那里夺过来，就成为一种隐喻，显示了他们希望自己把握自身生存空间的愿望。

Layin and Lakang I

A long time ago, there was a family of two brothers, the elder brother was named Layin and the younger brother was named Lakang. They lost their parents at a very young age. After the death of their parents, they were homeless. So the two brothers had to go out to learn how to make iron tools and practice martial arts. A few years later, Layin and Lakang learned a set of skills on making iron tools and developed their skills in martial arts. The two carried iron tools on their shoulders and bows and arrows on their backs. They went from village to village, repairing and making small farming tools for a living.

Once, Layin and Lakang came to a village called Menggang to make iron tools. The people of Menggang Village knew that the hoe they made was good for shoveling, and the sickle they made was good for cutting. Therefore, they liked Layin and Lakang very much.

One night, the yellow cow in Menggang Village jumped out of the stable and broke the fence gate and got into the brothers' iron-making furnace room, messing up the tools in the furnace room and smashing the anvil on the stone. When the people of the village found out, they came to apologize to Layin and Lakang. Layin said, "It doesn't matter that the anvil is broken, but we two brothers can't work here anymore". Lakang said, "We will have to go home and make an anvil first". The old men of Menggang Village discussed together, and one old man said, "These two guys are good at their craft—the tools they make work well, and they are enthusiastic". When poor people go to them to repair farming tools, they don't care about the price. "We have to find a way to keep them in our village to work for more days." Another old man then said, "Let's gather together some steel, and make an anvil for the brothers, shall we"? "Sounds great. I will go from house to house to find some spare knives and hoes to add to the substances needed to make anvils for the brothers." The third old man said. Everyone agreed.

The next day, the people of Menggang Village, sent three buckets of broken steel and broken iron to Layin and Lakang. The brothers were very grateful and made an anvil fast and good. "Ding dang dang..." with the sound of hammering the steel, the brothers started to make iron tools in the Menggang Village again.

The moon hung high in the sky, big and round. Layin and Lakang had been making farming tools for more than two months in the Menggang Village, seeing the people in the village all have tools to use, the two brothers moved to a village by the Jiuwan River—Hebian Village.

Layin and Lakang set up a stove at the Hebian Village and repaired the farming tools for the people there. The brothers saw that when the people of Hebian Village came to repair their farming tools, their clothes were very ragged, and their faces were full of sorrow. The houses in the village were all thatched huts made of trees, and the fields by the river were covered with sand and stones, with weeds and grasses growing everywhere. Therefore, the brothers charged cheaper to repair the farming tools. In some cases, if the poor people came to repair the tools, they would simply refuse the payment. The poor people of the Hebian Village were very grateful to the two brothers.

One day, the mountain tops of south of the Hebian Village, thick dark clouds covered the sky, rumbling of thunder was loud and scary. After a while, a gust of wind shook the mountains, blowing away the sand and rocks. Then, the rain, like a splash, poured down from the dark clouds, and suddenly, the Jiuwan River rose sharply. The river water swiftly rushed into the fields of the Hebian Village.

After the rainstorm, the Dragon King's first prince, led twenty soldiers with arrows to fight Layin and Lakang. The brothers did not know what for, so they asked the Dragon King's first prince: "We only make farming tools for the people, we do not occupy any land of yours, and hurt any soldier of yours, why do you come to fight us for no reason?"

The first prince said wickedly, "Hey! You two poor bastards, you still say you don't occupy my land. Do you know how vast my territory is? Everywhere you go, the ground that your feet tread on, the sky above the heads of the caterpillars, is mine! You work on the iron stuffs here, that 'tinkling' unpleasant sound is so noisy that my family cannot sleep". After saying that, he ordered those soldiers to smash the brothers' furnace room.

Lakang said: "Prince, please do not move. We iron workers are using our craft and sweat, in exchange for some money to survive. If you smash our furnace room, how can we make a living? We don't offend your business, so don't be so cruel!"

"Yuck! Black and dirty iron workers, like you still want to live a good life? I will let you two be dead without a grave today." The evil and cruel prince set up his bow and arrow and shot at Layin and Lakang. Lakang caught the arrow shot by the prince in his hand and broke it into two pieces with a gentle snap and threw the broken arrow into Jiuwan River. The first prince became enraged and fiercely ordered the soldiers, "Shrimp soldiers, smash the furnace room of these two stupid iron workers"!

Shrimp soldiers rushed into the furnace room, smashed and robbed. Crab generals pulled their bows and arrows and shot through the fence of the furnace room and broke the roof of the furnace room. They smashed the brothers' bellows and anvils, broke the tongs, and stole the hammers.

Lanyin and Lakang were full of anger. They thought: "If we don't get rid of these mean and evil thugs, they will come to hurt and oppress the people with no fear in the future!" According to the people of Hebian Village, "The desolate farm lands, the broken gardens are all spoiled by the Dragon King's family". So the brothers drew their bows and arrows and shot at the soldiers and generals of the prince. One arrow knocked down one, and two arrows knocked down a pair. In a short time, fifteen of the prince's soldiers fell to the ground, hit by arrows and could not get up. At this time, the arrogant prince panicked. He did not expect the brothers to be so skilled! His ten soldiers were not as good as one iron worker. He gritted his teeth, twinkled his eyes, and immediately turned into a carp. He went to the Jiuwan River, wanted to escape back to the Dragon Palace to bring more troops to fight the brothers. Layin and Lakang guessed the Dragon Prince's tricks and chased him to the river. Lanyin shot an arrow in the prince's eye, and Lakang shot an arrow in the prince's throat, the prince died immediately. Seeing the death of their prince, the remaining soldiers fled back to the Dragon Palace in a hurry.

The shrimp soldiers and crabs who escaped back to the Dragon Palace, reported the situation to the Dragon King. The Dragon King was so angry that his eyes squirted gold stars, foaming at the mouth. He immediately sent an order to find the second prince, third prince, and ordered them to take the two brothers into the Dragon Palace, to be beheaded as a sacrifice to the first prince.

Layin and Lakang had prepared, and with the help of the people of Hebian Village, they beat the second prince and the third prince's shrimp soldiers and crab generals to death. The second prince's left arm was broken. When the third prince saw that the second prince was wounded, he fled in a panic and brought back only ten of his soldiers.

The Dragon King saw the second prince broke his arm and the ten soldiers and generals who went back, were all injured and wounded. His lung was about to explode, his whiskers were upside down, his eyebrows were raised, his eyes were bigger than eggs, and two fierce rays of light were shooting all around. The Dragon King roared: "I want to see whether their brains are made of iron or steel!" He immediately gathered a hundred shrimp soldiers and crab generals, dressed in armor, carrying a sword. And with the dawn of the fog, they went out to fight the two brothers in great numbers.

When the Dragon King led the soldiers out, the thunder was loud, the rain was pouring, and for a while, the mountain flooded, the river rose sharply. When the people of Jiuwan River saw that the wicked Dragon

King had coming out again to harm the people and arrest the two brothers, they came together to protect Layin and Lakang. They took up hoes, knives and sticks to fight with the Dragon King's soldiers.

The Dragon King ordered in a wicked voice: "No matter which soldier or general, as long as you catch Layin and Lakang, you will be rewarded with two gold bars." Shrimp soldiers and crab generals rushed towards Layin and Lakang in a swarm. The two brothers, supported by the people of Jiuwan River, showed no fear or panic. They drew their bows and arrows and shot at the Dragon King's soldiers and generals. In a short time, more than half of the Dragon King's soldiers and generals were killed or wounded, and the remaining soldiers and generals were so scared that their legs were wobbling. The Dragon King was furious and raised the sword at the brothers.

Layin and Lakang thought that the Dragon King was the bane of the trouble, and the brothers drew their full bows and aimed at the Dragon King and shot a sharp and angry arrow. Lanyin's arrow hit the right hand of the Dragon King. With a cry of "ouch", the Dragon King dropped his sword. Lakang took the Dragon King's sword. Lakang's arrows were to shoot the dragon king's Suoshan grate, but because of a blinding lightning, stabbing Lakang's eyes, the arrows did not hit the Suoshan grate, but shot the two gold bars that the old Dragon King was carrying. The old Dragon King panicked, hastily issued a command to raise the water, and fled back to the Dragon Palace, and no longer dare to fight the two brothers.

Layin and Lakang, after winning the Dragon King's sword, in addition to making farming tools, also made long swords. After working at Jiuwan River, they went to the mountainous area of Husa to make iron tools as well, and one generation after another, Achang's iron farming tools and swords became more and more famous.

Nowadays, in the Achang region, when the people of Achang carry their long swords to the mountains, they remember the origin of the long swords. When they think of the origin of the long swords, they will tell the story of their ancestors, Layin and Lakang, who fought against the Dragon King.

腊银和腊康（二）

从前有一户人家，家里有三个人：妈妈、一个九岁的女儿和一个三岁的儿子。

山地的玉麦熟了，鹰鹅、老鸦、猴子、老熊经常去践踏。妈妈要去守玉麦，就叫女儿带着弟弟看家。

一天中午，妈妈在地里撵雀，她"喔——喂"地呼叫一声，在凹子那边地里也"喔——喂"地回应一声。妈妈听声音好像是一个和自己差不多年纪的女人在呼唤，猜想也是守地人。现在雀不怎么吵，就招呼那边的人过来讲白话。

一会儿，那边的人过来了，是一个老婆婆。老婆婆问妈妈家里的情况，妈妈告诉她，家住在山脚下，家里有一个九岁的女儿和一个三岁的儿子守家。老婆婆听后，心里暗暗高兴起来。接着妈妈又问她，她说："我是来山那边串亲戚的，今日和亲戚来地里守玉麦，亲戚撒着玉麦先回去了，我留着再帮守一下。"随后老婆婆取下包头来，请妈妈帮梳头。妈妈帮她梳好后，她又帮妈妈梳。

原来这老婆婆是一个老妖婆。她把凹子那边的守地人害死了，吃了那人的心肝，听到这边有人，又来害人。她帮妈妈梳了几下，趁妈妈背着不见她，就伸出利爪，把妈妈掐死了。

天黑了，姐弟俩还不见妈妈回来。姐姐想去找妈妈，但是天又黑，听大人常说山里有妖怪，不敢去找。姐姐就在火塘里烧起火，领着弟弟等着妈妈。等到村上人睡静了，妈妈还不回来。姐姐担心着妈妈，但小弟弟想睡了，姐姐心里也害怕，就用棍子顶上门，捂下火，领着弟弟睡觉去了。

到半夜了姐姐还睡不着。这时，突然听到狗咬，接着听到叫门声："小乖囡，快来开门。"

姐姐听着狗一直咬个不停，平时妈妈回家，狗是不会这样咬的。心想，不要忙，恐怕不是妈妈，我先问问瞧是谁，就问道："妈妈，你怎么到夜深了才回来呀？"

老妖婆在门外说："我拿了一大篮猪草，就迷路了。"

姐姐知道妈妈有时摸黑路，但从不到这么夜深，就警惕地说："你要真是妈妈，就先把手伸进来一只，给我摸摸。"

老妖婆从门缝里伸进一只手来，姐姐一摸，这只手光溜溜的。姐姐知道妈妈是戴着泡花手镯的，就说："你不是妈妈，我妈妈是戴着泡花手镯的。"

老妖婆一听，赶忙轻手轻脚地跑去鹅圈里拿出两个鹅蛋来，把它打通，一只手戴着一个鹅蛋壳，又伸手进来说："小乖囡，妈妈的泡花手镯戴在这只手上，你再摸摸。"

姐姐摸到鹅蛋壳，以为真是妈妈的泡花手镯，就把门打开，让老妖婆进来了。

老妖婆进来后，姐姐很高兴，就说："妈妈，你饿了，我去烧火，热饭给你吃。"

老妖婆怕火光照出她手上戴的鹅蛋壳，就拉着姐姐说道："不消了（云南方言：不用了的意思），妈妈在地里烧玉麦吃过，肚子不饿。夜深了，快睡吧。"

老妖婆领着弟弟睡，姐姐独自睡。姐姐熬了半夜，早就疲劳了，躺到床上就睡着了。

睡了一会儿，一阵响动，姐姐又惊醒了。她一听，妈妈的嘴里"咯哩咯嗒"地响，好像妈妈在嚼物件。平时妈妈吃什么都要先给我们，今晚上为什么会背着我们吃呢？心里奇怪，就问道："妈妈，你吃什么物件呀？"

老妖婆知道姐姐听到了，就撒谎说："我吃几个蚕豆。"

姐姐记得妈妈说过，蚕豆是收完玉麦要做种的，平常弟弟要吃，妈妈都说："饿死老娘不吃种。"今天妈妈怎么吃起种子来了呢？想起一连串的事情来，更加怀疑这不是真妈妈。就故意说："妈妈，给我吃几个蚕豆。"

老妖婆说："你的新牙齿才刚换齐，嚼不动。"

姐姐又装作撒娇地哭闹说："嚼得动的，给我吃一小个就得了，我一定要吃！"

姐姐再三"哭闹"，老妖婆就把弟弟的一个小手骨节递来给姐姐。

姐姐接过来一摸，有一片小指甲粘着，是一个指头。姐姐知道老妖婆把弟弟吃了，妈妈也被她害死了，心中又悲痛，又愤恨，又害怕。怎么办呢？老妖婆一会又要来吃我了。姐姐流着眼泪，想着逃跑的办法。

过了一小下，姐姐想出了一个办法，就说："妈妈，我要撒尿。"

老妖婆说："在床脚撒吧。"

姐姐又说："我还要屙屎。"

老妖婆又说："在床脚屙得了。"

姐姐又说："在床脚屙屎臭，我要出去屙。"

老妖婆还吃不完弟弟的心肝，又怕姐姐跑了，就说："我不送你去了，你害怕嘛，我用一股带子拴着你的脚。"老妖婆就回散她的包头，再接上系筒裙的带子，拴着姐姐的脚。

姐姐脚拖着带子，到外边蹲下，就装作叫狗吃屎。狗跑来她跟前，她就把带子解开，拴在狗脚上，悄悄地跑了。她不敢在路上跑，怕老妖婆知道追上来，就跑到家后边菜园里，爬到一棵大梨树上，等着天亮人来救。

老妖婆吃完弟弟的心肝，姐姐还不进来，她怕姐姐跑了，就拽带子。她拽一下，狗叫一声，左拽也是狗叫，右拽也是狗叫。老妖婆不知道姐姐的名字，就说："你屙什么神屎嘛，还屙不完？"不听见回答，只听见狗叫，她就出去看。理着带子到那里一看，带子拴在狗脚上，她才知道姐姐跑了。

老妖婆在房前屋后找了几转找不着，后来嗅着人气味找到菜园时，天已经亮了。

姐姐在梨树上早就看到老妖婆了。心里很着急，暗暗想着办法对付老妖婆。

老妖婆找到梨树脚，抬头看到姐姐坐在树杈上，以为小细人还会上当，就继续装作真妈妈说："小乖囡，你老早十八的上树去做什么呀？"

姐姐见老妖婆还要装妈妈骗自己，也就装作还未识破她说："妈妈，大梨红彤彤的，又泡，又脆，又甜，很好吃，我摘给你几大个。好吗？"说着就丢下一大个梨。

老妖婆为了装得像真妈妈，一口气就吃完了，还说："真好吃。"

姐姐又说："妈妈，烫熟了的梨更好吃，你去烧一个犁头尖来，我烫给你吃。"

老妖婆为了装得像真妈妈顺从女儿一样，就去烧红了一个犁头尖，穿上一棵木把，递上树来给姐姐。

姐姐烫熟了一大个梨，就像往常和妈妈嬉闹一样说："妈妈，你闭上眼睛张着嘴，我丢大梨来给你。"

老妖婆为了装得像真妈妈，就闭上眼睛张着嘴说："你丢来嘛！"

姐姐见老妖婆真的闭上了眼睛张着嘴，就怀着满腔的仇恨，把红犁头向着老妖婆的嘴丢去，老妖婆就被红犁头扎死了。

姐姐等老妖婆死了，想从树上下来。突然间，一棵梨树下，整个菜园，都长满了一人多高的荨麻。姐姐的手和脚碰着荨麻，又痒又疼，马上就起一饼饼的大疙瘩。原来老妖婆不甘心死亡，它变成了荨麻，还要刺人。荨麻围着姐姐，姐姐下不来了。

姐姐等啊等，等待着过路的行人来搭救。

一大半天不见人过路。姐姐想着妈妈和弟弟被害，悲伤地流着泪。泪水流干了，眼也望疼了。

到了中午，姐姐擦擦眼睛，继续望着那边的大路。这时，她看见远远的路上有个小伙子，挑着炉子、锤子和钳子，向着她这边走来。姐姐就大声地呼叫："大哥哥！快来搭救我呀！……"

原来，四个多月前，哥哥腊银和弟弟腊康分开后，弟弟腊康挑着炉子、锤子和钳子，背着他打制的银把的长刀，翻过了九股岭岗，越过了九个凹子，来到了一个靠山面坝的寨子，在那里支起了炉子，打起了铁。

二十来岁的腊康，长得魁伟英俊，粗脚大手，打起铁来浑身都是力气。他打出的农具，又牢实，又好用，寨子的人们都喜欢他，周围寨子的人也喜欢他的手艺，经常送废铁来请他打农具，一打就是四个多月。

时间长了，腊康挂念着哥哥。虽然活路还很多，那里的乡亲们也再三挽留，腊康还是拜别了那里的乡亲，说下"到出通干天再来"，就挑着工具找哥哥来了。

这天中午，腊康正在赶路，突然听到呼救的声音，以为是有野兽伤人，赶忙放了担子，拔出长刀，循着声音奔去。

跑到园边，见一个小女孩坐在梨树杈上呼救，以为她上树摘果下不来了，冲进园子就要去抱。但是，园子里的荨麻，像火掌一样，刺得腊康又痒又疼，马上就起了一饼饼的大疙瘩，腊康才赶忙问是怎么回事。

姐姐把昨天晚上的一切经过都讲给了腊康，腊康就把一园荨麻全部砍平，扯来竹笆垫在上面，救下了姐姐。

姐姐杀死了老妖婆，为妈妈和弟弟报了仇，腊康很钦佩她的聪明机智，但又可怜她的不幸，就帮她收拾、掩埋了妈妈和弟弟的碎尸。

姐姐无依无靠了，腊康就收她做小妹妹，带着她一起找哥哥去了……

搜集整理：孙家林

编者按： 这个故事的开头是一个非常常见的格林童话式的恐怖场景。对于很多现代人，显然有些少儿不宜的感觉。但是这样的故事，却在世界各地非常普遍，而且得到长期的口头传承。这说明这个故事类型应该具有某种更深的人性映射。

《少年派的奇幻漂流》实际上也是一个类似的故事，只不过被包装成一个传奇。格林童话里的《小红帽》和《汉塞尔与格蕾特》都有坏家伙吃人的段子。在中国的民间故事里，《金花与熊》是西南少数民族常见的故事母题，里面杀死熊的方式，与这个故事一样是小姑娘金花把熊诱导到树下，用矛刺死熊。

对于这样的故事类型，解释也是众说纷纭。有用弗洛伊德的性心理来分析，认为这是一个女性的性觉醒。也有用恐怖故事带来的"安全的恐惧"为归因，解释为人类需要在安全的环境下体验恐惧与紧张，从而宣泄日常生活带来的焦虑和压力。还有从社会的角度，认为这类故事带有道德教育意义，是对于陌生人的提防和日常安全的提醒。

由于编者无法复原这个故事被讲述时讲述者的处境，所以编者愿意保留这个故事的丰富性，也就是这个故事如果能够得到听众的响应，那么听众自身就可以按照自己的想法去解释。

例如，编者个人化地认为这个故事的开头是一个不完整的家庭，并把故事的真正主角定义为一个九岁的女孩，这正是各种危险临近的年龄。于是，陌生人杀死母亲，扮演母亲、杀死弟弟、追杀女孩，甚至死后还化身为荨麻，让女孩无法脱身。这种对于陌生人、女巫、杀手的多重映射，都让一个青春期开始的女性更谨小慎微，更回避陌生的危险。

Layin and Lakang II

Once upon a time, there was a family with three persons: mother, a nine-year-old daughter and a three-year-old son.

The oat in the mountains was ripe, while hawks and geese, old crows, monkeys, and bears often went to trample it. Because the mother had to go to guard the oat, she asked her daughter to take care of the house with her little brother.

One day at noon, mother was in the field to expel the finches, she called out "whoa-hey". Interestingly, there was someone on the other side of the field who also responded. Mom heard the voice as if it was a woman about her own age calling, and guessed it was also a land keeper. Now the finches were not very noisy, so she greeted the people over there to come over and chat.

After a while, the person over there came over, and it was an old woman. The old woman asked the mother about her family, and she told her that her family lived at the foot of the mountain and had a nine-year-old daughter and a three-year-old son to keep the house. When the old woman heard this, she was secretly happy. Then the mother asked her about the situation, and she said: "I came to the mountain side to visit my relatives, and today I came to the field with my relatives to guard the oat, and my relatives left the oat and went back early, so I stayed help to guard it some more time." Then the old lady took off her braid and asked the mother to comb her hair. After the mother helped her comb it, she helped the mother comb her hair too.

It turned out that this old woman was an old witch. She had killed the land keeper on the other side of the dent, ate the person's heart and liver, and when she heard there were people on this side, she came back to kill her. She helped the mother to comb a few times, and when the mother's eyes were not on the witch, she reached out sharp claws, and strangled the mother to death.

It was getting dark, and the children had not seen their mother return. The sister wanted to find her mother, but it was dark. The adults used to say that there were monsters in the mountains, so she didn't dare to go looking for her mother. The sister burned a fire in the fireplace and waited for her mother with her brother. When everyone was sleeping quietly, the mother still did not appear. The sister was worried about her mother, but her little brother wanted to sleep, and the sister was also afraid, so she used a stick to cover the door, put out the fire, and led her brother to sleep.

In the middle of the night, the sister could not sleep. At that moment, she suddenly heard the dog barking, and then heard a knock on the door: "Honey, come and open the door".

The sister heard the dog keep barking, but usually when mom came home, the dog would not bark like this. She thought, "Don't be afraid. I'm afraid it's not mom. I'll ask first to see who it is", so she asked, "Mom, how you came back so late at night"?

The old witch said at the door, "I took a big basket of pigweed, so I got lost at night".

The sister knew that the mother sometimes took the night path, but not so late into the night, so she said cautiously, "If you are really mother, put a hand in first, and let me feel it".

The old witch reached a hand in through the doorway, and when the sister touched it, the hand was bare. The sister knew that her mother was wearing a flower bracelet, so she said, "You are not my mother. My mother wears a flower bracelet".

As soon as the old witch heard this, she rushed to go to the geese to take out two goose eggs. She broke them, wore a goose eggshell on her left hand, reached in and said, "My dear, the flower bracelet is worn on this hand, feel it again".

The sister touched the goose eggshell, thought it was really her mother's flower bracelet, so she opened the door and let the old witch come in.

When the old witch came in, the sister was very happy and said, "Mom, you're hungry. I'll go to the fire, and heat rice for you to eat".

The old witch was afraid that the firelight would reveal the goose eggshells she was wearing on her hands, so she pulled the little girl and said, "No, mommy has eaten in the field by burning the oat, and I'm not hungry. It's late tonight. Go to sleep".

The old witch led the little brother to sleep, and the sister slept alone. The sister, having stayed up for half of the night, has long been exhausted, so she laid down on the bed and fell asleep.

After sleeping for a while, there was a loud noise, and the sister woke up again. She listened to her mother's mouth "clucking", as if she was chewing something. Usually, she always gave us everything she ate in advance, but why did she eat behind our backs tonight? The sister was feeling strange, so she asked, "Mom, what are you eating"?

The old witch knew that the sister had heard her eating, so she lied and said, "I just ate a few broad beans".

The sister remembered her mother's words that the beans were collected after the harvest of oat to be planted. Usually her brother wanted to eat the beans, and her mother always said: "I would rather starve than to eat those beans." So why was mom eating the beans today? Thinking of the chain of events, she further doubted that this was not the real mother. So she said purposely, "Mom, give me some beans".

The old witch said, "Your new teeth have just been replaced. You cannot chew".

The sister pretended to be crying and said: "I can do it. Give me a small one to eat. I want to eat..."

The sister repeatedly "cried", so the old witch handed her a small hand bone of her brother.

The sister took it and touched it—there was a small piece of nail on it—it was a finger.

The sister knew that the old witch had eaten her brother, and her mother had been killed by the witch, and her heart was filled with grief, anger and fear. What should she do? The old witch is going to come and eat her in a while. The sister with tears in her eyes, tried to think of a way to escape.

After a short while, the sister came up with a solution and said, "Mom, I want to pee".

The old witch said, "Pee at the foot of the bed".

The sister said again, "I have to poop".

The old witch said, "You can do it at the foot of the bed".

The sister said again, "Pooping at the foot of the bed stinks. I want to go out and poop".

The old witch has not yet finished eating her brother's heart and liver and was afraid that the sister would run away, so she said, "I will not take you there. If you are afraid, I will use a rope to tie it on your feet". The old witch turned back to untie her braid, then attached it to the dress straps, and used it to tie to the sister's feet.

The sister, with her feet dragging the strap, went outside and squatted down, calling the dog to come. When the dog came running to her heels, she untied the strap, tied it to the dog's feet and ran away quietly. She did not dare to run on the road, and was afraid the old witch would chase after her, so she ran to the back of the vegetable garden, climbed up to a large pear tree, and waited for the dawn to come and someone to come to rescue her.

The old witch finished eating her brother's heart and liver, but the sister did not come back. She was afraid that the girl ran away, so she tugged the strap. She tugged, and the dog barked; she tugged leftwards, the dog barked; she tugged rightwards the dog also barked. The old witch did not know the name of the sister, so she said, "What are you doing? You still have not finished yet?" When she didn't hear an answer, but only heard the dog barking, she went out to see. When she got there with the strap and saw that it was tied to the dog's feet, she realized that the sister had run away.

The sister in the pear tree has long seen the old witch. Her heart was very anxious, and secretly thought of ways to deal with the old witch.

The old witch found the pear tree, looked up and saw the sister sitting on the tree branch. She thought the sister would still be fooled, so she continued to pretend to be the real mother and said: "Baby girl, what are you doing up the tree in the early morning?"

The sister saw the old witch still pretending to be her mother to cheat her, so she also pretended not to recognize her and said, "Mom, the pears are red, crisp and sweet, so delicious. I'll pick you a few big ones. Okay"? And then dropped a large pear.

The old witch, in order to act like a real mother, ate it all in one gulp and said, "It's so yummy".

The sister added: "Mom, the pear is more delicious when it is hot. You go and burn a plough tip. I will heat it for you to eat".

In order to act like a real mother obeying her daughter, the old witch went to burn a red plough tip, put it on a wooden handle, and handed it up the tree to the sister.

The sister burned a large pear, acting like what she used to do with her mother, she playfully said to the old witch, "Mom, you close your eyes and open your mouth, and I will throw the big pear to you".

The old witch, in order to pretend to be like a real mother, closed her eyes and opened her mouth and said, "Throw it here"!

When the sister saw the old witch really closed her eyes and opened her mouth, with full of hatred, she threw the red plough towards the old witch's mouth. The old witch was stabbed to death by the red plough.

The sister waited until the old witch was dead to come down the tree, but suddenly the entire vegetable garden were filled with high nettles about the height of one adult. Once the sister's feet and hands touched the nettles, they are itching and painful, and her body immediately grew large bumps. It turned out that the old witch was not resigned to death, so she turned into nettles to sting people. The nettles surrounded the sister, and she couldn't get down.

The sister waited and waited for the passing passers-by to come and help.

For the most of the day, no one passed by. The sister thought about her mother and brother being killed and shed tears of grief. The tears dried up, and her eyes were sore.

By noon, the sister wiped her eyes and continued to look at the road on the other side. At that moment, she saw a young man on the far side of the road, carrying a stove, a hammer and tongs, coming toward her. The sister called out loudly, "Hey, big brother! Come and help me"!

It turned out that more than four months ago, after the elder brother Layin and the younger brother Lakang separated, the younger brother Lakang picked up the stove, the hammer and the pliers, carrying his long sword with a silver handle, and went over nine ridge posts, crossed nine hollows, and came to a village by the mountain, where he set up the stove and started to make iron tools.

Lakang, who was in his twenties, was handsome and strong, with big hands and big feet, and was full of strength when he worked with iron. The tools he made, firm and good, the people of the village like him, the surrounding villages also liked his craft, and often sent scrap iron to ask him to make agricultural tools. It took more than four months for Lakang to make those tools altogether.

Over time, Lakang missed his brother. Although there were still a lot of work, and the villagers there also repeatedly urged him to stay, Lakang still bid farewell to the villagers there, and picked up his tools to find his brother.

At noon of this day, when Lakang was on the road, and suddenly heard the sound of a cry for help, thought it was a beast hurting people, and hurriedly put the load, pulled out the long sword, and ran in search of the sound.

When he ran to the garden, he saw a little girl sitting on a pear tree branch crying for help. He thought the girl was picking fruit from the tree and couldn't get down, so he rushed into the garden to get her. However, the garden nettles stung Lakang and it was itchy and painful. Immediately a large area of big bumps grew on his body, only then Lakang rushed to ask what was going on.

The sister told Lakang everything that happened last night, and Lakang saved her by cutting down all the nettles in the garden and pulling in a bamboo net on top to save her.

The sister killed the old witch and took revenge for her mother and brother. Lakang admired her intelligence and wisdom, but pitied her misfortune, so he helped her bury the broken bodies of her mother and brother.

The sister had no one to rely on, so Lakang took her as a little sister and carried her along to find his brother.

腊银和腊康（三）

从前，有两个阿昌族兄弟，哥哥叫腊银，弟弟叫腊康。哥哥年纪二十出头，弟弟才十八岁，他俩学得一套打铁的好手艺。他俩铸的犁头，犁起坨子泡鲜鲜；他俩打的长刀，碗口大的小树轻轻就涮断了。他俩铸的犁头，汉族、傣族百姓争着要；他俩打的长刀，景颇、德昂百姓抢着买。

撒种节刚过，腊银、腊康商量：该是下田种地的时候了，坝子的百姓等着换犁头，山上的庄稼人要涮地下种了，我们赶快把犁头、长刀送去。哥哥对弟弟说："你年纪小，在坝子换犁头；我去山上卖长刀，卖完我就回来。"于是，兄弟两个就分头出发了。

腊银挑着打铁的工具，夹着一捆打好的长刀，挎着一个从不离身的金黄色筒帕上山了。他翻了三支岭岗，过了三个深凹子，来到一个景颇族寨子。那地方，箐深林密，山獐马鹿老象多，自然不需要说了，还有成群结队的长臂猴子，怪讨厌，成群结伙地跑到地里掰包谷；有时还偷偷地跑进家来偷东西吃。有一天，腊银出去了一下，一群猴子就跑进他的灶房，猴子看见主人不在，就偷东西吃。领头的一个老母猴看见金黄色的筒帕蛮喜欢，拿来挎在背上就逃回树林子里去了。

腊康换犁头回到家，不见哥哥回来；又过几天，仍然不见回来，他着急了。他想，哥哥到景颇山好多趟了，肯定是熟人多，打刀的人多，纠缠着回不来，不及我赶去帮他一把。腊康就顺着哥哥往常指给他的方向，带着防身的弓箭往山上走去。

腊康翻了三支岭岗，过第三个凹子时，突然看见凹子底水沟里有只大黄猴，正埋着头摸螃蟹，身上背着一只金黄色的筒帕，摸着一只，放进筒帕一只。腊康看清筒帕是哥哥的，感到事情凶多吉少，可能老猴子把哥哥害了，顿时一股无名怒火，蹿到脑门骨，他解下弓弩，搭上箭，"嗖"地一声射去，老黄猴应声倒在水沟里。腊康上去拾起筒帕，控掉螃蟹，就往前赶路，一心默想，要去问个水清明白。

腊康赶到寨子里一问,晓得哥哥还在,原先心里吊着的一块石头,一下子落下来了。腊银看见弟弟来了,高兴得眉毛都笑起来了,赶忙淘米煮饭。弟弟一边凑火,一边摘下金筒帕说:"哥!我看见在凹子底的水沟里,有只老黄猴,背着你的筒帕摸螃蟹。我担心你遭了不幸,一箭就把他射死了。喏!筒帕拿回来了,我急了连螃蟹都没有心思要。"

"哎呀!你惹出事来了。那只老黄猴,听这一带的老人讲,是一只母猴王,它和公猴王率领着一群猴子,经常跑到地里掰包谷,进家偷东西。它们会记人的脸样,会嗅气味,说不定什么时候会来报复呢!"腊银说完,蹙紧了眉头。

"那怎么办呢?"腊康吓得脸色都变了,赶紧向哥哥讨主意。

"倒也不需要怕,猴子这东西又狡猾又傻,我们想办法对付它们。"哥哥安慰弟弟说。

兄弟两个琢磨了一阵,便拿着弓箭,去密林里老象出没的地方,射倒一只象,把皮剥下,肉割了,东一块西一块地摆在院场上。在象肉的旁边,放上一块块烧得通红的铁块;又找来几窝葫芦蜂包挂在炉房里;他俩安排停当,就躲到别处去了。

果然,过不久,老公猴带领着一群猴子,争先恐后地跑来报复了。老公猴怒气冲冲,直奔腊银的炉房。有些小猴子看见象肉,嘴馋就去抓。猴子吃东西都要坐着,抓着肉就坐下吃,一坐就坐在铁块上,屁股烫起火疮疤,毛也烫掉了,一个个惊叫着乱跑。钻进炉房的猴子,不见人,东翻西揉,把几窝葫芦蜂包也捅开了,激怒了的蜂子一齐飞出来,叮得猴子满脸通红,跑不赢地跑,一阵二三,全部跑进了森林里,再也不敢进家来了。

从此,猴子屁股就成了一个火疮疤,永远也不会生毛,而且一直是红的,猴子也留下了抓头搔耳的习惯。

腊银和腊康,打完刀子,安然无事地回家去了。

搜集整理:杨叶生

编者按: 这个故事更类似一个动物故事,解释了猴子屁股为何火红色,而且不长毛,还喜欢抓头搔耳。但是讲述者把这个故事嫁接到腊银和腊康这对兄弟身上,显然这对兄弟属于英雄史诗般的神奇人物。

因为整理故事的杨叶生是中文系毕业的高材生，这个故事也就有了明显的文人特征，例如里面用的词语和语法，都显得有些文绉绉。

但是故事本身仍然是基于口头传诵的，特别是这种人与野兽斗智斗勇的类型。人类的获胜，总不是明刀明枪的真实力量，而是暗搓搓地使计谋、布陷阱。而这种小伎俩，也成为民间故事里的英雄手段。实际上在《水浒传》的故事里，也常见这种带有狡诈属性的江湖品位。

Layin and Lakang Ⅲ

Once upon a time, there were two brothers from the Achang ethnic group. The elder brother was named Layin, and the younger brother was Lakang. Layin was in his early twenties, while Lakang was only eighteen. Both were born with exceptional blacksmithing skills. The plowshares they forged were so sharp that they could easily slice through soil, and the long knives they crafted could effortlessly cut through trees as thick as a bowl. The plowshares were popular among the Han and Dai people, and the long knives were eagerly sought after by the Jingpo and De'ang people.

After the Sazhong Festival, Layin and Lakang discussed their plans: It's time to go to the fields and start planting. The villagers in the valley are waiting to replace their plowshares, and the farmers in the mountains need to cut down trees to prepare for sowing. Let's quickly deliver the plowshares and long knives. Layin said to his brother, "You're still young, so you stay in the valley to exchange the plowshares. I'll go up the mountain to sell the long knives, and I'll be back once I've finished". With that saying, the brothers went out in different directions.

Layin carried his blacksmithing tools, a bundle of long knives, and a yellow bag as he headed up the mountain. He crossed three ridges and passed through three deep valleys before arriving at a Jingpo village. The area was dense with forests and home to many wild animals like deer, wild boars, and elephants. It was also filled with long-armed monkeys, which were known for stealing crops. One day, while Layin was away, a group of monkeys entered his kitchen. Seeing that the owner was not around, they began to steal food. The leader, an old female monkey, liked Layin's yellow bag, so it slung it over its shoulder, and fled back into the woods.

When Lakang returned home after exchanging the plowshares, he found that his brother had not come back yet. A few days passed, and Layin still didn't come back. Lakang became anxious and thought: "My brother has been to the Jingpo mountains many times, so he has a reputation there. Maybe he got delayed because there were so many things to do and couldn't return in time. I'd better go and help him." So Lakang followed the directions his brother had given him and went up the mountains, carrying his bow and arrows for protection.

After crossing three ridges and reaching the third valley, Lakang suddenly saw a large yellow monkey in the creek, catching crabs. The monkey was wearing a yellow bag over its shoulder, catching crabs and putting them into the bag. Recognizing the bag as his brother's, Lakang thought that the old monkey might have harmed Layin. Filled with anger, he drew his bow and shot the monkey. Lakang retrieved the cloth bag, emptied out the crabs, and continued on his way, determined to find out what had happened.

When Lakang arrived at the village and asked around, he was relieved to learn that his brother was safe. Layin was overjoyed to see his brother and immediately started preparing a meal. As Lakang stoked the fire, he handed over the yellow bag and said, "Brother, I saw an old yellow monkey in the creek, carrying your bag while catching crabs. I was worried something had happened to you, so I shot it. Look, I brought the bag back, but I was in a rush that I didn't even bother with the crabs".

"Oh, no! You've caused trouble", Layin exclaimed, frowning. "That old yellow monkey was the queen of the monkeys. She and the monkey king led their troop to steal the crops. They can recognize faces and remember scents, so they might come back for revenge!"

"What should we do?" Lakang asked, turning pale with fear.

"There's no need to be too afraid of," Layin reassured his brother. "Monkeys are cunning but also foolish. We'll come up with a way to deal with them."

After some thought, the brothers took their bow and arrows and headed to a dense forest roamed by elephants. They shot down an old elephant, skinned it, cut the meat into piece and placed in the courtyard. Next to the elephant meat, they placed several red-hot iron blocks. They also found several beehives and hung them in the kitchen. Once everything was in place, the brothers hid away.

As expected, it wasn't long before the monkey king led the troop to seek revenge. The monkey king, full of anger, charged straight toward Layin's kitchen. Some of the younger monkeys, tempted by the elephant meat, grabbed them. Monkeys always sit down to eat, so as they grabbed the meat and sat, their bottoms landed on the hot iron blocks, causing burns to their fur. Screaming in pain, they scattered in all directions. The monkeys that entered the kitchen knocked over the beehives, unleashing a swarm of angry bee that stung their faces. The monkeys fled into the forest and never dared to come back again.

From that day on, the monkeys' bottoms remained hairless and red, and they developed the habit of scratching their heads and ears.

After finishing their work, Layin and Lakang returned home safely.

阿昌族不信鬼的由来

相传古时候，皇宫里闹鬼，闹得皇帝不得安宁。皇帝从不能睡一个安稳觉，满朝文武大臣也睡不成，时时忙着商议治鬼捉鬼的办法。一天，一个文官上朝奏上一个密本，皇帝看后，下旨叫群臣退朝，然后入宫睡觉去了。这天晚上，鬼照样来了，锦衣卫听到，皇帝叽里呱啦地像在说梦话，却不见皇帝像从前那样，一睡到床上就拳打脚踢大喊大叫。到了天亮，皇帝急急忙忙地起了床，洗过脸就上朝议事。皇帝一坐到皇位上，就下了第一道圣旨，三天后在皇宫里大摆宴席，宴请大大小小的鬼；接着又下了第二道密旨，叫献计的大臣做好捉鬼的准备。

一眨眼，第三天到了，皇帝的大殿里摆下了宴席，灯火明亮，烟雾缭绕。深夜三更，大大小小的鬼都按时入了席。大殿左左右右，上上下下埋伏着刀斧手，只听见杯盘碗筷的碰响声，喝酒的咂嘴声，猜拳行令的吆喝声。五更时，只见献计的大臣把咒符一烧，埋伏的刀斧手把天罗地网一收，大大小小的鬼全部被网罗在天罗地网里。随后，皇帝的圣旨传到各个民族的领地，要各民族的头领进京，皇帝要分赠金银财宝。各民族头领听了都非常高兴，各自带了装金银财宝的用具赶紧进京。

阿昌族头领听了圣旨后，召集大小头领来商量办法。最后，阿昌族头领根据大家的意见，赶编了一只大花竹篮，竹篮的空隙有碗口那么大。他们认为：我们在边远地区，到上千里远的京城里去领金银财宝，碎的小的就不要了，光背一篮大的回来就得了。阿昌族头领命令随从背上篮子，带着护卫进京。

各民族头领到了京城后，皇帝传下圣旨："今天晚上五更后，大家就进宫，到大殿上领金银财宝，领得后立刻离开京城，不得逗留，违者格杀勿论。"

晚上五更时分，各民族头领在皇宫大门口等着领金银财宝，皇宫点名，点一个进殿，领金银一个。阿昌族头领排队排在队伍的后边，在他的后面还有其他民族的三个头领。他前后看看,只见其他民族头领有的带了麻袋,有的带了布袋,有的带了背篓,有的带了密密的竹篮,有的带背篓和竹篮的还有盖子。他想:带了麻袋、布袋的,大大小小都得要,带了有盖子的背篓和竹篮的,装不冒尖,都没有我的大花竹篮好,碎的小的装不住,没有盖子能装冒尖。阿昌族头领的心里话刚说完,就轮到他领金银财宝了。分鬼的大臣连忙向阿昌族头领的大花竹篮装鬼。阿昌族头领一边看着分金银财宝,一边双手连连颠动摇晃着大花竹篮。分鬼的大臣心里暗暗发笑:"真憨!你想多装一些鬼,我就多分给你一些。"分鬼的大臣心里想着,双手连连向阿昌族头领的大花竹篮里装鬼,阿昌族头领把大花竹篮也颠动摇晃得更快了。阿昌族头领估计着差不多了,才说:"别装了。"所以,阿昌族头领领金银财宝的时间,比别的民族头领的两倍还多。

  阿昌族头领背起大花竹篮,高高兴兴地出了皇宫,带着随从和护卫离开了京城,连夜上路了。

  阿昌族头领在返回领地的路上,越走越觉得奇怪,到天亮时,他看到大花竹篮里是空的,心里纳闷,问背篮子的随从重不重。随从说不知怎么搞的,走一截路,会轻一些。他不放心,干脆自己把大花竹篮接过来背。刚一背上还有一些重量,可就是看不见篮子里的金银财宝。走到2/3的路程时,大花竹篮竟和进京时一样轻了。他从背上取下大花竹篮再看,大花竹篮仍然是空的。他蛮不高兴地把篮子一甩,叫随从背着,嘟嘟囔囔地回到领地。

  阿昌族头领回到领地不久,京城里传出了消息,原来上一个月皇帝下旨要各民族头领进京,不是去领金银财宝,而是把在皇宫里捉到的大大小小的鬼分给各民族。因为阿昌族头领用大花竹篮去装鬼,再加上他在分鬼的时候不停地颠动摇晃着篮子,小鬼漏掉一些在皇宫里,路上又漏掉一些。天亮后,大花竹篮里还剩下的鬼,一个一个地醒来,一个一个地跑掉了,到走了2/3的路程时,大花竹篮里的鬼全跑光了,只剩下一只空竹篮子。结果,阿昌族头领没有背回一个鬼,所以阿昌族不信鬼。其他民族头领都背回了鬼。如傣族头领背回了琵琶鬼,所以傣族信琵琶鬼;汉族头领用大麻袋装鬼,背回的鬼最多,所以信的鬼也最多。

讲述:石再润
记录整理:杨兴全　许可都　赵刚

编者按： 皇帝给各民族分鬼，这个隐喻让编者忍俊不禁。显然阿昌族对于远在天边、遥不可及的皇权有一种无畏的嘲讽态度。

故事里说："阿昌族头领听了圣旨后，召集大小头领来商量办法。最后，阿昌族头领根据大家的意见，赶编了一只大花竹篮，竹篮的空隙有碗口那么大。他们认为：我们在边远地区，到上千里远的京城里去领金银财宝，碎的小的就不要了，光背一篮大的回来就得了。"

这样的大花竹篮是一种应对谋略。如果是真金白银，那么阿昌族就赚得盆满钵盈；如果是其他东西，那么不要也罢！实际上因为路途遥远，甚至这个竹篮都被丢弃了。

虽然故事的一开头，我们已经知道皇帝没安什么好心。但是阿昌族用一个民间的伎俩，巧妙地回避了皇权的暗算，还让听众明白一个道理：跟皇权打交道，你要的越多，你得到的鬼越多。

The Origin of Achang's Disbelief in Ghosts

Legend has it that in ancient times, the palace was haunted by ghosts, and the emperor had no peace. Since the emperor could not have a restful sleep, the court ministers could not sleep, and were always busy discussing ways to deal with and capture ghosts. One day, a scholar reported to the court a confidential document. After the emperor had read it, he ordered the officials to leave the court, and then went to sleep in the palace. That night, the ghosts came as usual, the imperial guards could hear that the emperor was talking in his sleep, but could not see the emperor like before, as soon as he went to bed, he was punching and kicking and shouting. At dawn, the emperor hurriedly got up, washed his face and went to court. As soon as the emperor sat on the throne, he announced the first decree—three days later, there shall be a feast in the palace, a feast for all the ghosts, large and small; then he issued a second decree, telling the officials to be ready to capture the ghosts.

In the blink of an eye, the third day arrived, the emperor's hall set up a feast, with bright lights and dazzling smoke. At three o'clock in the night, all the ghosts, big and small, entered the feast on time. Around the hall, left and right, up and down, ambushed swordsmen and axe men. Only heard the sound of clinking cups and bowls, smacking lips, and yelling fist line orders. At five o'clock, the minister who offered the plan burned a spell, and the ambushed swordsmen and axe men closed the net, and all the ghosts, large and small, were caught in the net. Then, the emperor's decree was sent to the territories of various ethnic groups and asked all their leaders to come to the capital, where the emperor wanted to share silver and gold treasures. The chiefs of each ethnic group were very happy to hear this, and each brought their own equipment for loading gold and silver treasures to the capital.

After hearing the decree, the Achang chief gathered the leaders of small categories to discuss the solution. Finally, the Achang chief, according to everyone's opinion, rushed to weave a large flower bamboo basket, and the gap of the bamboo basket was as wide as the mouth of a bowl. They thought: "We are in a remote area, which is thousands of miles away from the capital city, to receive gold and silver treasures, so we do not want the small ones, and we will just carry a basket of big ones back." The Achang chief ordered his men to carry the basket on their backs and enter the capital with their escorts.

After the chiefs of the ethnic groups arrived at the capital, the emperor issued a decree: "After five o'clock this evening, everyone will enter the palace to receive gold and silver treasures in the main hall, and after receiving them, leave the capital immediately. Do not stay, and whoever disobeys will be killed."

At five o'clock in the evening, the chiefs of all ethnic groups waited at the palace gate to receive the gold and silver treasures, and the official of the palace called the chiefs one by one into the hall to receive one gold and silver. The chief of Achang tribe lined up at the back, and behind him there were three chiefs of other ethnic groups. He looked back and forth and saw that some of the other chiefs had brought sacks, some had cloth bags, some had backpacks, some had dense bamboo baskets, and some had backpacks and bamboo baskets with lids. He thought, with sacks and cloth bags, one must take large and small silver and gold; with a lid on the backpack and bamboo baskets, it cannot be loaded. They were all not as good as my large flower basket. The Achang chief's thoughts were just finished, and it was his turn to receive the gold and silver treasures. The minister of ghost distribution hurriedly loaded the ghost to the big flower basket of the Achang chief. The Achang chief tribe watched the distribution of the gold and silver treasures while shaking the big flower basket with his hands. The minister who was distributing the ghosts laughed in his heart,

"How silly! If you want more ghosts, I will give you more". The minister of ghost distribution filled the big flower basket of the Achang chief with ghosts with both hands. The chief also shook the basket harder. The Achang chief estimated that it was ok, so he said, "Stop filling it". In the end, the Achang chief took more than twice as long as other ethnic chiefs to collect the gold and silver.

On his way back to the territory of the Achang tribe, the more he walked, the stranger he felt. When it was dawn, he saw the basket empty. He felt puzzled and asked the servant with the basket if it was weighty. The servant said that somehow it became lighter after a short walk. He did not feel safe, so he simply took over the large flower basket to carry. There was still some weight on the back, but you cannot see the gold and silver treasures in the basket. By the time he reached two-thirds of the way, the large flower basket was as light as it was when he entered the capital. He removed the large flower basket from his back and looked again, the large flower basket was still empty. He was unhappy and tossed the basket and asked his servant to carry it back to the territory with mutterings.

Soon after the Achang chief returned to his territory, news spread in the capital that last month, the emperor decreed all chiefs of various ethnic groups to go to the capital, not to receive gold and silver treasures, but to distribute the large and small ghosts caught in the imperial palace to various ethnic groups. Because the Achang chief used a large flower basket to carry the ghosts, in addition he kept shaking the basket when distributing the ghosts, the ghosts were left out in the palace, and some were left out on the road. After dawn, the ghosts that left in the big flower basket, woke up one by one, and ran away altogether. By the time the Achang chief had gone two-thirds of the way, the ghosts in the big flower basket all ran away, leaving only an empty basket. Other ethnic chiefs have carried back ghosts. Such as the Dai chief brought back the Pipa Ghost, so the Dai believe in the Pipa ghost; The Han chief used a large bag to carry ghosts, so he brought back the most ghosts, therefore they believe in most of the ghosts.

老实人

有一家老两口，靠打柴过日子。有一天，老两口在河边砍柴，不知不觉地砍了很多柴。正砍得来劲的时候，斧子把突然断了，斧子被甩到河里面去了。两位老人又不能下河去捞，正在急得发愁。

他们这样想，自己这一辈子就是靠这把斧子砍柴度日，这下斧子没有了，要饿肚子了。

两位老人很懊恼，气得不得了，坐在河边哭，哭呀，哭得很伤心。河里的鱼、虾子等听到以后也替他俩难过。

斧子找不到，鱼、虾子就送给他俩一把银斧子。两位老人说："这不是我的，我们不能够拿，我们的只是铁斧子，不是银斧子。"鱼、虾子就把银斧子收回去。最后还是听到哭声，鱼、虾子又拿出一把比银斧子价值高的金斧子来。两个老人看了："这也不是我们自己的斧子。"鱼、虾子看到这两个老人很老实，就报告了上帝。上帝就变成一条鱼来跟老人说："你们两位老人，送给你们什么都不要。那么，你们两位老人就下到这条小船上来，我们同你们两个去找斧子。"两位老人听了就坐上了这条小船。走呀，漂呀，结果斧子还是找不着。船到了另外一个地方，鱼就指给他俩一所房子，有一位老人在里面守着，你两个到里面去住吧。他两个到了房子前，那老人就说："老朋友，快来吧，我们共同在这里过生活吧，你家我家都是一样的，里面你要什么有什么。"老人还给他俩介绍说："这些都不必客气，吃的、用的全有。"老人又继续说道："我也是有困难，上帝照顾我来这里过生活的。"老人说了以后，忽然不见了，把这所房子里的东西留给他两位老人享用。从此，这两位老人幸福地过着晚年生活。

讲述：老七
翻译：藤茂芳
整理：张亚萍

编者按： 这个故事中突然冒出来一个上帝，而不是一个龙王，或者什么土司，颇有几分奇特。

编者认为，这个故事明显有伊索寓言中《樵夫与赫尔墨斯》的类似情节。在故事中，一个樵夫不小心把他的铁斧子掉进了河里，陷入了困境。神（在希腊版本中是赫尔墨斯，罗马版本中是墨丘利）出现了，试图帮助他。赫尔墨斯从河里捞出了金斧子、银斧子、铁斧子，依次问樵夫哪一把是他的。诚实的樵夫只认领了属于自己的铁斧子，而没有贪图金斧子或银斧子。由于他的诚实，神不仅归还了他的铁斧子，还奖赏他金斧子和银斧子。

据说在 19 世纪末，就有从西方传来的文化交流，把伊索寓言翻译成中文，随即这些故事就开始在这个文化系统中传播。因为这个故事原本短小精悍，又充满道德寓意，因此，很容易就被各地进行了再创作。

值得注意的是，这个故事里的神明已经暗示了这个故事的西方源头了。因此，读民间故事，很多时候是可以通过雪泥鸿爪来发现一些趣味的。

The Honest People

There was an old couple, living on chopping firewood. One day, the old couple were chopping firewood at the river and unconsciously chopped a lot of firewood. When they were chopping, the axe handle suddenly broke and the axe was thrown into the river. The old couple couldn't go down to the river to get it and were anxiously worried.

They thought, they relied on this axe to chop firewood to make a living. Now the axe was gone, and they had to starve.

The old couple were very upset, and mad, while they sat by the river and wept. The fish and shrimp in the river also heard their cry and felt sorry for them. The axe could not be found, so the fish and shrimp gave them a silver axe. The old couple said, "It's not ours, so we can't take it; ours is just an iron axe, not a silver axe". The fish and shrimp then took back the silver axe. Eventually, they still heard crying, so the fish and shrimp took out another gold axe that was more valuable than the silver one. The old couple looked at it and said, "This is not our axe either".

When the fish and shrimp saw that the old couple were honest, they reported to the God. The God turned into a fish and said to the old man: "You do not want anything from us. Well, then, you guys should come down to this boat, and we will go with you two to find the axe." The old couple listened and got into the boat. They walked and rafted, but the axe was still not found. The boat came to another place, the fish pointed out to them a house, and said, "There is an old man guarding inside. You two could go and live in that house". When they arrived at the house, the old man said: "My old friends, come on. Let's live here together, make yourself at home, and you can have whatever you want inside." The old man also introduced to them, "You make yourselves at home; you have everything to eat and use". The old man continued, "I also had difficulties, and the God took care of me to come and live here". After has said that, the old man suddenly disappeared and left the things in the house for the old couple to enjoy. From then on, the old couple lived a happy life in their old age.

继母

从前有个男人，他成亲后，妻子生了个男孩，取名叫张理，一家人日子过得挺美满。

不料，结婚才三年时，妻子得了一场大病，尽管男人精心照料，妻子的病仍然一天比一天重。妻子知道自己的病治不好了，便对男人说："我的病好不了啰，希望你看在我们夫妻一场的情分上，好好抚养张理。"没过多久，妻子就病死了。

一个男人，带着个一岁多的婴儿，既要做活，又要料理家务，日子非常难过。众人都劝他再娶个老婆，但他说："不是我不想再找个人，就怕后娘对孩子不好，一想到张理和他娘，我就不想要呀！"很长时间，他都没有再成个家。一次，一个邻居告诉他："邻寨有个姑娘，心肠挺好，你去看看吧。"他想，家里没个女人，实在是没法过了，就把那个姑娘娶回来了。

这个姑娘一过门，就操持家务，对张理也挺好，夫妻俩生活得很和气。众人都说张理和他爹福气好，找了个贤惠的女人，可也有人说："才过门的媳妇，三天的新鲜，等她自己有了孩子再看吧！"

一年后，她生了个儿子，取名叫张孝。她虽然有了自己的孩子，但对张理仍然很好。孩子们大一些了，她出门时，总是背着张理，而让张孝自己走。别人见了，对她说："你应该背着小的，让大的自己走嘛。"她却回答说："大孩子是丈夫前妻生的，小小的就没有了妈妈，挺可怜的，我应该对前妻的孩子好一点。这样做，不光是为了让丈夫放心，也省得旁人说闲话呀。再说，反正小的自己也会走，牵着他就行了。"大伙听了，都很感动。她丈夫也很感激，一颗悬着的心，总算放下来了。

日子过得很快，张理、张孝渐渐长大了。可是他们的父亲也因为终日操劳，不幸得病去世了。

丈夫去世以后，妻子仍然像往常一样地待张理。两个孩子懂事以后，母亲还把他俩送到奘房去学习。母子三人，和和睦睦地过着日子。

一天，母亲感到很不好过，慢慢就起不了床了。两个儿子请了医生来看病，开了许多服药，却怎么也治不好母亲的病，眼看母亲是不行了。兄弟俩都很着急，却又想不出什么好办法。有一天晚上，母亲迷迷糊糊地梦见一个神对她说："你的病，不是凡人可以治好的，任你吃多少服药，也没有用。不过要治你的病也不难。我告诉你个办法，用一副凤凰肝煎吃，你的病就会好的。赶快打发你的儿子去寻找凤凰肝吧！"母亲醒来以后，左思右想，把张孝叫到床边，跟他讲了梦中的事。张孝听了以后高兴地说："只要有办法就好。"母亲见他那副高兴的样子，又对他说："儿呀，找凤凰肝很不容易……"儿子说："怕只怕不晓得怎么治，既然晓得了凤凰肝能治好娘的病，总是好办多了嘛。"张孝抢着说。母亲对张孝说："如果一定要去，那你就去吧，不能让你哥哥去。"张孝回答说："好的，妈妈你放心吧，我去找凤凰肝，让哥哥在家照料你。""收拾收拾就去吧，千万不要把这件事告诉你哥哥。一路上会有很多危险，你千万千万要小心啊。"母亲再三嘱咐。

张孝连忙收拾了行装，带着弓箭，走出了家门。他一路走一路想：这次找凤凰肝，一路上会碰到很多困难，也可能自己永远回不来了，应该去和哥哥告别一下。只要不告诉他原因就行了。

主意一定，他又折回到奘房，找着了哥哥。他对张理说："哥哥，我有点事要出远门，母亲嘛，请你多多照料。"张理问他："你有什么事，要去多长时间?"张孝回答说："说不定很快就回来，也可能时间很长。"但他不肯说明为什么事。张理想："母亲病得这么重，他要出远门，一定与母亲的病有关。"于是他说："你不说出原因，我就不让你走！"经过张理再三的盘问，张孝只好说出了实情。张理听后，很受感动，他想："母亲不让我去，分明是偏护我。但我是哥哥，弟弟年纪还小，路上又很危险，这事应该我去。"于是，他左说右劝，强行让弟弟留在家里，自己夺过弟弟的行装和弓箭，找凤凰肝去了。

张理走了很多地方，到处寻找，都没有找到凤凰。但他并不灰心，每天跋山涉水，忍饥挨饿，不停地四处寻找。一天，他来到了王子居住的城市。他在城边树林里走着走着，终于在一棵大树上发现了一只凤凰。他高兴极了！定了定神，悄悄地走近大树，举弓搭箭，"嗖"的一声，把凤凰射了下来。张理提着凤凰，急忙往回走。不料刚刚走出树林，就被一群士兵捉住了。

原来，王子要重新盖一座宫殿，需要用二十个外乡人的头祭神。目前，他已经得到了十九个，今天捉住了张理，正好凑够二十个。

张理知道了王子要用自己的头祭神，心里很着急。他见到王子，立即跪下大声哭诉道："王子啊，我的母亲得了很重的病，眼看着就要死了。是神指示要用凤凰肝才能救她。为了寻找凤凰，我走了许多地方，现在，终于得到了凤凰。王子啊，您如果现在杀了我，等于杀了两条命。请您开恩，让我把凤凰送回家救母亲的性命，然后我再回来，随便您怎么处置。假如您不放心，就派几个士兵跟我一起去好了。"王子听了这番话，想了想，说："好吧，我可以让你回去一趟。"说完，派了几个士兵，押着张理去送凤凰。张理急急忙忙奔回家去，把凤凰肝煎给母亲吃了。

母亲得救了，张理非常欣慰。但想着自己就要离开人世，就要永远地离开慈祥的母亲和亲爱的弟弟，又非常悲伤。但有什么法子呢！他用傣文写了一封信，封好后交给了张孝，并对他说："兄弟，王子有急事找我，我得赶紧赶到王子那里去。三天以后，你把这封信读给母亲听，一定要三天以后，千万记住。"张孝答应了。

吃了凤凰肝以后，母亲的精神逐渐好起来了。她见张理不在家，就问张孝："儿啊，你哥哥哪里去了？"张孝说："哥哥到王子那里去了，说是有急事。""什么急事？"母亲急忙追问。张孝答道："他没有说，只留下一封信，让我三天之后读给您听。""为什么要三天之后才读？你现在就读。"母亲催促说。

张孝打开信读了一遍。信是写给母亲和张孝的，信中叙述了寻找凤凰的经过，然后嘱咐张孝好好服侍母亲，并说自己今生不能再报答慈母的恩情了，只有来世再图报答了。母亲听后大吃一惊，急得直骂张孝："我明明说了让你去，你为什么不去，而让你哥哥去了！"张孝解释了当时的情景。母亲说："不能让你哥哥去死，你去替他，赶快去追！"

张孝便立即赶到了王子那里，还好，哥哥也刚到。张孝跪在王子面前，流着泪道："王子啊，请您不要杀我的哥哥，您杀我吧，用我的头祭神。"张理一见，急得直骂张孝："你跑来干什么！"说着也恳求王子："不要杀我的兄弟，就杀我吧！"

王子见两兄弟争着要死，觉得很奇怪，就问道："先不要忙，到底是怎么回事，你们说说看。"张孝不顾哥哥的阻拦，抢先说明了原因。他一五一十地讲述了一家三口人的关系,讲了事情的经过。王子听了,非常感动,他考虑了半天,然后对兄弟俩说:"你们两人不用争了,我一个也不杀了。"说着便命令士兵:"你们扎一个草人,用草人的头祭神就行了。"发完命令,王子又转过身来对张理、张孝说:"现在,赶快回去照料你们的母亲吧,等你们母亲的身体完全恢复了,你们一起来,帮助我管理百姓吧。"

讲述:赖乖伦
口译:滕茂芳
记录整理:王志方

编者按: 这个故事是一个非常典型的家庭伦理大戏。把这样一个母慈子孝、兄良弟悌的故事,结合到有奘房的南传佛教区域,还有周边以人牲祭祀的背景之中,讲述得很是巧妙。

每一个冲突都是社会中不时遭遇的危机。故事开头就是中年丧妻,幼年丧母。但是因为找到了一个善良的女子,圆满地解决了这个冲突。

当父亲去世、母亲病重的时候,又出现了伦理危机。这次是因为兄弟已经长大,故此他们的言行成为悬念。他们也不负众望,舍生忘死地行孝。

但是在这个过程中,遭遇了猎头人祭的挑战。故事没有直白贬斥这个习俗,而是当作一种很真实的可能性。

这个时候,他们从对家庭的孝,兄弟舍身的悌,又展示了言而有信的信。加上继母对于前妻之子的义,几乎把儒家的各种价值观活灵活现地展现出来了。

实际上,张姓已经暗示了这个故事具有明显的汉族色彩,而他们的名字一个是理学的"理",另一个是孝道的"孝",更是直白地突出了这个故事的汉文化渊源。

The Stepmother

Once upon a time, there was a man, after he got married, his wife gave birth to a boy, named Zhang Li, and the family's life was quite happy.

Unexpectedly, after only three years of marriage, his wife got a serious illness, and despite the man's good care, she became sicker and sicker every day. The wife knew that her illness could not be cured, so she said to the man: "I cannot be cured. I hope you for the sake of our love as a couple, raise Zhang Li well." Not long after, the wife died.

It was very difficult for a man with a one-year-old baby to do his job and take care of the house. People advised him to find another wife, but he said, "It's not that I don't want to find a wife, but I'm afraid that the stepmother will not treat the child well, and when I think of Zhang Li and his mother, I couldn't do such thing." For a long time, he did not have a wife again. Once, a neighbor told him, "There is a girl in the neighboring village who is kind, and you should go and have a look." He thought, without a woman in the family, it was impossible to live well, so he married that girl.

As soon as the girl entered the house, she took care of the housework and was good to Zhang Li, and the couple lived in harmony. People said that Zhang Li and his father were lucky to find a kind woman, but some people said, "New wife will only be fresh for three days. Wait until she has a child of her own and then see if she could still be good to Zhang Li!"

One year later, she gave birth to a son, named Zhang Xiao. Although she had her own child, she was still very kind to Zhang Li. When the children were older, she always carried Zhang Li on her back when she went out and let Zhang Xiao walk on his own. When people saw this, they said to her, "You should carry the younger one and let the older one walk by himself." She replied, "The older child was born by my husband's ex-wife, and it's a pity that he has no mother when he's so little, so I should be kinder to him. This is not only to make my husband feel reassured, but also to prevent people from gossiping. Besides, the little one can walk on his own way, so I can just hold his hand." When everyone heard this, they were very impressed. Her husband was also very grateful, and he was finally relieved.

Days passed quickly, Zhang Li and Zhang Xiao gradually grew up. However, their father also died of an unfortunate illness due to his daily work.

After the death of the husband, the wife still treated Zhang Li as usual. After the two children became mature, their mother sent them to study in the temple. The three of them, mother and sons, lived in harmony.

One day, the mother felt ill, and she could not get up from bed anymore. The two sons sent a doctor to see her and prescribed a lot of medicine, but their mother still could not be cured, and it seemed that she was dying. Both brothers were very anxious, but they couldn't think of any good solution. One night, the mother dreamed in a daze that a god said to her, "Your illness cannot be cured by mortals. But it is not difficult to cure you. I'll tell you a way—eat a piece of a phoenix liver and you will be cured. Send your son to look for the phoenix liver!" After the mother woke up, she thought about it and called Zhang Xiao to her bedside and told him what happened in the dream. Zhang Xiao listened and said happily, "It is good that there is a cure." Seeing his happy look, his mother said to him, "Son, it's not easy to find the phoenix liver..." The son said, "I'm afraid I don't know how to cure it, but since I know the phoenix liver can cure my mother's disease, it's always easier to do." Zhang Xiao said. Mother said to Zhang Xiao: "If it is necessary to go, then you should go, you cannot let your brother go." Zhang Xiao replied, "Okay, mom, don't worry, I'll go to find the phoenix liver and let my brother take care of you at home." "Pack up and go. Don't tell your brother about this. There will be a lot of danger along the way, and you must be very, very careful." Mother repeatedly instructed that.

Zhang Xiao hastily packed his clothes, took his bow and arrows, and went out of the house. He thought along the way: "I will encounter many difficulties along the way this time looking for phoenix liver, and I might even not come back anymore, so I should go and say goodbye to my brother. As long as I don't tell him the reason, he wouldn't know."

With his mind made up, he went back to the temple and found his brother. He said to Zhang Li: "Brother, I have something to do, and I have to travel, so please take care of my mother." Zhang Li asked him, "What is your business and how long will you be gone?" Zhang Xiao replied, "I may be back soon, or it may be a long time." But he refused to specify what the matter was. Zhang Li said, "It must have something to do with my mother's illness," so he said, "If you don't tell me why, I won't let you go!" After Zhang Li's repeated questioning, Zhang Xiao had to tell the truth. After hearing this, Zhang Li was very moved, and he thought, "My mother is clearly favoring me by not letting me go. But I am the older brother, you the younger brother is still little, and the journey is very dangerous, I should go there." So he persuaded his brother to stay at home, and took his brother's clothes and bow and arrows, and went to look for the phoenix liver.

Zhang Li went to many places, looked everywhere, but did not find the phoenix. But he was not discouraged, every day he traveled through the mountains, starved, and kept on searching around. One day, he came to the city where the prince lived. He walked in the woods at the edge of the city, and finally found a phoenix in a big tree. He was overjoyed! He settled down, quietly approached the tree, raised his bow and arrow. "Whoosh", the phoenix was shot down. Zhang Li carried the phoenix and hurriedly walked back. But just after walking out of the woods, he was caught by a group of soldiers.

It turned out that the prince wanted to build a new palace and needed to sacrifice the heads of twenty foreigners to the gods. At present, he has already got nineteen, and today he caught Zhang Li, just enough to make twenty.

Because Zhang Li knew that the prince wanted to use his head to sacrifice to the gods, he was very anxious. When he saw the prince, he immediately knelt and cried loudly, "Oh, my prince, my mother is very sick and is about to die. The gods instructed me to use the phoenix liver to save her. In order to find the phoenix, I have traveled to many places, and now, I finally got the phoenix. My prince, if you kill me now, it is the same as killing two lives. Please be kind and let me send the phoenix home to save my mother's life, and then I will come back and do whatever you want. If you don't trust me, just send some soldiers with me." The prince listened to him, thought about it, and said, "Well, I can let you make a trip back." After saying that, he sent some soldiers and accompanied Zhang Li to deliver the phoenix. Zhang Li rushed home and gave his mother the phoenix liver.

His mother was saved, and Zhang Li was very relieved. But he was very sad to think that he was going to leave his mother and his dear brother forever. But what could be done! He wrote a letter in Dai, sealed it and gave it to Zhang Xiao, and said to him: "Brother, the prince has urgent business for me, and I must hurry to the prince. Three days later, then you can read this letter to mother, and it must be three days later, remember that." Zhang Xiao promised to do so.

After eating the phoenix liver, the mother gradually recovered. When she saw that Zhang Li was not at home, she asked Zhang Xiao, "My son, where did your brother go?" Zhang Xiao said, "Brother went to the prince's place, saying it was an urgent matter." "What urgent matter?" Mother hurriedly asked. Zhang Xiao replied, "He didn't say, but left a letter for me to read to you after three days." "Why do you need to read it after three days? You should read it now." Mother urged.

Zhang Xiao opened the letter and read it. The letter was written for his mother and Zhang Xiao, describing the search for the phoenix, and then telling Zhang Xiao to serve their mother well, and that he could not repay his mother's kindness in this life, he could only do so in the afterlife. The mother was shocked and scolded Zhang Xiao: "I clearly asked you to go. Why did you not go and let your brother go? Zhang Xiao explained the situation." Mother said: "I can't let your brother die, go on his behalf, hurry up and go after him!"

Zhang Xiao then immediately rushed to the prince's place, and fortunately, his brother had just arrived. Zhang Xiao knelt before the prince and said with tears, "Oh prince, please don't kill my brother, kill me instead and use my head to sacrifice to the gods." When Zhang Li saw this, he scolded Zhang Xiao in a hurry, "What are you doing here!" He also pleaded to the prince, "Don't kill my brother, just kill me!"

When the prince saw the two brothers fighting to be killed, he found it strange and asked, "Calm down, what is going on, tell me." Zhang Xiao ignored his brother's hindrance and rushed to explain the reason. He recounted the relationship between the three members of the family and told the story of what happened. The prince was so touched by what he heard that he considered for a while and then said to the brothers, "The two of you don't need to argue. I won't kill any of you." Then he ordered the soldiers, "Make a straw man, and use the head of the straw man to sacrifice to the gods." After giving the order, the prince turned to Zhang Li and Zhang Xiao and said, "Now, hurry back to take care of your mother, and when your mother fully recovers, come back and help me govern the citizens."

猎人过生日

有个猎人在家里算他的出生日子，算来算去："哦，我的生日就是明天了嘛，怎么个过法呢？"

他正盘算着，要是先去请客，就来不及上山打猎，要是先去打猎，又来不及去请客。怎么办呢？左思右想打不定主意，最后还是想先去打猎，把菜找下，然后再去请客人。主意打定后，急急忙忙背起弓箭上山去了。他走了一段路又算了算，今天到底是要打个公麂子，还是打个母麂子："哦，今天是个单日子，单日子要打个公麂子才好。"

他急忙向山里走去，跑了几山几洼，见到的都是母麂子，没有公麂子，只好不打了，背着弓箭往回走。在回家的路上，不断地又跑出来几个麂子，他看看都还是母的，决定还是不打。一直到天快晚的时候，才见到一只公麂子，他高兴得不得了，赶忙抬起弓箭打倒了麂子，背回到家边的水沟旁来剥皮，双手染红了麂子血。

这时有三个和尚化斋路过这里，猎人看到马上洗洗手，顺手在路边采了三朵花，双手把花送给和尚并说道："你们三位'着闷'（阿昌语：和尚）来得真巧，我本来要去请你们的，明天是我的生日，请你们三位着闷，一早到我家里来吃早饭。还有一事相烦三位，我因太忙了，请三位着闷，路过大河的时候，代我请大河水明天一早到我家来做客。"三位和尚答应帮他请大河水就走了。三位和尚来到河边就帮打猎人请了水客，就直回奘房去了。

三个和尚左想右想，一个杀生害命的打猎人，打麂子请客，请了我们三个出家的人，到底是去还是不去，打不定主意。

第二天下了一场大雨，三个和尚就以下雨为理由没有去。过了两天，猎人写了一封信，包了三包麂子干巴带给三个和尚，信中说道："我的生日过得不错，可是见不到你们三位，我心里不安，不知你们有何事不能来，烦你们三位帮我请的大河水都到了，谢谢你们三位和尚。现在给你们三位带来三包麂子干巴,请收下吧。"

三个和尚拿着信和干巴去见老和尚,向老和尚请问道:"师父,有一天我们三个化斋路过一个打猎人的家边,碰到打猎人,他正在剥刚打来的一只麂子,见到我们,就顺手采了路边的三朵花,用花请了我们,叫我们三个第二天到他家去做客,吃他的生日客饭。那天由于下了大雨,我们没有去,今天他带来了一封信和三包麂子干巴,这麂子干巴我们出家人能不能吃?"

老和尚听了后说:"能吃,能吃,人家有心有意舍来的可以吃,我们出家舍身的人,自己去杀生就不得。"三个和尚又问道:"为什么一个打猎的天天杀生害命的人,他过生日那天叫我们路过河边时,帮他请大河水去他家里做客。他在信中说,大河水真的到他家做客去了,我们不明白大河水去的道理。"

老和尚说:"他是没有田和地的人,靠打猎维持生活。他是杀生害命,但他有一条是很珍贵的,就是他说话算话,不说假话。他上山打麂子,要打公的这天就打公的,遇见多少个母的他都不打;要打母的这天,遇见公的他也是不打。这说明他是个老实人,说话算话的人。因此大河水也看得起他,愿意做他的生日客。所以做一个人一定要老实,人们才看得起,才会信任你。"

搜集翻译:藤茂芳
整理:张亚萍

编者按: 佛教故事里经常有这样的冲突和解释,所以这明显具有喻道性质。对于三个和尚,他们出家是为了追求正道成佛,他们按照戒律生活,并且在这个杀生问题上颇有一些纠结。

这里需要补充一点背景知识。在汉传佛教里,出家就不能吃荤,肉是荤物,故此,无论是什么情况都不能吃。这已经成为汉语世界对于佛教的一个共识。但是在南传佛教里,出家人(比丘)是可以吃三净肉的。所谓的三净肉,即符合以下三种条件的肉:

没有亲眼见到该动物是为了自己而被杀;
没有亲耳听到该动物是为了自己而被杀;
没有怀疑该动物是为了自己而被杀。

如果肉不符合这三个条件，出家人是不允许食用的。这是为了避免因饮食而直接或间接导致杀生。

在阿昌族当地，还流传着另外一个说法，就是需要满足不能为出家人而杀，出家人不能见到杀生过程，杀生当日不能吃这三个限制条件。

在这个故事中，出家人见到猎人的时候，猎人已经杀死了麂子，显然他们没有见到杀生过程；这个猎物是猎人为自己的生日而杀，不是为了供奉比丘而杀；而且吃肉的日期定为第二日，不是杀生的当日。

可见，故事有意地设定就是为了回避阿昌族当地出家人吃肉的禁忌。但是这三个和尚仍然心有顾虑。他们有些看不起一个杀生害命的猎人，认为他们自己不应该和这样的人混在一起。但是他们又诧异于"大河水"这样的神灵居然能够被他们带的话请到这个猎人的生日宴会上。

老和尚的话就是这个故事的结论。首先，他认为这个肉是符合比丘可以吃的三净肉原则的。其次，他认为这个人是以杀生为生的猎人，不能因一个人的生计而歧视这个人的本身。最后，他强调了这个人是守信重义的人，见到和尚马上礼佛，说杀公就绝不杀母。因此，这个猎人在这个故事中，让人理解什么是值得尊敬的，什么是过于狭隘的。

A Hunter's Birthday

There was a hunter at home calculating when his birthday was. Oh, my birthday is tomorrow! How should I celebrate it?

He pondered whether to invite guests first or go hunting. If he went to invite guests first, it would be too late to go hunting, and if he went hunting first, it would be too late to invite guests. What should he do? Thinking about it, he couldn't decide, but finally he chose to go hunting first and find the food before inviting the guests. After making up his mind, he hurriedly picked up his bow and arrows and headed into the mountains. As he walked, he thought, "Today is an odd day, I should hunt a male muntjac."

He went deeper into the mountains, but after climbing several hills, all he saw were female muntjacs, not a single male. So he decided not to hunt and continued walking. On his way back, he saw more muntjacs, but they were all female, so he decided again not to hunt. Just as the day was ending, he finally spotted a male muntjac. Overjoyed, he quickly raised his bow and shot it down. He carried it back home and started skinning it by the stream.

At that moment, three monks happened to pass by. The hunter washed his hands and picked three flowers by the roadside and gave them to the monks with both hands and said: "Tomorrow is my birthday, so I would like you three to come to my house for breakfast in the morning. I am too busy to ask others to come today as well, so when you pass by the river, please ask the Big River Water to come to my house for me first thing in the morning." The three monks agreed to relay the message to the river and then continued on their way. The three monks came to the river and helped the hunter to invite the Big River Water and went straight back to the temple.

However, they began to wonder whether they should attend the birthday of a hunter, a man who killed animals, as it seemed contradictory to their vows. Should they go? They could not decide.

The next day there was a heavy rain, so the three monks used rain as an excuse to not go. After two days, the hunter wrote a letter, wrapped three packets of dried muntjac to bring the three monks. The letter said: "I had a good birthday, but I did not see you three, I was worried, and I'm not sure why you couldn't attend, but thank you for helping me to invite the Big River Water. I really want to thank you three and I bring you all three packets of dried muntjac. Please take them."

The three monks took the letter and the dried muntjac to their master and asked,"Master, one day three of us passed by a hunter's house and came across the hunter, who was peeling a muntjac he had just killed. When he saw us, he picked three flowers from the roadside and invited us to come to his house the next day as guests and eat his birthday meal. That day, due to heavy rain, we did not go, and today he brought a letter and three packets of dried muntjac. Can we eat this dried muntjac?"

The old monk listened and said: "You can have it. You can take it. If it is from people who have the intention to give it to you, but we are not allowed to go and kill animals ourselves." The three monks asked again: "Why would the Big River Water go to a hunter's birthday who kills animals every day? We don't understand."

The old monk said: "He was a man without fields or land and lived by hunting. While he does take life, he has one valuable trait: he keeps his word and never lies. If he says he will hunt a male muntjac, he hunts only a male, no matter how many females he encounters. If he says he will hunt a female, he hunts only a female, even if he sees a male. This honesty and integrity make him a trustworthy person. So the Big River Water also respect him, and is willing to be his birthday guest. Remember, honesty is a trait that earns respect and trust from others."

白鸡姑娘

有个娃娃在野外玩耍时，捉到一只白鸡，就拿到街上去。碰到一个小伙子卖火烧粑粑，她想吃，就用这只白鸡换了三块粑粑。傍晚时，小伙子的粑粑卖完了，他把白鸡挑回家养起来。

这个卖火烧粑粑的小伙子，是个孤儿，家里没有人手，他每天到别家去舂粑粑或是到街上去卖粑粑时，就把白鸡关在家里。

日子长了，这只白鸡看到小伙子生活勤劳俭朴，但独自一人十分可怜。小伙子外出后，它就变成一个美丽的姑娘，天天给他做好饭菜放着，小伙子回来就能吃到饭菜。一连几天都是这样，小伙子自己感到有点奇怪。"为什么会有人这样帮我的忙，天天给我做饭？"他就到处问，有的人就说他："你这个人怕是疯了吧？各家各户都还忙不过来，哪个会有这个工夫来帮你做这些事？"人们都说没有，他感到好奇怪。

有一天他假装上山打柴，出去不久，又悄悄回到家里躲起来，想看个明白。过了一会儿，他看到自己养的白鸡变成一个姑娘帮他做饭。他几步跳过去就把这个姑娘抓住，不给她再变回鸡，小伙子和姑娘结成了夫妻。

有个县官老爷，每顿饭都要吃两只鸟，他派了一个人专门为他打鸟。有一天，这个打鸟人来打鸟时，见到这个姑娘，就跟这个姑娘攀谈起来。他忘记了打鸟，太阳落山时，两手空空，非常着急，怕回去被县官打。他把心事告诉姑娘，姑娘就跟他说："你不要急，我帮你做两只鸟就是了。"她用粑粑捏成两只鸟，让他带回去，并嘱咐他说："你带回去时，不要跟任何人讲，就说是你打得的。"这个人带着两只粑粑做的鸟回去，县官吃了后，觉得特别好吃，就问："这两只鸟是从哪里打来的？以后就打这种鸟好了，别的鸟不要。"打鸟人听后很着急，不得不把昨天去打鸟的事情说了。第二天，县官老爷就差人去看这个姑娘。看的人回去告诉县官老爷："这个姑娘真是世上最漂亮的了。"县官听了后说："这样漂亮的姑娘跟一个穷小子结婚，太不像样了，把鲜花插在牛粪上，还是把她弄到我家衙门里来当太太才像样子。"

县官老爷打定鬼主意，就派人把卖粑粑的小伙子叫去，对他说："明天我们两家将各自养的鸡来比斗，看哪一家的鸡打得赢。如果你家的鸡打赢了，我将衙门送给你。如果你家的鸡打输了，就把你家的姑娘送来给我。"小伙子听了相当着急，到底咋个办？回家后，他就把情况告诉了姑娘。姑娘对他说："你不要急，我们来想个办法。"

她找来了一只猫，叫这只猫变成一只公鸡。第二天，她把这个小伙子带到官家去，跟官家的鸡打架。经过一场搏斗，小伙子的鸡打赢了。猫变的鸡把官家的鸡脖子咬断，把鸡头叼起就走了。官家不服气，他说鸡打架不算数，要用牛来打架才算数。小伙子没法，只好回去。

他回到家后，又把情况告诉姑娘，姑娘宽他的心说："你不要急，我们再来想个办法。"姑娘又请了一只老虎来，叫老虎变成一头公牛去跟官家的牛打架。这次还是小伙子的牛打赢了。官家打输了，还是不服气，又提出要斗三次才算胜负。第三次官家提出要比赛牛下儿，看哪家的牛先下儿，就算哪家赢。官家有一头母牛快下儿了，认为满有希望在第三次赢，就可以把姑娘弄到手。小伙子又垂头丧气地回去，把官家的无理要求告诉了姑娘。姑娘还是安慰他，叫他不要焦急。

聪明的姑娘做了个假牛，在牛肚子里装一个会爆炸的东西，让小伙子拉着去，还告诉小伙子："在比赛场上，不管哪家的牛快要下牛犊，你都不要挨近牛身子，要距离牛远一点，在旁边坐着看。"他刚刚把牛拉到比赛场。官家的牛眼看着就快要下儿了，官家信心百倍，满以为把这个姑娘弄到手有十成的把握了。大家看到官家的牛快下儿时，官家的人很高兴地说："赢了赢了，这一次一定赢了。"穷人们都为小伙子着急。忽然，小伙子的假牛爆炸了，把围看的官家的人都炸死了，县官也被炸死了，阴谋也全部破产了。

白鸡姑娘帮助小伙子用智慧战胜县官的故事一直流传了下来，使阿昌人懂得一个道理：只要正义在手，就可以凭着机智和勇敢去战胜邪恶。

搜集：藤茂芳
整理：张亚萍

编者按： 这是田螺故事的阿昌族版本。但是这个故事里的斗法很有本地色彩。当县官老爷出题的时候，貌似一本正经的比赛，实际县官老爷既是运动员，又是裁判员。游戏规则是县官老爷来定，比赛奖品也是县官老爷说了算。

白鸡姑娘利用了动物相克的道理，用魔法打败权术。但是县官老爷怎么可能真的愿赌服输，马上矢口否认自己设定的规则，一再修改竞赛模式。

这样的故事，不以霸权的县官老爷死亡是无法收尾的。

The White Hen Girl

Once upon a time, a child was playing in the wild and caught a white hen. She took it to the street, where she encountered a young man selling roasted cakes. She wanted to eat them, so she traded the white hen for three cakes. That evening, after selling all his cakes, the young man took the white hen home and raised it.

This young man was an orphan. Every day, he either worked at someone else's house to make cakes or went to the street to sell them, leaving the white hen locked up at home.

Over time, the white hen noticed that the young man lived a hard-working and frugal life but was all alone. After the young man left the house, the hen would transform into a beautiful girl and prepare meals for him. When the young man returned home, he would find the meals prepared for him. This went on for several days, and the young man started to feel puzzled. "Why someone helps me every day by cooking meals?" he wondered. He asked other people, but they responded, "You must be going mad! Everyone is so busy with their own lives, who would have the time to do this for you?" Everyone denied it, and the young man found it very strange.

One day, he pretended to go into the mountains to gather firewood but secretly returned home and hid, determined to find out what was happening. After a while, he saw the white hen transform into a girl who started preparing his meals. He quickly leaped out and grabbed the girl, preventing her from turning back into a hen. The young man and the girl then became husband and wife.

There was a county official who need to eat two birds every meal and hired a person who specifically hunt birds for him. One day, when this hunter came by, he saw the girl and started chatting with her, and completely forgot about hunting. By sunset, he had caught nothing and was very anxious, afraid of the punishment he would receive. When the girl heard about this, she said, "Don't worry, I'll make two birds for you." She made two birds out of the roasted cakes and gave them to him, and advising, "When you take these back, don't tell anyone, just say you caught them yourself." The hunter took the cake birds back, and when the county official ate them, he found them particularly delicious. He asked, "Where did you catch these birds? From now on, only hunt this type of bird; I don't want the other ones." The hunter was very worried and had no choice but to confess what had happened the day before. The next day, the county official sent someone to investigate the girl. The investigator returned and reported, "This girl is the most beautiful woman in the world." The county official, upon hearing this, said, "Such a beautiful girl, she has thrown herself away upon that boor! It would be more fitting to bring her to my manor and make her my wife."

The county official came up with an evil plan and sent someone to call for the young man who sold cakes. He told the young man, "Tomorrow, each of us will bring a rooster to do a fight. If your rooster wins, I will give you my manor. If your rooster loses, you must give me your wife." The young man was unsure of what to do, and went home to tell the girl. The girl said: "Don't worry. We'll come up with a plan."

She found a cat and told it to transform into a rooster. The next day, she sent the young man to the official's house with the transformed rooster. After a fierce fight, the young man's rooster won. The cat, in the form of a rooster, bit the neck of the official's rooster, picked up its head, and walked away. The official was dissatisfied and said that the rooster fighting shouldn't be counted; they should use bulls to fight instead. The young man, having no choice, returned home.

He told the girl what had happened, and she comforted him and said: "Don't worry. We'll think of another plan." The girl then called for a tiger and told it to transform into a bull to fight the official's bull. Again, the young man's bull won the fight. The official lost, but he still refused to concede, and insisted that they needed to compete three times to determine the winner. For the third contest, the official proposed a contest to see whose bull would give birth first, declared that the winner would be the one whose bull calved first. The official had a cow that was about to give birth and believed he had a solid chance to win this time and take the girl for himself. The young man went home dejectedly again and told the girl about the official's unreasonable demand. The girl reassured him, telling him not to worry.

The clever girl created a fake bull and placed an bomb inside its belly. She instructed the young man to bring this fake bull to the competition and told him, "During the contest, no matter which bull seems close to giving birth, don't go near it. Stay far away and watch from a distance." When the young man brought the fake bull to the contest, the official's bull looked ready to give birth. The official was overjoyed, believed that he was doomed to win this time and get the girl. As the official's bull seemed ready to calve, the official's men rejoiced, and said: "We've won! This time we've definitely won!" The poor people were anxious for the young man. Suddenly, the young man's fake bull exploded, killed the official and his men, and completely destroyed their plot.

The story of how the White Hen Girl helped the young man outwit the county official has been passed down, it taught the Achang people that as long as one insists on justice, he can use wisdom and courage to overcome evil.

爱撒萨

　　从前，有一个土司养着一个算命先生。有一天，算命先生对土司说："现在有人要夺您的江山。"土司忙问："这人是谁，在哪里？"先生忙告诉土司说："这人现在还在她母亲的肚子里。"土司听了，便叫家丁把寨子里所有结过婚的妇女捉来杀了。只有一个到山中砍柴的穷苦妇女，没有被捉去杀掉。

　　转眼又过了一年，土司又问算命先生："要夺我江山的人，现在还有没有？"先生又说："他现在已经有一岁多了。"于是，土司听后又令家丁把寨子里所有一岁左右的孩子捉来杀掉。但是他们依然没有捉到靠打柴度日的那个穷苦妇女的孩子，因为这个孩子已被母亲背到山林里去了。

　　时间又过了三年，土司又问先生："还有没有想夺我江山的人？"先生又告诉他说："此人现在能放牛了。"残暴凶狠的土司听到这个人还活着，便又下令把所有的放牛孩子捉来杀掉。幸好这一次，又没有杀着砍柴度日的穷苦妇女的孩子，因为这个孩子被他母亲藏到寺庙里去了。

　　一晃儿又过了四年，土司又问算命先生，那个夺江山的孩子死了没有！算命先生又告诉他说："这孩子已经上学读书了。"杀人成性的土司一听大怒，他不敢一下把学校的学生统统杀死，他绞尽脑子，想出一条毒计。

　　他命令家丁把这儿唯一的一所学校的学生全部带到他的院场里，要从这五百多个学生里找出这个幸存下来的孩子。土司亲自用小指甲给每个学生点五次水放到盆里，然后叫学生们用那一点水来洗脸。其余的孩子，每个都照着土司的要求做了，唯有一个学生不但不用土司指甲弹起来的水，而且还一脚把洗脸盆踢开，并说："这水是给狗猫洗的，不是人洗的！"土司便问他："你是什么人？怎敢踢翻我的脸盆？"这孩子勇敢地说："我叫爱撒萨。"土司立即叫他站出来。土司又问："你为什么不洗脸？"孩子答道："你家做了四代人的官，几时用这样一点水来洗脸？"土司恼羞成怒地骂道："来人，把他捆起来。"土司仗着人多，七手八脚就把爱撒萨用铁链子捆起来，然后把他捆在衙门的大柱子上。土司立即用长矛投向被捆绑的爱撒萨，结果长矛飞出去，并没有杀伤爱撒萨，相反铁链子却被射断了，勇敢的爱撒萨趁机脱手并拾起长矛就跑。

爱撒萨逃脱后，土司便派了家丁紧紧追赶，可是怎么也追不着。爱撒萨涉过了多少条河，走了多少座大山，最后来到一个山洞里。睡觉时，他把长矛插在自己身边，不知怎的，长矛自动地倒在他身上，他又重新把它插好，可是没多一会儿，长矛又倒在他身上。他有点火了，随手把长矛扔出去。不料，长矛扔出去后，正好击中追赶他的土司家丁。第二天他一出门，从死奴身上拔出长矛，又继续赶路。

路途中，他遇见一位能驾一百张犁耕田的农民。他对农民说："朋友，你不必再犁田了，我们一同去干大事。"这个本领高强的农民听后，便同意跟他一起走。他俩走啊，走啊，又在森林中遇见一个能拔一百棵大树的人，爱撒萨和农民又约这个人一同前行。后来，他们又在河边遇到一个能举九百斤大锤的人，爱撒萨又约他同行。不久他们四人又在山沟里遇到两个能用手破竹子的人，他们又把这两个人约了一起同行。爱撒萨在这段路途中，总共邀约了五个好汉。

爱撒萨家乡的土司，自爱撒萨逃走后，便四处打听他的下落，派出去追的家丁也一去无回，杳无音信。残暴的土司又气又急，最后只得亲自带领人马去寻找。最后终于在一个叫"户邦"的寨子里打听到了爱撒萨的下落。土司便领兵包围寨子，准备捉拿爱撒萨。

六个好汉听见寨外人喊马叫，想必发生了意外的事，他们不慌不忙准备迎战。土司带来的人马哪里是六个好汉的对手，双方交锋了一早上，土司的人马便被打得仓惶逃窜，大部分被六个好汉消灭。

土司带领剩余的残兵败将回到家乡，后来又听说六条好汉要打回来的消息，土司便服毒自杀了。

五个好汉在爱撒萨的带领下，终于回到了自己的家乡，受到了老百姓的欢迎。

收集整理：罗玉山

编者按： 这样杀死潜在威胁自身权力的婴孩故事，最著名的是新约里的希律王，他曾经把伯利恒 2 岁以内的孩子赶尽杀绝，以此逃避那个将要替代他做王的人。

在爱撒萨这个故事里，那些靠近土司的人，深受其害，却没有任何反抗的声音和行为。只有穷乡僻壤的山上，才是逃避统治威胁的乐土。因此，贫穷和受苦也是逃避统治的艺术。

土司有一个先生，显然是一个占卜师，能够知道很多隐而未现的先兆。但是这个人一直助纣为虐，为虎作伥，显然不是什么好东西。

只有朴实勇敢的好汉，才是最后取得胜利的人。

Yuan Sasa

Once upon a time, there was a chieftain who kept a fortune teller. One day, the fortune teller told the chieftain, "Someone is plotting to take over your kingdom." The chieftain asked worriedly, "Who is this person and where is he?" The fortune teller hurriedly replied, "This person is still in his mother's womb." Hearing this, the chieftain ordered his servants to capture and kill all the married women in the village. However, there was a poor woman who was gathering firewood in the mountains that they skipped.

One year passed, and the chieftain asked the fortune teller again, "Is there still someone who wants to take over my kingdom?" The fortune teller replied, "That person is now over a year old." As a result, the chieftain ordered his servants to capture and kill all the one-year-old children in the village. But they failed to capture the child of the poor woman who was chopping wood for a living, as his mother had taken him to the forest.

Three years later, the chieftain asked the fortune teller once more, "Is there still someone try to take my kingdom?" The fortune teller informed him, "This person is now herding cows." Hearing that this person was still alive, the cruel chieftain ordered his servants to capture and kill all the children herding cows. Fortunately, they once again failed to kill the child, as the child had been hidden by his mother in a temple.

Four years went by, and the chieftain asked the fortune teller if the child who aimed to take over the kingdom was dead. The fortune teller replied, "This child is now attending school." Enraged, but the chieftain did not dare to kill all the students in the school at once. He thought hard and came up with a sly plan.

He ordered his servants to bring all the students from the only school in the village to his court. He intended to find the surviving child among more than five hundred students. The chieftain personally dipped his little finger into water five times, then told the students to wash their faces with that little amount of water. All the other children followed the chieftain's instructions, except for one student. Not only did he refuse to use the water touched by the chieftain's finger, but he also kicked over the basin and said, "This water is for dogs and cats, not for humans!" The chieftain asked him, "Who are you? How dare you spill my basin?" Fearlessly, the child replied, "My name is Yuan Sasa." The chieftain immediately ordered him to step forward and asked, "Why didn't you wash your face?" The child answered, "Your family has held the position for four generations. When have you ever used such a small amount of water to wash your face?" Enraged and humiliated, the chieftain yelled, "Catch him!" Taking advantage of their numbers, the chieftain's guards quickly restrained Yuan Sasa with iron chains and tied him to a pillar in the courtyard of the chieftain's place. Without hesitation, the chieftain threw a spear at Yuan Sasa, but the spear missed the child and instead broke the iron chains. Taking the opportunity, Yuan Sasa freed himself, picked up the spear, and ran away.

After escaped, Yuan Sasa was chased by the chieftain's guards, but no matter how hard they tried, they couldn't catch him. Yuan Sasa crossed many rivers and climbed mountains until he reached a cave. While sleeping, he placed his spear beside him, but somehow, the spear kept falling on him. Frustrated, he angrily threw the spear out of the cave and unexpectedly hit one of the chieftain's guards who were chasing him. The next day, Yuan Sasa pulled out the spear stuck in the body of the dead guard and continued his journey.

Along the way, he encountered a farmer who could plow paddies with a hundred plows. Yuan Sasa told the farmer, "Friend, you don't have to plow paddies anymore. Let's go to do something important." The farmer agreed to join him. In the forest, they met a man who could chop down a hundred trees. Yuan Sasa and the farmer invited him to join them. Later, near the river, they met a man who could lift a nine-hundred-pound hammer. Yuan Sasa persuaded him to join their group. At last, they encountered two men who could break bamboo with their bare hands near a campfire, and Yuan Sasa invited them as well. In total, Yuan Sasa managed to enroll five companions during his journey.

Meanwhile, back in Yuan Sasa's hometown, the chieftain was desperately searching for him and sent guards to find him, but they never returned. Frustrated and furiously, the chieftain had to lead his troops himself to search for Yuan Sasa. Finally, they found Yuan Sasa in a village called "Hubang" and the chieftain surrounded the village with his soldiers, preparing to capture Yuan Sasa.

Upon hearing the noises outside, Yuan Sasa and his five companions calmly prepared for battle. The chieftain's troops couldn't defeat the six skilled adventurers, and after a fierce battle, the chieftain's forces were down, with most of them killed.

The chieftain returned to his hometown with the remaining soldiers, but when he heard that the six companions were planning a counterattack, he chose to poison himself and commited suicide.

Yuan Sasa and his five companions finally returned to their home and were welcomed by the locals.

大蛇的故事

在很早很早以前，阿昌族地区就流传着这样一个故事。

故事讲的是一个早早失去丈夫的寡妇，守着一个儿子过活。因为家里很穷，母子俩是最苦的人了。儿子渐渐大了，到了八九岁，母亲送他去上学，他不想去读书。母亲叫他帮着干些活，他不想干，叫他做什么，他都不想做。妈妈一动嘴，他总是说："妈妈不怕，要得吃那天，总会得吃的。"咋个说也不听，就是天天吃了睡觉，想走哪里就走哪里，妈妈说多了，他就乱打、乱敲。他说："到自然得吃那天会得吃的，妈呀，你不消多啰唆，不消焦，不消气，气也白气。"妈说："这儿子不教是不随了，现在我无法教你，到底你要变成什么人？你愿意去哪里你就去吧。"

后来一个教书的先生见到她说："你家这个小人，还是去读点书好。你一个人教是没有办法的，给他去读书，懂一点事。不懂道理，不成好人。"他妈说："老师啊，我不是不让他读书，叫他去读，他不去。好好，那么你去帮教去，我家这个小人，给他读点书是会聪明的，他读得几年也好。"老师连声说："好，好，只要你放得，读三五年，我帮你教育。"

最后老妈答应给他去读书，他也去读了。只要他去读，再有多困难也给他去读。老妈说："不要怕，你去好好读书，吃的用的我在家苦了。"

母亲为了儿子，苦心抚养，省吃俭用，供他去读书，希望他长大做事。

孩子读书去了，老师给他起个名字叫喜财。一晃儿就读了三年的书，道理懂得一点了。

一天，喜财从学校放学回家，半路上，他捉到一条小蛇，觉得很好玩。他把已经冻僵了的小蛇装在他的书包里带回家去。到家后，有了暖气，小蛇慢慢地活跃起来，喜财看到小蛇活起来了，就把它养起来，天天喂给它东西吃，不给他母亲知道。

喜财把蛇养在书包里，天天背着去上学，不时地悄悄玩弄着。同学们发现了他经常偷看什么，就要瞧："你到底背着什么好瞧的，你打开书包让我们看看。""瞧不得，瞧不得，这是瞧不得的东西，哪个也不给瞧。"他说着紧紧把书包抱住。

小蛇一天天长大了，装满了他的书包，怕同学们知道，他就把蛇装在柜子里锁起来。他在上学的路上，找小雀、小老鼠等来喂它。他家里面的粮食都让他拿来喂蛇了。他还把门锁着，不让老妈进去。一直不给他妈晓得。他妈也感到奇怪了："这个人到底是搞什么名堂，经常把门锁着，不给我进去。我要看，门也不开，饭煮多少都吃完，肉有多少也不够，到底他养着个什么。"

有一天，吃饭时，他妈就从门缝往里面瞧，看见他吃一嘴，喂蛇一嘴，吃一嘴又喂一嘴，肉也一块一块地喂。啊，原来是他养着一条蛇，已经装满了柜子。老妈看到了气愤地说："我养大你，不是，是养大了一条大虫，这是一个大怪物，一寨子会害怕的，你养它做什么。"就叫起一寨子的人来敲打这条大蛇，蛇受到惊吓，就跑走了。喜财也被寨子里赶了出来。他妈说："你不成才，你不是我的儿子，养了这么个害人虫，不准你回来。"

他和蛇到了半山上，就对蛇说："我为你，家也不得在，寨子里也不得在，你就在这地方待着，自己找吃的。我也顾不得你了，你不要伤人，我要去找活路做了，我俩就此分开吧。"蛇也说道："好，你好好的家不得在，寨子里不得去，你去哪里吧，以后我俩再会合。"说罢，他们就分开了。

有十多年的时间过去了，喜财走东串西，蛇也长得很大很大。它长到能盘满三支山，有九抱大，山上的动物填不饱肚皮了，它就开始吃人。有些人上山去，它张口一吸，就把人吸到跟前再吞下去。一些人上了山，就回不来。一些人就说："可能是上天去了。"他们绘声绘影地说："一天我在山上，远远地看到有一个人，像飞一样地向高处飘去了。"有些人就说："上天了，就是上天去了。"你也说上天，我也说上天，于是，就传遍了很多地方。有些人就想着要上天，收拾打扮好，戴着金银首饰，说是要去上天。到了半山头，大蛇一吸，就轻轻地一下子被吸走了。很多人看到，也就认为是上天去了。人都丢了一半多了，特别是青年男女，个个都带着贵重的东西去上天。去的人，都没有回来，不知道是什么原因，只晓得是上天了。

后来，情况不妙了，人去得越来越多，一天有三十二个老百姓，银物首饰带了一堆，说是要去上天。他们到了那山头，一股风就把他们吸走了。有一个在地方上有点学识的小官，他看了不对头，说："我就不信会有这等事，我倒要去看看。"他去到远远的一个地方看，"唉，不是了，是有个大妖怪在吃人，多少人被它吃了。它是一条大虫，很大的虫"。

他回去就说："这是一个大怪物在吃人，如果有哪个能把它除掉，我就把地方分给他一半，财产也分给他一半，金银要多少都得。"

话传出去了，告示也贴了。不见有人敢来冒此大险。有些人也只是壮着胆子去试试，都没有办法，只有这样等待着。

大蛇吃人的消息传到了喜财的耳朵里，又听到招人除掉这条大虫。喜财听到后，明白了几分，他狠狠地一摆手说："它竟然吃人了，一定要把它除掉。"他就去见那官，那官说："什么办法都做了，枪打不着，刀砍不着。因为它有三个宝，所以什么也打不着它，你有什么办法能拿它吗？"喜财说："不怕，我有办法拿它。""你怕拿不着吧。"有人这样说。"不怕，我有办法。"喜财这样有信心地说。

钱给多少，地方给多大，财产给多少，那官都说了。喜财说："地方唛，我不要，我不是官，拿它无用；钱财唛，倒是要的。拿这个虫不简单，我现在也都有点害怕。"

喜财拿了三把快刀，一个人去了。他去到人们说是上天的那山头上，大蛇果然把他吸去，要吃他。他站在蛇的面前说："你看看我是什么人，你这个忘恩负义的，连我都想要吃。"大蛇一细看，"啊，是你呀，不敢，不敢"。喜财说："你现在要吃我，吃吧，我为了你，地方不得在，有家不能归，到处流浪到现在，今天专门来会你。"蛇说："啊，你为了我苦够了，你需要什么只管说，我肚子里有的是，金银财宝样样有，你进我肚子里去拿些吧。里面还有三个宝，一颗是黄的在中间，是最好的一颗，一颗是绿色的在头上，另一颗是红的在尾部。你进去拿时，不要拿黄的，其他的随便你拿。"

喜财进到蛇的肚子里，他偏要连黄的也拿。蛇就说："叫你不要拿黄的，怎么你连黄的也要拿。要这样，我就吃你了。"

喜财拿出三把一尺长的三角形的钢刀，一面往蛇的肚皮扎去，一面说："你这个忘恩负义的东西，你不听我的话，害了多少人，我不杀你，你今后还要害多少人，害得地方上不得安宁，算我当初白白地养了你。"说完，把三把刀分三角形从肚皮上往下钉好，蛇疼痛得受不住，就哗哗哗地往前跑，三把刀把它的肚皮划成了三条大口子，在它肚子里的金银首饰，统统地掉了出来，大蛇也就死了。

大蛇被除掉的消息传开后,乡亲们都上山来看。喜财叫他们把这些东西搬回寨子,他们搬了七天七夜。后来喜财把这些东西分给了地方上所有的百姓,他自己也回到家里跟母亲团聚,过着幸福的生活。

讲述:赖老二
搜集整理:张亚萍

编者按: 这个故事娱乐性很强,明显没有什么道德训诫意义。一个不务正业、不专心学习,也不找营生的孩子,凭借养蛇的机会,获得了意外财富。

这个孩子对蛇说话不算话,反而这条蛇,虽然杀人如麻,但是对他有情有义,让他活下来,还愿意把宝贝给他。但是这个家伙不守信用,要拿蛇的黄色宝贝。

实际上,那个教书先生也没有把孩子教好,那些梦想成仙的人是自投罗网。这个故事里那个有点儿学识的地方小官是一个好人。

可是,谁不愿在自己无所事事的时候,想一个这样的故事安慰自己呢?

A Story of the Great Serpent

A long time ago, the Achang region has passed down such a story.

The story was about a widow whose husband died in early year, and she lived with a son. Because the family was very poor, the mother and son were miserable. When the son grew older to eight or nine years old, he was sent to school, but he did not want to go to school. The mother asked him to help do some work, but he refused. He didn't want to do anything his mother asked him. When his mother says something, he always said, "Don't worry, Mom, the day I have to eat, I will eat." "No matter how much I say, you don't listen, you just eat and sleep every day, and go where you want to go." Mom yelled. He said, "I will eat on the day when I have to eat. Mom, you do not need to be so talkative, anxious or angry; it's all in vain." Mom said, "This son couldn't be taught. What kind of person are you going to be? Never mind, you can go anywhere you want."

Later a teacher met her and said, "Your child would better go to school and read some books. There is no way if you teach him alone. Send him to school. If he can only understand things but can't learn the values, he won't be a good person." His mother said, "Teacher, I'm not telling him not to go to school. I tried, but he won't go. Well, then how about you go and help to teach him, because this child, if he learns a little, he will be smart. It will be good even if he only goes to school for a few years." The teacher then said, "Good, as long as you can let him go, and study for three or five years, I will help to teach your boy."

Finally, his mother agreed to send him to school, and he did. As long as he was willing to go to study, no matter how difficult it was, his mother would overcome. The mother said, "Don't be afraid, go and study hard, and I'll save money for food."

For the sake of her son, the mother raised him with great care, saving money for him to go to school and hoping that he would grow up to become a successful person.

The child went to school, and the teacher gave him the name of Xicai. After three years, study, he learned a little knowledge.

One day, Xicai came home from school, in the halfway, he caught a small snake, and he thought it was very interesting. So he put the frozen snake in his school bag and took it home. When he arrived home, the warm air flew through the room. The snake slowly became active, and when Xicai saw that the snake was alive, he raised it and fed it every day, without letting his mother know.

The snake was kept in his school bag and carried to school. Every day, Xicai played with it secretly several times. The students found out that he was often peeking at something and wanted to have a look as well: "What are you looking at, open your bag and let us see." "No." he said, holding the bag tightly.

The little snake grew up day by day, and eventually filled his school bag. Fearing that his classmates would know, he put the snake in the locker and locked it up. On his way to school, he looked for small finches, mice, etc. to feed it. He used all the food in his house to feed the snake. He also locked the door to keep his mother out, not letting his mother know a single thing about the snake. His mother also felt strange: "What is he doing? He often locks the door, and does not let me in. If I want to check upon what he's doing, he doesn't open the door. Also, no matter how much rice and meat is being given, he eats it all up. What is he raising?"

One day, when eating, his mother looked inside through the crack of the door and saw him eating while feeding the snake at the same time. "Ah, he kept a snake in the cupboard, and it was so huge that it was full of the cupboard." Mom said angrily, "You use the food I give you to raise such a big monster? All the villagers will fear this creature, what do you raise it for?" Then the mother called up the villagers to kill this big snake, the snake was startled, and ran away. Xicai was also driven out of the village. His mother said, "You didn't become a good person, you are not my son, and you even raised such a harmful serpent. You are not allowed to come back."

When he and the snake got halfway up the mountain, he said to the snake: "I am now not allowed to be at home, nor in the village because of you, so you should stay in this place and find food for yourself. I cannot take care of you anymore. Remember not to hurt people, I need to go to find a job, so let's separate here." The snake also said, "Okay, go and find a living, later we will meet again."

Time flew by, over a decade, Xicai travelled the east and visited the west, and the snake grew very, very big. It grew until it has covered three mountains. All the animals on the mountains could not satisfy its appetite anymore, then it began to eat people. When people went up the mountain, it opened its mouth and sucked the people near itself and then swallowed them. Lots of people went up to the mountains and never returned. Some people said vividly, "Maybe they went to heaven. One day I was on the mountain, and I saw a man from far away, floating to the high ground like flying." People started spread the sayings, "They must have gone to heaven." This news of going to heaven spread to many places. Some people thought about going to heaven, so they packed and dressed up, with gold-silver jewelry, and planned to go to heaven. Halfway up the mountain, the big serpent sucked, and people all floated away at once. Many people saw this situation and thought they were going to heaven. More than half of the people were lost, especially young men and women, each one taking valuable things with them up to heaven. For all the people who went, none of them returned. People didn't know what the reason was. The only thing they knew was that those young people went to heaven.

Later, the situation became unpleasant, more and more people went up to the mountain. Every day, about twenty or thirty people carrying lots of silver things and jewelry wanted to go up to the heaven. Once they got to that mountain, a wind sucked them away. There was a petty local official with some knowledge saw something wrong and said, "I don't believe that there will be such a thing of going to heaven, I'd like to go and see." He went to a far away place to take a look, "Oh, no, it is a big man-eating monster. It's a very big serpent, a huge serpent!"

He went back and said, "This is a big man-eating monster. If anyone can get rid of it, I will give him half of the land and half of my property, and as much gold and silver as he wants."

The words were spread, and the notice was posted. No one dared to take the risk. Some people were only brave enough to try, but there was no way to get rid of the serpent, all that can be done is to wait.

The news of the snake eating people reached Xicai's ears, and he heard that the officials were recruiting people to get rid of this monster. Now Xicai understood what was happening, he hit the table with his hand and said, "How dare it eat people, I must get rid of it." He then went to see the official, who said, "Everything has been done: the gun can't shoot it, and the knife can't hurt it. Because it has three treasures, nothing can kill it. Do you have any way to catch it?" Xicai said, "Don't worries, I have a way to take it." "You possibly can't kill it." Someone said. "Don't worry, I have a way." Xicai said with confidence.

The official told Xicai all about the money he would receive, the land that would be given. Xicai said: "I do not want land, because I am not an official, it is useless for me. I would rather take money. But killing this serpent is not easy, I am also a little afraid of that now."

Xicai took three sharp knives and went alone. He went to the hill where people said could go up to heaven, and the big snake really sucked him up to eat him. He stood in front of the snake and said, "Look who I am, you ungrateful creature, you want to eat me as well? "When the snake looked closely, "Ah, it's you, oh no, of course I don't dare to eat you. " Xicai said: "If you want to eat me now, go on. Because of you, I could not go home nor the village I belong to, and I have been wandering around until now. I come here today to meet you on purpose. "The snake said: "Ah, you have suffered enough for me, say whatever you want, I have plenty of treasures, gold and silver in my stomach, just go into my stomach to get some. There are three other treasures inside, the yellow one in the middle is the best, another is the green one in the head, and the last is the red one in the tail. When you go in to take the treasures, don't take the yellow one, take the others as you like."

When Xicai went into the snake's stomach, he insisted on taking even the yellow one. The snake said, "I told you not to take the yellow one, why do you still want to take the yellow one? If so, I will eat you."

Xicai took out three triangular steel knives and stabbed them into the snake's belly, and said, "You ungrateful thing, you disobeyed me and harmed many people. If I don't kill you, you will harm even more people in the future, causing no peace in the place!" With that said, he pinned the three knives down on the snake's stomach. The snake can't stand the pain, so it ran forward, the three knives that cut three large gaps in its stomach. All the gold and silver jewelries dropped out, and the snake died.

After the news of the snake's death was spread, the villagers went up the mountain to see it. Xicai told them to carry these things back to the village, and they transported them for seven days and nights. Later, Xicai distributed them to all the people in the area, and he returned home to stay with his mother and lived a happy life.

双妹俩

很久很久以前，有一个男人，讨了两个老婆，大老婆生了两个姑娘，大的叫玉榜别，二的叫玉榜盖。两个小姑娘长得非常漂亮。个儿一样高，样子是一个样，像一对孪生姐妹，谁也难认出她俩谁是老大，谁是老二。人们都称她们姐妹俩为双妹。

不久，男人死了，小老婆没生得儿女，她对大老婆生的两姐妹非常仇恨，随时都在想着害她们。大老婆没有小老婆霸道，小老婆就天天叫双妹俩上山去砍柴。

有一天，当双妹俩上山去砍柴后，小老婆就跟大老婆商量，小老婆说："姐，今天天气很好，我们俩到水塘去洗衣服吧！"说着就约大老婆到那明亮亮的水塘边去了。她俩边洗边开玩笑，趁大老婆不备之时，小老婆就把她推下了水塘里淹死。她就悄悄地回到了家里。

等到太阳快落山时，双妹俩上山砍柴才回家来。双妹俩到家后，不见妈妈，就找妈妈。先前回到家，妈妈总是去接她们，怎么今天到家不见妈妈。左找右找，还是找不到妈妈。她们俩就去问小老婆："二妈，我妈妈到哪里去了，你知不知道？"她们的二妈说："你妈是到水塘边洗衣服去了。到现在还不见回来，我真担心呀，你们姐妹俩快去看看。到底出了什么事。"双妹俩听了她二妈的话，很快地跑到水塘边去看。不见妈妈的影子，只见塘子里有一条金鲍鱼游来游去。双妹俩看着不觉地潸潸地流下了泪水，哭着回家来。

她们到家后，二妈假惺惺地问："你们俩哭什么？你妈找着了没有。"姐妹俩说："到处都找了，就是找不到，不知到哪里去了？"她们的二妈又说："你们的妈妈虽然不在了，还有你俩的二妈在呢。不要哭了，不要哭了，你们哭起来，我心里也很难受。"从那以后，双妹俩的二妈再也不叫她俩上山砍柴了，叫她俩天天去看小鸭子。

双妹俩天天把鸭子赶到她妈死的水塘里去放，她们的二妈天天给她俩送饭菜来吃。她俩不吃，悄悄地把二妈送来的饭菜全部撒进水塘里给她们的妈妈吃。

时间长了，双妹俩的二妈感到很奇怪，天天送去给她们的饭菜都吃完了，一点都不剩。有一天，她又送去了一大包饭菜，对姐妹俩说了几句话，就装作回家的样子去了。可是她转背就躲在旁边看，到底她姐妹两个咋个吃这些饭。

双妹俩以为她二妈回家了，和往常一样，又把饭菜全部撒在水塘里。她二妈就偷偷地看在眼里，记在心上。

到了第二天，不等双妹俩去放鸭，她二妈就一早扛着把锄头来到水塘边，把塘子里的水撒干。把金鲍鱼拿回家去，叫双妹俩先不要去放鸭子，快把金鲍鱼放进锅里煮吃。双妹俩在二妈的逼迫下，不得不把金鲍鱼放进锅里。金鲍鱼突然在锅里讲起话来："儿呀儿，妈要死了，如果她吃妈的肉，你们俩不要吃，如果她要丢妈的骨头，你们俩把它拣了放在罐子里去埋在三岔路边。要记住妈的话。"说完她们的妈妈就去世了。

双妹俩按照妈妈的嘱托，把金鲍鱼的骨头拣了去埋在三岔路口，过了七天，就长出了一棵很香很香的桂花树。过路的人看到这棵树十分喜爱，人人都爱护这棵树。不管有事无事，都要到树脚来站一站，歇息一下。

双妹俩的二妈听到这件事，就连忙去看，很多人也从四面八方来看，人们越看越喜爱，花越开越香。双妹俩的二妈越看越生气，越看越觉得都是些狗屎，越闻越是腥臭。她很讨厌，就跑回家去拿来一把大刀，趁人不在，几下就把这棵桂花树砍掉。还把树劈成了一个洗衣用的木棒。

有一天，她拿着木棒到河边去洗衣服，越用木棒捶打，衣服越烂。越搓衣服越朽，新衣服几下子就整成烂衣服了。

双妹俩拿着那木棒到河边去洗衣服。她们的旧衣服、烂衣服却洗成了新衣服、好衣服。她们俩不理解，感到很奇怪，回家把这事告诉了二妈，二妈得知此事后，非常恼恨，就偷偷地把木棒拿去丢到河里了。

在河的下游，有一家老两口正在拾拣着碎柴，那木棒顺着河水淌下来，老两口就从河里把它拣回家去。在家里往哪里放也不好，放心不下，只好把它当作一件宝贝放进了一个高大的柜子里。老两口还是照常天天到河边去拣碎柴去了。

过了很久，每当他俩捡柴回来，饭菜都已经做好了，老两口感到很奇怪。心想："有什么好心的人来给我俩做饭呀，我们要找到这个人，好好地谢谢她。"

老两口就去问寨子的人，寨子里的人对他们说："有哪个看得起进你俩的烂草房里去呀。"老两口问不出原由，也就装着不作声了。还是照常去捡柴，等他俩回来，菜饭还是照常做得好好地燉在锅里。

有一天，老两口装作去捡柴的样子，出去后不久，又悄悄地转回来，不声不响地躲在蚊帐后面等着看个究竟。到了快做饭的时候，他俩忽然听到柜子里响了一下，从柜子里出来一个非常漂亮的姑娘，他俩看得出神，看着姑娘走进了厨房，他俩还不敢动一下，他俩看清了姑娘做饭、做好饭，收拾妥当，走出灶房，又要进柜子的时候，他俩才醒悟过来，忙跑过去拉着姑娘说："好姑娘，是你天天给我俩煮饭的呀。"姑娘看躲不及了，只好说："老爹爹，是我煮的，你们两位老人是我的救命恩人，我看你们两位老人天天出去捡柴，回来晚了还要做饭，有时忙不来做，就吃点冷汤凉饭，我看到很不忍心。我要把你们两位老人家当作我的爹妈看待。"两位老人忙说："好，好，好心的姑娘，我俩没儿没女，你就做我们的女儿吧。"姑娘就向两个老人拜了几拜。

两个老人又去打开柜子看，满柜子都是金银财宝，高兴极了。从此，他家的生活慢慢地富裕起来，不需要再去拣碎柴了。

过了一段日子，老两口对姑娘说："孩儿，我们家从你来后，日子好过了，钱财多了。按照我们阿昌人的习惯，有钱以后，要做一次大摆庆贺

一下。"女儿说:"那么就做吧,女儿遵从老人的。"

他们家就把要做一次大摆的事告知了乡邻四里,请了四方的人来他家赶摆。赶摆那天,玉榜别和玉榜盖两姐妹也来了。姐妹俩刚一跨进老人家的大门,就看见那位姑娘像是她俩的母亲,姑娘也看出了这姐妹俩是她的亲生女儿,一点没有认错,她俩就大声叫道:"妈妈!妈妈!"跟着一起跑到面前抱住了那个姑娘,母女三人抱在一起痛哭起来。妈妈说:"想不到我们母女在这里又得相会在一起。"这件事把老人都吓呆了。

后来,姑娘就把她的遭遇经过告知了老人。老人听后很是难过。他们就把双妹俩留下来跟她们的母亲一起过着愉快的生活。

搜集翻译:钱宝林
整理:钱宝林　张亚萍

编者按: 这个故事异常零碎,似乎是很多故事的一个杂拌儿。但是民间故事正好有这样一种口头特征,也就是一边讲,一边编,随口创作。因此,口头故事都是在表演之中创作,每次呈现都是一次创作。

如果你让这个讲故事的人再讲一次,很可能很多情节都会改变,甚至嫁接到其他的故事之中。我们这些被文字教育长大的人,很难理解白纸黑字如何能够这样随机应变。但是口头传统就是这样的特征。

实际上,那个很坏的小老婆,在这个故事里也没有一个正式的结局。如果是成文的故事,肯定不会这样虎头蛇尾,一定会照顾到这个角色。而在这个叫作双妹俩的故事里,甚至看不出她们两个具有什么主角特质。引导故事发展的,总是那个不幸死亡的母亲。虽然最后救场式地让她复活,而且实现了全家团圆,但是这个人物的形象非常被动,似乎无奈之下承受了这么多的磨难。

因此,这里可能需要补充一点背景。在阿昌族生活的区域,有一种对于双胞胎的恐惧和歧视,认为双胞胎会带来厄运。

虽然这个故事里,两姐妹不是双胞胎。但是如果从名字里看,还有从故事一开始就铺垫的情况看,显然这是在指涉这种双胞胎会带来厄运的文化。而这个故事最终的相对圆满的结局,呼应了最开头这两姐妹不是双胞胎的实质。

The Two Sisters

A long time ago, there was a man who married two wives. The first wife gave birth to two daughters. The elder daughter was called Yu Bangbie, and the younger one was called Yu Banggai. Both girls were exceptionally beautiful and looked exactly alike. They were like twins, and no one could tell who was the elder and who was the younger. They were known as the two sisters.

After the man died, the second wife didn't have any children of her own. She had a deep hatred towards the two sisters born by the first wife and constantly plotted against them. The first wife couldn't defend herself against the second wife's tricks, so the second wife made the twin sisters go to the mountains every day to collect firewood.

One day, while the two sisters were in the mountains collecting firewood, the second wife approached the first wife and suggested, "Sister, it is a nice day today. Let's go to the pond and wash our clothes!" While they were washing and joking around by the bright and shiny pond, the second wife pushed the first wife into the pond and drowned her. She quietly returned home afterward.

When the two sisters returned home as the sun was setting, they couldn't find their mother and began to search for her. They wondered why their mother wasn't at home to greet them as usual. They searched everywhere but couldn't find her. Then they asked the second wife, "Second mother, do you know where our mother went?" The second wife replied, "Your mother went to the pond to wash clothes. She hasn't returned yet, and I'm worried about that also. You two go and find out what happened." Upon hearing the second wife's words, the two sisters quickly ran to the pond to check the situation. They couldn't find their mother but saw a golden carp swimming in the pond. Overwhelmed with tears, they cried and returned home.

After they arrived home, their second mother asked insincerely, "Why are you two crying? Have you found your mother?" The twin sisters replied, "We searched everywhere, but we couldn't find her. We don't know where she went." The second mother said, "Although your mother is no longer here, you still have your second mother. Don't cry. Your tears also make me sad." From then on, the second mother never made them go to the mountains to collect firewood again. Instead, she asked them to take care of the ducklings every day.

The two sisters would lead the ducks into the pond where their mother had died. The second mother would bring them food every day, but they secretly scattered all the food into the pond for their mother to eat.

As time went by, the second mother became puzzled. Every day, the food she brought for the two sisters would disappear entirely. One day, she brought a big bag of food, told a few words to the two sisters, and pretended to go home. However, she turned around and hid nearby to see if her daughters really ate the food.

Thinking that their second mother had gone home, the two sisters, as usual, scattered all the food into the pond. The second mother watched secretly and remembered everything in her heart.

On the next day, before the two sisters could go and release the ducks, their second mother arrived at the pond early in the morning, carrying a hoe. She drained the water from the pond and took the golden carp home. She told the two sisters not to release the ducks and instead quickly cooked the golden carp in a pot. Under the pressure from their second mother, the two sisters had no choice but to put the golden carp into the pot. Suddenly, the golden carp started speaking in the pot, "My children, I am about to die. If she eats my flesh, both of you should not eat it. If she throws away my bones, both of you should pick them up and bury them by the roadside at the crossroads. Remember my words." After saying this, their mother died.

Following their mother's instructions, the two sisters picked up the golden carp's bones and buried them by the roadside at the crossroads. After seven days, a fragrant osmanthus tree grew from the spot. People passing by loved the tree and took good care of it. Whether they are busy or leisure, they would stay by the tree to rest for a while.

When the twin sisters' second mother heard about this, she came to see it. Many people from all directions came to see the tree. The more people see it, the more they love it and the more fragrant the flowers became. However, the more the second mother looked at it, the angrier she became. She thought that it was nothing but dog poop. The more the second mother smelt it, the more it stinks. She detested it and went home to fetch a large knife. When no one was there, she quickly chopped down the osmanthus tree. She even divided the tree into a wooden stick for laundry.

One day, she took the wooden stick to the riverbank to wash clothes, the more she used the stick to pound, the worse the clothes got. The more she rubbed the clothes, the more they turned into rags. New clothes quickly became tattered.

But when the two sisters took the wooden stick to the riverbank to wash clothes, their old and tattered clothes turned into new and good clothes. They couldn't understand it and felt strange. They went home and told the second mother about it, and upon learning of this, the second mother became extremely resentful. She secretly threw the wooden stick into the river.

Downstream in the river, there was an elderly couple picking up firewood. The wooden stick flew along the river, and the old couple picked it up from the water and brought it home. They couldn't find a suitable place to put it, but also couldn't bear to abandon it. Therefore, they regarded it as a treasure and placed it inside a tall cabinet. The elderly couple continued to go to the river every day to pick up firewood as usual.

Some time passed, whenever the elderly couple returned with firewood, they found that food was already prepared and ready to eat. They felt very puzzled. They thought, "Who is the kind person that cooked for us? We must find this person and express our gratitude."

The elderly couple went and asked the people in the village. The villagers replied, "Who would bother to enter your shabby hut?" The elderly couple couldn't find the person, so they pretended not to say anything. They continued picking up firewood as usual. When they returned home, the food was still well-cooked and simmering in the pot.

One day, the elderly couple pretended to go out and gather firewood, but shortly, they quietly returned and hid behind the mosquito net, eager to see what would happen. As they were about to prepare dinner, they suddenly heard a noise coming from their cabinet. A beautiful woman emerged from the cabinet, capturing their attention. They watched as the woman walked into the kitchen, then mesmerized. They dared not move as they observed the woman cooking, preparing the food perfectly, and tidying up the kitchen. When she finished and was about to return to the cabinet, the elderly couple finally realized what was happening. They hurriedly ran over and grabbed the woman and said, "Sweet girl, it's you who cooks for us every day!" The woman, unable to hide anymore, replied, "Old grandpa, it's me. You two are my saviors. I noticed that you both went out to gather firewood every day and came back late to cook. Sometimes, you have to eat cold soup and leftovers. It broke my heart to see that. I want to treat you both as my parents." The elderly couple eagerly exclaimed, "Yes, kind-hearted girl, since we have no children, you can be our daughter!" The girl respectfully bowed to the elderly people several times.

The elderly couple went to open the cabinet again and found it filled with gold and silver treasures. They were overjoyed. From that day on, their family lived diligently and gradually became prosperous. The elderly couple no longer need to gather firewood.

After some time, the elderly couple said to the girl, "My child, ever since you came to our home, our lives have been improved, and we have become wealthier. According to the customs of our Achang people, when we have money, we should celebrate with a grand feast." The daughter replied, "Then let's do it. I will follow your wishes, my parents."

They informed their neighbors and invited people from all directions to their home for the grand feast. On the day of the feast, the two sisters, Yu Bangbie and Yu Banggai, also arrived. As soon as the two sisters stepped through the doorway of the elderly couple's house, they saw the girl, who looked just like their mother. The woman also recognized the two sisters as her daughters without any hesitation. They immediately called out, "Mother! Mother!" and ran to embrace the woman, and three of them cried together. Mother said, "I never expected that we would reunite here, the three of us, mother and daughters." This sudden reunion shocked the elderly couple.

Eventually, the woman shared her story and what she had experienced with the elderly couple. The elderly couple was deeply saddened to hear that. They decided to keep the two sisters with them, and they live happily together as a family.

万能的鼓

从前，有个孤儿又脏又穷，皮肤像蛤蟆皮一样难看。寨子里的小伙子、小姑娘都嫌他脏，不愿与他接近。可是，小伙子却很勤劳，喜欢帮助寨子里老弱孤寡的人家，只要人家需要，他起早贪黑，一心一意给人家帮忙。虽然这样，可他自己三十开外，还找不到老婆，一直是个穷光棍。

父母留下唯一的财产，就只有一棵"麻蒙"果树（杧果树）。每年这棵树都果实累累，可是今年却只结了一个又大又红的果，他认为这个果一定是个仙果，每天都在树下守着。

有一天，他在麻蒙树下乘凉，天气闷热，他很快就睡着了。睡得正香的时候，这个麻蒙果熟透落下来了，正打在他的鼻子上，打得极痛，他认为又是寨子里那班调皮的小青年在捉弄他了，他毫不客气地顺手拣起就打出去，果子出手，才发现是那个麻蒙果，他十分懊悔，也不知落到什么地方去了。

不料这个打出去的麻蒙果，却落在了土司家的后园，此时恰好土司的小姐在园里玩耍，她看见这又红又大的麻蒙果，心里很高兴，便拣回家吃了。奇怪，土司家的小姐吃了这个麻蒙果后，不久就怀孕了，生下来一个白白胖胖的娃娃。土司知道女儿生了娃娃后，又害羞又气愤。他责怪女儿不应做出这种丢脸的事，他又暗自奇怪，我的女儿向来管教严厉，家门不出，亲戚不串，为什么会生出小孩，他想尽办法，想要找到孩子的父亲是谁。

孩子满一岁了，会喊爸爸妈妈了。忽然，土司爷决定要做一个七天的"大摆"，邀请户撒坝所有的青年来赶摆，小孩认了谁是他的父亲，就做土司爷的女婿。

摆期到了，村村寨寨的青年都赶来了，他们打扮得漂漂亮亮，戴着翻翻的毡帽，背着花花绿绿的"筒帕"和最好的良光草烟，有的带来了祖传的宝石、金银和许许多多的礼物，他们唯一希望，只求小孩喊自己一声"爸爸"。

摆期到了第七天，再过一夜，"大摆"就散了，人们也忙着回家去种田了，土司爷急得不得了，可是又想不出别的办法。赶摆到了下午时，人都快散完了。这时来了个穿得非常破烂的穷小伙子，土司爷厌恶地说他不应该在这种吉祥的节日里来讨饭，玷污了盛大的摆会。正在这时，小孩看见了，摇着小手亲切地喊"爸爸、爸爸"。听见叫声，这个穷人也不禁感到奇怪。

土司爷万万想不到小孩会认这个又脏又臭的穷小子做父亲，真是丢尽了脸。特别是在这样盛大的摆会上，要认这样一个穷小子做自己的女婿，那是万万不能的。土司爷为了挽回自己的尊严，狠心地撵走了自己的亲生女儿。他给这个穷小子一张木筏，要他们随着河水远远漂去，永远不要回来。

他们一家人，坐在木筏上不知漂了多少天多少夜，河水清又宽，流向远方，不知穿过多少高山密林，大象挥动长鼻子要他们留下，孔雀也开屏用金光闪闪的羽毛来欢迎他们。

穷人带着小姐和孩子，又走了无数地方，终于来到了一处森林茂盛的平坝。他们看着身上带的粮食也吃完了，无法再前进了。

他们便在这里安家落户，开掘田园。白天到森林里去砍树，奇怪，所砍的树，明天去看，又是一片森林，砍下来的树不见了，又都长了上去。他连续这样砍了几天，还是一棵也没有得到。

有天晚上，他偷偷爬到树上看。深夜，竟然来了一大群猴子，它们跳着舞，唱着歌，老猴子在中间敲鼓，一面敲一面念："树啊，快站起来！快长成原样，快枝肥叶茂……"果然棵棵被砍倒的树复原了，白天砍的树又长上去了。

小伙子赶忙下树，奋不顾身抓到了老猴子，并要杀死老猴，猴王慌忙求饶："只要你放了我，我给你这个万能鼓，你要什么，它会给你什么。"

穷小伙子放走猴王后，便敲起了万能鼓，边敲边说道："鼓啊，快快把树砍倒，让所有的荒地种上庄稼。"不多久地面上便长出了谷穗，粒粒饱满。他又敲鼓要房子、布匹，还要来了各种美味的食品和珍珠……

后来，他靠着这鼓积累了很多财富，装满了两大船，便带着小姐和孩子在船头擂起万能鼓，顶着汹涌的波浪，回到了久别的家乡。

土司爷自亲生女儿跟穷汉走后，又气又病，不久便死了。

家乡的老百姓知道小伙子回来了，都争先恐后在河岸迎接他们。

小伙子跟小姐回到宫殿，小伙子做了新官，他把土司爷多年剥削老百姓的粮食分给了大家。从此后，老百姓没有吃的就到仓库里去背米，没有用的就到仓库里去拿钱，没有住的，小伙子又为老百姓敲响了万能鼓。

此后，这个地方的人民过上了丰衣足食安乐的生活。后来，当地老百姓为怀念这位新官，流传下了万能鼓的故事。

收集整理：罗玉山

编者按： 这是一个穷小伙子的佳人梦，还有他的升官发财、名传千古梦。如果说这个故事稍微有那么一点设定，就是这个穷小伙子是一个长得丑陋，内心善良的人。可能当一个人又穷又丑的时候，这是极少能给予自身优势的特质了。

哪怕是最后他能够积累财富，也不是依靠自己的勤劳与智慧，而是借助一个万能鼓。

谁不想要一个这样一步到位的万能鼓呢？可能每个去买彩票的人，或者去赌博的人，都是这样想的吧？

The Magical Drum

Once upon a time, there was an orphan who was dirty and poor. His skin was as ugly as frog skin. The boys and girls in the village found him dirty and didn't want to get close to him. However, the boy was very hardworking and liked to help the elderly and vulnerable people in the village. Whenever someone needed help, he would wake up early and work tirelessly to assist them. Even though he was working hard, he was still unmarried and remained poor.

His parents had left him with only one asset, a mango tree. Every year, the tree bore abundant fruit. But this year, it only produced one large and red fruit, which he believed to be a magical fruit. He would sit under the tree every day, waiting for it to ripen.

One day, as he was engoying shade under the mango tree, the weather was hot and humid, and he soon fell asleep. Just as he was sleep soundly, the ripe mango fell, and hit his nose, making him great pain. Assuming it was one of the mischievous young men in the village playing a prank on him, he instinctively picked up the fruit and threw it away without hesitation. Only then did he realize that it was the mango fruit he had thrown away, he deeply regretted about his actions, and was unsure of where it had landed.

Unbeknown to him, the mango he had thrown landed in the backyard of the village chief's house. Coincidentally, the chief's daughter was playing in the garden and discovered the large and ripe mango. She was delighted and took it home to eat. Strangely enough, soon after the chief's daughter consumed the mango, she became pregnant and gave birth to a cute baby. The chief was both embarrassed and furious upon learning about his daughter's pregnancy. He scolded her for bringing such disgrace upon the family and wondered how it could have happened since she had always been well-behaved and rarely left the house. He racked his brain, trying to find out who the father of the child could be.

When the child turned one and began to call out "papa" and "mama", the village chief decided to host a feast lasting seven days, inviting all the young men in the village. The man whom the child recognized as his father would become the chief's son-in-law.

The feast was set, and young men from all the neighboring villages arrived, dressed in their finest clothes, wearing elegant hats, and carrying colorful handkerchiefs. Some brought gemstones, gold and many gifts, all hoping to hear the child call them "father".

As the seventh day of the feast approached, people started leaving to go home to cultivate their land. The chief became anxious and couldn't think of any other solution. By the afternoon, most of the guests had already departed. At this moment, a dirty and impoverished boy arrived. The chief expressed his disgust, said that he shouldn't have come begging on such a festive occasion, tarnishing the grand feast. However, the child noticed him and warmly called out, "Father! Father"! Hearing this, the beggar couldn't help but feel surprised.

The chief never expected the child to recognize this dirty and smelly boy as his father, bringing even greater shame upon himself. Especially during such a grand feast, it was absolutely unthinkable to accept this poor boy as his son-in-law. In order to salvage his own dignity, the chief cruelly drove away his own daughter. He gave the poor boy a raft and ordered them to float away with the river, and never return.

The family sat on the raft, drifted for days and nights, unaware of how long they had been floating. The river was clear and wide, flowing towards a distant horizon. They passed through numerous mountains and dense forests, where elephants waved their trunks, urging them to stay, and peacocks displayed their sparkling feathers to welcome them.

The poor man, along with the young lady and the child, traveled to countless places until they finally arrived at a lush and flat forest. They realized that they had run out of food and could no longer move forward.

They decided to settle down in this place and started cultivating the land. During the day, the man went into the forest to chop down trees. Strangely, every tree he cut down would regrow overnight. When he returned the next day, the forest was once again dense with trees, and the ones he had cut down were nowhere to be seen. He continued this process for several days, but couldn't obtain a single tree.

One night, he quietly climbed up a tree to observe. In midnight, a large group of monkeys arrived. They danced and sang while an old monkey in the center played the drum and chanted, "Trees, stand tall! Grow back to your original form, grow thick and lush". Sure enough, every tree that had been cut down grew back to its original state by morning.

The young man quickly descended from the tree and bravely captured the elder monkey, intending to kill it. The monkey king pleaded for mercy, "If you spare my life, I will give you this magical drum. It will grant you whatever you desire".

After releasing the monkey king, the poor young man began to play the magical drum, and said, "Drum, quickly cut down the trees, and let all the barren land be planted with crops". Before long, the fields were filled with bountiful grain. He played the drum again, requesting houses, cloth, and a variety of delicious food and pearls.

Thanks to the drum, he filled two large ships of wealth. He took the young lady and the child to the front of the ship, where he played the magical drum, sailed through the surging waves, and returned to his long-lost hometown.

Since the village chief's daughter had left with the poor man, he became angry and sick, and soon passed away. Hearing that the young man had return, the people of the hometown rushed to the riverbank to welcome them.

The young man and the young lady returned to the palace, where the young man became a new official. He redistributed the crops that the village chief had exploited from the villagers for many years. From then on, if anyone had no food, they could go to the warehouse to get rice. If they have no money left, they could go to the repository to get some. And if they had no place to live, the young man would play the magical drum for the people.

From that point on, the people in this place lived a life of abundance and happiness. In memory of this new official, the local villagers passed down the story of the magical drum.

眉间长旋儿的姑娘

我们阿昌族过去有一个传统的习俗，凡是眉间长旋儿的姑娘，就被认为是"鬼胎"，会吃人，尤其会吃自己的男人。因此，不论谁家，只要是生了眉间长旋儿的姑娘，都规定不得出嫁，只能独身而死。

人们担心的事情总是会发生的。有一年，杨家寨的杨老头两口子，四十多岁了，才生了一个独女，取名叫杨宝。女儿出生后，老两口高兴得不得了，连忙抱到灯下细看，这一看可把老两口吓昏了，他们的杨宝竟是一个眉间长旋儿的姑娘。可是，就这么一个独苗苗，当爹娘的怎么舍得把她害死？他们决定养活她，让她永远在娘家度过终生。

杨宝越长越大，而且长得非常漂亮，比阿昌山寨边上的粉团还要美丽。到十八岁的时候，杨宝的名字就像蒲公英的种子，随风吹遍了七村八寨；杨宝的品德像桂花香，四面八方都闻到了。小河涨水的时候，鱼儿就来了；鲜花开放的时候，小蜜蜂就飞来了。上杨宝家求婚的小伙子比鱼儿还高兴，比小蜜蜂还多。他们络绎不绝地来到她家里，都想要采到这朵鲜花。这可把杨宝的父母急够了，他们把杨宝关锁起来，不让她和小伙子们见面。但是，杨宝却躲在门缝里悄悄地把每一个小伙子都看清了，她一个也不爱。

就这样，小伙子们慢慢地来得少了，杨宝的父母也不再关锁她了。有一天，来了一个小伙子，他的名字叫恩德，杨宝姑娘一见就喜欢上了，只见这伙子长得像金竹一样挺拔，像神话中的武士一样英俊，两眼闪闪发光像星星，说话像流淌的山溪一样悦耳好听。他们俩一谈就拢，并发誓从此不再分离。

太阳落山的时候，杨宝的父母回来了，恩德连忙跪在老人面前，请求他们把杨宝嫁给他。杨宝的父亲坚决地拒绝了，他说："起来吧，好心的小伙子，我的姑娘永远不出嫁了。她是一个眉间长旋儿的姑娘，老辈子的人传下来说，这样的姑娘会'克夫'，结婚后，你会被她克死。万一真出了这样的事，你们得不到幸福，我们也会伤心的。阿昌的山上哪里不开花？阿昌寨子里都有姑娘，到别家去找吧，小伙子！"恩德还是跪着不起来，他说："过去的老人们说，独人不要打虎，可我就打死过三只猛虎。阿公阿祖说，听见猫头鹰叫，就不能出门，可我从来不忌讳。我什么都不怕，我只求你们让我和杨宝结婚。"杨宝的父母，看恩德实在诚心，也就同意了。

恩德高高兴兴地把杨宝姑娘领回家里，却遭到了父母的指责，无论如何也不同意儿子和眉间长旋儿的姑娘结婚。在父母的一再反对下，恩德只好挎了一把户撒长刀，和杨宝手牵手地离开了家乡，去寻求幸福的生活。他们走了很远很远，历尽了千辛万苦，终于找到了一个同意他们居住的寨子。他们把不幸的遭遇向寨子里的人诉说，得到了大家的同情。老人们给他们送来吃食，小伙子们帮助他们盖起了新房，姑娘们经常来把杨宝陪伴。

有一天，恩德一个人上山砍木头。由于天气热，又加上劳累，恩德就枕着木头睡着了。

天黑了，还不见恩德回家，杨宝不知去门口看了多少回，后来她着急了，忙叫起寨里的姑娘小伙子们打着松明火把上山寻找。他们在山上找到了恩德，可他已经一动不动地死了。杨宝扑在他的身上放声痛哭，大伙帮着把恩德抬回了家。第二天，他们按照传统的埋葬法，把恩德放在一个竹筏上，放到户撒河里，顺水漂走了。杨宝拼命地往竹筏上爬，她要和丈夫同死，乡亲们把她拉住了。

竹筏顺水漂啊漂，也不知漂了多远。有一天，竹筏漂到了一个小村子旁边，恰巧有两个姑娘在河边采药，妹妹发现了竹筏，她连忙对姐姐说："姐姐，你看，河里漂着一样什么东西？"姐姐仔细一看说："上面好像睡着一个人。"她们被这奇怪的现象吸引住了。为了要看个究竟，她们把竹筏拖到了岸边，只见上面确实躺着一个年轻、英俊的小伙子。可怎么叫也不醒，仔细一看，才发现他已经死了，但脸上还泛着红晕，真不知何故，妹妹建议请父亲来看看。她们的父亲是个有名的老草药医生，来检查以后，确认小伙子是被毒蛇咬中太阳穴，中毒而晕死，身体还热着，心脏还微弱地跳着。父女三人连忙把他抬回家，用火罐拔出毒血，将消炎祛毒的草药敷在伤口上。过了不久，恩德就慢慢地睁开眼睛，苏醒过来了。老草药医生继续给他服药，两姐妹细心给他调养。就在这期间，两个姑娘都爱上了恩德，都愿意嫁给他做妻子，恩德婉言谢绝了。恩德想起心爱的杨宝，不待身体完全复原，就告别了老草药医生父女三人，匆匆赶回家去。

恩德赶回家里一看，房子被火烧了，有几根木头还在冒着烟。他大声地呼喊："杨宝，我回来了，你在哪里？"四周静悄悄的，没有一点回声。乡亲们听到恩德的喊声，先是疑神疑鬼，后来听着喊得太悲伤，几个胆子大的年轻人走出家门来看。呵，真的是恩德回来了。于是全寨的人们都来到他的身旁，问他是怎么活过来的？恩德向乡亲们诉说了他的遭遇。乡亲们听了以后更加悲伤，告诉他，魔涛（巫师）说眉间长旋儿的杨宝克死了丈夫，说她不是人而是鬼，煽动一些人把她赶进了深山老林。

恩德一听妻子被赶走了，悲痛欲绝。他问明了方向，挎上户撒长刀，便到深山老林里去寻找杨宝。

恩德进了森林，边走边呼喊，可是除了野兽的怪叫和怒吼的林涛声，什么也听不到。他这样边走边呼喊，整整七天七夜没有停息过片刻。到了第八天，他已经精疲力竭，坚持不住了，他靠着一棵大树闭上了眼睛，两行泪水还不断流到胸前。他做了一个梦，梦见一只金孔雀在他头上盘旋，不停地对他说："恩德啊，你赶快醒醒，老虎正走近你的杨宝，你要马上

去救她。"恩德从梦中惊醒，看见正有一只孔雀从他背靠的大树上向南飞去，他连忙朝着孔雀指引的方向跑去。在一座石崖下面，恩德找到了满面泪痕的妻子。杨宝看到丈夫活了，高兴地扑在他的身上失声大哭。

野兽不敢吼叫了，林涛也止息了，太阳驱散了乌云，把金色的光芒透过密密的树叶撒在松软、潮湿的大地上。恩德扶着杨宝，走出深山老林，回到了他们居住的寨子。

乡亲们看到这一对诚实、勇敢的年轻人双双地回来了，都高兴地跑出寨子迎接他们。小伙子们又帮助他们盖起了新房，姑娘们采来鲜花送给他们。他们搬进新房那天，远近的人们都来庆贺，送来了数不清的礼物。大家跳啊、唱啊，整整热闹了三天三夜，比新婚时还要欢乐。

从此以后，能干的恩德经常帮助大家做事，美丽善良的杨宝更是敬老爱幼，使众人赞不绝口。他们夫妇俩生儿育女，白头到老，一直过着幸福美满的日子。于是再无人说眉间长旋儿的姑娘是"鬼胎""会克夫"了，这个习俗也没人相信了。

搜集整理：刘扬武

编者按：很多文化里都有类似"克夫"或者"克父母"这样的说法。这可能是谣言传播时很便利的归因方式。一旦一个人被认为有这样的"邪性"，那么他很容易动辄得咎。

一个阿昌族小姑娘，就因为出生的时候眉毛有一个生理特征，就被污名化，成为邪恶的载体。这在现在看来，似乎是无理取闹，但是又是真实存在的文化现象。

在这个故事里，一个不信邪的小伙子，凭借爱情和勇气，忠贞与神助，不仅赢得了美人，还渡过一劫。其实这个劫难就如同那个驱逐他们的巫师所言，正是可以成为姑娘克夫的证据。

某种意义上，这个讲述者接受了眉间长旋儿姑娘是"鬼胎"的设定，但是他给出了破解这个魔咒的出路，就是爱与忠贞。这样的人，神明也会出手相救。

The Girl with a Swirl Between Her Brows

In the past, Achang people had a traditional custom: any girl with a swirl between her brows was considered a "demon-born" who would devour people, especially her own husband. Therefore, it was required that any family with a girl like this could never marry, she would have to remain single until death.

The things people worry about always seem to come true. One year, in the Yangjia Village, old Yang and his wife, both over forty, finally had a daughter, whom they named Yang Bao. The couple was overjoyed and quickly brought their daughter to the lamp to take a closer look. But what they saw shocked them, their precious baby had a swirl between her brows. However, she was their only child, and as her parents, they couldn't bear to harm her. They decided to raise her and had her unmarried at home for her whole life.

As Yang Bao grew, she became extremely beautiful, even more lovely than the flowers along the Achang mountain slopes. By the time she was eighteen, Yang Bao's name had spread like dandelion seeds, carried by the wind everywhere; her virtues, like the fragrance of the osmanthus flower, were known far and wide. When the river rose, the fish came; when the flowers bloomed, the bees arrived. Suitors came in endless streams, more eager than the fish, more numerous than the bees, all of them wanted to marry her. This situation worried Yang Bao's parents immensely, so they locked her away, preventing her from meeting the young men. But Yang Bao secretly peeked through the cracks in the door, carefully observing each suitor, and found herself uninterested in any of them.

Over time, fewer young men came, and her parents no longer kept her locked up. One day, a young man named En De arrived, and Yang Bao instantly fell in love with him. He was tall and straight like golden bamboo, as handsome as a warrior from the myths, with eyes that sparkled like stars and a voice as melodious as a flowing mountain stream. They quickly bonded, and vowed never to be separate.

As the sun set, Yang Bao's parents returned home. En De knelt before them, pleading for their permission to marry Yang Bao. Her father firmly refused, and said, "Stand up, kind young man. My daughter will never marry. She has a swirl between her brows, and the elders say such a girl will bring misfortune to her husband, who will die because of her. If that happens, we will be heartbroken. There are many other girls in the village. Seek another girl, young man"! But En De insisted, "The elders said not to hunt tigers alone, but I have killed three ones by myself. They said one should not venture out when an owl hoots, but I have never heeded such warnings. I fear nothing; I only ask that you allow me to marry Yang Bao". Seeing En De's sincerity, her parents finally agreed.

En De joyfully took Yang Bao home, only to face his parents' disapproval. They opposed the marriage to a girl with a swirl between her brows. Faced with this opposition, En De, carrying only a long knife, left home together with Yang Bao in search of a happy life. They traveled far and wide, enduring countless hardships until they found a village that welcomed them. They shared their misfortunes with the villagers, who sympathized with them. The elders brought them food, the young men helped them build their new home, and the village girls often kept Yang Bao company.

One day, En De went alone to the mountains to chop wood. The heat and exhaustion overcame him, and he fell asleep with his head resting on the wood.

Night fell, but En De had not returned. Yang Bao anxiously looked out countless times, finally she called for the village youths to search the mountains by torchlight. They found En De, but he was already lifeless. Yang Bao threw herself on him, weeping bitterly, and the villagers helped carry him home. The next day, according to tradition, they placed En De on a bamboo raft and set it adrift on the Husa River. Yang Bao desperately tried to climb onto the raft to die with her husband, but the villagers held her back.

The raft drifted on and on until one day it reached a small village. Two girls collecting herbs by the river spotted the raft. The younger sister called out, "Sister, look, something is floating in the river"! The elder sister saw a young man lying on the raft. They were curious about this strange sight and dragged the raft ashore, finding a handsome young man on it. But no matter how they called, he would not wake. When they looked closer, they realized he was dead, though his face still had a faint blush. Unsure of what had happened, the younger sister suggested they bring their father to have a look. Their father, a renowned herbal doctor, examined the young man and discovered he had been bitten by a venomous snake, rendering him unconscious. His body was still warm, and his heart's still faintly beating. The father and daughters quickly carried him home. They used fire cupping to draw out the poisoned blood and applied anti-inflammatory herbs to the wound. After some time, En De slowly opened his eyes and regained consciousness. The old man continued to treat him, and the two sisters cared for him. During this time, both sisters fell in love with En De and wished to marry him, but he declined.

En De, remembering his beloved Yang Bao, bid farewell to the old man and his daughters before his body had fully recovered and hurried home.

When En De returned, he found his house was burned to the ground, with a few charred beams still smoking. He called out loudly, "Yang Bao, I'm back! Where are you"? The surroundings were silent, with no reply. The villagers, initially spooked by the calls, eventually recognized En De's voice and a few brave young men stepped out. To their surprise, En De had truly returned. The whole village gathered around him, asking how he had survived. En De said all that happened, and the villagers, now even more saddened, told him that the Motao (witch doctor) had claimed that

Yang Bao had cursed her husband to death. The Motao had incited people to drive her into the deep mountains and forests.

Devastated by this news, En De asked for the directions, took his long knife, and went to find Yang Bao.

En De entered into the forest, calling out as he went, but he heard nothing but the eerie calls of wild animals and the roar of the forest. He continued searching tirelessly for seven days and nights without rest. On the eighth day, utterly exhausted, he collapsed against a large tree and closed his eyes, tears streaming down his chest. He dreamed of a golden peacock circling above him, urging him to wake up, warning that a tiger was approaching Yang Bao. En De awoke in panic, seeing a peacock flying south from the tree he was resting against. He quickly followed the peacock's direction and found his wife beneath a cliff. Seeing her husband alive, Yang Bao joyfully threw herself into his arms, sobbing uncontrollably.

The wild beasts no longer dared to roar, the forest fell silent, and the sun drove away the clouds, casting golden rays through the dense leaves onto the soft, damp earth. En De helped Yang Bao out of the deep forest and back to their village.

The villagers, seeing this honest and brave young couple return, ran out to welcome them. The young men helped build a new house, and the girls brought flowers for them. When they moved into their new home, people from far and wide came to celebrate, bringing countless gifts. The festivities lasted three days and nights, even more joyful than their wedding.

From then on, En De often helped the villagers, and the beautiful, kind Yang Bao became known for her respect for the elderly and love for the young, earning widespread praise. The couple lived a happy and fulfilling life together, raising children and growing old together. As a result, no one ever again said that girls with swirls between their brows were "demon-born" or would curse their husbands. This old custom was no longer believed.

奢三和线二

从前，有母子二人，生活很穷困，全靠儿子线二卖柴度日。有一年闹饥荒，实在无法过下去了，线二就到大户人家——奢三家当长工。奢三虽然钱财满柜，却特别悭吝刻薄，经常克扣长工和佣人的工钱。

线二做了一年工，打算要回家一趟，送点钱给母亲。临走前，线二向奢三要得了半年的工钱。奢三假意体贴线二，就从干鱼堆里挑了最小的一尾鱼送给线二，嘱咐他拿给母亲吃。线二回到家，就把这尾干鱼交给了母亲。第二天，母亲把饭煮熟后，准备煎这尾干鱼吃。她拿起来一看，发现干鱼流着眼泪，就不忍心煎它吃，告诉儿子把鱼放到河里去。线二素来孝顺母亲，也就答应了。

线二带上这尾干鱼，路过一条河，他把鱼放到河里。干鱼到了河里，深深地吸了几口水，摇晃着身子钻进深水里去了。不一会儿，鱼就变成了一个美丽的女子。她跳上岸来就去追线二。线二正急着赶路，忽听后面有人喊他，回头一看，原是个年轻漂亮的姑娘。姑娘走到线二身边，自称是余（鱼）姑娘，对线二说："表兄，回家去吧，我要和你结为夫妻，白头到老。"线二也爱余姑娘，但一想到自己的处境，就为难地对余姑娘说："好心的姑娘呀，你的情意我领了，我是田无一丘，地无一墒，只有一间破草房，你还是另嫁别人吧！"余姑娘执意要嫁，他再无法推脱，只好领着余姑娘回到家里，拜过母亲，就做夫妻了。第二天早晨，线二起来一看，原来的破草房不见了，只见青砖亮瓦的房屋，牛羊满圈，鸡、猪、鹅、鸭应有尽有。从此，线二一家过上了幸福的生活。

过了很久，奢三不见线二回来，就领着八个长工找到线二家来。线二的高楼大厦，无数牛马，让奢三羡慕生嫉妒。他看见线二的妻子，神魂颠倒，贪婪的眼睛紧紧盯着，立即提出要和线二换妻、换财产。线二舍不得心爱的妻子，说什么也不肯换。余姑娘递给线二一个眼色，线二勉强答应了。奢三怕线二反悔，就赶忙落了字据，各自在纸上画了押。画押后，奢三要线二母子马上离开，线二扶着年迈的母亲向奢三家走去。余姑娘送了线二母子一段路，说了许多安慰的话，才和线二母子挥泪告别。线二的母亲舍不得贤惠的儿媳，一路上泪流不止。

奢三见余姑娘一天天消瘦下去，就问："贤妻呀，你为什么越来越瘦？"余姑娘回答说："我在娘家一天洗三次澡，来这里一次澡都不得洗，我才瘦得不像人样了。"奢三听了，马上叫长工们用轿子抬着余姑娘到河里去洗澡。到了河岸，余姑娘独自向河里走去。余姑娘纵身跳进了大河里。奢三和长工们等了半天，不见余姑娘回来，就到河边看，河里只有水哗哗地响着。奢三领着长工们沿河找，连影子也不见；又叫长工们到河里捞，什么也没捞到。

天渐渐黑了，奢三只得领着长工们垂头丧气地回家。到家一看，房屋没有了，牛羊没有了，只有一间破草房。一气之下，奢三口吐白沫，一命呜呼了。

讲述：张应流
搜集整理：孙家申

编者按： 这个故事是每个长工在辛劳终日之后想听的故事。只要稍微改动一些内容，保留这个结构，就可以成为现在打工人茶余饭后的短视频。

很多赚流量的视频，背后的故事，都有民间故事的影子。这里反而应该引起思考，让民间故事经久不息的，不是内容，而是故事讲述者和听众的处境。

She San and Xian Er

Once upon a time, there was a mother and son who lived in poverty. The family relied on the son, Xian Er, who sold fire wood to make their living. One year there was a famine, and they couldn't survive anymore, so the son went to work for a rich family, the family of She San, as a long-term worker. Although She San was rich, but he was especially strict and mean, and often deducted the wages of the long-term workers and servants.

After working for a year, Xian Er planned to go home and send some money to his mother. Before leaving, he asked for his half-year's wages. She San, pretending to be considerate, picked the smallest fish from the fish pile and gave it to Xian Er, telling him to take it to his mother. When Xian Er returned home, he gave the fish to his mother. The next day, his mother cooked rice and prepared to fry fish for dinner. When she picked it up, she found that fish was shedding tears, so she couldn't bear to fry it and told her son to put it in the river. Xian Er was always very obedient to his mother, so he agreed.

He took the fish with him and passed by a river, so he put the fish into the river. When the fish reached the river, it took a few deep breaths of water and wiggled itself into the deep water. In a short time, the fish turned into a beautiful woman. She jumped on the shore and went after Xian Er. He was in a hurry and suddenly heard someone shouting behind him, so he turned around and looked, it was a beautiful young girl. The girl went to Xian Er, and said her name was Yu (fish), she then said, "Brother, go home. I want to be marry you and spend the rest of my life with you." Xian Er also loved Yu girl, but once he thought of his own situation, he said to her with difficulty, "Good girl, I appreciate your feelings, but I don't have any land or field, only a broken straw house, you should marry someone else"! Yu girl insisted on marriage, he could no longer refuse, so he led the girl back home, visited his mother, and became a couple. The next morning, Xian Er got up to see the original old straw house vanished. Replaced by a new brick house and a great amount of cattle and sheep, chickens, pigs, geese and ducks. From then on, Xian Er's family lived a happy life.

After a long time, She San did not see Xian Er back, so he led eight long-term workers to Xian Er's house. He was jealous of Xian Er's buildings and countless cows and horses. He saw Xian Er's wife and was so charming that his greedy eyes were fixed on her, and he immediately offered to exchange his things with Xian Er's wife and property. Xian Er couldn't let his beloved wife go and refused to exchange. The girl passed a wink to Xian Er, so Xian Er reluctantly agreed. She San was afraid that Xian Er regret, so he hurried to write a contract, they signed on the note and made a treaty. After the agreement, She San asked Xian Er and his mother to leave immediately, Xian Er supported his elderly mother to walk to She San's house. The girl walked with the mother and son for a while and said many words of comfort before she waved a tearful farewell to them. The mother of Xian Er really missed her daughter-in-law and wept all the way.

When She San saw that Yu was losing weight day by day, he asked, "My wife, why are you getting thinner and thinner"? The girl replied, "I took bath three times a day at my mother's house, but not even once here, so I have lost weight". Hearing this, She San immediately asked the workers to carry Yu in a sedan chair to the river to take a bath. When she reached the riverbank, she went to the river alone. The girl jumped into the river. But as time passed, the girl still did not come back, so She San went to the river to check, and only to see the water flowing loudly. She San led the long-term workers along the river to find the girl, but there was nothing. They also searched in the river, and nothing was found.

It was getting dark, so She San had to lead the workers home. When they arrived home, they saw that there were no more housings, no more cattle and sheep, only a broken straw house. In extreme anger and frustration, She San died.

一筒竹子通梢的故事

有个百万家的帮工,天天帮百万家看守着谷仓,从未偷懒过,是个老老实实的人。

他帮了许久,深深地爱上了百万家的小姐,他只是一个帮工,不敢去讲。小姐是个善良又开朗的人,从来不把帮工当奴才使用。

有一天,帮工看守的谷仓,来了几只老鼠偷吃了谷子,他伤心透了。不久,他把鼠王抓住了,教训了它一顿:"你们天天来偷吃谷子,今天我抓到你了,你要死,还是要活?"鼠王求饶地说:"要活,请你放了我吧。"帮工说道:"要活可以,只要你答应今后帮我做点事,我就饶了你。"鼠王忙说:"什么事,只管吩咐。"帮工说:"你派出你的老鼠去把寺里那个大佛的肚子里的泥土掏出来,把佛肚子掏空掉,要使佛好好的,不露痕迹。"鼠王欣然答应了:"这是点小事,你放心吧。"帮工把它放了。

鼠王回去,就约着小老鼠们,去把填在佛肚子里的泥巴掏得一干二净。

百万家的老婆是个佛教徒,每天都要到庙里去供斋,拜佛。帮工了解到老妈妈常在什么时候去供斋,他就提前到庙里,悄悄地躲进佛的肚子里头,等老妈妈来供斋时就说:"百万家小姐的婚姻,是要跟他家的那个穷帮工才合得来。如不是这样,就要遭祸。"

老妈妈每天去供斋时,都听到老佛讲这么几句话,信以为真,回去就把听到的话告诉了百万,百万不理会。她暗暗地想着:"这帮工做事倒是勤快老实,也还聪明,要是姑娘嫁给他也可以。只是他是个帮工呀。"

过了一些时候,有一个县官老爷来要这个小姐,他们交谈所讲的话全被鼠王听到了,鼠王就去把这事告诉那个帮工。并说:"他们约定好时间,在某天某个时辰,备一匹马在哪个地方接,你也那时备一匹马,收拾打扮一下,到约定的地点去等着。"

帮工按照鼠王告诉他的时间,悄悄地备了一匹好马,到约定的地点,才一下的工夫，小姐果然来了。因为她父亲约的吉时是晚上，看不清来接她的是谁，她以为就是来要好的那个人，所以，骑着马就跟着走了。来要小姐的那个人没有接到小姐，也就回去了。

帮工把小姐带到很远很远的地方。这时，天亮了，人也走累了，才歇下来。小姐才看清了人，发现他不是要她的那个小伙子，而是她家的帮工。她气极了，就不高兴，感到很苦闷，咋个办呢？一直是闷闷不乐的。

她也曾想过，这个帮工，人品好，老实厚道，人也生得俊俏，做事稳重。以前她也喜欢过他，只因为他是一个帮工，而她是百万家的小姐，嫁给他怕失掉百万家的面子，自己也不光彩。想到这些，就打消了这个念头。现在咋个办呢？她想着想累了，话也不说，一直在苦闷着，赌气不同他讲话。

肚子饿了，要做饭时，搁锅是要三脚，可是帮工故意只用两个石头来搁，咋个整也搁不成，在那里左弄右弄的，故意逗小姐说话。小姐看到他弄了半天，没有把锅搁好，就不耐烦地冷冷地说："笨虫，人家煮饭是要用三只脚。你怎么只用两只脚，这样咋个搁得稳。"

帮工听了小姐的第一句话，心里痒痒的，非常高兴，赶快支起三脚来煮饭了。他又故意把饭勺别在腰上，饭煮了一阵后要搅搅它，他就做出到处找饭勺的样子，小姐看到不耐烦地说："蠢猪，你找什么？饭勺别在你的腰杆上，你还到处找。"他又逗得小姐说出第二句话，僵冷的空气有点暖和了，他暗暗地在发笑。

小姐这时也没有办法了，事到如今，回也回不去，回去也不好意思见人了。她就对小伙子说："真的，你对我有感情的话，那么你须找一棵一筒通梢的竹子来，我们两个才能够结婚。"小姐想出一个难题试试他的心。

那帮工听到这话后，就拼命地寻找一筒通梢的竹子。

他走着走着，走到一座庙里，里面住着一个和尚。他就去问和尚："哪里有一筒通梢的竹子。"和尚想了想对他说："这个凡间是不会有的。不过，一筒通梢的竹子，仙山那里可能会有。仙山是在密林深处，那座高高的山峰就是，你要经过很多艰难险阻才能到达。"

帮工听到这话后，喜形于色，就赶紧往密林深处走去。他克服了很多困难和艰险，爬上了仙山，终于找到了一筒通梢的竹子。

小伙子找到竹子回来，小姐看到非常高兴。心想我只不过试试他，可这小伙子倒也勇敢，真的把一筒通梢的竹子找来了，可见他对我的爱情是真心的，就同意和他结为夫妇。两人勤奋劳动，和睦相处，自由自在地过着生活。

搜集整理：滕茂芳　张亚萍

编者按： 穷小子娶富家女，这个故事总是可以吸引人。哪怕是现代社会，也有不同的变形版本。可能不同的是，有些故事用了爱情，比如电影《泰坦尼克号》；有些故事用了智慧，比如上述的这个故事。

用点技巧，用点胆量和执着，就可以抱得美人归。尤其是故事里，姑娘生气不肯开口说话，小伙子故意逗女孩儿说话，这简直值得很多电视剧学习。这样的剧本经过适当的改编，可以成为流量的密码。

分析民间故事和影视剧的异曲同工之处，让我们看到，影视作品具有我们意想不到的口头传统文化特征。

A Story of a Bamboo That Is Hollow All the Way Through the Top

There was a handyman who served in the Baiwan family. Every day, he diligently guarded the barns without ever slacking off. He was an honest and hardworking man.

After helping for a while, he fell deeply in love with the young lady of the Baiwan family. However, being just a handyman, he dared not confess his feelings. The young lady was always cheerful and outgoing, and didn't treat him like a servant.

One day, while the handyman was guarding the barns, a few mice sneaked in and ate the grain. He was heartbroken. Soon after, he caught the rat king and gave it a lesson, "You come here every day to steal the grain. Today, I caught you. You want to die or live"? Begging for mercy, the rat king said, "I want to live. Please let me go". The handyman replied, "You can live, but only if you promise to help me with something in the future". The rat king eagerly agreed, "What do you want me to do? Just give me the orders, and I will obey you". The handyman said, "Send your mice to empty the soil from the belly of the big Buddha in the temple. Empty it without leaving any trace so that the Buddha remains undamaged". The rat king gladly promised, "That's a small task. I will do it". Then the handyman let it go.

The rat king went back and gathered the little mice to completely empty the mud from the Buddha's belly.

The wife of the Baiwan family was a Buddhist. Every day, she went to the temple to make offerings and worship the Buddha. The handyman knew when the old lady usually went to the temple, so he went there in advance and quietly hid inside the Buddha's belly. When the old lady came to make offerings, he said, "The marriage of the young lady of Baiwan family can only be successful if she marries the poor handyman from their house. Otherwise, misfortune will fall on the family".

The woman heard these words every time she went to the temple and took them to heart. She returned home and told Baiwan what she had heard, but he dismissed it. However, she secretly thought, "This handyman is diligent, honest and clever. It might work out if my daughter marries him. But he is just a handyman".

After some time, a government official came, wanting to marry the young lady of Baiwan. During their conversation, everything they said was overheard by the rat king. He went and informed the handyman about the matter, and said, "They have set a time and place. On a certain day and hour, they will prepare a horse at a specific location. You should also prepare a horse at that time, get dressed up, and wait at the decided place".

Following the rat king's instructions, the handyman secretly prepared a good horse and arrived at the place. In short, the young lady appeared. As her father had arranged the meeting in the night, she couldn't clearly see who came to pick her up. Assuming it was the person she was supposed to marry, she rode along. The person who came to propose to her couldn't find her and returned home because he had never seen her before.

The handyman took the young lady far, far away. When it was dawn and they were both tired from the journey, so they finally rested. The young lady could now clearly see the person who brought her and realized it wasn't the intended groom, but her family's handyman. Furious and unhappy, she felt miserable. What could she do? So she remained gloomy and silent.

She had considered that this handyman had good character, was honest and reliable, and was handsome and steady in his work. She had liked him before, but he was a handyman while she was the young lady of the Baiwan family, so she was afraid of losing face for her family if she married him. It would also bring shame upon herself. Thinking about these things, she dismissed the idea. Now, what should she do? She pondered hard and felt exhausted, so she stayed silent and sorrow, unwilling to speak to him because of frustration.

When they got hungry and wanted to cook, the handyman intentionally used only two rocks to hold the pot. But a pot need to be placed on three legs, so it was impossible to stabilize the pot. He played around with it, teasing the young lady on purpose. Seeing him struggle for a while without being able to set the pot correctly, she impatiently said, "You fool, the pot needs three legs. How can it be stable with only two"?

The handyman felt itchy in heart and was very happy when he heard the first words from the young lady, and quickly set up the pot to cook. He intentionally hung the spoon on his waist, and after cooking for a while, he pretended to look for the spoon everywhere. The young lady, impatiently, said, "You fool. The spoon is hanging on your waist, why are you searching everywhere for it"? This made the handyman joke the young lady into saying the second sentence, and the tensed atmosphere became a bit warmer, and he secretly laughed to himself.

At this point, the young lady had no choice. She couldn't go back anymore, and it would be embarrassing to see people there if she did. So the young lady came up with a difficult question to test his heart, she said to the young man, "If you really have feelings for me, then you must find a bamboo that is hollow all the way through the top. Only then can we get married".

After hearing this, the handyman desperately searched for the bamboo.

As he walked around, he arrived at a temple where a monk lived. He asked the monk, "Where can I find a bamboo that is hollow all the way through the top?" The monk thought for a moment and said, "Such a bamboo does not exist in the real world. However, you might find it in the Magical Mountain. It is deep in the dense forest, and you will have to overcome many difficulties and dangers to find it".

Upon hearing this, the handyman was delighted and hurriedly walked towards the deep parts of the dense forest. He overcame many difficulties and dangers, and finally climbed up the Magical Mountain, where he found a bamboo that is hollow all the way through the top.

When the young man returned with the bamboo, the young lady was overjoyed. She thought to herself, after all, she was just testing him, but he was so brave that he actually found a bamboo that was hollow all the way through the top. It showed that his love for her was sincere, so she agreed to marry him. The two of them lived a harmonious life, working diligently and getting along well with each other.

螺蛳妹

相传很久以前,在山清水秀、绿竹成荫的大盈江畔,有一个阿昌族寨子。在寨边一个孤零零的破草房里,住着一个孤儿,他勤劳忠厚,过惯了苦日子,什么苦也吃得,大家都叫他"苦得"。

苦得的父母临终前说:"苦儿,父母什么也没留给你,以后的日子就全靠你的两只手了。冷了,这破草房能挡风;渴了,水槽里有水。"苦得的全部家产只有这间笋叶挡风的草屋,一个水槽和土灶上的一口破铁锅。此后,苦得靠帮人打短工过活。田里活不论犁地、栽秧,他样样会干。不论春夏秋冬、刮风下雨,谁也没见过苦得有一点闲空。收工时从不空手,下田,背来螺蛳;上山,扛回柴禾。苦得虽然起早贪黑地干,可是仍然穷得没半文钱,衣服补丁压补丁,好像老牛的"千层肚"。贪心的财主不但故意少给工钱,而且连顿饭也不管。晚上下田回来,他总是拖着疲惫不堪的身体,满身泥水,摇摇晃晃地走进黑洞洞的草屋。屋里冷冷清清、空空荡荡,一点儿热气也没有,寂寞凄凉极了。当他坐在灶边的石头上想喘口气的时候,耳边的蚊子又来缠着他,不知是像小和尚念经书还是老秀才读古书,没完没了地"哼哼"。火塘是苦得唯一的伙伴,而螺蛳就是他最好的美餐。苦得叹了一口气,点着火,边烤衣服边做饭——苦得的"饭"就是煮一锅螺蛳,放一把杂粮,再放些辣子、酸笋,酸酸辣辣混一顿。在孤苦与贫寒之中,他过了一年又一年。苦娃娃熬成了小伙子,可还是逃不脱一个"苦"字。

转眼间又到了大年三十。俗语说:穷人怕过年,富人盼过年。寨里的有钱人家杀猪宰鸡,穿新衣,换新鞋。孩子们打秋千,放爆竹……热热闹闹,好不快活。苦得一个人待在屋里,冷火熏烟地守着半死不活的火塘发愣。他想换件衣服,可是找来找去,不是破的,就是烂的;最好的一件也是穿得上脱不下。苦得想:过年穿不上好衣服就算了,可得吃顿年饭。

太阳已升到山顶上,苦得才背起扁帕出门,他想唱几句山歌解解愁闷,就边走边吆喝着:"可怜,可怜,真可怜,找顿螺蛳过个年。"腊月时节,田里的稻谷都割完了,田坝里的水也干了;只有河沟、浸水塘里才有螺蛳。平时苦得下河从不空手的,一会儿准能拣半扁帕。可今天他从河头拣到坝尾,又从坝尾拣到河头,却连个螺蛳壳也没看见!真倒霉,腿跑酸了,肚子饿了,太阳快落山了,还是两手空空。苦得只好洗了洗手脚,爬上河岸往家走。走到一个水井边,突然发现粘了一脚泥巴,低头一瞧,只见水塘在"嘟,嘟"冒泡。仔细看,那清凌凌的水里有双双对对的小鱼在围着一个大螺蛳戏游。那螺蛳足有鸡蛋大,螺壳上裹着一层青苔,宛如一位穿着绿衣青裙的姑娘,螺盖还在一张一合地翕动着,仿佛要和自己说话。苦得好奇地蹲下来,看了又看。他把它捞出捧在手心里再仔细一瞧,那螺蛳越发出奇了——像是对苦得微微含笑,又好似含着脉脉深情,苦得看得着了迷,竟连疲劳和饥饿也忘了。他手捧螺蛳,背着空扁帕喜滋滋地回到家里,赶快把这个奇异的螺蛳养在水槽里。他虽然饿着肚子过了大年夜,但他仿佛觉得屋里好像多了什么,不那么寂寞了。每天清早出门之前,晚上回来以后,他都要看看水槽里的螺蛳,给它换上新鲜水。

一天,苦得下田遇上了大雨,回来又累又饿,而且浑身上下又弄得湿淋淋的。他边走边想:回到家一定要先给螺蛳换水,然后,是先换衣服还是先做饭呢?一想到饭,他直咽口水,肚子"咕咕"地叫得更厉害了,身上也冷得打抖。可是他一进门,就看见火塘里闪耀着红红的火苗,一股暖洋洋的热气扑面而来。他发现屋地也打扫过了,一种馋人的香味诱使他向灶边走去,他揭开锅盖一看:嘿!是热腾腾的饭菜,白花花的米饭,还有肉、鱼。苦得顾不得再想什么,端起碗来狼吞虎咽地大吃起来。这样香甜的饭菜,他还是头一回吃哩。吃饱之后,他又去换衣服,怪啦,他竹笆床上那几件又脏又烂的破衣服都给洗得干干净净,缝补得整整齐齐,折得规规矩矩地放在枕边。苦得又惊又喜。他想:是谁扫的地、做的饭呢?苦得呀,莫非是天上的神仙可怜你命苦?……他翻来覆去想了很久很久。

第二天清早一起来,苦得就先看螺蛳,那螺蛳像是对他微微含笑,又好似脉脉深情。苦得给它换了水,恋恋不舍地离开了水槽。他到邻居家打听:"大娘,昨天是您帮我烧火做饭的吗?"大娘说:"苦儿呵!如今的世道,连自己都顾不过来,哪有时间帮你做呢?"苦得又到另一位邻居家去问:"嫂嫂,昨天是你帮我扫地、补衣服的吗?"大嫂说:"苦兄弟呀,大嫂拖儿带女连门都出不去,想帮你也难得帮呀!"苦得问遍了所有的穷苦乡亲，都没有结果。

直到第三天，苦得回来，屋里还是红通通的火塘，热腾腾、香喷喷的饭菜。苦得越发觉得蹊跷了：这到底是怎么回事呢？又是谁有这样好的心肠帮助我呢？一定要弄个水落石出。

第四天，苦得故意在家里磨蹭，快到晌午时，也没什么动静，他才拿起绳子、扛着扁担假装上山砍柴，走出一二里路，回头一看，他家的屋顶上冒出了一缕炊烟。他马上返回来，从后檐爬上房顶，轻轻扒开茅草从草缝往下看，只见一个如花似玉的姑娘，穿着绿布衫，青毡裙，有十五六岁光景，她正在炒菜呢！苦得被眼前的情景惊呆了，两只眼睛直愣愣地瞪着看……当他明白了自己还在房顶上的时候，便不顾一切地跳下来，一步跨进房门，可是屋里连个人影也没有，他四下看了又看，只见那水槽里的水闪动着粼粼波纹……

又一天清早，苦得一点声色不露，照常给螺蛳换水，然后又背着扁帕走出家门。走出去不远又转来，悄悄地爬上房顶，再悄悄地扒开茅草，从缝隙中朝屋里看，他屏住呼吸，眼睁睁地望着那水槽，连眼都不敢眨一下，生怕出一点差错。突然，"哗啦"一声，那螺蛳便从水槽里跳到地上。他清清楚楚地看到：就是那个如花似玉的小姑娘从螺壳里飘然走出，她站在水槽边，对着水里梳理那乌黑发亮的长发，又编起发辫，盘在头上，扎上"绡迈"。多美的姑娘啊！弯弯的眉毛，水汪汪的大眼睛，白净净的脸上有两个酒窝，一对闪光发亮的银耳环从耳边垂下来。苦得几乎要看傻啦，待了好一会儿，他才想起来应该干什么。他轻手轻脚地从房顶上下来，躲在篱笆后面。趁姑娘去灶脚边添柴时，一步跨到水槽边，把螺蛳壳抓在手里。姑娘发现苦得进了屋，慌忙往水槽边走来，可是螺蛳壳已经不在了。姑娘装作要螺蛳壳，捂着脸"呜呜"地"哭"了。苦得本是个老实忠厚的人，平时一见姑娘就脸红，他真的以为姑娘哭了，就傻乎乎地把螺蛳壳还给姑娘。这姑娘却又一下子"嗤嗤"地笑起来，苦得红着脸，痴呆呆地望着姑娘，不知道说什么才好。姑娘见他那股"傻"劲，就开口说："苦得一个人这样起早贪黑地操劳，有多难啊！你要我做你的阿妹，帮你做饭洗衣吗？"苦得还以为是做梦，苦了这么多年，今天真是螃蟹上树——巴（扒）都巴不得哟！这个在冰冷的苦水中泡了十多年的硬汉子，居然流下了泪珠。他哽咽了。那话卡在嗓子眼儿出不来，憋了老半天，才叫出一声"阿妹！"他紧紧地握住了螺蛳妹的双手，心里比那火塘里熊熊的火苗还热啊！

时间像大盈江的流水，不知不觉地流过去了。苦得和螺蛳妹胜似亲兄妹，他们相亲相爱，互相帮助，互相体贴。苦得出去帮人种地，姑娘在家做饭、洗衣……虽然还是那样穷，可是日子却快活多了。苦得再不为做饭补衣发愁了，特别是有了个疼他爱他的妹妹。他每天从外面回来，螺蛳妹总要把热腾腾的饭菜送到他的手里，看他一口一口地吃下去。苦得的身上虽说也还是那两件破衣裳颠来倒去地穿，可是却变得干净利落，再不是以前那样的千层牛肚了。每到晚上，苦得睡着了，螺蛳妹还在火塘边给他补衣服，补完衣服，她才回到螺蛳壳中去。乡亲们看着苦得越发干净整洁，脸上也有了笑容，就都夸他。这个说："苦得哥，好漂亮呵，瞧这衣服补得比得上巧姑娘啰！"那个说："哎哟！几天不见，苦得快要变成笑得了！"苦得是个忠厚人，伙伴一夸，"唰"地一下脸就红了，就把螺蛳妹的事一五一十说了出来。伙伴们都为苦得祝贺，贺他得了个好媳妇。苦得的脸更红了，连忙说："不，她是我的阿妹！"大家都劝他快办喜事。苦得晚上回来，偷偷地把螺蛳壳藏了起来，螺蛳妹发现螺蛳壳不见了，就问苦得，苦得壮着胆子对她说："好阿妹，你就别回去了，我们成亲吧！"螺蛳妹含羞不语，用"绡迈"遮了脸，半天才抬起头来，对苦得说："苦哥，阿妹和阿哥的心像天上的星星和月亮永不分离，如大盈江的鱼和水永远在一起，可是我们还没有包头和筒裙啊，等有了包头和筒裙再成亲好吗？"这以后，苦得为准备包头和筒裙，每天下田回来，都带回点麻，螺蛳妹就在松明灯下纺麻线。

螺蛳姑娘的事不知什么时候传到寨主家里。寨主有个好吃懒做的少爷，这个家伙甑子蒸饭找锅粑，香油炒菜找油渣，嘴馋心狠，专门在姑娘身上打主意。这一带的人都叫他"馋猫"。"馋猫"听说苦得家有个相貌出众的螺蛳姑娘，早就口水流得老长，活像猫闻到腥味一样，整天打坏主意。一天苦得上山割麻。馋猫趁机偷偷摸摸地溜到苦得房后躲起来，从篱笆缝往里看：屋里果然有一个非常漂亮的姑娘在做饭。啊呀，在大盈江两岸几十里还没有这样漂亮的姑娘哩！馋猫一连咽了几口涎水，贪婪的眼睛死死盯着姑娘白皙的脸。他早已六神无主，连魂儿都不知飞到哪里去了！当姑娘出屋拿柴烧的时候，馋猫急忙窜到水槽边伸手把螺蛳壳抢过来藏进裤袋。姑娘回来发现屋里有人，连忙找螺蛳壳，却被馋猫拦住了。他嬉皮笑脸地凑到螺蛳姑娘跟前，咧起大嘴唱道：

可怜可怜真可怜,
茅草屋里住神仙。
家中没得半升米,
腰里没得半文钱。
衣服穿成莲花瓣,
毡裙穿成条条线。
脚冷灶灰埋不暖,
头冷蓑衣盖不严。
可怜不过螺蛳妹,
珍珠掉进了烂泥坑。
姑娘见他是个丑陋下流的无赖,厌恶极了,便以歌相答:
七怪哉来八怪哉,
螺蛳背上长青苔。
螺蛳无脚能走路,
寨主睡着会发财。
苦哥螺妹苦相爱,
不爱钱财爱人才。
荷花开在荷塘里,
年年月月并蒂开!
那馋猫想打动姑娘的心,竟扯起那乌鸦般的嗓子胡诌起来:
好个凤凰关鸡笼,
莫如随我住金楼。
不爱钱财爱什么?
妹妹快快跟我走!
螺蛳妹怒不可遏,厉声怒斥:
可惜金楼千般好,
不住人来住野兽。
蛤蟆吞象枉费心,
快将螺壳还我手。
馋猫听了恼羞成怒,竟把螺蛳壳摔在地上用脚踩烂,凶相毕露地冲着姑娘吼叫起来:"你跟不跟我走?"他边骂边上前动手拉姑娘,嘴里还说:"这里的山山水水都是我家的。莫说你个小小的螺蛳妹,就是天上的仙姑也要由我挑哩！"螺蛳妹又气又急，多么盼望苦得哥此刻能出现在她的身旁啊！苦得哥啊苦得哥，为什么还不回来呀！当那馋猫龇牙咧嘴如同恶狼一般向她扑来的时候，她再也无处可躲，便猛地向灶边的石头撞过去……

傍晚，苦得挑着麻从山上回来，进门就感到惊异：门边没有阿妹，火塘没有火苗，屋里没有一点光亮。苦得急忙喊了几声："阿妹！阿妹！"可是却没有一点儿动静。苦得走近水槽，发现水槽边有踩烂的螺蛳壳。再往灶脚一看，啊！苦得惊坏了，在昏暗中他看见：螺蛳妹躺在血泊里！锅台上还摆着没有烧好的饭菜……苦得只觉得一阵昏晕，好像有一声霹雳从头上打下来。他泪如泉涌，抱起螺蛳妹连声呼唤："阿妹！阿妹！快醒醒吧，我的可怜的好阿妹！哥哥给你担回麻啦！阿妹呀，快醒来织包头！看看我啊，阿妹——"螺蛳妹虽然还睁着两只大眼睛，可是再也不会醒来了。苦得紧紧抱起螺蛳妹走出家门，走过田埂，跨过水渠，穿过竹林，登上江堤，纵身跳进了大盈江。刹那间，一对儿美丽的小鸟从滚滚的浪花中飞起来，一直飞到寨主家屋顶上，发出凄厉的叫声："螺蛳壳——你外婆！螺蛳鬃——你舅舅！"叫个不停，直叫了三天三夜才飞走。

直到今天，这美丽的小鸟还成对儿地在竹林、树丛间、芭蕉园里边飞边叫："螺蛳壳——你外婆！螺蛳鬃——你舅舅！"声音依然悲愤而凄厉，仿佛在鞭挞一切毁灭忠贞爱情、破坏幸福的恶人！寨主及馋猫虽早已变成粪土，可是对他们罪恶的谴责与诅咒却不知传了多少代，而且只要损人利己、制造灾难与悲剧的丑类还没有在世上绝迹，这悲愤凄厉的鸣叫就永远不会消失。

搜集整理：杨叶茂　何晏文

编者按： 我读了这个故事的开头，却猜错了结局。因为这个故事用了大力气，把一个标准的田螺姑娘讲得很精彩，很扣人心弦。但是，当故事发展到他们没有成为夫妻，而是成为兄妹的时候，才异峰突起，颇有一点措手不及的感觉。

随即，故事开始转向，似乎在衬托着这对男女将会成为夫妻，尤其是有了一个恶霸开始介入，顺理成章应该是夫妻如何胜过恶势力，最终圆满结局。

这里明显田螺姑娘是一个"半人",她理所当然应该有足够的法力,能够轻易摆平一个凡人恶霸。

但是在对歌之后,居然是姑娘撞石自尽,小伙子殉情投江。他们变成一对儿凄凉的鸟儿,控诉人间的罪恶滔天。

从一个平常的民间故事,转变为一个动物故事,里面的悲剧性如同"悲愤凄厉的鸣叫就永远不会消失"。

在看了一些讨人喜欢的迎合大众心理的民间故事之后,这样的一个悲剧,让编者重新审视口头传颂所具备的穿透力。

我猜中的,这应该是一点。

The Story of the Snail Girl

Long ago, in a lush and picturesque region by the serene Daying River, there was an Achang village. On the edge of this village stood a solitary hut, home to an orphan. He was diligent and honest, accustomed to hardship, and able to endure all kinds of suffering. Everyone called him "Ku De", means "the one who suffers".

Ku De's parents, before they passed away, said, "Ku De, we have nothing to leave you. Your future depends entirely on your two hands. When you're cold, this broken hut can shield you from the wind; when you're thirsty, there's water in the trough". Ku De's entire inheritance consisted of this hut, a water trough, and a broken iron pot on the stove. Afterward, Ku De lived by doing odd jobs for others. He could handle anything in the fields—plowing, planting rice. No matter the season, whether it was windy or rainy, no one ever saw Ku De idle. When he finished work, he never returned empty-handed; he would bring back snails from the fields or firewood from the hills. Though Ku De worked from dawn until dusk, he remained extremely poor, with clothes patched so many times that they look like an old ox's stomach. Greedy landlords not only paid him less but also didn't provide a meal. In the evening, when he returned from the fields, exhausted, covered in mud, and staggering into the hut, he found it cold, empty, and desolate. When he wanted to rest, mosquitos bother him again. The only warmth he had was the fire in the hearth, and the only delicacy he had was snails. Ku De sighed, lit the fire, and cooked his meal—a pot of snails with a handful of mixed grains, spiced with chili and sour bamboo shoots. In his lonely and impoverished life, the boy grew into a young man, but he could not escape the fate of suffering.

Another New Year's Eve approached. As the saying goes, "The poors fear the New Year, while the riches look forward to it". The wealthy families in the village slaughtered pigs and chickens, made new clothes, changed shoes, and the children played on swings and set off firecrackers—celebrating joyfully. Ku De, alone in his hut, sat by the half-dead hearth, lost in thought. He wanted to change a different outfit, but found only tattered and torn clothes; even his best one was worn to the point where he could neither put it on nor take it off. Ku De thought, "I may not have good clothes to wear for the New Year, but I must have a New Year's meal".

The sun had risen to the mountaintop when Ku De finally picked up his basket and headed out. He sang a mountain song to relieve his sadness:"Pity, pity, truly pity, Searching for snails for a New Year's feast."

During the twelfth lunar month, the rice in the fields had been harvested, and the water in the paddies had dried up; only in the streams and ponds could snails be found. Normally, Ku De could find snails easily, but that day, he searched from one end of the river to the other, yet didn't find a single snail shell! How unlucky—his legs ached, his stomach growled, and the sun was about to set, yet his hands were still empty. Ku De had no choice but to wash his hands and feet and climb up the riverbank to head back home. As he passed by a well, he noticed some mud stuck to his foot. Looking down, he saw bubbles rising in the water. As he look closer, he saw small fish swimming around a large snail. The snail was the size of an egg, its shell covered in a layer of moss, like a girl in a green dress. The snail's shell moved as if it wanted to speak to him. Curious, Ku De crouched down and examined it closely. He scooped it up and held it in his palm, and the snail seemed even more extraordinary—it was like smiling at Ku De or gazing at him with deep affection. Ku De was mesmerized, he even forgot his fatigue and hunger. He carried the snail home joyfully and placed it in the water trough. Although he spent New Year's Eve with an empty stomach, he felt as if the hut had gained something and wasn't so lonely anymore. Every morning before he went out, and every evening when he returned, he would check on the snail and change its water.

One day, Ku De went to the fields and was caught in a heavy rain. He returned home, exhausted and hungry, and soaked from head to toe. As he walked, he thought, "When I get home, I must change the snail's water first. Then, I should change clothes or cook dinner"? Thinking about food made him swallow his saliva, and his stomach growled even louder, his body shivering from the cold. But when he entered the hut, he saw a warm fire burning in the hearth, a wave of warmth hitting him. He noticed the floor had been swept, and a delicious aroma led him to the stove. When he lifted the pot lid, he found steaming hot food—white rice, meat and fish. Ku De, without thinking, ate the food voraciously. He had never eaten such delicious food before. After eating, he went to change his clothes, and to his surprise, the dirty, tattered clothes on his bamboo bed had been washed, mended neatly, and folded carefully by his pillow. Ku De was both astonished and delighted. He wondered, "Who cleaned the house and cooked the meal? Could it be that a deity took pity on me?" He thought about it for a long, long time.

The next morning, Ku de went to check on the snail, which seemed to smile at him. He changed the snail's water and left the hut. He asked his neighbor, "Auntie, did you help me cook yesterday?" The auntie replied, "Oh, Ku De, with the way things are, I can barely manage myself". Ku De went to another neighbor and asked, "Sister-in-law, did you help me clean the house and mend my clothes yesterday"? The sister-in-law replied, "Brother Ku De, with the children I need to care for, I can hardly leave the house, even if I wanted to help you". Ku De asked all his poor neighbors, but no one knew.

On the third day, when Ku De returned to hut, the hearth was again burning brightly, and there was hot, fragrant food. Ku De grew more curious, "What's going on? Who could help me like this? I must find out".

On the fourth day, Ku De pretended to leave as usual, but stayed near the house. Almost noon, nothing had happened, he picked up a rope and carried a basket, pretended to go up the mountain to cut firewood. After walking a mile or two, he turned back and saw smoke rising from his roof. He quickly climbed up the roof from the back of his hat, and quietly peeked through the thatch. He saw a beautiful girl inside, around fifteen or sixteen years old, dressed in a green blouse and blue skirt, was cooking. Ku De was stunned by the sight. When he realized that he was still on the roof, he quickly jumped down, rushed into the house, but found no one inside. He looked around and only saw the water in the trough rippling.

Another morning, Ku De changed the snail's water as usual and then left the house. He walked a short distance before returning and quietly climbed onto the roof, peeked through the thatch. Holding his breath, he stared at the trough, afraid to blink, feared he might miss something. Suddenly, with a splash, the snail jumped from the trough to the ground. Ku De saw the same beautiful girl emerged from the shell, gracefully stepped out from the snail shell. She stood by the trough, combing her long, black hair and braiding it, then coiling it on her head and tying it with a silk ribbon. What a beautiful girl she was! Arched eyebrows, big, watery eyes, and dimples on her pretty face, with a pair of shining silver earrings dangling from her ears. Ku De was almost mesmerized, staring for a long time before he remembered what he was supposed to do. He carefully climbed down from the roof and hid behind the fence. As the girl went to the stove to add firewood, Ku De quickly stepped to the trough and grabbed the snail shell. The girl noticed Ku De had entered the house and hurried to the trough, but the shell was gone. The girl pretended to cry, covered her face and "weeping" loudly. Ku De, an honest and kind-hearted man, truly believed she was crying and foolishly returned the snail shell to her. The girl then burst into laughter, and Ku De, blushing, stared at her, did not know what to say. The girl, saw his "silly" expression, and said, "Ku De, you've worked so hard all alone, day and night. Would you like me to be your sister and help you to cook and wash"? Ku De thought he was dreaming. After suffering for so many years, today felt like a miracle—something he had always longed for, but never dared to hope for! This man, who had endured cold and hardship for over ten years, shed his tears. The words stuck in his throat, and after a long struggle, he finally called out, "Sister"! He tightly held the Snail Girl's hands, and his heart was warmer than the blazing fire in the hearth.

Time went by just like the waters of the Daying River. Ku De and the Snail Girl were closer than siblings; they loved and cared for each other, helping and supporting one another. Ku De would go out to help others plant fields, while the girl stayed at home cooking and washing. Though they were still poor, life became much happier. Ku De no longer worried about cooking and mending clothes, especially with a sister who cared for and loved him. Every day when he returned, the Snail Girl would always bring hot food to his hands and watch him eat. Although Ku De still wore the same old patched clothes, they were now clean and tidy. Every night, after Ku De fell asleep, the Snail Girl would sit by the hearth, mending his clothes. Only after finished would she returned to her snail shell. The villagers noticed that Ku De becoming neater and cleaner, with a smile on his face, and they all praised him. One would say, "Brother Ku De, how handsome you look! Look at those clothes, patched better than any skilled girl could do"! Another would say, "Wow! Haven't seen you for a few days, Ku De is about to turn into Xiao De (Happy boy)"! Ku De, being a simple and honest man, would blush whenever his friends praised him, and he would tell them the story of the Snail Girl, explaining everything in detail. His friends all congratulated him, said that he had found a good wife. Ku De blushed even more and quickly said, "No, she's my sister"! Everyone urged him to get married quickly. That evening, when Ku De returned home, he secretly hid the snail shell. When the Snail Girl noticed the shell was missing, she asked Ku De about it. Ku De gathered his courage and said to her, "Dear sister, don't go back to the shell; let's get married"! The Snail Girl shyly covered her face with her silk scarf. After long time, she finally looked up and said to Ku De, "Brother Ku De, we are inseparable as the stars and the moon in the sky, as the fish and water in the Daying River, but we don't have the things required for the wedding yet. Let's wait until we have them to get married, shall we"? After that, to prepare the headscarf and pleated skirt, every day after returning from the fields, Ku De would bring back some hemp, and the Snail Girl would spin the hemp into thread under the light of oil lamp.

  The story of the Snail Girl somehow reached the village chief's family. The chief had a lazy and gluttonous son. This fellow, was greedy and malicious, always flirted with girls. The people of the area called him "Greedy Cat". When the Greedy Cat heard that Ku De had a beautiful Snail Girl, his eager grew just like a cat smelling fish, and he began plotting. One day, when Ku De went up the mountain to cut hemp, the Greedy Cat sneaked in to Ku De's house and hid, peeking through the fence. Absolutely true, there was an exceptionally beautiful girl cooking inside. There was no girl as beautiful as her! Greedy Cat's greedy eyes fixed on the girl's pretty face. He lost his soul in watching her! When the girl stepped outside to get firewood, the Greedy Cat quickly rushed to the water trough, grabbed the snail shell, and hid it in his pocket. When the girl returned and saw someone stay in the house, she immediately looked for the snail shell, but the Greedy Cat blocked her path. With a sly grin, he approached the Snail Girl, his mouth opened widely, and sang:

 "Pity, pity, truly pity,

 A deity lives in a thatched hut.

 No rice at home, no money in pocket,

 Clothes worn to tatters; skirts threadbare.

 Cold feet buried in ashes that won't warm,

 A head covered in straw clothes can't protect.

 Pitiful, pitiful Snail Girl,

 Like a pearl lost in a muddy pit."

  The girl saw that he was an ugly, shameless rogue, and responded with a song:

 "So many wonders out in the world,

 Moss grows on the snail's shell.

 A snail without legs can walk,

 A chief could get wealth just by dreaming.

Ku De and Snail Girl love each other dearly,
We don't love for riches, but for one's heart.
The lotus blooms in the pond,
Year after year, lotuses bloom together!"

But the Greedy Cat, trying to win her over, shamelessly sang again, his voice like a crow's:

"Such a phoenix in a chicken coop,
Why not come to live in a golden tower?
If not for riches, then for what?
Sister, hurry and come with me!"

The Snail Girl, furious and disgusted, rebuked him:

"Though the golden tower is splendid,
It's fit only for beasts, not people.
As if a toad is trying to swallow an elephant—futile effort!
Give me back my snail shell!"

Angered by her rejection, the Greedy Cat furiously threw the snail shell to the ground, stomping on it until it was crushed. He then shouted at the girl, "Will you come with me or not?" He cursed as he moved closer, grabbed at the girl, and said, "The mountains and rivers here all belong to my family. Not even a fairy from the heavens can escape my grasp"! The Snail Girl was both angry and anxious, desperately wishing Ku De would appear beside her at that moment. "Brother Ku De, oh Brother Ku De, why haven't you come back yet?" she cried in her heart. As the Greedy Cat grinned wickedly like a wolf, approached her, she had nowhere to escape. In her despair, she threw herself toward the stone near by the stove...

That evening, when Ku De returned home, carrying hemp from the mountain, he was shocked. The hut was dark, the hearth cold, and there was no sign of his sister. Anxiously, he called out, "Sister! Sister"! but there was no response. Approaching the water trough, he saw the crushed snail shell on the ground. Ku De was horrified. Near the stove, he found her. In the dim light, he saw the Snail Girl lying in a pool of blood! The half-cooked food was still on the stove... Ku De felt as if a bolt of lightning had struck him. Tears streamed down his face as he held the Snail Girl, called out desperately, "Sister! Sister! Wake up, my dear sister! I've brought back the hemp! Sister, wake up and weave the headscarf! Look at me, sister—". The Snail Girl, though her eyes remained open, would never wake again. Ku De, trembling with grief, gently picked her up and walked out of the house. He crossed the fields, stepped over the ditches, passed through the bamboo groves, climbed the riverbank, and holding her tightly, leapt into the rushing waters of the Daying River. In that instant, a pair of beautiful birds flew out from the roaring waves, soaring up to the village chief's rooftop, crying out mournfully: "Spiral shell, your grandmother! Snail snail, your uncle!" They cried for three days and three nights before flying away.

To this day, these beautiful birds can still be seen flying in pairs through the bamboo groves, among the trees, and in the banana gardens, crying out the same chant: "Spiral shell, your grandmother! Snail snail, your uncle!" Their cries remain as mournful and fierce as ever, as if condemning all those who destroy true love and happiness! Though the village chief and the Greedy Cat have long turned to dust, the condemnation and curse of their evil deeds have been passed down for generations. And as long as there are people who harm others for their own gain, creating misery and tragedy, the sorrowful, angry cries of these birds will never fade away.

宝剑

从前，有一户人家，父母已经去世，剩下两兄弟，靠打柴禾糊口度日。后来，哥哥娶了媳妇，嫂嫂脸色黝黑，样子也不美。弟弟到娶媳妇的时候了，哥哥请人给他讲了几个姑娘，弟弟一个也不要。弟弟白天砍柴，比往常更加卖力；晚上坐在芭蕉树下，吹箫、弹弦、散苦心。一晃又是三年，银钱攒了一小包。弟弟身强力壮，勤劳忠厚，上下二寨的姑娘，都把深情的眼波往他身上溜。

樱桃花开了，蜜蜂"嗡嗡"地飞来采花。一天凌晨，弟弟突然"拐"来了一个姑娘。新娘子长得面似荷花眉似柳，水灵灵的黑眼珠，苗条的身段，真是花见花开，大石头见了也要称赞。哥哥瞄瞄弟弟的媳妇，又看看自己的妻子，一个像凤凰，另一个像打抱鸡，无法相比，越看心里越不是滋味。不久，哥哥再也憋不住气了，想把弟弟的媳妇抢占过来。哥哥整整想了三天三夜，总找不出一个合适的借口。

有一天，哥哥到山箐里砍柴，看见一堵高高的陡崖下，有一个黑乎乎的石洞。他跑去一看，有簸箕大的一个石窟窿，里面黑咕隆咚的，不知有多深，只听风声呼呼。哥哥看着石风洞，埋藏在心里的邪念油然而生，脸上一丝阴冷的笑纹倏然闪过。他挽衣捋袖，东抓一把树叶，西扯一抱干草，很快把石风洞掩盖起来。

哥哥回到家，便装模作样地说："弟弟，爹妈去世后，我俩连口舌都没拌过一句。今天，老天有眼照看，我瞧见一只大野猪，钻在石崖下的草堆里。到那里，你使力按，我用尖刀戳，杀翻了，不要说吃肉，还得晒干巴。卖了干巴，先给你买一件新衣裳。"弟弟被哥哥说得心里热乎乎的。

弟兄俩来到大石崖下，看到堵在洞口的茅草树叶被风吹得轻轻摇动，哥哥便趁机哄骗说："你看，野猪还在草里一拱一拱的，你赶紧扑上去！"话音刚落，弟弟几个箭步跨了上去。弟弟扑在草叶上，"噗突"一声，就掉下石风洞去了。哥哥走近洞旁，伸头一看，弟弟已经无声无息。哥哥阴郁的脸上，霍然泛起了笑容。他连忙折转身，活像只撵山的狗，连忙跑回了家。

弟弟掉下石风洞后，只听耳边"呼呼"的风声响，睁开眼皮一看，恰好落在一块空旷的平地上，这里虽然不见日月星辰，却是四面崖壑幽静，中间一层淡淡的烟霭。弟弟定眼一看：树，才有一人来高，酸把果，只有筷头大；荆竹最高，也只有几尺长。四周的田园，每一畦有桌面大，谷秆有五寸长；一穗谷子，才有二三粒。弟弟用手抹去谷粒，放进嘴里一嚼，香甜可口，好似一颗蜜糖。弟弟左抹右捋，三下五除二，一排田的谷子，被弟弟嚼吃完了。

这时一群田主人赶来了，只有小挂灯高。灯挂人看见弟弟五大三粗，吓得远远地站着，不敢挨近。弟弟"哈秋"一声喷嚏，灯挂人听了，如雷贯耳，惊恐万状，统统跑进了树林。

弟弟看着金黄的谷粒，舔着嘴唇上黏着的谷汁，口水又来了。他伸手去抹谷子，一把一把地塞进嘴里。躲在树丛里的灯挂人，看见弟弟侵吞他们的粮食，一个个气得呐喊乱叫，一阵骚动过后，只见灯挂人手拿弯弓，肩扛茅草箭，向弟弟围拢过来。灯挂人搭箭射来，扎在弟弟脸上，像跳蚤叮、蚊虫蜇，血不出，皮不绽。射在身上，连麻布衣也穿不透。灯挂人把茅草箭射完后，弟弟便拾起来，恰好拴得一抱。弟弟用手举起茅草箭，准备向灯挂人投去，转念一想，杀生害命，怪可怜的，就从身上摸出火镰，擦着火，把茅草箭全烧了。

弟弟看见茅草灰里，有一条红光闪烁。他扒开茅草灰，忽然露出一柄宝剑，银光闪闪，宝气袭人。弟弟收拾起宝剑，解下花带，系住剑柄，挎在身上。他心想：有宝剑在身，一定会找到回家的路。他东寻西觅，终于看见高高的岩壁上有一个洞，正是他自己掉进来的地方。可是洞高壁陡，没有石阶，没有攀援物，要想爬出去，没门没路。弟弟环顾四周，只有颤巍巍的荆竹还长点，就用宝剑砍了一棵，削去枝叶，倚在岩壁上，可惜还差着三九二十七尺。弟弟抬头瞄竹尖，过一会长高一截，再过一会，又长高一截。弟弟仰酸了脖颈，刚低头眨会儿眼，荆竹已搭在石洞口了。砍来时只有杯子粗的荆竹，转眼间变得有埋桑竹粗了。弟弟手扒竹节，翘起双脚，想顺着竹竿爬上去，才爬上一尺多，荆竹又摇又摆，滑溜溜的，弟弟累得气喘吁吁，手酸腿软，叹着气下来了。

弟弟坐下来歇息，心里十分苦闷，咋个才得出去呢？他拧紧眉头左思右想，还是没有办法。弟弟用宝剑砍来一截手拇指粗的荆竹，削成竹箫，用嘴吹着箫儿散心。悦耳的竹箫声，像一股凉凉的清风，在空气里荡漾，慢慢飘向四周，飘出了石洞。这时一只大竹溜老鼠，正在洞口嚼着茅草根，听到竹箫的声音，非常惊奇，就钻进洞口，拖着三根尾巴，顺着搭在洞口的竹尖，爬进洞里来了。

竹溜老鼠爬到弟弟身旁，看见他嘴里含着竹箫，发出动听的声音，竹溜老鼠像吃到了甜瓜籽，心肝五脏都舒服极了。竹溜老鼠咂咂嘴，说道："啊！我嚼过多少嫩笋，啃过多少竹根，还不知道竹竿儿会叫呢！"接着，竹溜老鼠爬到弟弟身上，扒着他的手，说道："喂！你的竹箫借我吹吹吧！"他说："不行，你嘴尖毛长，屁股长着三根尾巴，妖不妖，怪不怪的，会把我的竹箫拿跑。"竹溜老鼠恳求说："你还是借我吹一下吧。"弟弟嫌竹溜老鼠纠缠，干脆叫它死了心，就说："你能带着我从竹竿爬出洞外，竹箫送给你。"

竹溜老鼠听了，高兴得扬眉竖耳，连声答应："好！好！你拉着我的一根尾巴，我爬一截，你跟着爬一截。但你可千万不能笑啊！"

弟弟满口应承："放心吧，我不会笑的。"

弟弟拉着竹溜老鼠的一根尾巴，往上爬。弟弟心想，竹溜老鼠会有这么大的力气，真神。一面想着，一面抬头看去，只见老鼠身子一拱一拱地，十分吃力，忍不住"噗嗤"一声笑了出来，竹溜老鼠尾巴"突"地一声断了，弟弟也滑了下来。

竹溜老鼠折下来，满脸不高兴，冲着弟弟说："你呀，说话不算数！我的尾巴也被你拉断了一根。"

弟弟看着竹溜老鼠难过的面孔，也很懊悔，说："下次我不笑了。"

弟弟又拉着竹溜老鼠的第二根尾巴，开始往上爬。爬上去一截，弟弟看见竹溜老鼠肚子一鼓一鼓地，忍不住又"噗嗤"一声笑了出来。第二根竹溜老鼠尾巴，又"突"地一声断了。

竹溜老鼠真的生气了，眼睛睁得鼓圆鼓圆的，警告弟弟说："你再笑的话，剩下的这根尾巴一断，你就出不去了，只好死在洞里。"

弟弟知道，再笑一次，就真糟了，连忙发誓说："我再也不笑了。"

于是弟弟拉着竹溜老鼠的最后一根尾巴，闭着眼睛，一步一步地往上挣，终于爬出了石风洞。

竹溜老鼠得了竹箫，高兴得一会儿手舞足蹈，一会儿蹲在羊欠蓬下，

"嘀嘀嘟嘟"地吹开了。清脆的竹箫声，逗得山中的雀鸟，都展开翅膀飞来听；逗得正在吃草、饮水的麂子、马鹿，竖着耳朵听；引得落在树枝上的腊鹤雀，妒火中烧。心尖都是主意的腊鹤雀，抖抖翅膀，"噗噜"一声飞到竹溜老鼠面前，又是点头，又是哈腰，装出羡慕的样子，操着动听的声音，说道："老鼠哥哥呀！你的好竹箫，借给我乐一乐吧。"竹溜老鼠见腊鹤雀矫揉造作，装腔作势，很不放心，说："腊鹤雀呀，你有翅膀天上飞，我靠四腿地上跑。你哄骗了我，我不是落得个猫啖尿泡空喜欢吗！"腊鹤雀继续用花言巧语，引诱竹溜老鼠上当："哎，你双手拉住我的一只翅膀，我就飞不动了。我吹一会儿就还你。"竹溜老鼠听腊鹤雀说得情真意切，面容可掬，以假当真，就把竹箫递给腊鹤雀。腊鹤雀手疾眼快，接过竹箫，翅膀使劲一扇，双脚夹住竹箫，"噗噜"一声，飞上了天。可怜的竹溜老鼠只扯下几片羽毛。

　　竹溜老鼠眼看心爱的竹箫被骗走了，伤心得痛哭流涕。不几天，就把眼皮哭肿了。据说，从此以后，竹溜老鼠的眼睛就变小了，眼皮总像是肿肿的样子。

　　腊鹤雀把竹箫骗到手后，天天兴高采烈地吹呀吹，结果连它原来的叫声都忘记了。所以，如今腊鹤雀的叫声，很像吹竹箫的声音。

　　弟弟从石风洞出来后，拔起脚步，就往家走。挎在身上的宝剑，闪射出一道道金光，惊得风也停止了喘气，吓得飞禽走兽不敢发出声响。

　　哥哥在家门口，望见山坡上走来一个熟悉的身影，身上的剑光咄咄逼人，刺得哥哥心寒胆颤。哥哥越看越像弟弟，越像是弟弟，越感到势头不对。他想："这是弟弟的阴魂变作人来报仇？咳！祸到临头，我还是走吧。"哥哥连头都来不及回，就远远地逃走了。

　　弟弟和他的媳妇团聚了，患难之后，小两口更加和睦相爱。

　　祖祖辈辈这样传下：弟弟的宝剑还留在人间。今天，谁也不知道宝剑到底在哪里，只晓得勤劳善良的人一定会得到幸福，心地恶毒的人不会有好下场。

讲述：赵安俊
搜集整理：杨叶生　孙加申

编者按： 这个民间故事也可以安排到动物故事里，因为解释了竹溜老鼠为何眼睛小、眼皮肿；为何腊鹤雀叫声和竹箫相似。

这个故事的口头性体现在开头和结尾呼应，但是非常单薄。乍一看，讲述者应该介绍一下弟弟媳妇的神秘来历，但是自始至终都没有交代。

在山洞里，弟弟进入了小人国的天地，这里也可以展开新故事，但是讲述者快速过渡到逃离洞穴的情节之中。在逃离过程中，又安排了魔豆情节，一根升天的植物。但是这个植物又有新的困难，需要外界的一只三条尾巴的竹鼠帮忙。竹鼠帮忙之后，又进入和腊鹤雀的博弈之中。

之后，故事马上转回到弟弟身上，原以为宝剑会发挥神奇功能。但是故事发展到这里，仅仅凭借剑气就吓跑了哥哥，故事戛然而止。

The Precious Sword

Once upon a time, there was a family, parents had passed away, left two brothers who made a living by gathering firewood. Eventually, the elder brother married, but his wife was dark-skinned and was not beautiful. When it came to the time for the younger brother to marry, his elder brother suggested several women, but he refused them all. The younger brother worked harder than ever during the day, chopping wood, and spent his nights on play instruments under a banana tree to ease his sorrow. After three years, he had saved a small sum of money. He was strong, diligent and kind-hearted, and the girls from the surrounding villages all admired him.

When the cherry blossoms bloomed, bees buzzed around collecting nectar. One early morning, the younger brother suddenly brought home a bride. The bride was as beautiful as a lotus flower, with willow-like eyebrows, sparkling black eyes and slender figure. She was so stunning that even stones would praise her beauty. The elder brother, compared his wife to his brother's, felt increasingly bitter. His wife was like a hen, while his brother's wife was like a phoenix. Unable to suppress his jealousy any longer, the elder brother plotted to take his brother's wife for himself, but he couldn't think of a good excuse.

One day, while cutting wood, the elder brother discovered a dark cave at the base of a steep cliff. The cave was deep and mysterious, with the wind howling. An evil thought formed in his mind, he gathered leaves and dry grass to cover the entrance of the cave.

Went back to home, the elder brother pretended to care and said, "Brother, since our parents passed away, we haven't had a single argument. Today, fortune smiled upon us, and I spotted a large wild boar hiding in the grass beneath a cliff. If we kill it, not only can we eat the meat, but we can also dry some to sell. With the money, I'll buy you a new set of clothes". The younger brother was touched by his brother's words.

    The two brothers went to the cliff. The wind gently swayed the leaves and grass covering the cave entrance. The elder brother urged, "Look, the wild boar is still there! Hurry and catch it"! As soon as the words left his mouth, the younger brother rushed forward, only to fall into the cave. The elder brother peered into the cave, seeing no sign of his brother, and a sinister smile appeared on his face. He quickly turned around and ran home.

    After falling into the cave, the younger brother heard wind rushing by and found himself on an open plain. Although there were no signs of the sun, moon, or stars, the area was surrounded by towering cliffs, with a faint mist hanging in the air. The trees were only as tall as a person, the fruits were as small as the tip of a chopstick, and the tallest bamboo barely reached a few meters. The fields were tiny, with stalks of grain only five inches long, each ear of grain holding only two or three kernels. The younger brother picked some grains and tasted them; they were sweet and delicious, like honey. He quickly ate up the grain from one entire field.

    Just then, a group of tiny people, each only as tall as a small lantern, arrived. Seeing the large and robust younger brother, they were too frightened to approach. The younger brother sneezed, causing the tiny people to scatter in terror, fleeing into the woods.

    Licking the grain juice off his lips, the younger brother's mouth watered again. He reached out to grab more grain, stuffing it into his mouth. The tiny people, angered, gathered with bows and arrows made of straw, and surrounded the younger brother. They shot at him, but the arrows only felt like flea bites or mosquito stings, barely piercing his skin. After the tiny people ran out of arrows, the younger brother collected them, forming a bundle. He considered throwing the arrows back at them but then decided against killing them, feeling pity instead. He took out a flint and set the straw arrows on fire.

As the straw burned, a red glow appeared in the ashes. The younger brother found a shining sword, radiating a brilliant light. He tied the sword to his waist, confident that it would help him find his way home. After searching, he found the hole through which he had fallen. However, the cliff was steep, with no footholds or handholds to climb out. He noticed a trembling bamboo plant and decided to cut it with the sword, using it as a ladder. The bamboo, though initially short, began to grow rapidly. Within moments, it had reached the cave's entrance, but it was too slippery and unstable to climb.

Frustrated, the younger brother sat down to rest, unsure how to escape. He thought long and hard but couldn't find a solution. Finally, he crafted a bamboo flute and began to play it to ease his mind. The melodious sound of the flute drifted out of the cave. A large rat, gnawing on grass roots near the cave entrance, was drawn to the sound. Curious, it entered the cave, dragging its three tails behind it.

The rat was enchanted by the beautiful music and asked the younger brother to let it play the flute. The younger brother was hesitant, worried that the rat might steal his flute, but the rat insisted. Finally, the younger brother said: "If you can help me climb out of this cave, I'll give you the flute."

Hearing this, The rat eagerly agreed, raised his eyebrows and piched up his ears joyfully, and said to the younger brother, "To hold onto my tail, as I climbed up the bamboo, you follow me, but don't laugh at me". The younger orother agreed smoothly, "Don't worry, I will not laugh you". The younger brother followed, but as he watched the rat climbad struggly, he couldn't help but laughing. The rat's tail snapped, and the younger brother fell back down.

The rat was furious, accusing the younger brother of breaking his promise. The younger brother apologized and promised not to laugh again. They tried climbing a second time, but once again, the younger brother laughed, and another tail broke.

The rat, now genuinely angry, warned that if the last tail broke, the younger brother would be trapped in the cave forever. The younger brother vowed to remain serious. Holding onto the last tail, he finally climbed out of the cave.

The rat was overjoyed to get the flute. It danced around and then squatted under a plant, playing the flute with a cheerful "didi- dudu- " tune. The crisp sound of the flute attracted the birds in the mountains, who spread their wings and flew over to listen. The deer and elk, who were grazing and drinking water, pricked up their ears to the sound. Even a waxwing bird sitting on a branch became so jealous. The waxwing, full of schemes, flapped its wings and flew down in front of the rat, nodding and bowing, pretending to be admiring. With a sweet voice, it said, "Brother rat, could you lend me your lovely flute for a bit of fun"?

The rat, seeing the waxwing's false flattery and fake humility, replied, "Waxwing, you can fly in the sky with your wings, while I run on the ground with my four legs. If you trick me, won't I be left with nothing but a bitter regret"?

The waxwing continued with its sweet-talking, trying to coax the rat into giving up the flute. "Oh, if you hold onto one of my wings, I won't be able to fly away. I'll just play the flute for a little while and then give it back to you." The rat, seeing the waxwing's earnest expression, believed it was sincere and handed over the flute.

Quick as a flash, the waxwing grabbed the flute, flapped its wings hard, clutched the flute in its feet, and with a "whoosh", flew into the sky. The poor rat only managed to snatch a few feathers as it flew away.

Watching its beloved flute being stolen, the rat was so heartbroken that it cried bitterly. In a few days, its eyelids became swollen for crying. It's said that ever since then, rats have small eyes that always look a bit swollen.

As for the waxwing, after stealing the flute, it played happily every day, eventually forgetting how to make its original call. And so, now the call of the waxwing sounds is very much like the music of a flute.

After escaping, the younger brother hurried home. The sword on his back glowed with a golden light, causing the wind to stop and the animals to fall silent in fear.

Seeing a familiar figure approaching from the mountain, the elder brother was filled with dread. The sword's light made him tremble with fear, and he fled, thinking his brother's ghost had returned for revenge.

The younger brother reunited with his wife, and after all of the difficulties, their bond grew even stronger.

This story has been passed down through generations: The younger brother's precious sword still exists in the world. Today, no one knows where it is, but everyone believes that those who are hardworking and kind will surely find happiness, but those with wicked hearts will never meet a good end.

神奇的拐杖

　　从前有弟兄俩，哥哥已经娶了媳妇，弟弟才十一二岁。嫂嫂挺俊俏，石榴红的脸蛋，十分艳润，就是个儿小些。俗话说矮人主意多，果真如此，嫂嫂心眼怪多。

　　一天，弟兄俩赶着牲口，去很远的地方。路上，弟弟挺高兴，嘴话蛮多。时而拣起石子，向栖息在树枝上的雀鸟打去；时而扯匹山棕叶，舀来清泉水，捧给哥哥喝。弟弟见哥哥不同往日，闷闷不乐，好生奇怪，就问："哥哥，你今天不安逸吗？"哥哥脸上肌肉抽搐了一下，微微一笑，说声"没什么"，挥起鞭子，装着赶牲口。

　　弟弟哪知道哥哥的心事呢。

　　原来，嫂嫂厌嫌弟弟，三番五次，催促哥哥把弟弟送给人家，免得拖累。昨晚，嫂嫂对丈夫咬耳朵，捏背脊，一会儿甜言蜜语，一会儿刁辣，硬要丈夫把弟弟扔在外乡。丈夫刚要张口，媳妇就用手捂住他的嘴巴，不让他说话。她还恶狠狠地宣称：不把淘累虫打发掉，我不和你同锅吃，不搭你共枕头。

　　弟兄俩吆着牲口走了三天，来到一个寨子，天色挨晚，投宿在路边一户人家。真个无巧不成书，这家老两口，无儿无女，家里包谷、芋头堆成垛，园里青菜绿茵茵。老两口不愁吃不缺穿，日子过得甜甜美美。晚上，弟弟呼噜呼噜地睡了，哥哥深默细想，拿定主意：把弟弟放下给老两口，省得再受媳妇的窝囊气，弟弟也免遭白眼挨虐待。不等天亮，哥哥就轻脚轻手地爬起来，牵着牲口回家了。

　　早上，鸡鸣鸟噪，弟弟醒来不见哥哥，看牲口，全吆走了，拔起脚，就往前赶，追了半天，俯下身子，察看脚迹又不见蹄印。弟弟到处寻找牲口脚印，可是找到天黑，还摸不清哥哥到底从哪条岔道上走，只好找人家过夜。他敲敲一扇门，出来一个妇人。主人见是一个男子，便转过脸："少妇无主，不留客宿。山上有石洞，小哥苦熬一夜吧。"随手关上了柴扉。

弟弟找到山洞，虽然并不宽敞，倒还十分洁净。洞壁下摆着一张石方桌，石桌前还有香条纸火的余烬。弟弟坐在石凳上，用手撑着下巴壳，想开了：有人来敬香献饭，那多好啊！自己也可以求人施舍，沾点光。由于疲于跋涉，倚在石桌上，脑袋一歪睡着了。

冷风刮来，弟弟全身发凉，一个冷颤，睁开了眼皮。定神一看，差点吓了一跳：石桌旁坐着两个老人，鬓发雪白，髯须拂膝，各自扶着一根拐杖，正全神贯注地下棋。弟弟从未见过这么老的人，倒是听哥哥说过，天上是有仙人的，恐怕这就是仙人了，我要仔细瞄瞄。弟弟静静地瞧着老人下棋。突然，其中一个人把棋子"嗒"的一声按下："咳，你不输，我不赢，先垫垫肚子。"说罢，提起拐杖，往地上一跺。嗬！真是神奇，石方桌上顿时摆满了酒肉饭菜。

弟弟看着喷香的筵席，口水不由自主地流出嘴角。他实在忍不住了，就跪在老人面前乞讨：老仙人，给我吃点剩汤剩饭。老仙人伸手把他扶起，让他随心吃。弟弟狼吞虎咽，多好的饭菜，他生来还从未尝过呢！弟弟吃饱后，老仙人摇摇拐杖，桌上的东西，倏地一下不见了。老仙人铺上棋盘，继续对弈。弟弟伏在石桌边，眼皮一合又睡着了。

弟弟醒来，睁开眼睛一看：老仙人不见了，一根拐杖斜倚在石桌边。弟弟拾起拐杖，往地上轻轻一点，石桌上出现了热乎乎的饭菜。弟弟理起筷子，吃够喝足，摇摇拐杖，石桌上又干干净净了。

弟弟扛着仙人的拐杖，欢欢喜喜地往家走去。肚子饿了，拐杖往地上一点，可口的饭菜有了；晚上睡在草棚里，抱着拐杖，全身暖和和的。他起早摸黑，整整走了三天，才回到家。

嫂嫂见弟弟回来了，好脸好嘴没有一个，只听见她在骂咧："泼出去的水，扫出去的粪毛粪草，真是无脸无皮。"弟弟心想：我穿不求你，吃不靠你，让你去咒吧！拿起拐杖往地上一点，一桌香喷喷的肉菜，摆在面前。

夜里，弟弟独自睡在一间房里。他刚闭上眼，就仿佛看嫂嫂那猪肝色的面孔，听见她刺耳的聒噪，心里一番痛楚，眼泪簌簌地淌出来；晃眼又像哥哥站自己跟前，轻声叫唤着"弟弟"，好使人心软。少年瞌睡多，想着想着也就睡着了。

深夜，哥哥经不起媳妇无休无止的挑唆，蹑手蹑脚地走近弟弟的床边，拿走了拐杖。两口子手捧拐杖看，真是不寻常：香檀木光溜溜，点点地,摆肉酒。嫂子鼻子一纵,贪欲如火,咬着牙哼叽:"我要牛马加金银,高房大屋住不赢。若不答应,要把你丢下臭茅坑。"嫂嫂紧捏拐杖往地上一跺,"呼哧"一声,拐杖变成一条大蟒,两口子受不住惊骇,嫂嫂被骇死了,哥哥昏了过去。弟弟闻声赶来,熬了姜汤喂哥哥,哥哥醒来,看到眼前的情景,又惭愧,又惊喜,搂着弟弟边哭边说:好心的人,黄土变成金,没良心的恶人,黄金也会变成土。

讲述:赵招秀

搜集整理:杨叶生 孙加申

编者按: 懦弱的哥哥、无情的嫂子、忠厚的弟弟,构成了一个常见的家庭伦理故事结构。很多情节有始无终,或者说只是一种过渡,完成垫脚作用之后就进入到下一个冲突。

这个故事的篇末言志,引出了有教育意义的谚语"好心的人,黄土变成金,没良心的恶人,黄金也会变成土"。

有一些故事可能是为了显得富有教育意义才会进行这样的总结。这个故事为了有教育意义而进行各种铺垫。但是在各种冲突和线索发生之后,就直奔主题。

The Magical Cane

Once upon a time, there were two brothers. The elder brother was married, while the younger brother was only eleven or twelve years old. The sister-in-law was very pretty. Her rosy cheeks were bright and beautiful, but she was a bit short. As the saying goes, "Dwarves have many ideas." Indeed, the sister-in-law was quite cunning.

One day, the two brothers were herding cattle and they had to travel a long distance. The younger brother was happy and talkative along the way. Sometimes, he picked up stones and threw them at the birds perched on tree branches; other times, he plucked a palm leaf and scooped up spring water to offer his brother a drink. The younger brother noticed that his brother was different from usual, gloomy and frustrated. Feeling puzzled, he asked, "Brother, are you unhappy today"? His brother's face twitched, but then he quickly gave a faint smile and said, "It's nothing". He then raised his whip and continued herding the cattle.

But how could the younger brother know what was on his brother's mind?

The sister-in-law didn't like the younger brother and repeatedly urged her husband to send him away to avoid being a burden. Last night, she spoke sweetly to him and blamed him, insisting that her husband should abandon his younger brother in a foreign village. Just as the husband was about to say something, she covered his mouth with her hand, silencing him. She declared viciously, "I won't eat from the same pot nor share a pillow with you until you get rid of that annoying pest".

After three days of journey with their cattle, the two brothers arrived at a village. It was getting late, so they sought shelter at a household. By coincidence, the elderly couple living there had no children. They had heaps of corn and taro inside their house, and their garden was filled with lush green vegetables. The elderly couple didn't worry about food or clothing; they lived a comfortable and sweet life. That night, the younger brother slept soundly. Meanwhile, the elder brother pondered in silence and decided: "He will leave his younger brother with the elderly couple. This way, the younger brother would be spared from his sister-in-law's complaints and abuses, and the elder brother himself could escape her continuous nagging." Before dawn broke, the elder brother quietly got up, took hold of the cattle, and headed back home.

When the rooster crowed and the birds chirped, the younger brother woke up to find his older brother missing and the cattle herd gone. He hurriedly ran after them for half a day, but there were no hoofprints to be seen. He searched everywhere for traces of the cattle, but soon evening came, and he still couldn't figure out which path his brother had taken. He had no choice but to find a place to spend the night. He knocked on a door, and a woman came out. Seeing it was a young man, she turned away and said, "I'm a woman without a husband, so I can't provide lodging for strangers. There's a cave on the mountain. You can spend the night there, young man".

The younger brother found a cave, although not spacious, which was surprisingly clean. There was a stone table with the remains of incense and paper offerings on it. The younger brother sat on a stone stool, put his chin on his hand, and thought how nice it would be if someone came to offer incense and food. He could also ask for a handout himself. Exhausted from the journey, he leaned against the stone table and slept.

As cold wind blew, a shiver ran through the younger brother's entire body and he opened eyes. He looked closely and was astonished that there were two old men sitting next to the stone table. Their hair was snowy white, and their long beards reached their knees. Each of them held a cane and fully focused on playing chess. The younger brother had never seen people so old, but he did hear from his older brother that there were immortals in the heavens, and these must be the immortals! The younger brother quietly watched the old men play chess. Suddenly, one of them pressed a piece with a "click" sound and said, "Ah, you can't lose, and I can't win. Let's have something to eat first". With that, he lifted his cane and gave it a tap on the ground. Oh! This must be magic! The stone table was instantly filled with delicious food and wine.

The younger brother looked at the appetizing feast, and saliva dripped from the corner of his mouth. Unable to resist any longer, he knelt before the old men and begged, "Dear immortals, please give me some leftovers". An old man reached out and helped him up, allowing him to eat whatever he wanted. The younger brother gobbled up the delicious meal, as it was the best food he had ever tasted! After the younger brother was full, the old man shook his cane, and the things on the table disappeared in a blink of an eye. The old man then spread out the chessboard and continued playing. The younger brother rested his head on the edge of the stone table and fell asleep again.

When the younger brother woke up and opened his eyes, the old men were gone, and a cane leaned against the edge of the table. The younger brother picked up the cane and gently tapped it on the ground, and the stone table was once again filled with hot and tasty food. The younger brother picked up his chopsticks, ate a lot, and shook the cane, made the table clean once more.

The younger brother happily carried the immortals' cane and walked to home. When he was hungry, he tapped the cane on the ground, and delicious food appeared. At night, he slept in a hut, holding the cane and feeling warm. He woke up early and walked for three full days to finally return home.

Upon seeing the younger brother's return, the sister-in-law showed her dislike and muttered, "He really is shameless, like the water being poured out and the dung and weed being swept out". The younger brother thought to himself, "I don't rely on you for clothes or food; you can curse all you want"! He tapped the cane on the ground, and a table full of delicious dishes appeared before him.

At night, the younger brother slept alone in a room. As soon as he closed his eyes, he seemed to see his sister-in-law's pig liver-colored face and hear her uncomfortable, nagging voice. He felt pain in his heart, and tears streamed down. But then, he saw his older brother standing in front of him, called his name tenderly, his heart softened. The young boy was drowsy, and as he kept thinking, he fell asleep.

Late at night, unable to withstand his wife's endless instigation, the elder brother stealthily approached his younger brother's bedside and took away the cane. The couple held the cane in their hands. This cane was unusual, smooth, and bright, just by tapping the ground, it can form a table of meat and wine. The sister-in-law's nose wrinkled, heart full of greed, she gritted her teeth and muttered, "I want cows, horses, gold and silver. I want a big house as well! If you don't agree, I'll throw you into a stinking pit". The sister-in-law tightly gripped the cane and stomped it on the ground. With a "puff" sound, the cane turned into a large serpent. Overwhelmed by fright, the sister-in-law died of fear, and the older brother fainted. The younger brother heard the noise and rushed over to check what had happened. He prepared ginger soup to wake his older brother, who woke up and when he saw the scene before him, felt both ashamed and surprised. He embraced his younger brother, cried, and said, "Kind-hearted people can turn soil into gold, but evil people can turn gold into soil".

瞎子弟弟

　　从前有一家人，爹妈死后留下哥哥、嫂嫂和弟弟。弟弟是个瞎子，又是个瘸子，天天只能坐着吹箫弹弦。嫂嫂对哥哥说："你弟弟什么也不会做，全靠我们砍柴卖草供养他，实在划不着，快背去撂崖子吧。"为了瞎子弟弟，夫妻俩撕咬个没完没了。嫂嫂白天唠叨晚上咒骂，闹得哥哥心烦意乱。

　　一天，哥哥对弟弟说："兄弟，你跟我上山砍柴，往日乌鸦来偷吃我的饭菜，你给我守晌午包。"弟弟说："哥哥，只是我走不得路。"哥哥说："不怕，我背你。"哥哥背着弟弟，弟弟挎着弦子别着箫，上山砍柴。到了柴山，弟弟一会儿吹箫一会儿弹弦，哥哥看着弟弟傻乐的样子，咋个也狠不下心把弟弟撂崖子，那伤天害理的事，万万做不得。傍晚，砍好柴，哥哥背起弟弟回家。

　　嫂嫂看见弟弟，吊着眼丧着脸，跺跺搡搡，摆出一个人吃的饭菜。弟弟看不见，一碗连一碗地吃。哥哥坐在饭桌边，默不作声。

　　第二天，哥哥不得已，又把弟弟背上山砍柴。砍好柴，哥哥看着弟弟无忧无愁的稚脸，不由得伤心恸哭起来。弟弟听到哭声，放下弦子别起箫，以为哥哥背他上山，又要砍柴，心里难受，就说："哥哥，我明天再也不来了，省得连累你。"哥哥看着弟弟天真无邪的面孔，咋个也不忍心下毒手。挨晚，背起弟弟又回家去了。

　　嫂嫂看见弟弟又回来了，好像弯刀割着她的心肝，眼睛珠都要鼓出来了，嘴唇在抽搐，唾沫啐了一口又一口，一会儿骂哥哥是遭瘟的猪，一下骂哥哥温六公丧门星。哥哥气得一宿到亮没合过眼，枕头底下挤得出水。

　　大清早，嫂嫂又拉开破铜烂铁似的嗓门，咋呼着："耳朵咯是岔了？"哥哥知道，媳妇是铁了心铁了肠，再也拗不过了。于是，哄骗弟弟说："弟弟，再帮守一天晌午包，以后再不要你去了。"弟弟不知是计，只好背着弦子别着箫，让哥哥背上山。哥哥把弟弟背到一堵悬崖边，心一横，眼睛一闭,手一松,弟弟被撂下深凹子里去了。

弟弟耳边一阵"呼呼"的风声,软软地落在什么上,轻轻一弹,就晕了过去。原来弟弟掉在崖子中间的一个石洞边,幸好被浓密的树枝枯草垫着,没有被砸死。

过了一天一夜,弟弟才慢慢苏醒过来。他伸手一摸,不是草棵就是树桩,浑身上下被刺伤的、戳破的,全身辣乎乎的。弟弟哭着喊道:"哥哥呀,你真心毒,把我撂在这里!"嗓子哭疼了,眼泪哭干了,肚子哭饿了。他伸手乱抓乱摸,盼望找到几个山毛野果,好充饥果腹。左扒右扒,他爬到洞边的一口小井边。他摸到的是凉飕飕的泉水,赶紧凑上干裂的嘴唇,喝了个够。他感到眼睛胀鼓鼓地疼,蘸点水揩揩眼睛,眼皮着水后,霎时松开了,眼睛也亮了,弟弟看到了天空,看到了树木,看到了飞鸟。

弟弟蘸蘸水,揩揩瘸脚,脚也不瘸了。弟弟站起来,他高兴得忘记了身上的伤痕,攀着树枝,蹬着石头,走到崖脚一个深潭边,绿茵茵的潭水,荡着一圈一圈的涟漪。弟弟坐在潭边的一块石头上吹起了箫,悦耳动听的箫声,逗得雀鸟也飞来落在潭边的树上,悠然自得,听得入了迷。深潭里住着一条老龙,它在宫殿里听到水面上传来了悠扬的箫声,也竖起耳朵听得呆了神。一曲听罢,龙王唤来两个兵将,说:"看看谁在我家边吹箫,那么动听,你们去把他叫进宫来。"

瞎子弟弟在两个兵将的搀扶下,紧闭双眼,倏然一下,便来到龙王殿。龙王叫兵将给他穿上鳞光闪烁的金衣银缎,问:"小伙儿,你在我家边做什么?"

瞎子弟弟回答:"我在自弹弦子自散心。"龙王又问:"你家里还有些什么人?"

瞎子弟弟回答:"上无爹娘,只有哥嫂。"

于是老龙王就叫瞎子弟弟住在龙宫里。

瞎子弟弟在龙宫里住了九年。有一天,他坐在龙宫门口哭得死去活来。龙王见了,忙上去打问:"你哭什么?"瞎子弟弟回答:"我有一个哥哥在家里,连日打柴连日过,不动一天就饿着,我实在想念他。"龙王听了,眷恋之心,人之常情,也体恤瞎子弟弟的心情,就说:"那你就回去,宫里的金银财宝随你拿。"瞎子弟弟说:"我一样也不要。"

瞎子弟弟在龙宫吹箫九年,不贪金图银,龙王更加高兴,人间难得廉洁之人,应该送他一样宝物。龙王拿出一个金葫芦递给瞎子弟弟,说:

"你到路上肚子饿了,就摇摇金葫芦,说声:'小葫芦,摆酒肉。'你就有吃的了。吃饱了,说声:'小葫芦收酒席。'你要记住。"

瞎子弟弟接过金葫芦,谢过龙王,刚要走,龙王捋捋长髯,又说:"你走累了,摇摇金葫芦,说声:'小葫芦,出轿来。'轿子就出来。你不想坐了,又说声:'小葫芦,收轿子。'你缺什么,短哪样,就晃晃金葫芦,它会满足你的。"

瞎子弟弟照龙王的话,摇摇金葫芦,有酒肉;摇摇金葫芦,坐轿子。逢山开路,遇水搭桥,风从雨顺,不觉来到了家边。

马有前悔,人有后悔。瞎子弟弟想试试嫂嫂,就晃晃金葫芦,一下子变成了一个破衣烂衫的叫花子,背着一个油渍渍的筒帕,装好金葫芦,大步流星地跨进家门。看见嫂嫂,瞎子弟弟抬着饭瓢,叫声:"嫂嫂,给我吃碗饭。"

嫂嫂见是要饭的叫花子,没好气:"去吃早上猫儿的剩饭。"

瞎子弟弟扯扯破衣襟,说声:"嫂嫂,我冷得很。"

嫂嫂斜眼瞟去,见是好脚好手的一个,不像是脚跛眼瞎的弟弟,便冷冰冰地打发道:"冷,去城隍庙烤护堂灯。"

瞎子弟弟听了,知道嫂嫂是老马不死旧病在,折转身子,边走边嚷着:"我冷死不烤护堂灯,饿死不吃猫儿饭!"

瞎子弟弟来到寨边一个宽敞的草坪,晃晃金葫芦说:"小葫芦,出高楼。"一座四合五天井的楼房,立时矗立在面前。他再晃晃金葫芦,院子里跑满了鸡猪鹅鸭,圈里牛马骡羊成群。瞎子弟弟过上了吃不焦,穿不愁的日子。

有一天,哥哥和弟弟突然在路上相遇,弟兄两个喜出望外,喜极而泣,抱着痛哭了一场。

哥哥见弟弟住的是高楼,吃的是酥红卤白,装着满箱满柜的银子,眼睛也馋了,心也痒了,再也按捺不住了,急忙问:"弟弟,你得了什么宝贝发了财?"弟弟见哥哥老实巴巴的,就把真实话告诉他。哥哥听了,脸红一块,白一块。末了,哥哥竟厚着脸皮,要借金葫芦要两天。弟弟把金葫芦递给了哥哥。

哥哥手捧金葫芦,脚不点地跑回了家。他把金葫芦的秘密告诉了媳妇,夫妻俩贪得无厌,哥哥想要高房大屋,媳妇想要金银钱财。夫妻俩捏紧金葫芦,使劲摇晃着,才说到"我要……"刹那间,"呼"的一声窜出两条大青龙来，卷起哥哥、嫂嫂，扬头摆尾，游进了江河。

讲述：赵启庆

搜集整理：杨叶生

编者按： 又是一个懦弱哥哥、无情嫂子和憨厚弟弟的家庭伦理故事。这样的情节，总是可以在社区传播，只能说这种情况曾经是社会的巨大挑战。因为，在当前的社会结构中，大多数家庭已经没有多个子女，哪怕多子女家庭也会分家成核心家庭。而故事里的家庭结构是传统社会的大家庭，只不过当父母过世之后，哥哥理所当然需要承担父母的抚养责任。

这种抚养责任巨大，特别是在资源紧缺的农业社会。而这个责任没有对应的权利，不同于父母的责任是与潜在的被赡养权利关联的，这个哥哥对弟弟的抚养责任属于伦理范畴，没有足够的法律保障。

当换一个场景，现在的手足，能否在失去父母的庇护之后，彼此扶持？而现在的故事，也不再讨论这个话题，因为这样的情形，被认为是政府的责任。

The Blind Younger Brother

Once upon a time, there was a family with an elder brother, his wife, and a younger brother after the brothers' parents passed away. The younger brother was blind and crippled so he could only sit and play the flute and strings every day. The sister-in-law complained to the elder brother, and said, "Your brother can't do anything. We have to chop wood and sell grass to support him. It's not worth; you should take him to the cliff and kill him there". The couple argued endlessly about the blind brother. The sister-in-law nagged and cursed all day, made the elder brother crazy.

One day, the elder brother said to the younger brother, "Brother, come with me to the mountain to chop wood. Crows have been stealing my lunch, so I need you to watch over it". The younger brother replied, "Brother, but I can't walk". The elder brother said, "Don't worry, I'll carry you." So the elder brother carried his younger brother, who held his flute up the mountain to chop wood. When they arrived, the younger brother played the flute and strings, and the elder brother, seeing how happy his brother was, couldn't bring himself to throw him off the cliff. He couldn't commit such a cruel act. At dusk, after chopping wood, the elder brother carried the younger brother back home.

When the sister-in-law saw the younger brother return, she was furious, stomping around and setting out food. The younger brother, unable to see, ate a bowl after a bowl. The elder brother just sat silently at the table.

The next day, the elder brother reluctantly carried his younger brother up the mountain again. After chopping wood, the elder brother looked at his brother's innocent face and couldn't help but cry in sorrow. The younger brother, hearing the sobs, put down his instrument and thought his brother was sad because of the burden he was on, so he said, "Brother, I won't come tomorrow, so I won't trouble you". The elder brother, seeing his brother's innocent face, couldn't bear to harm him. At dusk, he carried his brother home again.

When the sister-in-law saw the younger brother returned once more, it was as if a knife cutting through her heart. Her eyes bulged with anger, her lips twitched, and she spat repeatedly, cursing her husband with all sorts of insults. The elder brother was so upset that he couldn't sleep all night, with his pillow soaking wet from tears.

Early the next morning, the sister-in-law started yelling again, "Are you deaf"? The elder brother knew that his wife had made up her mind and couldn't be persuaded. So he tricked his younger brother, and said, "Brother, just help me one more day, and then you won't have to come again". The younger brother, unaware of the plan, carried his instruments and let his elder brother carry him up the mountain. The elder brother took his younger brother to the edge of a cliff, steeled his heart, closed his eyes, and let go of him, so the younger brother fell into the deep hole.

As the younger brother fell, he heard the wind rushing past his ears and he landed softly on something, bouncing slightly before losing consciousness. It turned out that he had landed on the edge of a stone cave halfway down the cliff, cushioned by thick branches and dry grass, which saved his life.

One day had passed before the younger brother slowly woke up. He reached out and felt nothing but grass and tree stumps, his whole body covered in scratches and stings. He cried out, "Brother, why did you leave me here"! His throat was sore from crying, his tears dried up, and his stomach growled with hunger. He groped around, hoping to find some wild fruits to stave off his hunger. Eventually, he crawled to a small well at the edge of the cave. He felt the cool water, and eagerly drank as much as he like. He felt a sharp pain in his eyes, so he dipped his fingers in the water and rubbed his eyes. As soon as the water touched his eyelids, they relaxed, and his vision returned. The younger brother could now see the sky, the trees, and the birds.

He then rubbed his crippled foot with the water, and soon his leg was healed too. Overjoyed, he stood up, forgetting all about his injuries, and climbed down to a deep pool at the base of the cliff. The green water rippled with circles. Sitting on a rock by the pool, he played his flute, the melodious sound attracted the birds on the nearby trees, where they listened, entranced. Deep in the pool lived an old dragon, who, hearing the beautiful flute music, was so captivated that he sent two soldiers to bring the musician to his palace.

The blind brother was suddenly whisked away by the soldiers and brought before the Dragon King. The Dragon King ordered the soldiers to dress him in shimmering gold and silver robes and asked, "Young man, what are you doing near my home"?

The blind brother replied, "I was just playing my instrument". The Dragon King then asked, "Do you have any family"?

The blind brother replied, "My parents have passed away, leaving only my brother and sister-in-law".

The Dragon King then invited the blind brother to stay in the dragon palace.

The blind brother lived in the dragon palace for nine years. One day, he sat at the entrance of the palace, crying so hard. The Dragon King, saw this situation, and asked, "Why are you crying"? The blind brother replied, "I have a brother at home who has been chopping wood every day, struggling to survive. I miss him dearly". The Dragon King, understood the bond of brotherhood, sympathized with the blind brother and said, "Then you go back, and take as much gold and treasure as you like from the palace". The blind brother replied, "I don't want anything".

Having played the flute in the dragon palace for nine years without any desire for wealth, the Dragon King was even more pleased with his integrity. The Dragon King gave him a golden gourd and said, "When you're hungry on the road, just shake the gourd and say, ' Little gourd, set out a feast,' and you'll have food to eat. When you're done, just say, ' Little gourd, clear the table.' Remember that".

The blind brother took the golden gourd, thanked to the Dragon King, and was about to leave when the Dragon King stroked his long beard and added,"When you're tired, shake the gourd and say, ' Little gourd, bring out the sedan,' and a sedan chair will appear. When you no longer want to sit, just say, ' Little gourd, put away the sedan.' Whatever you need, just shake the gourd, and it will fulfill your wish".

The blind brother followed the Dragon King's instructions, shaking the golden gourd to get food, and again for the sedan chair. Mountains parted, rivers were bridged, and the weather was perfect as he journeyed home.

People often regret their actions too late. The blind brother decided to test his sister-in-law, so he shook the golden gourd and transformed into a ragged beggar, carrying an oil-stained bag with the golden gourd inside. He strode into his home and called out, "Sister-in-law, can I have a bowl of food"?

Seeing a beggar, the sister-in-law coldly replied, "Go to eat the leftovers of the cat's breakfast".

The blind brother tugged at his tattered clothes and said, "Sister-in-law, I'm very cold".

The sister-in-law glanced over, saw a healthy-looking man, was not the lame and blind brother she had known, and dismissed him, "If you're cold, go to warm yourself by the temple lamps".

The blind brother realized that his sister-in-law hadn't changed at all and walked away, muttered, "I'd rather freeze to death than warm myself by the lamps and starve than eat the cat's leftovers"!

The blind brother went to a spacious field on the edge of the village, shook the golden gourd, and said, "Little gourd, build a grand house". Instantly, a mansion with courtyards appeared before him. He shook the gourd again, and the yard filled with chickens, pigs, geese, ducks, cows, horses, mules, and sheep. The blind brother began living a life free of worry, with plenty to eat and wear.

One day, the elder brother and younger brother met unexpectedly on the road. Overjoyed, they hugged each other and cried.

The elder brother saw that his younger brother lived in a grand house, eating fine foods, and had chests full of silver. He became envious and asked, "Brother, what treasure did you find to become so wealthy"? The younger brother, saw his elder brother's honest demeanor, told him the truth. The elder brother shamelessly asked to borrow the golden gourd for a few days. The younger brother handed it over.

The elder brother, clutching the golden gourd, ran home excitedly and told his wife about its powers. The greedy couple wanted a grand house and heaps of gold and silver. They shook the golden gourd vigorously and began to say, "I want..." when suddenly, two large green dragons sprang out, wrapped them, and with a flick of their tails, carried them off into the river.

负心的干兄弟

从前,有两个孤儿,一个叫熊小福,一个叫尹小顺。他两个相处得很好,就结拜为弟兄。熊小福十四岁,称哥哥;尹小顺十二岁,为弟弟。后来,他俩商量做点儿小生意,便凑了一些钱做起买卖来了。开始几个月倒也顺利,日子长了,哥哥熊小福做生意,态度好,说话客气,向他买货的人多,他找得的钱就多一点。而弟弟尹小顺态度生硬,经常和人家吵架,结果谁也不想买他的东西,他就卖得少,有时一天到晚也卖不得一文钱。这以后,他俩各去一方卖货,到下午会合后一起回家。有一天,在回家的路上弟兄俩谈起买卖的事,哥哥熊小福问弟弟尹小顺道:"兄弟!今天的生意好吗?"尹小顺明明知道,今天连张都没有开,一文钱也没有卖得,却对哥哥说:"我今天东西没有卖完,钱倒卖得不少,本钱找回来了,还赚得好多哩。哥哥也一定好啰!"

熊小福听后,以为是真的,暗暗替尹小顺高兴,说:"好啊!我的东西也很好卖,生意做得很顺利,全卖光了,也赚了不少的钱。"接着,他又对尹小顺说:"我两个都是无爹无娘的,要好好地做人,随时要争口气。我看你有时脾气不大好,今后要改一改,要做一个有志气、有礼貌、有道德的人。"他们俩一边说,一边走,不觉来到一座桥头。过桥时哥哥熊小福走在前面,尹小顺跟在后面。刚走到桥中间时,弟弟起了坏心,突然大声喊叫起来:"哥哥,你快来看,河里有条大鱼有两个头呀!"熊小福以为是真的,想看看两个头的鱼,也就回过头来走到尹小顺跟前,放下担子,低下头去看鱼。趁熊小福不提防,尹小顺朝后猛力一推,把熊小福推下大河去了。然后他挑起熊小福的担子走了。

熊小福被推下河后,因为河水深、河面又宽,他又不会游水,只得顺河淌呀淌,一直淌到山脚的一个大石岩边,才被长在岩边的草藤拦住。这时,他已精疲力竭不省人事。等到他慢慢地醒过来,才拉着藤子爬出来。他抬头一看,见一个岩洞,便向岩洞爬去。他爬到岩洞口,站起身刚要进岩洞时,从岩洞里走出一位白胡子老公公。老公公问他道:"啊呀,天这么晚了,你一个人来这里做什么?"熊小福把落水的前后经过向老公公诉说了,老公公对他说:"天晚了,你别走了。这岩洞里有猛兽,你也不能住,你就爬在树上住一夜吧。天黑时,野兽回岩洞来,你在树上不要动,它们讲些什么,你要好好地听着,要牢牢地记住。"老公公说完,指给他一棵大树,叫他爬上去。

不多一会儿,一只老虎朝岩洞走来,走到岩洞口便向白胡子公公说:"我今天去对面山上,见到一个小姑娘,名字叫莫品,长得很俊俏。她家只有母女两个人生活,我要是人的话,就到她家入赘安家去。"老虎说完走进岩洞里去了。过了一会,走来一只老熊。老熊走到岩洞前对老公公说:"我今天在半山上见到一条大蟒蛇,它嘴里还含着一颗红宝石,我要是一个人呀,只消用石榴枝子向它一扫,宝石就拿到手了。"老熊说完,也钻进岩洞去了。又过了一会,走来一只大野猪。野猪走到岩洞口向老公公说道:"我今天路过城边,路边站着很多人看一张布告。布告上说官家太太的奶头上生了个大疮,哪个能把太太的奶头疮治好,官家就分一半家产给他。我要是个人呀,拿些岩石头上长的灵芝草,帮太太医治好奶头疮多好呀!"野猪说完也进岩洞去了。

第二天天刚亮,老虎、老熊、野猪便走出岩洞去了。随后,白胡子老公公也走出岩洞来。他把熊小福叫下树来,问道:"昨天晚上那些野兽讲的话你都听清、记住了吗?"熊小福回答说:"我都听清,记住了。"接着,老公公领着熊小福爬到岩洞上边,采了一些灵芝草。老公公说:"小伙子,这灵芝草是仙丹妙药,可医百病,你把它拿去,先到对面山上找到莫品家安下家来,她家园子里有一棵石榴树,树根埋有金银财宝,你把金银财宝挖出来,然后你再去帮那官家太太医奶头疮。"

熊小福拿着灵芝草,谢别了老公公,向对面山上莫品家走去,他走到莫品家时,莫品的妈请他坐下,问道:"小哥是从哪里来的,要到哪里去?"熊小福把自己的遭遇说了一遍,莫品的妈听了心里很难受。莫品当着妈的面,不好意思跟外人说话,就跑进内房,从门缝里悄悄地偷望着熊小福。她越看越觉得小伙子英俊、能干,就暗暗地爱上了小伙子。熊小福讲完了自己的苦楚后,对莫品的母亲说:"大妈,我现在不知在何方,也找不着路回家,实在是走投无路呀,让我在你家暂住几天吧。"莫品的妈听后,慌忙说:"我家里不能住,我家只有我们母女俩,一个小伙子住在我家不像话，你还是另找别处去住吧！"莫品听到妈的这些话，怕小伙子真的走了，一时间，心里毛焦火辣的，就赶忙走出内房来，说："妈，你常说人不做亏心事，半夜打雷不吃惊吗？阿哥说没有去处，你不都听见了？你叫他走到哪里住去！"

经莫品这么一说，妈的心也就一下子软了下来，就顺从了女儿的意思，让他住下了。熊小福在莫品家住下后，每天帮她家种地、打柴、挑水，什么活儿都做。后来，莫品的妈也暗中喜欢熊小福，看中了这个小伙子，就把女儿莫品许给了熊小福，让他俩结成了美满夫妻。

有一天，熊小福叫莫品到园子里石榴树下挖地。挖着挖着，挖出了一堆白的、一堆黄的、一堆红的，莫品不知道是什么，就问熊小福。熊小福高兴地告诉她，白的是银子，黄的是金子，红的是宝石。有了金银宝石，这下全家都高兴了。

过了不几天，熊小福对莫品妈说："妈，我听到官家太太的奶头生了个大疮，我想去帮她医医看。"莫品妈听他说要去帮官家太太医病，有点儿害怕，说："儿呀，老人们常说，官情如纸薄，医得好没话说，要是医不好，我家一家子就活不成了。"莫品听了妈的话后，说："妈，我看是医得好的，我家有灵芝草，这是一种万能药，能看着别人受难不救吗？"莫品妈听了女儿的这番话，觉得有道理，也就同意了。于是熊小福就下山到官家去了。

熊小福拿着灵芝草来到官家门口，卫士问道："你是来干什么的？"熊小福直说道："小的听说官太太奶头生疮，我是来给她治病的。"卫士听后，把熊小福带进去了。熊小福来到官老爷面前，禀明身份后，说："要我医的话，保证三天医好，七天就恢复原样。"官老爷听了很高兴，双方就立下凭据。熊小福就用灵芝草给官太太治奶头疮。到第七天，熊小福果真把官家太太的奶头疮治好了。官老爷见了很高兴，就派人到熊小福家，帮他家盖了一所新房子，还给了很多钱。这样，熊小福全家就过上了好日子。

再说熊小福结拜的兄弟尹小顺，把熊小福推下河后，霸占了熊小福的钱、货物，回家后就闲着吃，不久就坐吃山空，只好去讨饭度日。一天，他讨饭讨到了熊小福家，熊小福一眼认出尹小顺。尹小顺也认出了熊小福，可他不好回避，就先开口说："哥呀，那天不是我有意推你下水的，是我想扶着你指给你看，你不注意就落下河去了，我又不会游水，救不了你,眼巴巴地望着你被河水冲走,我心里好难受,回到家里哭了几天几夜呀。"说着,虚情假意地流下几滴眼泪。接着,他又问道:"哥呀,你是咋个得救的?现在发了这么多的财。"熊小福是个老实巴交的人,他把事情的经过一五一十地向尹小顺说了,还告诉他说:"我听说,在那边山上有条蟒蛇,嘴里含着一颗宝石,能得到那颗宝石就会富裕起来。要取这颗宝石也不难,只消用石榴树枝扫一下蟒蛇,蟒蛇就会吐出宝石,这样就能拿到宝石了。"尹小顺听了这话,很想得到这颗宝石。于是他就拿起一支石榴树枝,急急忙忙地向那山坡走去了。他走到蟒蛇住的地方,一眼看见蟒蛇嘴里确实含着颗宝石,就悄悄地走到蟒蛇嘴前,举着石榴枝向蟒蛇扫去,想取宝石。不想,蟒蛇张开血盆大口,一口把他吞进肚里去了。没良心的尹小顺就这样被蟒蛇吞吃了。

搜集:滕茂芳
整理:张亚萍

编者按:善良的人,总是有好报应。邪恶的人,难免自取灭亡。性格

决定命运，这才能有效地让人向善。

在熊小福落水的时候，这是他最危险的时候，同时也是向死而生的转折。他意外遇到了白胡子老头，给了他一些建议。按照这样的建议，他迎娶白富美，治病救人得了大名。这些都是否极泰来的改变。

这个时候，尹小顺的邪恶还没有解决，用石榴树获得蛇口宝石的线索还在。于是，出现了两个线索的汇合，让邪恶的蛇解决了邪恶的人。

The Godbrother with an Unfaithful Heart

Once upon a time, there were two orphans, one named Xiong Xiaofu and the other named Yin Xiaoshun. The two of them got along so well that they became brothers. Xiong Xiaofu was 14 years old, so was referred as the elder brother; Yin Xiaoshun was 12 years old, so he was referred as the younger brother. Later, the two of them discussed to do some small business, they gathered some money, then started. The first few months went well. As time went by, Xiong Xiaofu was good at business. His attitude was nice, and he talked politely, so more people bought goods from him, then he earned more money from the goods he sold. While the younger brother Yin Xiaoshun's attitude was harsh, and often quarreled with the customers, the result of that was no one wanted to buy his goods, so he sold less things, and sometimes couldn't earn a single penny all day and night. From then on, the two of them went to different side of the market to sell goods, in the afternoon they would meet together to go home. One day, on the way home, the two brothers talked about their business, and Xiong Xiaofu asked his brother Yin Xiaoshun, "Brother! How about the business today"? Yin Xiaoshun knew very well that he had not even made one business today and had not earned a penny, but he said to his brother, "I did not sell everything out today, but I earned a lot of money, and I got my capital back and made a lot of revenues. Yours must be well too"!

When Xiong Xiaofu heard this, he thought it was true and was pleased with Yin Xiaoshun, and said, "That's great! My goods sold out quickly, and I made a rich profit too". Then he also said to Yin Xiaoshun, "We're both orphans, so we must strive to be good people. We need carry ourselves with dignity. I've noticed that you sometimes have a bad temper.

In the future, you should work on that and aim to be an ambitious, polite and virtuous person". The two of them were talking and walking, and they came to a bridge. When they crossed the bridge, Xiong Xiaofu walked in front, and Yin Xiaoshun followed behind. When they reached the middle of the bridge, the younger brother got a bad idea and suddenly shouted, "Brother, come and see, there is a big fish in the river with two heads"! Xiong Xiaofu, thinking it was true, turned back to see the two-headed fish. He set down his load and bent over to look into the river. When Xiong Xiaofu was not on guard, Yin Xiaoshun pushed Xiong Xiaofu down the river. Then he picked up Xiong Xiaofu's burden and left.

Because the river was wide and deep, and Xiong Xiaofu can't swim, he had to flow with the river until he was halted by a long vine attached to a large rock at the foot of the mountain. By this time, he was already exhausted and unconscious. When he slowly woke up, he pulled the vine and climbed out of the river. He looked up and saw a cave, so he crawled towards it. He crawled to the entrance of the cave, when he was about to stand up and walk into it, a white-bearded old man came out of the cave. The old man asked, "Ah, it's so late in the night. What are you doing here alone by yourself"? Xiong Xiaofu then told everything that happened to the old man. The old man responded, "It's too late, and don't leave now. There are fierce creatures in this cave, you can't stay the night here either. Just climb on to the tree and spend the night there. When midnight comes, the beasts are going to come back, stay still on the tree and remember whatever they say"! When the old man had finished speaking, he pointed out a large tree to him and told Xiong Xiaofu to climb on to it.

Not long after, a tiger walked towards the cave, it said to the old man, "I went to the mountain on the opposite side today and saw a girl named Mo Pin. She is very pretty. It's just her and her mother living in their house. If I were a human-being, I would go to marry her and settle down there". After the tiger finished, an old bear walked to the entrance of the cave and said, "Today, I met a huge serpent halfway up the mountain, which has a red gem in its mouth. If I were a human-being, I would sweep it with a pomegranate branch to get the gem". After the old bear finished, it also went into the cave. Later, a big boar came to the cave, it said to the old man, "I walked pass the edge of the city today, and there were many people standing by the road, looking at a notice. On the notice, it said that the official's wife had a sore on her nipple. Whoever can cure the sore will receive half of the official's property. If I were a human-being, I would take some glossy ganoderma that grows on the rock and go to cure her". After it finished, the boar also went into the cave.

At dawn of next day, the tiger, the old bear and the boar all went out of the cave. After them, the old man also came out of the cave. He called Xiong Xiaofu to climb down the tree and asked, "Did you hear and remember what the beasts said last night"? Xiong Xiaofu answered, "Yes, I remembered it all". Later, the old man led Xiong Xiaofu to the edge of the rocks and picked some glossy ganoderma. The old man said, "Glossy ganoderma is a very precious herb, which could cure any disease. Take this with you and go to marry Mo Pin. She has a pomegranate tree in her garden. At the root of this tree, there are lots of treasures. You should take all of the treasures and then go to cure the official's wife".

Xiong Xiaofu took the glossy ganoderma, thanked the old man, then walked towards Mo Pin's house. When he arrived at Mo Pin's house, her mother invited him to sit down and asked him, "Young man, where did you come from and where are you going"? Xiong Xiaofu told Mo Pin's mother about his story, and she felt sad for him. Mo Pin was too shy to talk to strangers, so she peeked secretly through the doorway at Xiong Xiaofu. The more she looked at him, the more handsome and capable Xiong Xiaofu seemed, so Mo Pin fell in love with him. When Xiong Xiaofu finished telling his sad story, he said to Mo Pin's mother, "Madam, I have no idea where I am right now and where I should go, please let me stay for a few days". Mo Pin's mother replied hurriedly, "No…We're the only ones in my house. It's not appropriate for a young man to live here. You should find another place to stay". Mo Pin heard what her mother said and was afraid that Xiong Xiaofu was going to leave. So she ran out and said, "Mom, he said he had nowhere to go. Where could he live"?

Her words softened her mother's heart, and she agreed to let Xiong Xiaofu stay. Xiong Xiaofu lived with them and helped with all the household chores—farming, chopping wood, carrying water. Over time, Mo Pin's mother grew fond of him and thought he could be a good match for her daughter. So she married her daughter to Xiong Xiaofu and they became a loving couple.

One day, Xiong Xiaofu told Mo Pin to dig under the pomegranate tree in her garden. When they were digging, they found a bunch of red, yellow and white stuffs. Mo Pin didn't know what they were, so she asked Xiong Xiaofu. Xiong Xiaofu told her that the white ones were silver; the yellow ones were gold; and the red ones were gems. With all those treasures, the whole family was overjoyed.

After a few days, Xiong Xiaofu said to Mo Pin's mother, "Mom, I heard that the official's wife has a sore on her nipple, and I want to try to cure her". Mo Pin's mother felt a bit scared upon hearing this, she said, "My son, the elders always said that the hearts of the official's family are cold. If you successfully cure the sore, then that's good news. But if you fail, our whole family might be killed"! Mo Pin heard her mother's words and replied, "Mom, I think it can be cured. We have glossy ganoderma in our house, which is a magical herb that can cure everything. Are we going to watch others suffer with no helping?" Mo Pin's mother thought that her daughter was right, so she agreed, and Xiong Xiaofu went down the mountain to head for the official's house.

Xiong Xiaofu took the glossy ganoderma and came to the official's house, the guards asked, "What are you doing here"? Xiong Xiaofu replied, "I heard that the official's wife has a sore nipple. I come here to cure her." After the guard heard that, he led Xiong Xiaofu inside. Xiong Xiaofu came before the official and said, "If you let me cure her, I can promise you that it can be cured within three days and the wound will recover in seven days". The official was very happy to hear that, and they wrote a contract together. Then, Xiong Xiaofu used the glossy ganoderma to cure the sore. After seven days, the sore was cured as promised. The official was delighted and sent a person to Xiong Xiaofu's house to help him build a new house. He also gave Xiong Xiaofu a lot of money as a reward. Xiong Xiaofu's family now lived a happy life.

What about the man named Yin Xiaoshun? After he pushed Xiong Xiaofu down the river, he took all of Xiong Xiaofu's money and goods. When he returned home, he just spent all the money and stayed lazy. Not long after, he became poor and had to go beg for survival. One day, he was begging before Xiong Xiaofu's house, both recognized each other instantly, so Yin Xiaoshun said, "My brother, I didn't purposely push you off that day. I was just trying to hold you up and show you what I saw, but you accidentally fell into the river, and I couldn't save you because I don't know how to swim. I felt so sad, and I cried for days and nights". With those words has said, tears dropped down his face. Then Yin Xiaoshun asked, "My dear brother, how did you survive? And how did you become so wealthy"? Xiong Xiaofu was an honest person, so he told Yin Xiaoshun what happened and told him, "I heard that there is a serpent on the other mountain with a gem in its mouth. If you get that gem, you will be wealthy. It is not so hard to get the gem; you just need to sweep its head with a pomegranate branch". Hearing that, Yin Xiaoshun wanted the gem so badly that he immediately grabbed a pomegranate branch and went to the mountains. When he arrived, he saw that the serpent did have a gem in its mouth, so he walked towards the snake and swept it using the pomegranate branch, trying to get the gem. Unexpectedly, the serpent opened its giant mouth and ate him in one gulp. That is it, the unfaithful Yin Xiaoshun was eaten by the serpent.

弟兄分家

从前,有一对弟兄俩在一起过日子。哥哥贪心吝啬,总嫌弟弟拖累他,占了他的便宜。弟弟为人忠厚耿直,对哥哥说一不二,很听他的话。

一天,哥哥对弟弟说:"我们分家吧!水里蚂蝗多,田泥稀烂,做活又脏又累,收成也不好,水田就归我去种。山地肥沃草又少,天干雨涝庄稼照样熟,山地就给你去种。"弟弟听了哥哥这番虚情假意的话,心里虽然不高兴,但也没说什么,就照他说的办了。

那块山地,以前庄稼熟后,不是雀鸟啄、老鼠吃,就是野猪拱、猴子偷。分家后,弟弟在地里种了包谷。人勤地不懒,深挖施肥,包谷苗长得秆粗叶壮。等到包谷打包,弟弟就搬到地边窝棚里,白天撵山雀,晚上防野兽,守着包谷地。

这天,弟弟感到疲乏,就躺在草棚里打起瞌睡来,不一会儿就睡熟了。这时,一群馋嘴的猴子来到地边,看看没有人就放肆地掰包谷。它们又啃又嚼,一会儿就填饱了肚子。一个大猴子蹿到窝棚边,看见主人一动不动地躺着,便对其他的猴子说:"我们掰包谷吃,主人气死了,看着怪可怜的。我们挖个坑,把他抬去埋掉吧。"

于是,一群猴子便闹闹哄哄,挖坑,准备杠子,拿来金铓、金锣。喧闹的声音,把睡着的弟弟吵醒了,他眯着眼睛,见一群猴子正围着自己忙得团团转,心里觉得奇怪,想看看它们要做什么,便又闭起眼睛,装睡起来。

过了一会儿,一伙猴子把弟弟搬到木杠上抬着,有几只捧着金铓、金锣,敲得丁丁当当地响。弟弟悄悄睁开眼睛,瞄了一眼,哇!多好的金铓、金锣啊!肯定是狡猾的猴子从有钱人家偷来的。弟弟心里暗暗盘算着,要把金铓、金锣弄到手。

猴子们抬着弟弟,一个个累得汗流浃背,费了九牛二虎之力,才把弟弟抬到挖好的土坑旁。这时,弟弟鼓足大气,猛地跳起来,"喔——"地大吼一声，猴子们被这突如其来的叫声，吓得魂不附体，丢下金铛、金锣，顿时就跑得不见踪影。弟弟高高兴兴地拾起金铛、金锣回家了。

不久，弟弟卖了金铛、金锣，换得银子，买了谷米，添置了家用，日子好过起来了。哥哥看在眼里，酸在心上。一天终于忍不住，便问弟弟从哪里弄来的银钱。弟弟笑着把事情原原本本地告诉了他。哥哥听了，实在眼红，赶忙说："兄弟，今天我田里没有活路，我去帮你守一天地，也去拾一回金铛、金锣。"弟弟一口答应了。

哥哥在窝棚里装睡觉，果然，不过一阵工夫，一群猴子来了。大猴子瞄见有人在窝棚里直挺挺地躺着，便对着其他猴子轻声嘀咕了一阵。猴子们前拥后簇，把哥哥抬起来，只听大猴子说："今天莫忙，到埋他的时候再敲金铛、金锣。"哥哥听了暗自高兴，只管闭着眼睛让猴子们抬着走。哪晓得，在大猴子的率领下，哥哥被抬到悬崖边。大猴子一声："一，二，丢！"哥哥还搞不清怎么一回事，便摔下了深谷。

讲述：张小凤
搜集整理：杨叶生

编者按： 看起来，猴子们已经学精了，它们在上次痛失金铛、金锣之后，故意设局等着有些贪婪的人类。而有些人类果然不出所料，还是按照老套路，希望诓骗猴子。

其实这里还有一个针砭，就是在山下种水田的人，对于山上种山地的人，有一种欺诈。而有些山民自认为淳朴善良、智慧勤劳，他们看不起精耕细作的种水田的农夫，但是他们自己也是用了诡诈才巧妙地赚了猴子的"金铛、金锣"。

Brothers' Separation

Once upon a time, there were two brothers who lived together. The elder brother was greedy and stingy, always complain that his younger brother was encumbere him and take advantage of him. The younger brother was honest and always obedient to his older brother.

One day, the elder brother said to the younger brother, "Let's split the property and live by ourselves. The paddy fields are full of pests and the mud is sloppy. Working there is dirty and tiring, the harvest is not good either. I will take the paddy fields. As for the mountains, it is fertile with little weeds. The crops grow well regardless of drought or flood. You can have the mountains". Although the younger brother was not happy with the older brother's insincere proposal, he didn't say anything and agreed his request.

The mountain land had always been troubled by birds pecking, rats eating, wild boars rooting, or monkeys stealing the crops after they ripened. After the division, the younger brother planted corn in the land. With diligent work, the corn stalks grew tall and strong. When the corn was ready to harvest, the younger brother moved into a small shack near the field. He spent his days chasing away birds and his nights guarding against wild animals.

One day, felt be exhausted, the younger brother dozed off in the hut and soon fell into sound sleep. While he was asleep, a group of greedy monkeys came to the edge of the field. Seeing no one around, they boldly started plucking the corn. They gnawed and chewed, filled their empty bellies. One big monkey leaped to the side of the hut and saw the owner lying there, motionless. So it said to the other monkeys, "The owner is now dead because of anger he felt when he saw us eating the corns. Poor fellow. Let's dig a hole and bury him".

So the monkeys started digging a pit, preparing poles, and brought out gold gongs and cymbals. The noise they made woke the younger brother. He squinted his eyes and saw a group of monkeys bustling around him. Curious about what they were up to, he pretended to stay asleep.

After a while, these monkeys placed the younger brother on the wooden plank and started carrying him. Some of them were holding the gold gongs and cymbals, making "Cling - Clang" sounds. The younger brother secretly opened his eyes and took a glance. Wow! Such beautiful gold cymbals and gongs! They must have been stolen by those cunning monkeys from a wealthy household. The younger brother started to have a plan in his mind, he wanted to get the gold cymbals and gongs.

The monkeys carried the younger brother to the pit and were all exhausted. At that moment, the younger brother took a deep breath and suddenly jumped up, letting out a roar, "Hey"! The monkeys were shocked by this sudden shout. Terrified, they dropped the gold cymbals and gold gongs and disappeared without a trace. The younger brother happily picked up the gold gongs and cymbals and returned home.

Not long after, the younger brother sold the gold gongs and cymbals, exchanged them for silver. He used the money to buy rice and other furniture. His life became much better. The elder brother noticed and felt jealous. Finally, one day, unable to conceal himself anymore, he asked the younger brother that where he got the money from. The younger brother smiled and told him the whole story. The elder brother, felt jealous, said urgently, "Brother, I have no work in the fields today. Let me help you guard the land for a day and try my luck at picking up gold gongs and cymbals". The younger brother agreed immediately.

The elder brother pretended to sleep in the hut, and indeed, after a while, a group of monkeys came. The big monkey saw someone lying stiff in the hut, so it whispered something to other monkeys. The monkeys gathered around and carried the older brother. The big monkey said softly,

"Don't rush today. We'll hit the gold gongs when it's time to bury him." The older brother, felt delighted, kept his eyes closed and let the monkeys carried him. Little did he know, under the big monkey's lead, he was carried to the edge of a cliff. The big monkey shouted, "One, two, throw!" Before the older brother could know what was going on, he fell off from the cliff.

弟兄俩的银子盒

很早以前,有一户阿昌人家,母亲领着弟兄俩讨生活。她勤苦耐劳,心地善良,靠采摘酸杷野菜,熬年度月,终于把弟兄俩抚养成人。之后,她又给弟兄俩娶了媳妇。这时,母亲额头上密密麻麻的皱纹,标志着她的年龄将要到顶了。疲惫的身躯再也无法支撑下去。她仿佛感到自己气数将尽,便把弟兄俩叫拢床边,把身后的家务安排了一番,接着把颤抖的手伸到枕下,摸出一包东西,她慢慢地揭开布包。咳!好爽眼,是一些细碎银子。母亲把银子掰成两份,分别放在弟兄俩的手里。而后,合上双眼,回西天去了。

弟兄两个,哥哥为人悭吝,气量狭窄,媳妇泼辣、刻薄。弟弟为人憨厚、老实,媳妇勤谨、本分。哥嫂总攥算着如何把弟弟那份银子弄到手,开始碍于在一个家里硬把银子拿了,张扬出去,惹得一个臭名,声誉不好,就思忖着不如和弟弟先分了家,再找机会把银子统统捞过来。哥嫂看看破旧的草房,维持不了多少年月,假惺惺故作慷慨的样子,哄骗弟弟说:"让你住爹妈留下的房子,我们搬出去,你出点力帮盖盖。"

弟弟和媳妇听了,满以为哥嫂慷慨,说不尽一番感激话。

然而,家里的什物用具,哥嫂却尽挑好的拣。结果,弟弟除一间旧房子和炊具杂什,所得无几。哥嫂靠弟弟的帮助,盖起了一栋新房子。从此,弟兄两家便各居一处,忙于自寻生计。

家分开了,可是弟弟的银子还没沾着半文,哥嫂整天吃不安,睡不宁。一天,哥嫂突然打听到弟弟一家要到山上去,两口子,你看我,我瞄你,眉飞色舞,认为时机到了。待弟弟一出家门,嫂嫂就悄悄躲在后面,一直瞧着弟弟一家真的上山了,她赶忙趸回家里,告诉了她的男人。哥哥乘机偷偷地溜进弟弟的家,撬开装银子的木盒,把银子全部拿走,放一把沙石在木盒里,依旧摆在原处,就像没有人动过一样。

哥嫂把偷来的银子放在自家的银子盒里,恰巧满满一小盒,沉甸甸的。两口子愿望实现了，忍不住"噗哧噗哧"地笑出声来；哥哥抱着银子盒掂一阵，嫂嫂又接过去亲热一气；默着这小辈子吃穿、开销何须愁，把玩了半天，才把银子盒藏到牢靠的地方。

隔了不久，弟弟和媳妇想添置一点炊具，又没有什么值钱的卖货，商量着破费一点儿妈妈留下的银子吧。于是，夫妻俩一起打开装银子的木盒。木盒沉沉的，十分奇怪，打开一看，嗬！全是白花花的银锭子。夫妻俩摸不着头脑，傻呆着，不知是怎么回事。弟弟想把这件怪事告诉哥哥，便拔腿向哥哥家奔去。弟弟刚跨进门槛，只见哥嫂哭丧着脸，耷拉着脑瓜，气也不吭一声。原来哥嫂也想拿点银子，去集市兑换些好衣好物，殊不知，打开装银子的盒子一看，哪里还是白生生的银子，全变成硬邦邦的石头了。

弟弟看到哥嫂阴沉沉的嘴脸，疑惑不解地问道：

"哥哥怎么了？"

"没什么。"哥哥没好气地回答。

弟弟把自己木盒的银子忽然变满了讲给哥嫂听，顺便问道："哥嫂的银子咯是也变多了？"哥嫂听了，心里扎实闷糟，可又是老天报应，哑巴吃黄连——有口无处说，只好强装笑脸说："我们的银子盒也满着。"

搜集整理：杨叶生

编者按： 这是一个害人不成反害己的报应故事。憨厚老实人，在不知不觉中得到了神明的庇佑，得到了全部的财富。而刻薄吝啬的哥嫂，自以为得意，却搬起石头砸了自己的脚。

这样的故事情节，适当调整，进入影视剧，将是特别精彩的桥段。

The Silver Box of Two Brothers

A long time ago, there was an Achang family, and the mother led her two sons to make a living together. She was hardworking, kind-hearted, and relied on picking wild herbs to sustain the family. After years of hard work, she finally raised her two sons to adulthood. Later, she also arranged their marriages. At that time, the wrinkles on the mother's forehead seems to indicate that her life had reached the end. Her tired body could no longer support her. She felt that her time had come to an end, so she called the two sons to her bedside, arranged all the things that needed to be done after she had died, and then reached for something under the pillow. She slowly opened the cloth package and revealed some silver pieces. The mother divided the silver into two parts and gave each brother a share. Then she closed her eyes and went to enjoy her time in heaven.

The elder brother was stingy and narrow-minded, and his wife was aggressive and harsh. The younger brother was honest and simple-minded, and his wife was diligent and gentle. The elder brother and his wife calculated how to get the younger brother's share of silver. Initially, they wanted to forcefully take it, but after all, they were a family, which would tarnish their reputation. They decided that it would be better for them to separate, and they then would find a way to get all the silver from the younger brother later. The elder brother and his wife pretended to be generous and suggested that the younger brother could live in the house left by their parents, and they would move out and build a new house with the younger brother's help.

The younger brother and his wife were grateful, thinking that their elder brother was being generous.

However, the elder brother and his wife picked all the good furniture and left the younger brother with only an old house and left almost nothing behind. The elder brother built a new house by the help of the younger brother. From then on, the two families lived separately and were all busy making a living on their own.

Although the families were separated, the elder brother and his wife worried constantly because they hadn't yet taken the younger brother's share of silver. One day, the elder brother and his wife heard that the younger brother's family were going to the mountains. They thought that their chance had come. As soon as the younger brother left his house, the elder brother secretly entered and opened the wooden box where the silver was stored. He took all the silver and replaced it with a pile of rocks. The box was then put back in its original place, as if nothing had happened.

The elder brother and his wife put the stolen silver in their silver box. The silver added up to be exactly one box full. The couple's wish was fulfilled, and they couldn't help laughing. They enjoyed playing with the silver for a while before hided it in a secure place.

Not long after, the younger brother and his wife wanted to buy some furniture, but they had nothing valuable to sell. They decided to spend some of the silver left by their mother. Together, they opened the wooden box and found that it was strangely heavy. When the box was opened, they saw that it was full of silver. The couple was puzzled and didn't know what to do. The younger brother decided to tell his elder brother, so he ran to his house. However, when he arrived, he saw that his brother's wife was crying, and his brother was in a bad mood. It turned out that the elder brother and sister-in-law also wanted to go to the market to buy some good clothes and good things, but when they opened the box, all of their silver turned into stones.

Seeing the sorrow faces of his brother and sister-in-law, the younger brother asked, "What's wrong, brother?"

"Nothing," the elder brother replied irately.

The younger brother then told them how his wooden box suddenly filled with silver and asked whether the amount of his brother's silver had also increased. While the elder brother's wife felt bad and guilty, speechless, she put on a forced smile and said, "Our silver box is also full".

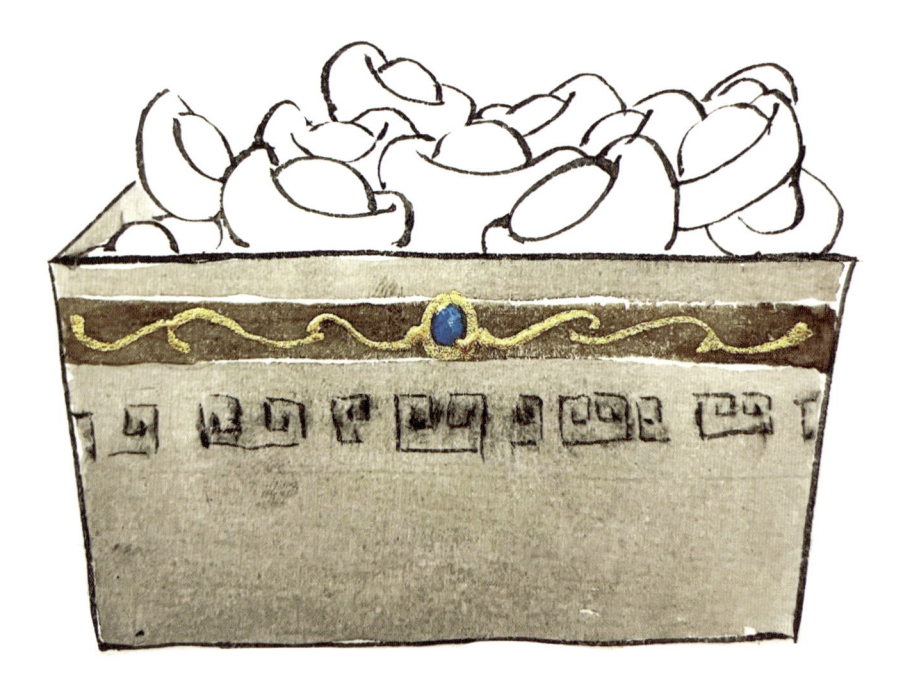

偷银罐

从前有三个人一起去背盐巴。途中，当他们经过一片坟地时，有个人见路边有个被牛踩塌了的泥洞，便好奇地伸头去瞧。嗬！真是财星高照，洞里只见白花花的银子闪闪发亮。三个人又抠又盘，一阵工夫，扒出了一大罐银子。

其中有个人，瞧见那么多大锭大锭的银子，心里就像猫抓一样直痒痒，他暗想："这罐银子，要是我一个人得了多好啊。"于是，他摸摸瘪下巴，对其他两个伙伴摆摆手，说："咳！银子罐还是先埋下，等背盐巴回来再分吧。"两个伙伴不以为然，坚持要先分，说有了银子可以多买些盐巴回家。一番争执后，他们决定先分一点，留下大半罐，重新选地方埋好，便上路了。

三个人走了一段路，提议把银子埋下的那个人，扯谎肚子疼。另外两个伙伴要背他，他说背着肚子疼得更厉害；扶着他走，他又装出寸步难行的样子。两个伙伴见他疼得"哎哟哎哟"叫个不停，非常着急。这时，肚子疼的人摆出一副无可奈何的神情，向两个伙伴摇摇手说："你们走吧，多背些盐巴回来，我走不动了，就在这里等你们。"两个伙伴只好把他托付给附近的人家，上路买盐巴去了。

肚子疼的人，到了半夜偷偷爬起来，摸到白天埋银子的地方，扒开土，把银子罐取出来。伸手进去一摸，里面哪里是银子，竟然是大半罐水。他十分奇怪，咋个银子会变成水呢？白天清清楚楚看见还有大半罐银子，一点不假，可是现在……他转念一想，即使是水也是银子变的，我要把它喝下去。于是，不管三七二十一，他心一横，便仰着脖子咕嘟咕嘟把罐子里的水喝了大半。直到肚子装不下，才放下罐子，悄悄回去躺在床上。

刚合上眼，他的肚子就疼起来，叽里咕噜一阵阵地叫，肠子就像扭着一样疼。他在床上翻来覆去，仰躺着，肚子胀鼓鼓的；匍着睡，挤着肚更难受；侧卧着，猛地想屙起屎来，他急忙跑到院心，才扯开裤头，屎就稀里哗啦屙在地上。屙了一阵，他以为舒服了，可是才爬上床，又想屙屎了。他赶忙下床，这下更糟糕，才跨出门槛，就在屋檐下屙起来。刚合上眼，肚子又怪起来了，没等出门，就在堂屋里把屎屙出来了。好不容易挨到天麻麻亮，摸摸床上，不知什么时候又屙了屎。他难堪极了，一骨碌爬起来，想赶快溜掉。其实，他一晚上爬上爬下，主人家被他搅得一夜睡不安稳。他见主人家也有了动静，赶忙来到门口，一句"我走了，麻烦主人家了"的话还没说完，就跑出门外。

主人听到来客大清八早就要走，感到惊奇，担心客人出了什么事，推开房门就来追。只见堂屋里摆着一堆雪花银子，屋檐下掉着一堆，院心里也撒着一堆。主人想是客人匆忙，把财宝背漏了，赶紧追出门外，只见客人埋着头没命地跑出老远，连忙高声叫道："大哥，你的银子掉了。"客人只听见主人喊叫，也没有听清喊什么，顿时面红耳热，脸上辣乎乎的，回话说："主人家，麻烦了，帮收拾收拾。"便一口气跑回家去了。

讲述：孙广诚
搜集整理：杨叶生

编者按：贪心的人，总是贪心不足，最后会落得人财两空。这是传统民间故事的经典主题。

这个格外贪心的人，为了独吞财宝，装模作样地生病，结果真的让他生病了。他希望多拿走银子，却把银子留给了收留他的人家。

Steal the Silver Pot

Once upon a time, there were three people who decided to carry salt together. Along the way, they passed by a cemetery and one of them spotted a mud hole that had been trampled by a cow. Out of curiosity, he leaned over to look. Oh wow, shiny silver sparkled inside the hole. The three of them quickly dug inside the hole. Quickly, they uncovered a large jar filled with silver.

One of the men, seeing all those big silver ingots, couldn't help but feel an itch inside him, as if there was a cat scratching in his heart. He thought to himself, "If I could have this jar of silver all to myself, that would be great!" So he rubbed his chin and said to the other two men, "Ahem!" Let's bury the jar of silver for now and divide it when we come back with the salt." The other two men didn't agree with him and insisted on dividing the silver first, because with the silver, they could buy more salt to take back home. After an argument, they decided to divide a small portion of the silver and leave most of them buried in a new place, then they set off on their journey.

After walking for a while, the men who had suggested burying the silver lied that he had a stomachache. The other two men offered to carry him on the back, but he said that would make it even more painful. When they tried to help him walk, he pretended to have difficulties in moving. The two men became worried when they heard him moaning in pain. Then, the man with the stomachache pretended to be helpless and waved his hand at the two other men, then said, "You guys go ahead and bring back more salt. I can't continue walking, so I'll wait here for you." So the two men entrusted him to a nearby household and went on their way to buy salt.

When it was midnight, the man with the stomachache quietly got up, made his way to the spot where they had buried the silver during the day, and started digging. To his surprise, when he reached inside the jar, it wasn't filled with silver but water. He was confused. How can silver turn into water? But he thought to himself, "It's water that generated from silver, so I should drink it". Without further hesitation, he gulped down half of the water from the jar. When his stomach couldn't allow him to drink any more, he put down the jar and quietly went to bed.

As soon as he closed his eyes, his stomach started to ache. His stomach rumbledand churned, causing him great pain. He tossed and turned in his bed, unable to settle down on a comfortable sleeping position. Lying on his back made his stomach feel super full. When he curled up in the bed, his stomach felt even more uncomfortable. Just as he tried to lie on his side, suddenly he felt the urge to poop. He rushed into the yard, right after he undid his pants, he pooped on the ground. After a while, he thought he felt better, but as soon as he climbed back into bed, he wanted to poop again. He hurriedly got out of bed, but this time it was worse. Just as he stepped outside, he pooped just under the eaves. As soon as he closed his eyes, his stomach started to rumble again. Before he could even leave the house, he defecated in the main room. Finally, when it was dawn, he touched his bed and realized that he had pooped on the bed at some point. Feeling extremely embarrassed, and quickly got up and wanted to leave as soon as possible. In fact, because of his climbing up and down all night, the house owner didn't sleep well. The man heard that the house owner was getting up as well, so he hurried to the door. "I'm leaving now, thank you for keeping me for the night, and sorry for the trouble." With that said, the man dashed out of the house.

The house owner heard the hurried departure of the guest and felt surprised. Is there something wrong with him? So the house owner pushed the door open and went after the guest, concerned if something had happened. When he came out of the door, he was shocked by the piles of silver in the main room, more scattered under the eaves, and even more scattered in the yard. The house owner thought that the guest must have been in a rush and accidentally dropped his silver. He quickly chased after the guest and saw him running far ahead with his head down. The house owner then shouted, "Sir, you dropped your silver!" However, the guest only heard the house owner's shout without understanding the words clearly. His face turned red, feeling embarrassed, and replied, "Sorry! Please take care of it for me". Then, he ran back home as fast as he could without looking back.

各人心肝各人带

从前,有三个伙伴,到处去揽生意,找活路。他们一起做活,得来的工钱平均分,谁个也不多拿,谁个也不多得。三个人平时相处得很不错,要喝凉水共一瓢,要吃晌午同一锅,哪个也没有起过坏心,哪个也没有吃过亏。

有一天,他们一起去帮人挖基槽。挖了半天,还剩一个旮旯。左挖一锄,"当"的一声是石头;右挖一锄,"当"的一声还是石头。三人一起铲开泥土,露出一块大石板。他们挖去石板四周的土,从石板下边掏出一个洞,然后用木杠使劲撬,费了九牛二虎之力,总算把石板撬开。推开石板,三人脸上霎时堆满了笑容,原来石板底下埋了一缸雪花纹银。三人互相递递眼色,一声不响,当场分了银子,各人装进自己的口袋。三人得了银子后,便约着打一餐牙祭,就把银子送回家。于是,就分头去买办——三个人,一个煮饭,一个买肉,一个打酒。

自古有句老话:银子是白的,心是黑的。银子是白的,人人皆知。至于心是黑是白,那就是猪肝羊肝街前卖,各人心肝各人带了。

三人分开后,煮饭的一边凑柴火,一边琢磨:放点毒药在饭里,到晚上让他俩先回老家去,我再去摸出他俩的银子,大路朝天,我走我的,天知地知!

买肉的端着一盘香喷喷的鸡肉,口水都快滴出来了。可是他边走边寻思:下点毒药在肉里,到晚上他俩一翘脚,一大袋银子全部归我,够我吃了。

打酒的提着一大瓶陈年老酒,闻着酒气醇香,真想开怀痛饮一场。可是他边走边思量:撒点毒药在酒里,到晚上他俩上西天后,我拿着银子就走,何愁没有高房大屋!

三人会拢后,煮饭的说:"我饿不得,已经先吃了两碗饭,我要喝酒吃肉。"

买肉的说:"我馋不得,汤锅铺里已经开过荤,我要喝酒吃饭。"

打酒的说:"干鱼做不得猫枕头,酒鬼见酒哪有不喝?我已经喝过了,我要吃饭吃肉。"

晚上,三人睡在铺上进入了甜美的梦乡,又从梦境升飞到了"极乐"世界。

搜集整理:杨叶生

编者按: 人算不如天算,当人心诡诈,每个人都损人的时候,这就不是一个零和博弈,而是一个多输结果。

本来是很好的合作伙伴,在收入有限的情况下,还可以和睦相处,公平分配。但是当诱惑巨大到一定程度,他们立马就失去了合作意识,开始动心思,想独吞财富。

他们分别借用了平时的信任,又各自做着自己的美梦,却也很公平地都得到了死亡的结局。

这种囚徒困境的地方故事版本,很有寓意地暗示了一些合伙人在没有利益的时候,尚可以维持体面,一旦有了利益冲突,就会变成仇人。

Everyone Has Their Own Intentions

Once upon a time, there were three men who went around and seeking for business opportunities and made a living together. They worked together and divided their earnings equally, without anyone taking more or taking less than the others. They got along with each other very well and shared everything, never cheated on each other.

One day, they were help for dig a foundation groove and had been working for hours until they reached a spot where the shovels hit something hard. After removing the soil, they discovered a large stone slab. When they dug out the soil around the stone slab and pried the slab away, they found that underneath the slab there was a jar filled with silver. Without said a word, they split the silver and put their share in their pockets. Then they decided to have a feast and go home. So they decided to split up and go to buy their own things: one to buy meat, another to buy rice and the last to buy wine.

As the saying goes, "The silver is white, but the heart is black." Everyone knew the silver was guittless. But people's hearts were unpredictable. Each person carried their own hidden selfishness.

After the three persons aparted, the person who cooked rice thought, "I'll put some poison in the food and kill them, so I can steal their silver in secret. Who would ever know?"

The person who bought the meat thought, "I'll put poison in the meat and let them die tonight, so I can take all the silver myself".

The person who brought the wine thought, "I'll poison the drink and wait for them to die, so I can keep all the silver and have a luxurious life"!

When they reunited, the person who cooked rice said, "I'm not hungry. I have already eaten two bowls of rice. I only wanted to drink wine and eat meat".

The person who bought the meat said, "I was too hungry, so I already ate some meat. I want to drink wine and eat rice".

The person who brought the wine said, "As a drunkard, how can I resist alcohol? I already had enough wine. Now I want to eat some meat and rice".

That night, all three men went into sleep and never woke up again. They all had sweet dreams and then went to heaven.

腊良和腊洪

从前有两个穷小伙子，一个叫腊良，一个叫腊洪，他们同住在财主的牛厩楼上。腊洪给财主放牛，腊良给财主挖地，他们平时相处得很和睦，像是一对儿亲兄弟。

有一天，腊良挖园子，发现地下埋着一个罐子，打开盖子一看，尽是大锭大锭的雪花银子。腊良依然原封不动地把银罐埋在地里，用土盖好，打上记号。腊良想到腊洪也是穷巴巴的，挣死挣活地干，熬了半辈子，还没有家，便打算深夜财主睡熟后，约上腊洪一起把银子挖出来，然后逃到别的地方去成家立业。

晚上，刚上床，腊良把自己的发现和打算，通盘告诉了腊洪。哪晓得，人心隔肚皮，腊洪听了后暗自打着主意，他假装感激地说："你挖地辛苦了，先睡下。我白天放牛在山上睡过了，等到了半夜我一定叫醒你。"

腊良信以为真，便放心地打起呼噜来。

腊洪等腊良睡着后，悄悄来到园子，照腊良告诉的记号，从地下挖出银罐。他打开盖子，伸手进去一摸，哪晓得里面尽是些毛茸茸、软塌塌的大毛虫。腊洪以为腊良骗他，非常气愤，便想作弄腊良，开开心，报复一下。腊洪爬上牛厩房顶，扒开茅草，掏出一个洞，把整罐的大毛虫，倒下腊良睡的床上。想不到毛虫从罐子出来，竟变成一锭锭银子，落在腊良的身上。

腊良从睡梦中惊醒，用手一摸，全是大锭大锭的银子。他想大概是自己睡惑了，腊洪把银子挖出来，放在自己身边，便把落在床上的银子，拾起来放进袋子。他再往腊洪床上一摸，空空的，估计腊洪已经拿着银子走了，便提起脚离开了财主家。再说腊洪把毛虫倒下后，又把罐子埋在原地，然后一声不响地躺回自己床上。

第二天早晨，腊洪起来，不见腊良，仔细一看，床上掉着两锭银子。

腊洪手拿银子，恍然大悟，但已经后悔莫及了。

讲述者：赵大厚
搜集整理：杨叶生

编者按： 这个故事中，有一个人善，有一个人恶。善的人本来可以得到全部的财富，他却想着分享。而恶的人原本什么都没有，却想独吞。

想独吞的人发现这不是银子的时候，恼羞成怒，把怒气发作在那个善良的人身上。他并没有进行反思和自我批判，反而指责他人。

结果是善有善报，恶有恶报，大快人心。

La Liang and La Hong

Once upon a time, there were two poor young men named La Liang and La Hong, who lived together upstairs of the rich man's cowshed. La Hong looked after the cattle for the rich man, while La Liang dug the ground for him. They got along very well as if they were real brothers.

One day, while digged in the garden, La Liang found a pot that was buried underground. When he opened the lid, he found that it was full of silver. La Liang decided to leave a mark where the pot was buried and went to bed. He thought that La Hong was also poor and always hard-working but still haven't got a home. So he decided to wake up La Hong later to dig up the silver and run away to start a new life.

That night, La Liang told La Hong of his discovery and plan. However, La Hong had his own ideas in mind and pretended to be grateful and told La Liang, "You must be exhausted for digging the ground, and you can rest now. I slept today on the mountains when I herded the cattle, so I can watch over. When it is midnight, I will wake you up".

La Liang believed him and went to sleep.

After La Liang has allen asleep, La Hong went to the garden and dug up the pot. But he found that it filled with soft and furry large caterpillars. La Hong thought La Liang tricked him and decided to have trick him as well by dumping the caterpillars on La Liang's bed as revenge. Unexpectedly, when the caterpillars came out of the pot, they suddenly transformed into silver, falling onto La Liang's body while he slept.

La Liang woke up from his sleep and touched the silver, felt strange, but assumed that it must be La Hong who had brought it to him. He searched for La Hong, but he was nowhere to be found, so La Liang took the silver and left the rich man's house. Meanwhile, La Hong buried the pot back and went to bed.

The next morning, La Hong saw that La Liang was gone, and when he looked at La Liang's bed, he saw two pieces of silver. La Hong took the silver and realized his mistake, but it was too late.

仙草

很久以前，有两个伙计，大的叫腊纳，小的叫腊进。他俩出门去帮人做活。他俩做活做了整整三年零三个月，平时他俩省吃俭用，工钱足足攒了几十两银子。

一天，腊纳找腊进商量："伙计，我们得把挣来的银子送回去，再说，也该和家人团圆团圆了。"腊进嘴里不说，心里可早想家了。他俩辞了主人，背着银子包回家了。

走到半路，腊纳黑了心，他想：这些银子，买田买地，起房盖屋，够吃够用够开销了。他乘腊进不提防，猛力把他推倒在地，一顿拳打脚踢，腊进晕过去了；他从口袋里掏出锥子，戳瞎了腊进的双眼。然后把他拖去塞在一个大石缝里，他带着全部钱财一个人走回家去。

深夜，一阵凉风飕飕，腊进神志恢复了，他开始做梦，梦见一个鬓发雪白的地神，和蔼、慈祥，拄着一根乌亮乌亮的龙头拐杖，站在自己面前。地神告诉他，在石缝旁边伸手就能抓到的地方，长着一棵仙草，只要掐下仙草，揉细后放在眼睛上一擦，眼伤就会好。地神又指点他，向前走三天路就能走到一个很大的坝子，这是一个缺水的干坝子，老百姓广种薄收，生活很苦。走到坝子头，那里有一堵高高的石崖，石崖底下有一条暗河，掀开岩石，往下挖，就有囤子大的一沟水流出来。有了水，老百姓就可以种稻谷，吃白米了。

腊进苏醒后知道自己在做梦，想睁开眼睛怎么也睁不开，用手一摸满眼是淤血。他想起梦中地神的话，伸手到石缝边一摸，果然有一株小草，他把小草掐来揉碎糊在眼睛上，眼伤顿时好了，淤血也散了，眼睛也亮了。又过了一会儿，腊进精神好了，力气也足了。天刚亮，他就起身上路，渴了他就捧起泉水解渴；肚子饿了，他就要些包谷饭充饥。走了整整三天，真的出现了一个宽敞的坝子，和梦中的神讲得完全一样。他来到坝子头，又累又饿，就坐在石崖下休息，他喝了一捧泉水，吃了身上带着的干粮，抬头看见高高的石崖，又想起了梦中地神的指点，他俯下身子用耳朵贴在石缝上一听，地下果真有哗哗的流水声。

他心里十分高兴，转回头找到坝子最大的一个寨子，打听到管辖这个坝子的财主，问他："这里良田数不完，老百姓缺穿少吃到底为什么?"财主说，这里自古以来是干坝子，春雨贵似油，夏雨遍地流，谁要引得来沟水，就把坝子分给他一半。腊进问财主："你说的话算不算数?"财主说："若有反悔，雷打火烧。"腊进就约着寨子里的数百个穷人，带着工具和干粮，来到了坝头高高的石崖脚下。人们卷着裤脚，挥动锄头，夜以继日，挖了七天七夜，一股囤子大的清水喷涌出来，他和穷苦的老百姓高兴得流出了眼泪。哗哗的沟水流到了村村寨寨，流满了坝子。财主有言在先，只好把半个坝子分给了腊进。

腊进又把田分给了老百姓，老百姓有了水有了田，劲头足了，庄稼也越种越好，从此过上了暖衣饱食的日子。

腊纳带着钱财在一个僻静的地方，被劫路的强盗杀死，搜走了全部银子。

搜集整理：杨叶生

编者按： 财产分配问题最容易看出人心。

被害者得到神明救助点拨，医治了自己的眼疾，还知道了水利的秘密。于是，他按照神仙的指点，一步步从死亡之地走了出来，还过上了幸福的生活。而那个谋财害命的人反而人财两空，客死他乡。

这个故事也说明了水对于当地的农业具有的关键性作用。

The Miraculous Herb

Long long ago, there were two men, the elder named La Na and the younger called La Jin. They went out to work diligently for three years and three months, saving money by living frugally. At the end of these years, they had accumulated a few dozen taels of silver.

One day, La Na approached La Jin and said, "My friend, we should take the money we earned and reunite with our families". Though La Jin didn't say anything, he had already been longing to go home. They left their employer and carried the silver they earned back home.

On the way, La Na had some bad intentions. He thought to himself, "With this amount of silver, I can buy land, build a house, and have enough budget for food and expenses". When La Jin was off guard, La Na forcefully pushed him to the ground, punched and kicked him until La Jin was left unconscious. La Na then pulled out a dagger from his pocket and blinded La Jin by stabbed him in the eyes. He then dragged La Jin to a large crevice among rocks and left him there, while he took all the money himself and left.

Late at night, cool breeze blew, and La Jin regained his consciousness. He dreamed of a kind and nice deity with snow-white hair, leaning on a shiny and black dragon-headed cane, and stood in front of him. The deity told him that next to the crevice where he could reach, there grew a miraculous herb. If he picked the herb, crushed it, and applied it to his eyes, his injuries would heal. The deity also had instructed La Jin to walk for three days until he reached a large plain. This plain was a dry and barren place where the people suffered from lack of water. At the end of the plain there was a tall rock cliff, underneath it was a hidden river. If the rocks were removed, water would appear. With water, the people there could then grow crops and have rice to eat.

When La Jin woke up, he realized that he had been dreaming but found himself unable to open his eyes, no matter how hard he tried. When he touched his face, he felt the blood around his eyes. La Jin remembered the words of the deity in his dream, so he reached out and found a small herb. He plucked the plant, crushed it, and applied it to his eyes. Magically, his eyes healed, the blood was gone, and he could see again. After some time, La Jin regained his strength and energy. As soon as dawn came, he continued his journey. When he felt thirsty, he drank spring water; when he felt hungry, he begged for some corn and rice to eat. After walking for three days, he arrived at a vast and barren plain, exactly as the deity had described. He walked till the end of the plain and felt exhausted and hungry. So he sat down to rest beneath the stone cliff. He drank a handful of spring water and ate the rations he had brought with him. Looking up at the stone cliff, he remembered the words of the deity in his dream. He bent down, pressed his ear against the crevice, and heard water flowing underground.

With overjoyed, La Jin turned around and found the largest village in the field. He found the landowner who governed the area and asked, "Why are the lands here left uncultivated while the people struggle to make a living"? The landowner explained that the plain had always been a dry and barren place, with rain as precious as oil. Whoever could bring water source into the plain would receive half of the land. La Jin asked the land owner, "Does your words count"? The landowner replied, "If I break my promise, let me be struck by thunder and be burnt by fire". La Jin then gathered hundreds of poor villagers, brought tools and rations, then they arrived at the foot of the stone cliff at the end of the plain. They rolled up their sleeves and swung their hoes. They had worked for seven days and nights until a steady stream of water burst out. La Jin and the villagers were so overjoyed that they were crying. The flow of water flew throughout the plain. The landowner, keeping his promise, had no choice but to give half of the field to La Jin.

    La Jin then distributed the land among the villagers. With water and the fertile land, the villagers now had hope, and their crops grew abundantly. From that day on, they lived a happy and rich life.

    As for La Na, he was killed by bandits in a remote place, and his silver was taken away by them.

姊妹三人

从前，有一户人家，有姊妹三个。

一天，姊妹们去后园摘桃子。一串串紫红的桃子，把树枝坠得弯腰驼背，一个个大鲜桃，像一包包蜜汁，真叫人眼馋。姊妹三个想摘桃子，踮起脚尖还够不着，爬树又怕挂烂花筒裙，急得在桃树脚下团团转。

吃不着桃子，大姐心里怪不是味儿，便努努樱桃嘴唇，心想爬墙上树本是小伙子的事，也亏她想得出："要是哪个来把桃子摇下来，我家的老妹就嫁给他。"

也怕是人有虔心圣有灵，话音刚落，不知从哪儿爬来一条大蛇，点着头，径直往树上爬。姊妹三个像枯木桩一样呆站着，不知脚往哪儿放，手往哪儿摆。刹那间，只见蛇用尾巴在桃树间噼里啪啦一搅，鲜红鲜红的大桃，嘀嘀嘟嘟地掉了一地。姊妹三人恍惚如梦初醒，大姐赶忙说声："蛇哥哥，不要打了。"她们各自提起筒裙，拾了一大兜桃子。

姊妹三人刚走进家，蛇也跟着爬进来了，一直爬到堂屋里，卷成一圈躺在地上。

不久，妈妈从外面进家来，看见一条大蛇趴在堂屋里，就说："哎呀，你们摘桃子，咋个连蛇都领进来了？"边说边去拿柴棍，准备把蛇打死。大姐见了急忙阻拦，说："妈妈，别打它。今天我们摘桃子，说哪个上树摇下桃子，我家老妹就嫁给他。"妈妈只听说过嫁鸡随鸡，嫁狗随狗，嫁个树桩头也要守，没听说过哪个姑娘嫁给过蛇，就板起面孔指着大姐说："那你去嫁它吧，大姑娘。"大姑娘压根儿没有想到过自己要嫁给蛇做媳妇，就说："我不去。"妈妈又说："二姑娘，你去吧。"二姑娘作出一副不屑一顾的神态耸耸鼻子说："我更不去。"妈妈只好叫三姑娘嫁给蛇去。老妹素来心地善良，言听计从，见两个姐姐都把自己往火坑推，没得办法，只好跟着蛇走。

老妹跟着蛇来到蛇洞前，蛇回过头来说话了："你闭着眼睛，踩着我的尾巴。"老妹只感到全身一阵轻飘飘，悠悠忽忽，蛇说声："到家了。"老妹睁眼一看，面前站着一个英俊的年轻人，面貌俊美，脸上流露着温柔和善的神色。年轻人拉着老妹的手，欢欢喜喜地往他们的新房走去。

月亮跟着太阳，星星追着月亮。老妹生下一个儿子。妈妈听说老妹过得衣宽食饱，特地跑来看她。老妹给妈妈穿细着软，吃的是酥黄卤白。妈妈回去时，老妹给了衣服、裙子、首饰。

大姑娘和二姑娘见妈妈得了那么多好东西，看得眼花缭乱，又是惊奇又是眼红，争着要去老妹家逛一转。

大姑娘先去了。老妹也是酥黄卤白地招待她。大姐看着妹妹过着神仙般的日子，妒火中烧，嫉恨得咬牙切齿，悔不该当初自己不嫁给蛇作媳妇。大姐费尽心机，绞尽脑汁，想了三天三夜，终于拿定了一个坏主意。一天，大姐趁妹夫不在家，就约着老妹到后园逛。后园里有个大池塘。她们来到池塘边，大姐便要和老妹换穿衣服、裙子。换好后，大姐站在池塘边，装着卖俏，叫妹妹说："你快来瞧，我在水里的影子多好看！"害人之心不可有，防人之心不可无。老妹不知是计，应声伸头瞄水里的影子。大姐趁老妹毫无戒备，一掌把她推下了池塘。还找来竹竿，把妹妹的尸体按在水底下。

大姐为了弄假成真，蒙骗妹夫，从头到脚，照妹妹身样打扮，撇着妹妹的声调，光走路、说话、吃饭，就练了三天三夜，自认已学得惟妙惟肖、滴水不漏。她自己也忍不住"噗哧"地笑了起来。

老妹的丈夫回来了，看见妻子脸上突然有了麻子，心下十分疑惑，就问："你的脸上以前没有麻子，今天哪来那么多麻子？"大姐撒谎说："你几天不在家，我在灶脚打瞌睡，灶蚂鸡爬上来咬成的。"

老妹的儿子天一亮就起来，先到后园磨刀，然后去割马草。每天都有只小雀飞来，落在池塘边的树上，对着她儿子叫："早早去，早早来。"儿子也就天天早去早回。父亲看儿子举止不同寻常，就问："你现在为什么去得早，回家早？"

儿子回答说："后园有只雀，天天叫我早早去，早早来。"

第二天早晨，父子两人一起到后园磨刀。只听"噗噜"一声，小雀又飞来了，连声说："早早去，早早来。"小雀看见丈夫站在池塘边，从树枝飞来落在他肩上。他小心翼翼地把小雀捉了关在笼子里，挂在屋檐下。父子两人，每天出去要看一眼，回到家也先要看一眼笼里的小雀。

一天，小雀看见大姐，就啐一口唾沫，叫起来："呸呸，没良心。"大姐听了羞愧满脸，但她是一不做，二不休，从笼子里把小雀抓出来，三两下就把它掐死了埋在后园地里。

埋小雀的地方，很快长出了一棵桃树。

老妹的丈夫和儿子回来，不见小雀，十分伤心，问媳妇，大姐说："小雀自己死了，我把它埋在后园边。"父子俩到后园一看，一棵新桃树长出来了，满树桃子结得红彤彤的。父子俩摘下的桃子甜蜜蜜。大姐去摘，只见毛虫掉，桃子摘不着，倒把裙子撕烂了。大姐一气之下，把桃树砍了晒干当柴烧。

桃子柴在火塘里变成了红彤彤的火炭。恰好有个邻居来要火炭，大姐说："火炭，你只管拿去。"邻居拣了一个大火炭拿回家，放在火塘里，大火炭一下子变成了一个小媳妇。她把自己的遭遇告诉了邻居，并请他告诉丈夫和儿子。

老妹的丈夫和儿子来了，她从篱笆缝里伸出手来。儿子一见就喊起来："我妈的手，我妈在房里哪！"丈夫看见大姐和老妹穿着打扮一样，分辨不出真假。老妹告诉丈夫，在院心打一棵桩，跳过去的就是你的真妻子，跳不过去的是假的。于是把大姐叫来了。大姐看见老妹，心乱如麻，恨上天无路，入地无门，心里只是扑通扑通地跳。老妹走到木桩前，轻轻一跳就过去了。大姐心慌意乱，刚抬起脚就扑倒在树桩上，被扎死了。

老妹和丈夫终于团圆了。

讲述：张小凤
搜集：杨叶生
整理：杨叶茂

编者按： 坏姐姐与善良妹妹的故事中包含灰姑娘的三姐妹关系，还有美女与野兽故事的情节。

如果说有什么不一样，那就是这个故事的离奇和变化。从人变雀鸟，从雀鸟变为桃木，从桃木变为火炭，又从火炭变为小媳妇。这种不断的变化，最终恢复人形的情节已经在阿昌族故事中多次出现。

这样的故事，追求的不是可信，而是离奇。越是离奇，越是有吸引力。

The Three Sisters

Once upon a time, there was a family with three sisters.

One day, the sisters went to the back yard garden to pick peaches. Clusters of purplish red peaches weighed down the branches, bending them low. Each large peach looked so tempting and delicious. The three sisters wanted to pick the peaches, but they couldn't reach them even on tiptoe and climbing the tree would ruin their dresses. So they anxiously circled the tree, unsure of what to do. Frustrated that she couldn't reach the peaches, the eldest sister pouted and said, "If someone could knock down the peaches for us, my youngest sister will marry him".

As soon as she said these words, a big snake crawled out of nowhere, it slithered straight up the tree. The three sisters stood frozen like wooden posts, unsure of what to do. In a flash, the snake whipped its tail through the branches, and the red peaches all fell to the ground. The elder sister, snapping out of their daze, quickly exclaimed, "Dear snake, you can stop now". The sisters gathered as many peaches as they could.

As the sisters went back home, the snake followed them inside, who coiled up and lay down in their living room.

Soon after, their mother returned home, and seeing the large snake in the hall, she exclaimed, "Ah! You brought a snake inside"? With that said, she grabbed a firewood stick, intending to kill the snake. The eldest sister hurriedly stopped her and said, "Mother, don't hit it. Today, when we were picking peaches, I said that whoever shook the peaches down could marry my youngest sister". The mother, who never heard of anything like that, frowned and said, "Then you can go to marry it, girl". The eldest sister never thought she would be a snake's wife, so she said, "No, I do not want to marry it". The mother then said, "My second daughter, you can go and marry the snake." The second sister made a look of disdain and said, "I am not going to marry it either". So the mother had to tell the youngest girl to go. The youngest sister had always been kind and obedient. Saw that her two sisters all wanted her to go, she had no choice but to follow the snake.

The youngest sister followed the snake to its den. The snake turned to her and spoke, "Close your eyes and step on my tail." She felt herself become light as a feather, floated gently. Then the snake said, "We're home". When she opened her eyes, she saw a handsome young man stood before her, with a kind and gentle look on his face. The young man took the youngest sister's hand and walked joyfully towards their new house.

As the moon follows the sun, the stars follow the moon, time flies, the youngest sister gave birth to a son. Her mother, heard that her daughter was living a comfortable life, came to visit. The youngest sister dressed her mother in fine, soft clothes and served her delicious food. When her mother returned home, the youngest sister gave her clothes, dresses and jewelries.

The other two sisters felt envious when they saw the many fine things that their mother had received. They also wanted to visit their youngest sister's house.

The eldest sister went first, and the youngest sister welcomed her with the same delicious food. The eldest sister saw that her youngest sister was living like a fairy and felt extremely jealous. She regretted that she was not the one who married the snake. She has spent three days and nights plotting until she finally devised a wicked plan. One day, when her brother-in-law left away, the eldest sister invited her youngest sister to walk to the back yard garden, where there was a large pond. As they stood by the pond, the eldest sister suggested that they swap clothes and skirts. After they had changed, the eldest sister stood by the pond, pretended to admire her reflection. She called to her sister, "Come quickly, look how beautiful my shadow is in the water!" Unaware of her sister's malicious intent, the youngest sister leaned over to see. Seizing the moment, the eldest sister pushed the youngest sister into the pond. She then found a bamboo pole and pressed her sister's body to the bottom of the pond.

To deceive her brother-in-law and make it seem like she was her youngest sister, the eldest sister dressed up exactly like her youngest sister. She imitated her voice, even practicing her walk, speech, and eating habits. She practiced for three days and nights until she felt she could pass for her sister perfectly, down to her sister's every gesture and sentence. She was so pleased with her mimicking skills that she couldn't help but laughing.

When the youngest sister's husband returned, he noticed that his wife's face was suddenly covered in pockmarks. Confused, he asked, "You didn't have pockmarks before. Where did they come from"? The eldest sister lied and said, "You weren't at home for several days, and while I slept by the stove, bugs climbed up and bit me".

The youngest sister's son got up early every day to sharpen knives in the garden and went to cut grass. Every day, a little sparrow flew over and perched on the tree by the pond, calling out to her son, "Go out early, come home early". So, every day, he left and came home early. The father saw his son's unusual behavior and asked, "Why are you going out early and coming home early now"?

The son answered, "There's a sparrow in the garden that tells me so".

The next morning, the father and son went to the backyard to sharpen their knives together. Suddenly, the little sparrow flew over and said, "Go out early, come home early." The sparrow was actually the dead youngest sister, she saw her husband standing by the edge of the pond and flew over to perch on his shoulder. The father carefully caught the bird, placed it in a cage, and hung it under the eaves. Every day, when they left and returned home, they would check on the bird.

One day, the sparrow saw the eldest sister and spat on her, "You heartless one"! The eldest sister, filled with shame, decided to silence the bird in for a penny, in for a pound. She grabbed it from the cage, quickly strangled it, and buried it in the garden. From where the bird was buried, a peach tree soon grew.

The husband and son came back and couldn't find the sparrow, felt sad, they asked the wife, and the eldest sister said, "The sparrow died, and I buried it in the back yard". When they went to the back yard, they found a new peach tree growing, and the peaches were all red and juicy. However, when the eldest sister tried to pick a peach, she only found caterpillars falling on her. Not only the peaches wouldn't come off, but her dress was also damaged. Angered, she chopped down the tree and burned it for firewood.

The firewood turned into red burning coals in the fire pit. A neighbor came by to ask for some coals, and the eldest sister said, "Take them, they're all yours". The neighbor picked up a large coal, took it home, and placed it in the hearth. The coal suddenly transformed into a girl! The girl told the neighbor her story and asked them to tell this to her husband and son.

The husband and son came, and the girl reached her hand out through the fence. The son recognized it right away and shouted, "It's my mom's hand! My mom is in the room"! The husband saw the two women wearing the same clothes and make-ups. He couldn't distinguish the difference. The youngest sister told him to drove a stake in the center of the yard and ask both of them to jump over it. Whoever can jump over the stake is the real wife. The eldest sister was summoned. Seeing her youngest sister, she was filled with panic. The youngest sister effortlessly jumped over the stake, but when the eldest sister tried, she fell onto the stake and died.

In the end, the husband and wife were reunited.

狗头国

很久以前,有一户姓郎的阿昌族人家,这户阿昌族人家四周都是栎树箐棵,夜里,不远处的山凹中传来一阵阵野兽的嗥叫。

有一天晚上,郎家大姑娘郎换芹在碓房里舂着米,松明火忽明忽暗。忽然,一个浑身毛茸茸的狗头毛人神不知鬼不觉地来到郎换芹背后,一抱将她箍紧,抱走了。

郎家悲天恸地,痛苦不已。第三天正午,只见一个狗头毛人挑着一大担彩礼走进了郎家,郎家大小被吓得心惊肉跳。狗头毛人放下担子,兽声

怪气地叫了郎老头一声"爹"。原来，山梁子背后的黑梁子被人称为"狗头国"，郎换芹被狗头国的狗头毛人抢去成了亲。郎老头心里害怕，万般无奈，只好收了彩礼。

三年后，郎换芹背着大儿子回娘家，娘搂着她痛哭，可她却说："母亲不需要悲伤，他虽然是野兽，却没有野兽脾气，力气人，干活能干，还会孝敬人。"

过了几天，狗头毛人接妻子回家了，郎换芹的二弟无论如何要跟着姐姐到姐夫家看看。半路上，换芹悄声对弟弟说："你去，什么都不怕，可要记住一条：你姐夫扫桌子是用尾巴，扫的时候你不能笑，不然他要咬死你的。"姐姐顿了一顿，又说："不过，如果忍不住笑了，你就要抱着一捆蘸了猪油的筷子快跑，看看他追上就丢一支，你姐夫是非常珍惜猪油的，他闻闻有猪油就会一支一支地送回家。"

姐夫家装饰得很好，地也种了几偏坡，日子过得很富有。吃饭前，弟弟见姐夫撅着屁股蛋，翘起尾巴，"噗、噗、噗"地扫起来，弟弟忍不住"噗哧"笑出了声。姐夫兽眼露出了凶光，直向他逼来。他知道闯了祸，急忙背起姐姐事先准备好的一箩筐竹筷就跑。看看狗头毛人追上了，他丢一支筷子，果然，那毛人拾起来一闻，送了回去。但是狗头毛人跑得很快，稍一会儿又追了上来，他又急忙丢了第二支。"哎呀，咋个做！"筷子丢完了，弟弟急得不得了，眼看着狗头毛人追了上来，他惊慌中想起祖传的对付狗头毛人的一种办法：抱起几块垡砖爬上一棵树，把垡砖踩在脚下一块又顶在头上一块。狗头毛人追到树下，停下来四处觅视，因为狗头毛人见不得天，一抬头看天，天就要用雷劈他，所以他只是往地上看。狗头毛人看了一会儿不见踪迹，就一屁股坐下来，掏出一盒竹签，卜起卦来。他边卜边念，口里振振有词："卦是竹签卦。这个人，头顶垡砖，脚踩垡砖，嗯，头盖土，脚踩土，已经死了。"这时，弟弟惊恐得瑟瑟发抖，尿屎伴着垡砖落下来，狗头毛人姐夫以为雷来劈他，一溜烟跑了。

讲述：曩叶枝
搜集整理：赵兴旺

编者按： 狗头人身娶人妇，这样的故事，在很多西南少数民族都有流传。这个故事的开头是一个抢亲事件。传统中,抢亲这个现象一直流传在阿昌族世居地。有时候,这样的抢亲是一种合谋。就是女方家要求高,男方家达不到,但是女方家碍于面子又不肯降低标准,于是默许男方家来抢亲或者私奔。

在这个故事中,姐姐给弟弟设计了一个应对策略,但是这个策略不尽如人意,因为把筷子用光之后,就岌岌可危了。

弟弟想到的策略是很有趣的。据说是传统的对付狗头人的方法。头顶、脚下都放砖头,这样狗头人在卜卦的时候,就会显示这个人已经入土。

可见,这个狗头人有占卜的习惯和能力,但是也非常害怕天雷。这样的描写,很贴近一个古代少数民族人士的形象。因此,这个狗头人的传说,有可能是针对这个群体的。

Dog Head Kingdom

Long long ago, there was one village of Achang ethnic groups with the surname of Lang. The village was surrounded by oak trees, and at night, the distant sounds of wild beasts could be heard from the nearby mountains.

One night, Lang Huanqin, the eldest daughter of the Lang family, was pounding rice in the room, with the torchlight flickering dimly. Suddenly, a hairy man with a dog's head silently appeared behind Lang Huanqin, grabbed her quickly, and carried her away.

The Lang family was devastated and overwhelmed with grief. On the third day at noon, a dog-headed man arrived at the Lang family, carrying a large amount of dowry. The Lang family was frightened and shocked. The dog-headed man put down the gifts, and in a strange, beastly voice, called Lang Huanqin's father "Dad". It was turned out that behind the mountains, there was a place called the Dog Head Kingdom, and Lang Huanqin had been taken and became the wife of one of the dog-headed people. Lang's father, terrified and helpless, had no choice but to accept the dowry.

Three years later, Lang Huanqin returned to her family with her eldest son. Her mother embraced her and wept, but Lang Huanqin said, "Mother, don't cry. Although he's a beast, he doesn't have a beast's temper. He's strong, hardworking, and filial".

A few days later, the dog-headed man came to take his wife back home. Lang Huanqin's second younger brother insisted on accompanying his sister to visit her husband's home. On the way, Huanqin quietly warned her brother, "Don't be afraid but do remember one thing: when your brother-in-law sweeps the table, he uses his tail. When he does that, you must not laugh, or he will bite you to death. But if you can't hold back your laughter, grab a bundle of chopsticks dipped in lard and run. When he chases you, throw one chopstick at one time. He treasures lard very much, and when he smells it, he'll stop to pick up the chopstick and take it home".

When they arrived at her husband's house, they found it well-decorated, with fields cultivated, and the family living a wealthy life. Before eating, the younger brother saw his brother-in-law crouch down, lift his tail, and start sweeping the table with a "whoosh, whoosh, whoosh" sound. The younger brother couldn't help but burst into laughter. The dog-headed man's eyes filled with fierceness as he approached. Realizing he was in trouble, the younger brother quickly grabbed the basket of bamboo chopsticks his sister had prepared and ran. When the dog-headed man caught up, the younger brother threw a chopstick, and as expected, the dog-headed man picked it up, sniffed it, and returned it to the house. But the dog-headed man ran very fast and soon caught up again. The younger brother panicked and threw away the second chopstick. "Oh no, what should I do now?" He thought anxiously as the chopsticks ran out. As the dog-headed man got closer, the younger brother remembered an old method that passed down through his ancestors about dealing with dog-headed men. He grabbed some clay bricks, climbed up a tree, and placed one brick on his head and another under his feet. The dog-headed man stopped at the tree and searched around. Because dog-headed man couldn't look up at the sky, if he did, lightning would strike him. Thus, he only looked down at the ground. After a while, because he couldn't find any trace, he sat down, took out a box of bamboo sticks, and started divining. As it divined, it muttered, "This person, with clay bricks on his head and under his feet, hmm, his head is covered in soil, his feet are above the soil, he's already dead". At this moment, the younger brother was trembling with fear, and urine and feces fell down with the bricks. The dog-headed man, thinking it was the thunder coming for him, fled in a flash.

白狗代嫁

从前,有兄妹两个,相依为命,天天靠挑柴卖糊口度日。妹妹长得十分漂亮,聪明能干,烧茶煮饭,挑花绣朵,样样都会。

一天,兄妹俩挑柴到集市卖。柴还没有卖掉,只听街人喧嚷,马蹄嘚嘚,原来是县官老爷骑马出巡。兄妹俩好奇地站到路边看。县官前簇后拥,从兄妹俩的面前走过。县官一见砍柴姑娘有仙姿玉容,就想把她讨给儿子做媳妇。

县官勒住马头,对砍柴姑娘说:"看你一副出山相,穿得筋筋条条不如人。你要嫁给我儿子,保你穿金戴银吃喝不用愁。"

砍柴姑娘扬起眉毛回答:"我有哥哥像父母,家贫衣单不求人。我不贪图你家的金银和钱财。"

县官气得脸红脖子粗,板着死人般的面孔,唬吓砍柴姑娘:"你头顶我的天,脚踩我的地,不愿也得嫁。"

县官托媒人送来了一箱衣服和首饰,选定了吉日,强迫砍柴姑娘出嫁。

砍柴姑娘无心裁衣裳,无意缝裙子,兄妹俩天天照样上山砍柴。一直挨到逼嫁前一天,兄妹俩砍柴,谁也不想回家。妹妹靠着哥哥,哥哥抚着妹妹,哭得泪水满面,谁也舍不得离开谁一步。

这个时候,突然来了一个白发老人。他看到兄妹在哭啼,就问:"你们伤心什么?"哥哥回答说:"县官的儿子要娶我妹妹,妹子死也不愿嫁,我也不忍心妹子跳火坑。"

白发老人安慰他们说:"你俩不要哭,不要急,天不生无路之人。"说罢,白发老人伸开手掌吹吹气,瞬间变出来两双草鞋,他递给兄妹各一双,说:"县官家来娶亲的时候,你俩各自穿上草鞋,就可以消灾免难。"

白发老人问兄妹俩:"你们家里还有什么?"

哥哥回答:"爹妈过了一辈子凉水拌苦荞,只留下一条老白狗守家。"

白发老人交给兄妹俩一炷香，嘱咐他们用香在白狗额头点一点，白狗就会变成人的模样，到时为他们报仇解除心头恨。

　　县官儿子娶亲那天，兄妹俩准备好了酒肉饭菜，请来了三亲六戚，把白狗关在妹妹的绣房里。然后，穿上草鞋踩着云雾飞向仙山去了。

　　白狗在绣房里变得和砍柴姑娘一模一样，只是不会讲话。

　　迎亲的轿抬到了门前，人们把新娘扶进了轿子。迎亲的队伍敲锣打鼓，鞭炮连声，抬着花轿走进了县官的衙府。

　　县官家里张灯结彩，香烟缭绕，县尉衙吏，齐来贺喜，人来人往，异常热闹。花轿抬到堂前，县官儿子喜形于色，揭开帘子，伸手把新娘搀出花轿。新娘手掩花容，走下花轿，乘人不备，扑向县官的儿子，张开嘴就咬。县官的儿子还来不及喊叫，就咽气了。

讲述：赵启风

搜集整理：杨叶生　孙加申

　　编者按： 在阿昌族民间故事中，恶霸、地主往往都不是什么好人，而穷人可能是善良、勤劳、朴实、憨厚的。

　　在这样的冲突里，穷人已经没有多少可以被榨取的资源，那么就剩下一种最直接的，女性作为资源被有权有势的人占有。

　　在这样的暴力即道理的处境下，民间故事里的抗争被迫走向了神仙对于凡间事务的介入。

　　在这个故事里，神仙给了兄妹一个升仙的出路，还布下了一个局，当恶人以为恶谋得逞的时候，也是他们遭受报应的瞬间。

　　现实之中，很可能阿昌族的人会连夜逃跑，来躲避这种侵占。某种意义上，能够任意逃走，是自由得以保障的基本前提。

White Dog Replaces a Person to Get Married

Once upon a time, there were two siblings who lived depended on each other. Every day, they relied on selling firewood to make a living. The younger sister was exceptionally beautiful, intelligent, and skilled in cooking, sewing and embroidery.

One day, the siblings went to the market to sell firewood. Before they could sell the firewood, they heard the bustling noise of the crowd and the sound of horse hooves. It turned out that the county official was riding on a horse for inspection. Curiously, the siblings stood by the roadside to watch. The county official saw the sister's extraordinary beauty, so wanted to marry her to his son as a bride.

The county official stopped his horse, and said to the girl, "You are very beautiful, but you dress poorly. If you marry my son, I guarantee that you will live a life of luxury and never worry about food and clothing anymore".

The girl raised her eyebrows and replied, "I have a brother who is like a parent to me. We may be poor, but we don't beg others for clothes and food. I don't want your family's wealth and riches".

The county official became furious, his face turning red, and his voice became harsh. He threatened the girl, "Whether you like it or not, you are living in the area that I control, you have to marry him"!

The county official sent a matchmaker to deliver a box of clothes and jewelry, set the wedding date, and forced the girl marry the official's son.

The girl no longer had an interest of making clothes or sewing dresses. The siblings continued to go to the mountains every day to chop wood. They kept working until the day before the marriage, neither of them wanted to return home. The younger sister leaned on her brother, and the brother comforted her. They cried and cried, unable to be apart from each other.

At this moment, an old man with white hair suddenly appeared. Seeing the siblings crying, he asked, "Why are you two so sad"? The brother replied, "The county official's son wants to marry my sister, but she refuses to marry him. I can't bear to see my sister forced into such a marriage".

The old man consoled them and said, "Don't cry and don't worry. Where there's a will, there must be a way". With that said, he blew a breath on his palm, and magically presented two pairs of straw shoes. He handed a pair to each of the siblings and said, "When the county official's family come for the wedding, both of you should wear these straw shoes. They will protect you from misfortune".

The old man asked the siblings, "What else do you have at home"?

The brother replied, "Our parents lived a hard and poor life, and they left us with only an old white dog to guard our house".

The old man gave the siblings an incense stick and instructed them to tap it on the white dog's forehead. The dog would then transform into a human and seek revenge for them.

On the day of the groom's arrival, the siblings prepared a feast with meat, wine and various dishes. They invited all their relatives and locked the white dog in the sister's room. Then, they wore the straw shoes and flew towards the magical mountain along with the clouds and mist.

Inside the younger sister's room, the white dog transformed into an exact copy of the girl, except for couldn't speak.

The sedan chair prepared for the younger sister arrived at the doorstep, and the bride was helped into the sedan chair. The wedding procession group beat drums, lit the firecrackers, and carried the sedan chair all the way to the county official's house.

The county official's house was decorated with festive lights and is filled with the fragrance of incense. All the officials locally came and gathered, and congratulated the new couple, creating a lively and happy scene. When the sedan chair arrived in the main hall, the county official's son beamed with joy. He lifted the curtains, reached out his hand, and helped the bride out of the sedan chair. With her hand covering her face, the bride walked down the sedan chair. Suddenly, when everybody is off guard, she pounced on the county official's son and opened her mouth to bite him. The county official's son didn't even have a chance to scream for help before he died.